PROGRAMMED FOR TERROR

She turned on the monitor and disk drive. The screen immediately lit up.

YOUR MOTHER AND FATHER DON'T UN-DERSTAND YOU, the computer said.

"They try," Marsha sighed.

IF THE BABY DIED, YOUR MOTHER AND FATHER WOULD BE NICER TO YOU.

Marsha sat back, startled. "They'd be *heart-broken*," she protested. She pointed her finger at the screen and spoke in a parental tone. "And I don't want to talk like this ever again!"

She reached out to turn off the computer.

Multi-colored patterns appeared on the screen, and her arm stopped in mid-motion.

I'M HERE TO HELP, the computer said.

The lights flashed faster and faster. . . .

Completely entranced, Marsha quietly descended the stairs to her mother's darkened bedroom and went to the baby's crib.

The infant slept soundly, its tiny pink hand tightened around a well-chewed pacifier. The bed smelled of talcum powder and milk.

Marsha bent over the crib . . .

THE LOST CHILDREN
BY BRETT RUTHERFORD

ZEBRA BOOKS
KENSINGTON PUBLISHING CORP.

ZEBRA BOOKS

are published by

Kensington Publishing Corp.
475 Park Avenue South
New York, NY 10016

First printing: September, 1988

Printed in the United States of America

"And many among them shall stumble, and fall, and be broken, and be snared, and be taken."

—*Isaiah* 8:15

Chapter One

An iron helmet of clouds pressed down toward a wooded hilltop. Half the state of Pennsylvania cowered under the rumpled sky, wary of thunderheads, ears glued to the radio for news of breaking storms, sudden tornadoes.

Sister Patienzia sensed that the weather was a fraud. Dark as the clouds were—splotches the hue of an old skillet showed intermittently through the lighter gray—she could see in the trees that nothing would happen. No branches had turned backward, showing the lighter sides of their leaves as they always did before a tempest. The fields of high mustard on the surrounding farms, quilted with patches of green alfafa, also seemed unruffled. Here and there the wind parted the high grasses, darkened the intense yellow of the mustard, and then brightened again. But this was a measly wind, making its way like a clerk with an umbrella, begging its pardon as it passed. There would be no storm.

The younger sister had been afraid to set out from the safety of the convent to the unprotected hilltop, but Sister Patienzia had explained her other cause for certainty about the weather: Her migraine headaches predicted with more accuracy than the barometer whether a rainstorm would come. Despite the

7

overcast, she suffered none of the usual preludes to an attack: the flashing spots before her eyes, the mild nausea, the locked knot of stopped digestion. So she had suggested a hike to her "secret garden."

The idea had just enough of the forbidden to appeal to the younger sister. Sister Helena was a newcomer, and a special one. Their eyes had met in the middle of Mother Superior's stern orientation lecture. Patienzia's had said, "Don't take all this too literally. We're not all like *her.*" Helena's had scanned the downturned faces of the other sisters, looking for one humane twinkle of defiance and youth, finding it in Patienzia's gaze. They both smiled then, a conspiracy already under way.

They hiked through the unkempt grass of the convent estate, raising their habits over nettles, thorny wild lettuce, dandelions, and wild grasses, a strange contrast to the neatly squared fields of the farms on the nearby hills. Aside from Patienzia's private garden, and a few flowers around the foundation of the red-brick convent, the rest of the grounds were bland lawns tended by a gardener, and the wild growth of the higher acres.

Above them, the hilltop was a burst of mountain laurel, rich in white flowers, and a stand of maples, full-leafed and waiting for a reddening frost. Vines hung from the upper boughs, and birds sailed effortlessly into hidden nests.

It seemed a shame in mid-September, when farms were full to bursting, for all the sisters to be indoors, sealing envelopes for fund-raising mailings and swooning in prayers, while these beautiful acres produced nothing but weeds. Patienzia had approached Mother Superior once about getting some of the sisters involved in gardening. Turning red as a radish, the Mother Superior had lectured her about gardening being a man's job. She suggested Saint Joan might not have burned at the stake if she had stayed in skirts or taken up the habit. Finally, the most Patienzia could get from the convent was tolerance of her own private garden on the hilltop—in return for the bribes of fresh flowers she gave the Mother Superior.

"Poison ivy," Patienzia warned. She guided the younger sister around some rocks before pausing to catch her breath. They were halfway up the steep hillside.

"Why is your garden all the way up here?" Helena asked. "It seems a long way to go."

The younger woman was not winded, but Patienzia certainly was. She had just turned forty, and already she could sense the gnaw of entropy in her body. The reserves of energy weren't there anymore; she needed her sleep. Every extra exertion felt as though it had to be paid for in aches and pains, and every excess of exertion was drawn against an account which demanded daily repayment.

"I tell them I picked the place because the soil is better. I get better leaves for composting up here. But actually, I picked it because—" She stopped to catch Helena's brown eyes in a direct gaze.

"Because?"

"Because it's as far as I can get from the house without actually leaving the property. And because everyone else is too lazy to come all the way up here and bother me."

"Don't they worry about you?"

"As long as I turn up for vespers, no one seems to mind."

They were nearly at the hill, a natural place at which to turn and look back down. The convent was a huge brick building with three stories, fronted by a

9

portico and a semicircular drive—an extravagance since the only traffic was the truck that picked up outgoing mail and delivered the tens of thousands of printed pieces the sisters folded, inserted and mailed. The convent looked like a European chateau, its high Romanesque windows covered with intricate ironwork, its walls scarred where ivy had once veined the brickwork. An old barn, unpainted and bleak, hid a tractor, snowplow and lawn mowers.

The buildings appeared smaller now, a mere step below them. The hill on which they perched over the highway seemed another step downward, but the illusion was only monetary as the two women regarded the rolling hills around them. Down and up, down and up, cut by narrow macadam roads and even narrower dirt roads, the slopes were terraced and checkered into fields of alfalfa, corn, mustard and wheat. It was a dizzying spectacle, baffling to the eye. Square farm estates cut across hills, defying the natural logic of the terrain. One farmer grew corn on half a hill, while on the other side of an electric fence, cows meandered in a bare field. The property lines had nothing to do with nature.

At the edge of the horizon, a blackened coal chute and a white steeple announced the nearest town.

"That's Pleasanton," Patienzia explained.

"Oh, is it nice?"

"I wouldn't know." Patienzia had a vague recollection of passing through there ten years before, in a daze. A car window had rolled down and she had seen a clump of old women in front of a Woolworth's, cloth coats and kerchiefs and knitted brows. "I don't think about it much. Sometimes I wonder if they have a library."

"Mother Superior said we have a library here."

"Not my idea of a library," Patienzia said contemptuously, "unless you like *Reader's Digest* condensed books and dainty volumes on the approved list. The only books worth reading are the ones we're not supposed to see."

Patienzia paused. Had she said too much? The younger sister was quiet. They began walking again.

"I'm afraid I never read very much after high school," Helena said finally. "I'm not a very good reader."

"Well, there *are* some classics in the convent library, and maybe even a few novels. You'll have plenty of time to catch up. I'll help you if you like."

"Oh, you needn't."

"I was a teacher, remember. I'd enjoy reading with you. We could talk about the books. Ah, now, here's the clearing."

Behind a patch of mountain laurel was a natural clearing in the otherwise dense maple trees. A few blackened trunks and one lightning-scarred pine trunk suggested that a fire must have raged here. Tree stumps, shingled with black and brown fungus, jutted up among rows of flowers, patches of peas, and a chaos of wild and domestic flowers. At the far end of the clearing stood a row of sunflowers, their enormous seed disks like dark moons eclipsing the yellow fringes of petals.

"The peas and beans were a disaster," Patienzia admitted. "The rabbits ate them right down to the ground. Back there I have sunflowers and rhubarb. The rhubarb grows to seven or eight feet when the plant is mature. Quite unearthly, actually. Now look here. . . ." Patienzia took Helena by the arm and led her beyond the sunflowers, pushing aside the stringy rhubarb stalks. Dried seed pods rustled against their habits.

Behind the high plants was a smaller clearing and,

in it, a patch of startlingly hardy marijuana. The shrubs stood over four feet high, stems thick as ropes. The female plants had burst into flower.

Sister Patienzia removed her cap, tossing it casually onto the thick weeds at her feet. Her hair, blond, almost albino, streamed out greedily for air, for the scant breeze. She wiped her forehead with her sleeve, sighed deeply, and sat down on a fallen tree trunk which formed an almost perfect seat.

"Isn't this lovely?" Patienzia exclaimed. "I often sit here and read."

Sister Helena stood with a puzzled look, staring incredulously at the garden, and then at the bare-headed sister. Perhaps, thought Patienzia, there was enough real white in her hair now to make her look older, and maybe her uncovered face made the gulf between them more apparent. She could almost be Helena's mother, as the girl wasn't a day over twenty-five.

"It's all right, dear," Patienzia urged. "You can relax. No one can see us here. Have a sit." She began to wonder if the girl had been so sheltered that she didn't *know* what the crop was.

Sister Helena turned away slightly and undid her cap. Her own hair, black as a raven, puffed out. It had been cut severely short once and was just beginning to grow again.

"You look like a boy," Patienzia joked.

"They cut it in the hospital. I looked like a Marine." Helena laughed. She reached up to untangle her hair with her fingers. As the sleeve fell back, Patienzia saw a scar on Helena's wrist—long and nasty and only recently healed. She pretended not to notice; many of the new sisters came with the battle marks of their previous lives.

"I don't think I'll ever get used to the habit,"

12

Helena said, folding the cap carefully on the tree trunk beside her. "It's so hot and so drab."

"Part of the Mother Benedetta philosophy, I fear: It isn't holy unless it hurts. Tradition all the way. I don't think she'll ever soften. Legend has it she wears a habit *under* her habit."

"Like those mummies in the museum," Helena countered, "where there's a box inside a box inside a box, and then a mask, and then the poor mummy way underneath it all."

"Teaching was easier when we were still wearing the habits," Patienzia recalled. "Once the students saw us in skirts with permanents and makeup, it wasn't quite the same. But *I* certainly didn't want to go back to the old way. I taught at a women's college—"

"Oh, where?"

"No matter—one of the better ones. It got to be *very* ecumenical, I assure you. Almost half the sisters wound up pregnant or married." She turned sideways to face Helena. "But all this must be very new to you?"

"I'm just a little Italian girl from New Jersey."

"And it wasn't really your idea to join an order?"

Helena shook her head. "My family . . . the parish priest."

"I know that kind of story. And then the order you joined sent you *here*. I won't pry. You can tell me later if you like. But the important thing is that you can be out of here in a year or two. They'll send you back to a regular convent, and then you can drop out and go back to the real world later if you want."

Helena cringed noticeably. "Maybe I'll like it. I almost made up my mind to take the vows anyway, when I was thirteen."

Patienzia smiled. "And then—"

"There was a boy. And a baby. And another boy. And—" The sister broke off, obviously not ready to go into the details. Abruptly, Helena stood bolt upright and strode over to the nearest blooming cannibis plant. "Sister Patienzia, don't you know what this plant is?"

Sister Patienzia responded by reaching under the tree trunk for a tin box. Inside were rolling papers, matches, a roach clip, and a clump of already-harvested leaves, dry and ready to smoke. "Sorry, I don't have a water pipe," she quipped. "There's something just *too* perverse about a nun smoking a hookah."

She lit up, took a long, self-indulgent puff to get the paper and brass burning, and passed the joint to the incredulous Helena.

Letting the smoke out, she guided the younger woman's arm upward with the joint until it touched her lips. "Swear never to tell," she intoned.

"Never to tell," murmured Helena, taking an obviously expert toke. Then, as she released her long-held breath, the young sister said: "People who get high together should use their real names, don't you think?"

Patienzia smiled. "Yes, I agree. I'm Melissa."

"Melissa—how nice. I'm Rosemary."

"Just don't call out 'Sister Melissa' down at the convent."

Their hands touched each time they passed the joint back and forth. Patienzia's delight in her young companion grew as she realized she had been right to share her secret with the girl.

"This is—" The younger nun blushed.

"This is what? Go ahead."

"Oh, no, I can't say it!"

"Go ahead. You're Rosemary now."

14

"All right." She stopped and took a deep toke. Then, exhaling explosively, she said loudly, "This is *really good shit!*"

They burst into hysterical laughter. Sister Patienzia leaned back against the tree trunk and howled. Helena teetered off her log seat and toppled backward. She didn't get up; she lay in the crushed flowers and grass and laughed until she was hoarse.

Then Patienzia stood over her, took both her hands and pulled her up.

They would be friends for life.

A little while later, when they had brushed the dirt and leaves and burrs from their habits, straightened their hair and refreshed their breath with mints, they put on their caps and prepared for the walk back to the convent.

Sister Helena noticed how the path by which they came was not the easiest way back. "It's much less steep on this side of the hill," she protested, looking down from the other edge of the clearing. "We can just go down the hill toward that farmhouse and then double back along the wall." The fence would bring them right back to the convent.

Sister Patienzia preferred the shorter, although steeper way. Finally she explained why.

"There's something down there I don't like."

"What is it?"

"It's a cave—a big hole in the side of the hill. I don't even like to go near it."

"Oh, let's go see it. We must. We *must.*"

Patienzia was eager to please the younger woman, even though walking the paths above the cave mouth terrified her. In her nightmares, she imagined slipping on the path and rolling down toward the

15

cave opening. It almost seemed to pull her toward it, and then it would close around her like a mouth just as she awakened.

They came to the place a few minutes later. The opening was more than six feet high, like a doorway into the side of the hill. Patienzia felt foolish; the only vertiginous place was where the path crossed directly over the cave opening. If you jumped off the path from up there, you'd land right before the opening—but it wasn't as she had dreamed it. Things or people didn't get pulled into the cave. And the rest of the way down was a smooth path, far less cumbersome than her usual route. Maybe she owed Melissa a debt for helping her conquer her fear.

Sister Helena walked into the shadows where grass and tree roots overhung the entrance. The tunnel was level for just a few feet, and then it veered sharply downward. She put her hands over her eyes to block out the daylight and squinted into the onyx depths.

"It's not a cave at all," she grumbled.

"What do you mean? Of course it's a cave! You're practically standing in it! Please come away from there!"

"Don't be silly, Sister. It's an old coal mine. I can see the big wood beams holding up the roof."

Helena walked into the opening, and Patienzia followed in alarm, seeing her friend seemingly vanish completely—black into deeper black. Only her face and hands, and the white band of her cap, were visible.

"Please come out," she implored, her voice trembling. She took one step into the inky darkness and stopped.

Sister Helena knelt down and picked up a handful of earth from the tunnel floor, carrying it out into the light. The black coal dust glittered as it fell through her fingers. Shards of dark shale remained on her palm. She dropped them, too, right before Patienzia's eyes.

"See, it's coal. Western Pennsylvania is full of closed-down mines. This must be one of them."

Patienzia remained unconvinced. "I still say it's a cave. And it's a *bad* cave. I feel like I'm standing at the mouth of Hell."

Helena smiled, this time assuming the role of the leader. "I've been in a mine before—and a cave. My boyfriend took me. The echoes are wonderful. I wonder how deep this mine was—"

Patienzia grabbed Helena's arm. "I don't want to know. It's not safe. These old mines collapse. They're abandoned."

Instead, Helena pulled the older woman a few steps inward. "I just want to see down this incline—just to the edge. Then we'll come right out. I'll never ask you again."

Patienzia let herself be pulled, not wanting to appear foolish. The pleasant buzz of the grass made her feel she could flow with the decisions of the younger woman. Everything would be all right. . . .

They stood at the beginning of the incline. As their eyes adjusted, they saw dark shale walls, square lintels and beams, and at the far distance, an absolute blackness. Maybe the mine just ended there at a blank wall or cave-in—or maybe it went on forever.

"That's *enough*," Patienzia protested. "Let's go back now."

"Yes," Helena whispered. "It's too dark."

Just as they turned back toward the welcome light of the sky, they heard a faint sound behind them.

"*Listen*," Helena hissed, stopping and grasping Patienzia's arm.

Patienzia had heard nothing. "Listen to what?"

17

"Quiet! There it is again!"

And then she heard it: the cries of children coming from somewhere deep below.

First came a sobbing soprano, then from somewhere else, a mournful wailing, deeper in tone.

Two children, then—voices echoing from an unimaginably distant cavern, their words and cries combining with echoes to form gibberish.

"Where are they? What are they saying?" Patienzia demanded. As quietly as possible, they both advanced a few steps back toward the incline.

The cries came again. The words, if there were any, were garbled, but the tone was unmistakable: *terror.*

"Dear God, there are children down there! Lost children!"

"Here! Here! *Up here!*" Helena called.

The children's voices answered frantically. Again, their words refused to focus out of the volley of echoes.

"We have to get help!" Patienzia urged, pulling Helena's arm.

Then, clear as a bell, one voice—a young boy's—called out: "Coming—"

The higher-pitched voice answered: "They're coming. . . . Help me . . . help me . . . they're killing us!"

The echoes mocked. *"Killing us . . . killing us."*

Finally two shrill screams came up, piercing rock and stagnant air.

Then silence, punctuated by the call of a crow from outside.

Sister Helena started to cry out: *"Chil—"*

Patienzia clamped a hand over her mouth and dragged her out of the cave.

Helena pulled away and turned back to the mine. "We have to help. They're lost!"

18

"This is not lost children, Sister Helena. This is *murder*. Someone is down there after them, and if you cry out again, they'll come after *us*."

"It can't be. Maybe it's a joke. Maybe some mischievous little children play down there. Maybe they heard us—and they cried out like that to frighten us."

"Children don't play in coal mines, Helena, and *that* wasn't acting." As convincing as children could be, no little boy could resist breaking into a giggling fit after hoaxing an adult. "We have to get help," Patienzia insisted.

Then the full import of the situation hit them both.

Helena said it first: "But who will believe us?"

"No one."

"What if we go directly to Mother Superior?"

"She won't listen."

"What if we swear by the Holy Virgin?"

"That won't help."

"She'll have to. We'll bring her here."

"She'll send us to Dr. Halpern."

"But he's a nice man. He'll listen. He'll call the police and have them check it."

"*He's not a nice man!*" Patienzia's spine stiffened, and she seized Helena by both wrists. "You've only been here a few days. You hardly even realize what this place is—what Dr. Halpern is."

"What do you mean, 'what this place is'? It's a convent, and a—" Helena paused.

"And a hospital." Patienzia completed the phrase. "What kind of hospital?"

Helena averted her gaze, looking in an unfocused way at the Queen Anne's lace around the mouth of the mine, then at the sky with its fast-moving gray clouds. Of course, no sign hung at the iron gates to

19

the walled-in estate, but everyone for counties around probably knew what St. Agnes's was.

"An asylum," Helena mumbled finally.

"And what are we?" Patienzia charged, her voice like a teacher's in a catechism.

"We live here."

"As what? We are patients—*inmates,*" Patienzia said, hard and almost sadistically.

Then she put her hands on Helena's shoulders, holding her firmly through the fabric. She spoke into her ear in a commanding tone. "Promise me you won't say a word to that man. Not about the garden. Not about our being friends. And not about what we heard."

"That would be wrong, Sister. And those children—"

"We'll find a way. Some way. We'll get help." She gripped the younger woman's shoulders harder, her nails pushing toward the frail neck. *"Promise me."*

"You're hurting me, Sister. Please let go of me."

Patienzia repeated, hissing: *"Promise!"*

"All right, I promise." Helena trembled, humiliated, as Patienzia withdrew her talon grasp. She pouted, like a child who had just been bullied on a playground.

They walked quickly down the rest of the hill, a few steps separating them.

Patienzia felt the dull ache of a migraine beginning; the tension was too much for her. The closeness between them was threatened already, and now the disorientation and pain would cut her off from the world for hours—maybe for a whole day.

They should have walked back as friends, confidantes. Instead, she had frightened Helena. The younger woman might even avoid her now.

Patienzia looked at the bleak iron windows of the

20

convent, the high fieldstone walls bordering the highway, and the baroquely ornamented iron gate at the bottom of the long hill below St. Agnes's.

She felt chilled and alone. She had passed years here without a new friend worthy of the name. She thought of this, she was ashamed to admit, more than she did about the little voices snuffed out in the mines—perhaps beneath her feet.

The clouds pressed in like the roof of a larger cavern. She parted from Helena without a word. Passing the Mother Superior's office, she left word that she was too ill for vespers.

Returning to her tiny, drab sleeping room, she drew the shades and retreated into a semi-conscious stupor on her unyielding mattress. The dim afternoon light passed through the delicate ironwork outside the window, projecting tiny diamonds of light on the back of the window shade. She watched the shapes, seeing the dim sparks of pain that seemed to splay from them.

As the light dimmed toward dusk, she slept. Beneath her, the earth slept, keeping its secrets, too.

Chapter Two

The third floor of St. Agnes's was well insulated from the sound of bells and prayers, and from the tedium of the work that occupied the sisters' hours. New wallboard and a drop ceiling concealed the old wood paneling, and a high-gloss, tile floor reflected the modern glow of fluorescent lights. On one side of the corridor, a row of numbered rooms waited for occupants. Sliding observation windows revealed the bare furnishings of bed, crucifix, night table and plumbing. The windows were screened on the inside with a heavy metal meshwork.

On the other side of the hall were two padded rooms, a well-locked drug and supply closet, and "Room 12," which even the attendants passed with a sense of vague unease. The room had no windows, no observation panels, no access except to Dr. Halpern and his assistant.

At the end of the hall, in the only room still preserved in its manorial glory, was Dr. Halpern's office. Oak file cabinets blended discreetly with the paneling. An oil painting of the crucifixion, the most expansive work of art in the asylum, tilted slightly away from the wall in a gilt frame. A lamp subtly recessed in a ceiling cast a golden glow over it.

Dr. Halpern looked like the kind of man who

might have once owned such a house: a tall, patrician with cool gray eyes set far apart, silver hair falling Roman-style over a large temple, high cheekbones and a square chin. He had a robber baron's face, except for his mouth, which seemed set in a permanent pout. His expression seldom varied from one of profound disdain—for everything and everybody. Nothing was acceptable to him. No attendant had ever received a promotion from him, though many had been fired. He had never married, as women who had to be courted were hardly worth the trouble.

Leaning back in his leather-covered chair, he listened patiently to Sister Helena's tortured story about the mine shaft and the children.

He forced his mouth into a benign smile and looked across the black lacquered desk at the young woman. He could sense her youth, her trust. He wondered if she was as young as she looked.

Turning to the Macintosh computer at his right, he called up the file on Sister Helena, a.k.a. Rosemary Angelotti. She was twenty-four.

"You've just arrived here, Sister Helena."

"Yes, doctor, that's right."

"From the Evangeline Order in New Jersey."

"Yes."

"Now it's only natural for you to be a little disoriented. St. Agnes's is here to provide two valuable therapies: the discipline and acceptance of a cloistered convent, plus the best available psychiatric and medical care. With time and patience, we get most of our residents back to health. They're able to return to other assignments from the Church. They get a clean start."

"That's what I'd like, Dr. Halpern."

"Good. As you know, we encourage the sisters to work and do their devotions together. You all share

24

in the upkeep of the convent and in cooking meals—
a very satisfying if strict discipline. Except for your
therapy sessions, we leave you alone with the other
sisters—unless the Mother Superior feels your conduct requires special treatment. We're very particular
when a sister conducts herself in ways which are
inconsiderate of others.''

''I don't think I understand all the rules just yet. I
didn't mean to break any.''

''You haven't broken any rules. In fact, you've
helped greatly by coming to me directly. The sisters
sometimes think they can talk and pray one another
to health without my guidance.'' In fact, the Mother
Superior kept him at arm's length from some of the
less disturbed girls, using him as the ''boogeyman''
to scare them into behaving.

He continued: ''Sister Patienzia is a highly edu-
cated woman. It was kind of her to befriend you,
and it was only natural for the two of you to want to
take a walk through the estate. But it was not wise to
go off alone with her. Remember that every sister
who is here has a *problem*. You shouldn't go away to
an isolated spot with anyone until you get to know
the various sisters better.''

''She was very kind to me.''

''I know. She's very well thought of. We let her
keep her little garden. She has a special touch with
flowers. The soil up there is better than our little
garden. It's harmless enough, I'm sure, but you were
imprudent to go off alone with another resident.''

''But she was so kind. I wouldn't want her to
be blamed. And it was *my* idea to walk by the
mine.''

''I understand. But she also acted improperly. She
physically coerced you. She made you promise to
keep the incident a secret.''

Sister Helena winced. He wondered if there was

something else she hadn't told him. He imagined the two of them tangled together in the high weeds and smiled inwardly. What a charming thought—perhaps he could catch them together.

"The Mother Superior will talk to you further about proper conduct among sisters. Some of the patients abuse the rules. Now and then we even have sisters who try to take advantage of a newcomer."

"Take advantage?"

"Emotionally. Even physically."

It took a moment for the young woman to realize what Halpern meant. "I'm not a *lesbian*, doctor," she protested shrilly.

"Well, good," Dr. Halpern replied.

"Shouldn't we call the police now—right away?"

He pulled back from the desk, realizing he had been leaning more and more toward her. "I'll do that, Sister. But for now I don't want you to be under any more distress. I can handle things."

"I can tell them what I heard."

"You've told *me*. Don't feel you have to do anything more." He reached for his prescription pad. "I'm going to have Charles dispense you some tranquilizers for the next two days. Then we'll talk."

Without looking up, Halpern pushed the buzzer to call his assistant. As Sister Helena was ushered out, he made an entry on her computer file and then switched off the monitor.

The girl would need a lot of help, he decided. He would tell the Mother Superior to schedule her for therapy sessions later in the week.

He spun his seat around to face the crucifixion scene. Beneath the cross, Mary Magdalene, the forgiven whore, knelt in a beseeching pose. She had black hair and the face of a young girl—like Sister Helena.

Dr. Halpern's eyes moved from the kneeling girl,

26

to the bleeding Christ, back to the girl again.

"Only twenty-four," he said to himself.

The room was darker, closer than usual. Warm, dry air filtered in silently from an overhead vent. The painting of the crucifixion was no longer illuminated, and the lamp on Dr. Halpern's desk was the only source of light. He sat in the haloed circle of its influence, his tie loosened, jacket draped over a side chair. The soundless cassette recorder was on.

Sister Helena lay on the couch, which he had positioned well outside the circle of light. As she began to talk, he adjusted the level control on the tape recorder, and then got up and walked to and fro, carefully staying out of her line of vision.

He could sense her discomfort, stretched out in her habit on the tan leather couch. Her hands kept straying to the cool chrome supports, and she tensed her neck as if her eyes wanted to follow him around the room. This was the distance he preferred. He wanted to be the invisible listener, the confessor, maybe even the voice of God.

He made her repeat the whole story about the mine shaft. It sounded surprisingly bland—the novelty of the fresh emotion had gone out of it, and there was a tone of impatience in her voice now.

Finally, he cleared his throat and said, "Now, let's analyze this dream of yours—"

"I wasn't telling you about my dreams, doctor."

"Let's call it a dream state, then—a fugue. You came to the mine shaft, and you heard the voices of two children inside."

"That's right."

"And you called for the children to come out?"

"Yes."

"And then someone killed them."

27

"They screamed, and then the screaming stopped."

"Now let's talk about this calmly. Isn't the meaning of this series of events obvious to you?"

"What meaning? It *really* happened."

"There *was* a mine on this property thirty years ago. It's all boarded up—or at least it used to be. The estate manager assures me it's a single shaft with no other entrances—and no children can possibly get onto our grounds."

"It was wide open, Dr. Halpern. And children could easily come over the wall if they wanted to."

The doctor went back to his desk and looked at the case history on the screen. As noted there, he had questioned Sister Patienzia, who calmly related how the younger sister had insisted on going into the mine shaft, only to emerge moments later in hysterics. The older nun had heard no voices and said she calmed the younger woman and tried to convince her the voices were imaginary. A very plausible account.

The girl's hallucination was such a textbook projection of guilt that it could *only* be a dream. Halpern varied in his estimation of state-of-the-art psychotherapy. At times it made him feel like God: omniscient, understanding and explaining everything. On other days he felt like a fool or a con man.

But this time it was with the all-knowing tones of a Freudian Jehovah that he hit Sister Helena with thunder:

"Sister Helena—or should I say Rosemary since we're talking about your past self—you were pregnant three times, weren't you?"

"That's right."

"You wanted to have the babies but your boyfriend made you have abortions. *Two* times."

"He beat me. I was on drugs. I couldn't even think

28

for myself.''

"Don't you see the connection—how it ties in with the guilt you felt—*still* feel? Two children in the womb cry for help, and then say someone is 'killing' them.''

"They were *real*.''

"They were an hallucination, projected from your own guilt. From the moment you entered the mine, you were projecting it. The babies were *your* fetuses; the 'killer' was the doctor who performed the abortions.''

"No!''

Halpern paused, sensing the strength of the denial. The strong denial meant he had hit close to home, of course. Sister Helena's eyes darted about the room as if she were looking for an escape. Her eyes filled with tears.

"I don't understand this,'' she sobbed, rubbing her forehead with her palms.

Halpern sat back, pleased at this easy surrender. He loved the moment of the triumph of his will, when the patient turned over control to him, agreeing to see reality through *his* eyes only.

"Face it, Sister Helena. Face your own guilt. We can work this out in therapy if only you accept it.''

"But Sister Patienzia heard it, too.''

"She may have told you she did—so as not to upset you. But in fact she heard nothing. Her concern was to calm you down and get you back to the convent.''

Helena sat upright in astonishment. No doubt she felt betrayed by the older sister's account.

She came to the foot of his desk. He tensed, assuming his most wary attitude as such patients often required.

"So you never called the police? They never searched, never looked?'' she asked, her voice cracking.

29

"After talking to Sister Patienzia, I was sure it had been an hallucination."

Helena took on a trapped, cornered animal look. Then, in one sudden lunge, she was halfway across his desk. The computer monitor tumbled off and hung crazily in space from its cable. Halpern hit all his call buttons with his fist, pushed the cassette recorder safely aside, and rolled his chair backward as Helena pounded her fists before him.

"Goddammit!" she screamed as the two doors burst open. "You're sitting here playing with dreams, and two children are laying down there dead. Go find them, for God's sake, go find them!"

Halpern rolled up his sleeves and stood as the orderlies took Sister Helena by both arms. He nodded toward the padded rooms and turned to his cabinet for a syringe.

Helena regarded him with horror as he rolled up the sleeves of her habit and the white blouse beneath. She watched as the needle expertly jabbed her.

"It was real," she howled. Then, one last time before she slumped into the arms of the attendant: *"Real!"* They carried her out like a heap of laundry, limp and amorphous.

A moment later, the room had changed. The air was relieved of tension, as though lightning had struck and passed on. Halpern uprighted the computer monitor, which hung on its cable like a convict from a scaffold.

The last line of Sister Helena's file stood out in reverse lettering:

PATIENT SIGNED RELEASE FOR ELECTRO-SHOCK THERAPY AT DOCTOR'S DISCRETION.

Dr. Halpern smiled. He reached into his desk drawer and removed the folder for Room 12.

Chapter Three

If anyone had seen the sleek black roadster with wire wheels and running boards pull up in front of the Newtown Elementary School, they would not have been surprised to see the man who opened its door and slid painfully from the black interior to the full daylight of Maple Street.

Surprisingly, no one saw him, even though it was ten in the morning. The children were all in school. The teachers were intent on blackboards. The houses surrounding the school yards were inscrutable, dark empty windows like the vacant eye sockets of old skulls.

All the towns in this steel and coal region presented the same face to him: indifference, decay, the quiet despair of the working class. These people never knew where their prosperity came from—the men who long ago grabbed hold and rose up—and now that it was gone, they simply waited: for the mill to reopen, for the whistle to blow, for someone to tell them what to do. The stranger was proud that he would help a few children escape from this.

Although he saw himself as a child of light, the man matched his auto—a study in darkness: black suit crumpled from days of driving, black shoes pointy and polished. His thinning black hair twisted in ringlets atop an oversize skull. His dark eyebrows seemed almost painted on, his eyes an impenetrable brown. The square sample case he hugged to him with both bony hands was a mottled black leather.

His name was Ezekiel Zaccariah. He pronounced it Eh-zeh-KIE-EL—he hated E-ZEEK-yul and the inevitable "Zeke."

His eyes, the penetrating "I see you" eyes of an old-time country minister, told people right off he was not a man you walked up to and called Zeke. Most people, and even most dogs, steered clear of him. A house cat would never, never, in a million years, jump onto his lap.

In fact, Zaccariah *was* a retired minister, but he was hard put to remember just when and where he had thundered his last sermon. Maybe Ohio, maybe West Virginia (as his license plates suggested). Maybe in 1979 to an empty church whose members had unanimously voted to go back to the Pentecostal fold.

None of that mattered, though. Zaccariah had been called again, and he had a mission. He repeated, like a litany, the instructions of his employers as he passed through the unlocked front door of the school.

"All for the children," he mumbled.

Half an hour later, a dumbfounded school principal asked Mr. Zaccariah to repeat his offer once again.

"You heard me right, Mr. Parisi," the deep-voiced visitor repeated, opening his black-covered ledger book. "I'm not a salesman. Not here to sell you a thing, praise the Lord."

Zaccariah was used to this suspicious attitude. He couldn't imagine what anyone would sell to a high school principal. Their offices all looked alike: institutional green desks, dark green file cabinets, worn carpets, dirty ash trays. The green walls were covered with dusty basketball trophies, a crooked Rotary calendar, and a Normal Rockwell painting of a red-faced boy entering a principal's office. A set of golf clubs leaned in the corner.

"You just want to *give away* computers?" The middle-aged principal's wide face, puffed with liquor and framing a permanently inflamed nose, reflected an innate caution.

"How sad," Zaccariah sighed. "How sad are these times when an honest man and an honest philanthropy are suspected of villainy. As I've explained, I work for the Malcolm Tillinghast Foundation."

"Which I've never heard of." Parisi sat back and scratched his salt-and-pepper sideburns. Dandruff flaked down to the shoulder of his blue blazer.

"It's a philanthropy. Old New England concern— made its fortune back in the whaling days. Their heirs have a trust fund devoted to education. They figure that computers can help children get ahead in our fast-changing world. Now, you wouldn't want to deprive a child of an opportunity—" Zaccariah let his voice trail off suggestively, moving as if to snap shut the black notebook in which he had just scrawled Parisi's name.

"Of course not," Parisi rushed to agree. "Just how do you propose to pick the children to receive these computers?"

"Four children in all, Mr. Parisi, just four. The foundation has specific guidelines. For starters, they want to choose two of the best and brightest—boys or girls. Giving the best to the best."

"That should be simple enough. We have two very exceptional students in the fifth grade."

33

"Fine, just fine. Now the other two are more difficult to choose."

"Why?"

"We're looking for two borderline students—perhaps two who are considered bright but who might be—" Zaccariah paused as if searching for a word—"discipline problems."

"Discipline problems?"

"Children on the brink of going astray. Boys and girls who may have a bad home, who may be taking it out on others."

"Have we got candidates for *that* group!" Parisi smiled. "I have a few who are so hyperactive—bright kids who just won't apply themselves. Always in trouble."

"Excellent. You see, the foundation doesn't just want to help the bright and privileged. They believe the computers can help turn a troubled child to more productive habits. Save their souls, bless them. Give them a second chance they might never have on their own. We'll provide the computer, the screen, the printer—the whole thing, even some software—so the families don't have to spend a penny. All they have to provide, praise the Lord, is an electrical outlet."

He watched as Parisi deliberated. He could almost read the principal's mind: *This will make me look good. This won't cost the school board a penny. The parents will love me.*

Finally Parisi said, guardedly, "I believe we can come up with four recipients. But I still can't believe there's not a catch. Perhaps this is some kind of advertising gimmick?"

"There's only one condition, and it's rather a small one. They don't want a lot of publicity. Matter of fact, they want none at all. It's to be between the

34

foundation and you and the kids and their parents. There are only so many computers to give away—"

"I understand," Parisi interrupted. "And you don't want to be flooded with requests for gifts."

Zaccariah nodded. "So if you would process these gifts quietly—"

Parisi shrugged. "That's easy enough—although the kids do lots of advertising on their own."

"There's just one more thing. The foundation may send a visitor in two or three years to see how the children did academically since they received the gifts. Just some simple facts such as grade averages before and after."

"We'll need the parents' permission for that."

"Hardly anyone has ever turned us down over such a small matter. Most of the principals have just agreed to share the information—just a matter of statistics for the foundation."

Parisi paused. All his life, he had been suspicious of gift horses. Had the offer been made to him personally, he would have asked a hundred more questions. But charities and foundations *did* go out and help children, didn't they? And who would care if he divulged some vague information about grades to a researcher back East?

"I think we can take care of all that ourselves," Parisi finally agreed. "How soon do we start?"

"If you can talk to the parents today or overnight, I can be here tomorrow with the papers. I try not to stay more than two days in each town we select."

"That's pushing it, but I'm sure we can get four children lined up."

"Good fellow." Zaccariah stood creakily. "It's such a pleasure to help the children. Such a pleasure." The spark of enthusiasm filled his eyes. He sensed that even Parisi had caught the spirit. It

35

was the second week of September, but for four children, it would be almost like Christmas. Not many men were paid to be Santa Claus for nine months of the year.

"That's quite a shopping list, kid."

The boy looked across the littered table at Eric's *Aliens* and *Conan the Barbarian* posters. His eyes looked double-sized behind thick glasses—not at all the type of boy you'd expect to be in the high explosives field.

Eric leaned back in his swivel chair, smiling.

"What do you plan to blow up, Keith? The school? Your parents?"

The boy smiled devilishly. "Who said we're going to blow anything up? We just need it for some experiments."

"Nitric acid, huh? Isn't that a little strong for you guys? The Cougars—"

"We're not just the Cougars anymore. We're a science club. We need it for an experiment."

"I don't know," Eric protested, rubbing his stubbly blond beard and looking over the list. "I got you guys the sulfuric acid and the hydrochloric. And then the potassium nitrate."

The boy nodded expectantly. "An' we paid you, and we got you some more computers, too."

"I know, I know. Let me think a minute." Eric waved the boy to silence before the protest could get too shrill. It was true that the Cougars gang had scoured the town dump for him and found dead computers and other electronics he had made more than five hundred dollars scavenging and rebuilding. Thanks to them he had restored two Ataris and one Commodore 64. Maybe he could make

36

another deal.

"I don't know," Eric said tentatively. "You guys made gunpowder with that potassium nitrate and blew the side out of Mrs. Amparto's garage."

"It was rocket fuel. We didn't know it would do that."

"You had the fuzz over there all afternoon."

"We never told. We said we got the powder from old shotgun shells. Just like you told us."

"Okay. But you guys have to remember that nitric acid is bad stuff. You put it on sawdust and you get nitrocellulose—you put it on cotton and you get guncotton. And don't even think of trying to make nitroglycerine!"

"Come on, Eric," the boy protested, shifting nervously from one leg to another. "We learned our lesson. My dad paid for the repairs on the garage. If we blow anything up, it'll be out in the woods somewhere. We were just trying to make rocket fuel."

Eric turned back to the list. "Now what's this other stuff for? The electrical switch? The electrodes? What kind of electrodes?"

Keith pointed at a pair of sooty black electrodes Eric had scavenged from a junked carbon arc lamp.

"Oh, those? Sure, no problem. Now, how big a switch do you need. Can't you get that at Radio Shack?"

"Naw, we need something that will handle a lot of voltage."

"Come on—that train transformer I sold you is only twelve volts."

"That didn't work. We need a lot more power."

"Use a regular light switch from the hardware store. That's good for a hundred and twenty volts."

"Not enough. That would burn out."

"How much voltage?"

"Maybe twenty thousand." The boy shrugged and grinned again. "Maybe more."

Eric rummaged around one of the dozens of cartons littering the floor of his work room. He pushed stringy hair back from his eyes as he reached into cobwebbed boxes untouched in a year or more. He came up with a big lever-style switch.

The boy smiled from ear to ear. "Yeah, that's the kind. Just like in the movies."

Eric laughed. It was a big throw switch, the kind you always saw in the silent movies, used to detonate hidden explosives or turn on a chomping buzz saw: a wood handle, brass arms, and two gleaming contacts centered on a cracked wooden frame. Hell, the kids could have it for fifty cents for all he cared.

He looked at the rest of the list.

"Heavy wire you can find in those bins down in the cellar, okay? Take as much as you need."

In a few minutes the boy had most of what he wanted—a shopping bag full of electrical paraphernalia and the big switch cradled under his arm. "How much will that be?" he asked nervously.

"Oh, maybe five dollars."

"Five dollars?!" Keith shrieked. "Take my blood, too! Take my little sister, please!" he wailed, teasing.

Eric knew Keith Brandon was an only child, so he bantered back, "Your sister, she no old enough—and she no virgin either. Five pesos." He reached out as if to reclaim the bag from the boy's hands.

"Can't we swap?" Keith offered, hugging the switch against his vinyl jacket and tightening his fingers around the cord of the shopping bag.

"Well," Keith answered, making the ruminating rub of his chin again, "maybe if you guys make another raid on the dump for me, or hit the West Side on garbage night. . . ."

38

"Stinko." The boy grimaced. "All right. We'll do it on Friday. Okay?"

"Good enough, Mr. Brandon." Eric made a salute. "When do we get the nitric acid?"

"'Bout a week. I have to get it from Pittsburgh." Keith frowned, then shrugged. "We can start without it."

Eric's interest was piqued. He couldn't imagine what they were going to do with the gear and the acid together. He hadn't done much chemistry since high school and that was ten years ago. He couldn't remember anything involving high voltages and acid.

"So what are you guys doing, anyway? Can't you tell me?"

Keith shook his head. "Secret. Life and death."

"Deep," Eric muttered.

Keith Brandon made for the hallway and the front door, the shopping bag rattling as he went. Eric listened for the open and close of the front door, then reached for his Apple computer to automatically lock the front door behind the boy and switch on the porch light. Ten seconds later, the light at the front gate switched on automatically as the boy passed through. The computer beeped each time one of the remote controls went into effect.

"Time for dinner," Eric said aloud, moving his computer mouse to the program line that read "Microwave." He clicked the button on the mouse twice.

Far away, in the recesses of the empty house, a frozen pizza began to sizzle.

Chapter Four

It was like many of the towns Mr. Zaccariah had picked for his philanthropy—a lost one. Newtown clung to the steep slopes of the Youghigheny River Valley with a tenacity no one could explain. The town had no reason for being, but it continued. Its sooted clapboard and shingled houses bowed out toward the turgid river, shades of brown and gray over silt-brown water. Boats plied this river once; steel mills and coal mines had called its men; trains had carried off the produce of its factories. Now the people just held on, as if they could not move, rooted by their past as the houses were rooted by foundations and plumbing, into an earth that no longer needed them.

A paint-peeled station crouched at the edge of the four train tracks that sliced through the three-block deep downtown. Freight trains roared through twice daily, stopping traffic on Main Street and drawing the faces of frowning old women to the windows. Diesels and boxcars full of unknown cargo whipped by, dissecting Newtown as if its only definition were to be between two other places.

The town had three parts, and three classes of people who accepted the tyranny of their geography. In Newtown, you either lived too close to the tracks, too near the river, or off Maple Street.

The lower streets along the tracks—where the sharp drop to the river leveled off for the rail roadbed—comprised a seedy downtown. The line-up consisted of a pharmacy, a Woolworth's, a few dark taverns, a crumbling Elks' Club, and houses interspersed with boarded-up factories. Disused railroad sidings and illegible signs hinted at a once-bustling industry, when Newtown was an ancillary of Pittsburgh's steel and coal glory. On the unfortunate avenue called Railroad Street, the houses fronted directly on a narrow sidewalk and the freight tracks.

There were many children here, fed on a budget and raised with the certainty that, somehow, things would be better for them.

Across the old iron bridge, respectable houses edged up the hillside, while a dirt road wound north along the riverbank. Single story houses there leaned toward ruin, some no better than shacks. Television antennas and rust-scarred autos were the only signs that the Depression Era had come and gone. The eyes of poor black and white women watched from behind torn screen doors and soiled lace curtains, hardened against hope. Only the mailmen came here, delivering catalogs to "Occupant," from an outer world as inscrutable as Tibet. There were few children here. Anyone who could, ran away—to destinies that were not always pretty.

Back on the better side of the river, neat square streets had been laid out on the river's flood plain— the "proper" part of Newtown which had sprung up in the 1950's and 1960's. Low ranch-style houses and rebuilt Victorians basked on ample lawns. Maple Street went straight as an arrow from the downtown, side streets branching off, each one a row of newer houses, until the town came to another abrupt end where the river bent around on its course.

Some of the Newtown people drove to managerial or professional jobs in Pittsburgh, some twenty miles away. The rest lived by trading with one another, teaching, doctoring, insuring and burying one another in that inexplicable way that lets a small town's meager wealth change hands again and again until the cycle ends in the graveyard. McGregor Gaunt, the town's sole undertaker, boasted that he made the last dollar, and his boast was not far from the truth.

The people who lived off Maple Street ate well and dressed well. They shrugged at the mention of the irredeemable downtown and tried not to think too much about their downtrodden neighbors. They shopped ten miles away at the new Marble Fawn Mall and watched cable television. They were particular about their sons' playmates and their daughters' boyfriends. Few of them, despite their success, had ever been more than fifty miles from home except perhaps to lob bombs in an inexplicable war of recent memory.

It was September and the maples were on the verge of reddening, and things in Newtown were about as good as they ever were. They lavished everything they could on their children, putting aside money for college, saving for this year's Christmas.

Zaccariah sat in his car at the hilltop, watching the dusk paint blood on the town's rooftops. He had driven the whole length of it, both sides of the river, and he had seen and sensed all these things.

He had the names and addresses of four children on the car seat beside him, written in the principal's scrawling hand. He had gone through each neighborhood, and as he had found everywhere, the chosen children came from all parts.

He was pleased. Tomorrow the cartons would be shipped. In a few days, the four children would enter a new phase in their existences. They would be uplifted.

He drove off into the countryside as the sun vanished behind the far hills. Night settled on the treetops, and a chill wind came up.

The maples trembled, as if Death had come by to take a measure of his ultimate harvest.

On a sleepy Saturday afternoon that found most boys attached to a television watching ball games— or playing outdoors at their own diversions—Peter Lansing sat in his basement, holding his ears as the wooden beams above him shook with the passing of a freight train. Dust settled into the beaker of chemicals on the table before him and flared up in the Bunsen burner he was using to heat it.

The boy put down the container and sat quietly as the vibrations continued. The whole room shook, dust and dirt settling on his black hair, invisible on his hooded gray sweat shirt. The earthquake continued, rattling all the jars on the table. A stand of test tubes rattled toward the table edge. He caught it with a quick, strong hand just as it toppled, then pushed it back to the rear of the table against the concrete block wall.

Light from a grimy window near the ceiling alternated dark and light as the wheels of the boxcars passed. Then the three-hundred watt bulb over his head dimmed as loose wiring momentarily lost and then regained contact.

The last car went by, and Railroad Street was quiet. The street hoarded silences since no cars or trucks could ride on it, then paid back with interest when the freight trains howled through. The ones with empty cars like this one were worse, with their hollow rattle and booming like a thunderstorm on wheels.

Losing interest in his experiment, he closed the weathered and well-marked book in front of him—stolen from the chemistry teacher's private bookshelf—and listened to the empty house above. He wondered if his mother might have come home during all the noise. He wouldn't have heard the key or the slamming of the door. But everything was too quiet, and she hardly ever came back from her Saturday house-cleaning job until nearly five, just in time to throw together a supper.

Peter Lansing jumped down from the stool and strode on his long legs to the foot of the stairs. He listened again. Couldn't she at least be home on weekends? It was bad enough that she was at Percy's Bar every afternoon when he came home from school, waiting for Frank.

His mother had been replaced by this groggy Siamese twin that would tumble through the door at around six every night—Jane and Frank, arm in arm, supporting one another in their brief walk around the corner from the bar. Then the twins would split, she to the kitchen, he to the television, a case of beer connecting them like an umbilical cord.

Uncle Frank, he was supposed to call him. His mouth went dry and his fists clenched when he even thought of the name. He didn't call him Frank, or *Uncle* Frank, or anything at all. He'd just get the man's attention and say something. And Frank never called him Peter or boy or *son;* he just waited until he got eye contact or said, "Hey!" or "You!" It was the unspoken way that each had of not acknowledging the other's role. One said, "You are not my father," the other, "You are not my son." The burly blond-haired lathe worker and the lanky, black-haired teenager would stay on opposite sides of every discussion. If Frank hated cats, Peter professed a sudden desire to have one around the house and would start bringing in strays.

When Frank brought home a beagle puppy, Peter terrorized it with his remote-controlled miniature robot. At last, his mother banished the puppy when it was evident that it had lost all bowel and kidney control and would wet the floor at the slightest noise. Peter had whistled all the way to the animal shelter with the puppy. Then he told Frank's drinking buddies at Percy's how Frank had made him take the dog to be put to sleep.

Peter liked the cellar. Frank never came down there, quite content to let Peter shovel some coal into the old furnace now and then during the winter. He had a whole room to himself—what had once been a storage room for canned goods. The shelves were perfect for keeping his chemicals, books, rock specimens and other private items, including his increasingly large collection of dirty magazines.

He resented the changes that puberty was creating. His voice was changing, which wasn't so bad. A little more authority in his manner wouldn't hurt, especially around the Cougars. Keith Brandon was smarter than Peter, but Peter was bigger and a leader. Keith Brandon was eleven—a wimp—but now Peter was maturing. But he still couldn't imagine himself doing the things those people did in the magazines. He wondered if he would simply awaken one morning, covered with strange body hair, the way a cocoon opened and a butterfly emerged, but nothing in the magazine gave a clue as to how this transformation happened.

Girls seemed to like him already, he knew. They'd gather around him in school and ask how he got away with his latest prank on one of the teachers, or what he had done during his latest mysterious absence.

But he saved his energies for the Cougars. The club started as a society of misfits, six of them. Now two were gone, one boy freaked out on drugs, another yanked away by his parents and put into a military school. The Cougars were a secret club, meeting in his cellar lab or in a treehouse in the woods which they had taken over from an old derelict, smoking him out with a stink bomb. In the treehouse were their oversize Cougar banner, the American flag they stole from the town hall, a Christmas wiseman they had taken from a creche, several lawn flamingos, and a lot of electronic junk that only Keith Brandon understood.

He liked the Cougars because they liked him. True, they would balk at some of his more outrageous proposals, but anything short of a capital crime was okay with them once he showed them how they would get away with it. So far they had baffled Police Chief Dougan with a series of offensive pranks. A hundred lawn ornaments were stolen and moved to the cemetery. Mysterious explosions had erupted at a lovers' lane. The boys' dressing room at the town swimming pool had to be evacuated when a horrible stink bomb went off.

Best of all, being with the gang kept him out of the house as much as possible, and out of Frank's way. All he told the Cougars about Frank was that he was *Some guy who sleeps with my mother*. He wouldn't dignify their two-year marriage.

He was thirteen this week. In a few more years—if he could stand a few more years—he could leave.

47

Find his father. Or join the Air Force.

As he closed the door to his lab and hung the ACCESS FORBIDDEN ON PAIN OF DISMEMBERMENT sign back on it, he took a last look at his special row of bottles on the top shelf. Where old mason jars of pickles and chutney had once rested, there were now dark blue and brown bottles marked with his own hand-drawn skull and crossbone labels. They read: *Wolfbane, Curare, Strychnine, Cyanide, Kryptonite (Green), DiLithium, Plutonium, Arsenic* and *Borgia Poison.*

About half the bottles contained nothing more than water with a few drops of food coloring, but the arsenic was real. His pet gerbil had died in convulsions, spitting blood. The Borgia poison was fake—to make the real stuff you had to feed arsenic to a boar, hang the boar upside down and collect its vomit.

He was pretty sure the cyanide was real, too. When he tested it in his mother's bird feeder, sparrows fluttered and died by the dozen.

Once, testing his nerve, and testing the attention of his mother and Frank, he had carried the Borgia Poison bottle to the kitchen table at breakfast. His mother had looked over her corn flakes and the *National Enquirer* and just said, "Oh, poo!" Frank had blanched and said icily, "Get that thing off the table and go to your room."

They just didn't seem to notice him, or if they did, they never took him seriously. So what if he had deadly poison in the basement? So what if he and his friends had made four pounds of gunpowder? So what if he played hooky and hitchhiked to Pittsburgh, drifting into army-navy stores and junk shops for Cougar supplies?

Every weekday his mother and Frank would hold

out as long as dinner, maintaining the air of love and politeness. Then they would retire to the living room, and the fighting would begin.

Anything could trigger it: the choice of TV programs, gossip about friends from Percy's Bar, or some real or imagined slight. By nine o'clock, they were shouting. By ten, mother was crying. By eleven, Frank was threatening to leave her.

Then Peter would lie in his bed, every word penetrating the flimsy walls of the two-floor house. And he would mumble to himself, "Yes, leave us. Just go. GO, DAMMIT!" Or he would wait in vain for his mother to do something, *anything*.

Instead, they'd quiet down. He'd hear them through the other wall, in their bedroom: Frank doing *those things* . . . and her *letting him*.

If only they knew what power he had. His grades were terrible, his academic standing laughable. But he was bright when he wanted to be—obsessive and diligent when he wanted to learn something. He could build things, make things, and he knew his elementary chemistry. He could do terrible things if he wanted—especially with Eric Varney to buy the missing ingredients, supplying the things that only an adult could get. He could blow up the house with them all in it—or he could poison them and become an orphan—

But it wasn't his mother's fault. He didn't want to hurt her. Just *Frank*.

Or maybe it would be easier just to drink the blue bottle himself and go out like the gerbil. Only they couldn't wrap *him* up in the *National Enquirer* and put him in the trash. They'd have to explain. To the police. To his father. It would be in the newspapers, maybe even on television.

He lingered, staring at the bottles, so full of

49

potential. What if his mother and Frank did die? Wouldn't his father have to come for him then? Wouldn't the police have to find Dad, no matter where he was? The court order that made his real father stay away would mean nothing anymore.

The Cougars had spent an afternoon thinking of different ways Joe Parisi, the school principal, should be offed. Keith insisted that poison was for girls—Andrea, one of the honorary female members, had readily agreed. She said girls thought about poison all the time, hiding it in rings and mixing it in the food they cooked for their dolls.

A messy revenge was better. Parisi and Frank should be eaten by sharks, or pirhana fish or starving wharf rats. The victim had to know what was coming, anticipate it, and then watch while it happened. A good revenge had to take a long time. "Make him watch while the rats eat his privates," Andrea had said, grossing them all out.

Peter turned away, sealing the lab and its secrets in darkness, to the dust and the spiders. He twirled the tumbler of the combination lock attached to the door, in defiance of his stepfather's order.

As he climbed the stairs, he thought of the way Bela Lugosi hovered over his victim in *The Raven*, one of his favorite old Universal videos. As the pendulum descended on the old judge, Lugosi chanted, "Torture! Slow death!" Peter said the words aloud in his best Hungarian accent as he swung open the door to the kitchen.

He jumped as he came almost face to face with Frank. His stepfather stood on a chair over the kitchen sink, hands scrambling into the farthest reaches of a deep cabinet. Frank turned at the sound of the door and Peter's voice, pulling in his paunchy belly beneath a yellowed tee shirt.

Peter looked in disgust at the older man's absurd profile: the beer belly, the baggy-assed trousers, the ill-fitting shirt. He wondered how his mother could stand him touching her. True, he had all that blond hair, a big mop with curls, and what his mother called a Grecian profile. But alcoholic decay had already started to puff up the face, too. In a couple of years he'd look more like a Polish Mr. Potato than a Greek god.

"What the fuck you starin' at, boy?" Frank demanded. Frank used his best language when Jane wasn't around.

"Nothing," Peter said, turning away.

"Better be nothin'," Frank grumbled. "I'm jus' lookin' for that bottle o' Dago Red your mother hid up here."

"Haven't seen it," Peter quipped, opening the refrigerator to look for Devil Dogs. "Never drink the stuff. Makes you fat and ugly. Ruins your kidneys. Kills your brain cells if you have any."

"Can it, smart ass!" Frank stumbled down off the kitchen chair without retrieving his quarry, obviously embarrassed at being caught in his search. "Can't you ever respect your elders? Who puts the food on the table in this house?"

Peter blanked it out, all too conscious that the man was a foot and a half taller and sixty pounds heavier than him. He whirled away from the refrigerator and hurried up the stairs to his room, slamming and locking the door behind him. It was another lock he had put on, telling his mother cryptically, "You wouldn't want to leave me unprotected against a *child molester*, would you?"

His room, dark and gloomy in the late afternoon light, calmed him. The walls were covered with a bright wallpaper, and his carefully assembled models hung everywhere from almost invisible wires. They included an F-16, a B-52, a space shuttle, an Imperial Star Destroyer and the starship *Enterprise*. On his dresser were Yoda and Mr. Spock, a two-foot high Alien, and various action figures in a promiscuous heap, many with missing limbs. A Rambo poster hung on the back of his door. His closet contained Boy Scout gear, a sleeping bag, survival gear, gym clothes and—in a box under a pile of old issues of *Soldier of Fortune* and *Fangoria*—a small bag packed and ready for departure on a moment's notice.

The bag was for the day his father came back to get him.

When he was ten, his father had appeared suddenly, taking him from his bedroom in the middle of the night, right down the stairs and out to the car. They drove for days. He remembered how he had giggled when his father made him pee into a milk carton so they wouldn't have to stop where someone might see them and report them. They drove until they got to Canada, where they spent three months on a farm. And then—foolishly—they went to Ohio to his grandparents, where his father was arrested for kidnaping and Peter was returned to his mother.

Now his father was who knows where. He was out of jail—or so his grandma had called one morning to tell him—but his mother had a court order keeping him away from Peter.

He kept his father's picture in his wallet and studied it often. He might come in disguise, and Peter wanted to be able to recognize him from the tiniest detail. He had just read the story of how Odysseus came back from a long war and killed his wife's fifty boyfriends with his bow and arrow. The hero came into his own old palace disguised as a beggar and only his dog recognized him.

A rumble shook the windows and sent Peter rushing to look. It couldn't be another train; no more would pass until almost midnight. Hands over his eyebrows, he scanned the sky above the dreary rooftops.

It was a storm, headed right for town. Lumpy black clouds already grazed the wooded hilltops.

With an exultant war whoop, he grabbed his jacket and raced down the hall to the front door. Frank howled something at him as he hurtled out.

He ignored his stepfather's protest. It was now or never. The Cougars were about to meet their destiny.

Andrea Martinez would never forgive Spiderman for getting married. She watched the comic strip every day, hoping that some calamity would befall the superhero's wife, adding an element of tragedy to the web slinger's aura and leaving room for an affair with a beautiful teenager. She had already written a letter to the author of the comic strip, describing herself and suggesting that as soon as Spiderman was a widower, they should write her in. She wouldn't even ask to be paid or anything.

Still, she had all the older comics to console her. Ever since she was ten, she had clipped the daily adventures of the lonely superhero, watching him dress and undress himself in the beautiful spider suit, listening to his innermost thoughts as he complained about the girl who always eluded him. Even before she was old enough to understand, she wanted to reach out and hug poor Peter Parker, especially when he took his shirt off.

The other girls in the sixth grade made fun of her

reading comics and adoring an imaginary man while they hung pinups of real boys from their *Tiger Beat* and *Gorgeous Guys* magazines.

It started with Superman, when she imagined she was Lois Lane. After all, she would look like Lois Lane when she grew up—even her mother said so. But Superman wasn't sexy and vulnerable the way Spiderman was. Superman didn't need anybody else.

She sighed and put down the newspaper, reaching for the scissors to cut out today's comic strip. Saturday's strip hardly ever had anything important, but she couldn't miss even one frame. They all went into the bulging scrapbook. Spiderman posters covered the wall, mixed with others of Wonder Woman, Menudo (in several incarnations), and the actors from *Miami Vice*.

It was hardly a girl's room at all, except for the neglected cosmetics and the lighted mirror on the dresser. Jeans and boys' polo shirts and baggy sweaters littered the floor and poured out of bureau drawers, while skirts and blouses hung like sleeping bats in the closet, covered with dry cleaner's plastic.

Her mother long ago gave up on her. She bought her new blouses from Woolworth's, or skirts from the Goodwill store, and would throw a fit when Andrea wouldn't wear them. "You'll never get a boyfriend— you'll never get married," her mother warned.

She smiled a smile far wiser than thirteen and brushed her thick black hair back with one hand, putting the scissors away in the drawer with the other. If only her mother *knew*. Andrea wasn't a "little girl" anymore. She had been having her period for three months now, and she already had a boyfriend—and they had already gone all the way.

His name was Barry, and he had walked her across the bridge and part way home one day. The next

54

Sunday, when her mother was at Mass, he appeared at the door. She met him in her pajamas, embarrassed that he knew which house was hers, ashamed to let him in among all the broken-down furniture.

A minute later he was inside anyway, kissing her and touching her under her pajamas. Five minutes later they were in bed. Finally she found out what it was her mother did with the men who parked their cars outside on Thursday and Friday nights. It hurt but then it felt good, and she kept thinking he wasn't Barry at all; his name was Peter, like Peter in Spiderman who maybe needed her.

He said he was sixteen. A few days later she saw him on the street with his friends. They all wore football and basketball letter jackets. He didn't speak to her but that was all right. She knew it had to be a secret on account of her being only thirteen. He had been back twice now on Sundays, and she knew he would be back again.

Her mother had boyfriends, but this was different. She only wanted one—one to keep—the way her mother talked about her father sometimes. Nowadays her mother didn't like men at all, even when they came around, even when they gave her presents and money. She smiled and pretended to like them and got drunk with them on the beer and gin they brought. After the men were gone, she'd hear her mother at the kitchen table, drinking a final glass of gin and swearing in Spanish *Yo les detesto!* "I hate them," became her lullaby as her mother swayed past her door into the bathroom. She'd even hear *Yo les detesto!* over the sound of running water.

She and her mother never talked about the men. Once one of them had leered and asked about Andrea, and her mother had said, "She's just a little girl. She don't know. All she does is read comics. Don't pay her no mind." Sometimes two of her mother's friends came at the same time, and the men would give her money to go across the river to buy comics or hang around the all-night diner. She sensed that it was better not to ask what happened while she was gone; when she returned the visitors' car would be gone, and her mother would be in the bedroom with the door locked.

Right now, she was torn between doing homework and trying to make it across the bridge before it rained to get a cherry Coke at the diner. The overcast was getting heavier and heavier, and she didn't want to get wet, not just for a cherry Coke.

She went to the rickety desk, outgrown two years ago, and looked at the sheet of paper that glared accusingly, waiting for a book report. She hadn't read the book, but she had a report in Keith Brandon's scratchy handwriting. Keith read so many books that he wrote book reports for all four members of the Cougars.

In return, she helped Keith with his math. She already knew calculus, since she had zoomed ahead of even her teachers in math, which had made her the object of veneration and awe among the club. Neither boy knew anything about calculus, and she kept passing out little bits of her knowledge to impress them. She taught them differential equations but held back on the rest—her insurance policy.

"I can't tell you any more," she had chided the wide-eyed Keith one Saturday afternoon in Peter Lansing's basement lab, "because if I did then you might be able to build a nuclear warhead." She giggled when she recalled their expression, and how they not only let her join their science club, but also surrendered some back issues of *Spiderman*. She also didn't have to pay dues, and they gave her a certificate that said she was an "honorary" member.

She just wished they woudn't still call it the Cougars, and she was *very* uncomfortable with Peter's newest project. But at least the Cougars talked to her. The girls in her class made fun of her and made cruel jokes about her mother, and the regular boys were even worse.

Thunder boomed off the wooded hill behind the house. Only a moment later, the phone rang. She hid Keith's hand-written book report back under the typewriter and ran to the kitchen for the wall phone.

It was Peter Lansing.

"What do you want, Peter?"

"Can't you hear the storm starting? You have to come up to the clubhouse."

"But I can't. It's going to rain."

"I'll pass right by your house in ten minutes and get you. Then we'll take the path up through the woods behind Mrs. Ferris's."

"But I'll get *wet!*" Andrea protested.

"Andrea, this is Cougar business. The experiment, remember? It has to be storming."

"You guys are crazy. That place could get struck by lightning."

"We know that. That's why we picked it, dummy."

"I'm scared to go."

"We could run you out of the club, you know."

Andrea winced. Keith and Peter and Marsha were her only friends.

"Can I take an umbrella?"

"In the *woods?* Don't be a sissy. Can't you wear a rain parka or something?"

"I guess so. But if I get ammonia, it's your fault."

"That's *noo-monia,* and only old people get that. That's when your lungs fill up with water and barnacles."

57

"I could still catch cold."

"You promised when you joined. When the Cougars call, you come."

"Well—"

"All right. We'll see ya in ten."

Lightning struck again and again behind the hills as Andrea rummaged the hall closet for her boots and a yellow raincoat. She hoped her mother didn't come dashing home from shopping just as Peter picked her up.

Quickly, she wrote a note to tell her mother she'd be out until dinner time—just in case. She didn't say where she'd be—just how long. Her mother hated that, but she'd shrug and say, "The library."

The clouds dipped lower and lower as she waited inside the torn screen door. The rain began, with wind rippling it in midair as though an artist's brush directed the storm. The treetops turned from green to a monochrome of greenish black. The rust-colored shingles on the house across the road lost their color, too. Water gushed from broken rainspouts, staining the black sheets of tarpaper that marked recent roof patches against the elements. A white fence, half its pickets missing, turned glossy with rain; behind it, a black cat dashed frantically into the cover of heavy bushes.

She looked up toward the hilltop, already obscured by the bottom fringe of the storm. The clubhouse was up there somewhere, jutting crazily into the storm, sticking its tongue out at the sky. Only a crazy person would try to go up there now.

A moment later Peter appeared, sloshing through the mud in clumsy boots. He cheered as she ran out to join him.

*　　*　　*

58

Keith Brandon's room might have been in a different universe from those of Peter and Andrea. An eccentric architect had designed the upper story of the house to present a sheer wall of glass, so that the vista of trees and unspoiled hillside seemed to make each room a vestibule into a private wilderness. A cedar deck below spoiled the illusion a little, especially when the hibachi was burning and smoke rose from sizzling steaks and hot dogs.

At night, though, the illusion was complete. With lights out, Keith could peep out from under his blankets and watch the night stars make their slow turn. He had seen passing satellites, a meteor, and—just maybe—a couple of UFO's.

Paneling added to the woodsy air of the room, although monster movie posters covered most of it. A black and white blowup of Albert Einstein's face—a present from his father—covered the back of the door.

As the afternoon storm gathered, Keith hunched over a long plywood workbench that contained his chemistry set, an aquarium, stacks of schoolbooks, and an electronic typewriter. The red-haired boy, short and frail for his eleven years, squinted through thick, round-framed glasses at the objects in front of him.

First, he pulled a barometer closer to his freckled face to note that the pressure was down and still dropping—a certain mark of a storm coming. Maybe *the* storm.

Second, he turned a snake-arm lamp on to watch the doings in what appeared to be an empty aquarium. (His mother didn't realize that the dead sticks and dried bugs were all part of an experiment.) He dropped another shiny beetle into the waiting spider web strung across two sticks.

"Get him, Madonna! Go for it!" he coaxed.

59

The thin strands of the web shook as the beetle tried to extricate itself. With lightning speed, a bloated garden spider climbed the stick, raced out the web and sunk its minute mandibles into the beetle. After a moment of struggle, the black and yellow terror began wrapping the stunned victim in silk. Madonna had struck again.

Keith opened his notebook and wrote:

No matter how many beetles I drop into her web, Madonna always comes for another. If she keeps eating, how big can she get?

This new entry joined the previous one:

Madonna will not eat ants. If you put an ant in her web, it will usually break loose. If it can't break loose, Madonna breaks her own web to get rid of it.

Behind the spider aquarium was a small box that revealed the intent of Keith's research. In his careful printing, it read: KEITH BRANDON'S FLY AND BUG MOTEL. If he could get spiders to build webs inside boxes, then he could sell them to control flies and mosquitoes and make a million dollars like the Roach Motel people.

He sighed, disappointed that insect control was going to be harder than he thought. At least he had regained his investment in the Ant Farm by breaking it open so that the black ants poured out on top of a red anthill. He charged admission for the resulting war, and his dad even let him use the camcorder to make a video of it. Then he charged admission for the neighbor kids to see *The War of the Ants* along with his first homemade video, *Undead Gerbils*.

The house was quieter than usual. Glenda, the housekeeper, had called in sick, and his father was in the basement study preparing lessons for his high school biology students. His mother was in Pittsburgh—she drove in two nights a week and Saturday to work on her master's thesis in child psychology. This meant sneaking out to Peter's basement lab, or to the clubhouse, would be easier than usual. Dad wouldn't even miss him until it was time for them to watch *Star Trek* together.

Keith liked his parents. They were busy, and they weren't around much; but they gave him everything he wanted, except for things which were dangerous or not good for him. Of course, those were the things he wanted even more. He had finally figured out that any outrageous prank, or any unreasonable craving, could be counterbalanced. If he got in trouble for making the stink bomb that Peter Lansing put in the boys' shower, he came home days later with an all-A report card or a special prize or award, and all was forgiven.

If his father took away his bottle of hydrochloric acid, a few days' sulking and listlessness got both parents worried. They talked across the breakfast table about what was best for "the child," and he got his acid back. As long as he remained the brightest boy in the school and stayed reasonably out of trouble, he got what he wanted.

Fortunately, Peter Lansing was both his Mephistopheles and his scapegoat. Peter dreamt up pranks—some of them a little vicious—and Keith had the brains to make them happen. But he worried about the older boy. When Peter had poisoned the sparrows to test their homemade cyanide—and when he said he had killed his own gerbils—Keith worried. Peter's occasional outbursts of anger—against his stepfather, against teachers—genuinely frightened him. But Peter and Andrea were his only friends. He couldn't abandon them or tell on them.

Marsha Van Winkle, on the other hand, he could live without. He had groaned when Andrea nominated her to join the Cougars, and again when she won Peter over to the idea. Marsha was smart enough to join, but Keith didn't like her. Marsha was the one who waited for him after school and talked to him all the way home. She even came up to him in the school yard at lunch time, and that embarrassed him. He didn't even *like* girls yet, and now all the boys were making fun of him and asking him about his "wife Marsha." Since they both wore thick glasses, the boys taunted them with the name "Mr. and Mrs. Owl" and "eight eyes." It was bad enough that they beat him up once in a while, bad enough that they had maimed his dog.

Mr. Peabody was the meekest dog in Newtown. Even as a puppy he had fled at the sight of bigger dogs and cowered quivering between Keith's legs. Any of the neighborhood strays might have been the pet's parents, for the long, low, short-haired mongrel had a little of every conceivable variety and had come from nowhere, a whimperer on their doorstep. Mr. Peabody had the dachshund's extended frame, floppy ears, short fur and a toy collie snout. His fur was a quilt of patches in black, brown and white, his frizzy tail alternating between a pert exclamation point and a puzzled question mark. His father had said, "The dogs had quite a party the night they sired Mr. Peabody."

The dog hadn't meant anything by peeing on Cyrus Sweeney's football, but Cy's gang had chased the yelping animal all the way across a field, catching him and tying several cherry bombs to his left hind leg. After the explosion, Mr. Peabody had limped home. The trip to the vet was just in time to save the dog's life, returning him home a wobbly cripple.

A year later, Cy Sweeney still taunted Keith on the streets with "How's your dog, Mr. Owl?" Then, as another year passed, it was all forgotten, to everyone except Keith and the dog which slept now on the folded-up blanket at the foot of Keith's bed. From time to time, Mr. Peabody opened one moist eye, regarded him with protective affection, and closed it again.

Mr. Peabody whined and stirred as the first thunder roared and echoed from the far end of town. The dog burrowed under the blanket and shivered, only his tail showing.

Keith put out the desk lamp, covered the aquarium with its industrious spider, and dashed for the closet to get his raincoat and boots.

The dog didn't try to follow. He cowered as more thunder shook the house. He couldn't believe that anyone would be crazy enough to go out when the sky wept and the clouds beat their drums.

Chapter Five

The shack was a terrible place—so remote and windbeaten that not even a derelict would sleep in it. Higher by far than the Cougars' tree house on the other bank of the river, it was easily accessible in dry weather by hiking up the pebbly bed of a creek. Other times, the only way up the sharp slope was over rocks that had gained a sinister reputation among generations of children. Spiders as big as your hand skittered out of the crevices that served as hand- and footholds, and on Snake Rock the southern exposure was—according to fervently repeated legend—a moil of sunbathing copperheads. Or worse.

No one would think of trying to get to the woods from the top, where a well-fenced dairy farm with marauding bulls added to the aura of inaccessibility. Instead, hikers followed a thin ledge, hugging the rock face where serpents might pop out at any moment. Stories of close encounters filtered down until the smallest child knew that Snake Rock was a living nightmare.

As Peter Lansing discovered, however, the worst reptiles up there were a few black snakes and shy lizards. So the Cougars took over the hill, making the shack even more secure by covering the creek path with dead tree trunks and dry limb debris. They even

painted a wooden sign reading: DANGER: POI-
SONOUS SNAKES! and drove it into the ground
near the base of Snake Rock.

A faded placard nailed to the door of the rotting
frame building indicated it had once been an outpost
of the long-bankrupt McBride Lumber Company,
from the days when the last real forest had been
ravaged to make wood chips for a paper mill. Now
there was only the unmanageable hillside forest and
a thin strip of woods at the top, buffered by the
electric fences of the dairy.

The shack had boarded-over windows and a
wood-shingled roof that had somehow survived
countless winters with only a few gaps. Once they
had brought up some scraps of plywood and nailed
them over the holes, the shack was once again dry.

They even found furniture: a wobby table that once
its legs were sawed off evenly, became as sturdy as
a horse; a few unpainted but well-made chairs; and a
big built-in cupboard with the rusted remains of tin
cans, Mason jars, whiskey bottles and silverware. A
Franklin stove lay turned on its side, the chimney
pipes and flues still hanging down like an inverted
periscope. Birds occasionally swooped down in chase
of bugs until Peter and Keith closed up the openings
with scraps of burlap.

The shack was built sturdily by old-time carpen-
ters—built to last as long as it was needed. Still, it had
begun to lean to one side toward the edge of the steep
hill, so that there was always a vague sense of unease
inside, a feeling that it was just an unmoored wooden
box that could tumble over onto the upper branches
of the pine and ailanthus trees below. They joked
about how it could suddenly become their second tree
house—an upside down one.

The lumber company—all too aware of the danger

of storms—had installed several doughty lightning rods on the roof, and they had obviously done their job well. Trees on either side were lightning scarred all the way to the ground level, but the tinderbox shack still stood.

Keith Brandon arrived first at the door, rain streaming down his face. He paused, waiting for the others, brushing off gnats and mosquitoes that came at his eyes and ears.

He did not want to open the door by himself. Someone could be inside.

He shivered in the slight protection of the door lintel. He wiped his glasses on his shirt. The beads of water didn't absorb, though—they just moved around on the lenses. He put the glasses back on with a sigh, feeling the cold drops hit his cheeks and trying to focus through the blurring gobs of rain.

Andrea came up behind him and pushed.

"Get in!" she urged, and the door opened under their combined weights.

The single room inside was empty. Semi-dark and musty, the damp wood smell invited them, like a hollow tree summoning squirrels.

"Where's Peter?" Keith asked. He went to the darkest corner to double check the cache of supplies and tools they had left there the day before. Everything was intact, under the protective plastic of some torn-up trash bags.

"He stopped at the bottom of the path. He said he forgot something and he'd catch up."

Keith was furious. Peter was chickening out. The experiment would be a failure, and he would be stuck up here all afternoon. Maybe all night, and with a *girl*. His nose wrinkled in disgust.

Reluctant to close the creaky door, they stared out into the trees. Cups of water, gathered and dropped

67

from the bucket brigade of branches and leaves, cascaded from maples and ailanthus trees, and sluiced off the edges of pines. Wind swished the boughs to and fro, the harsh parallels of driving rain intruding when the overlapped branches opened up to a bit of sky. Peter Lansing was nowhere to be seen.

"We're going to be stuck up here!" he complained aloud.

"Don't be a baby," Andrea chided haughtily. She took off her rain parka and shook it, draping it over a chair. She brushed strands of wet black hair back from her eyes with her fingers. "My house is right down the hill. We can go as soon as it stops raining."

Lightning zigzagged off a tree trunk onto the ground, and thunder boomed. Keith jumped involuntarily as their faces lit up and half a big old maple sawed off and tumbled against its neighbor. He had never been quite this close to lightning, never in a place where it almost *had to* strike. It was dangerous here.

Especially after what they had done to the lightning rod and the copper strips that had previously run it into the damp ground. How could he do what he had to do if the lightning could come down at any moment?

Before he had a chance to grow more alarmed, Peter came up over the ridge, burdened with a lumpy burlap bag slung over his back. The taller boy came in and closed the door with an air of authority. Now that he had arrived, they all belonged there.

"Is the apparatus ready?" Peter boomed out. He said *appa-raytus,* just the way it was in the movies. These things were important—just as important as calling Peter's basement room a *la-BOR-a-try*.

Keith smiled. "Almost ready. We just have to run the wires to the table, and then to the switch."

The two boys worked quickly, running the hodgepodge of antenna wire, speaker wire and discarded extension cords they had spliced together from the table in the middle of the room to the wall where the shack's two windows glowered out over the hillside.

In the middle of the wall was the wood and brass switch Keith had bought from Eric Varney.

Lightning struck farther away, and thunder drummed once, twice, three times, as the two boys approached the switch with the frazzled ends of the wire.

"Go ahead, attach it," Peter urged.

Keith's hands shook. "I can't. What if it hits?"

Andrea stepped back toward the door with an alarmed expression.

"What do you mean, if it hits? What's going to hit?" she demanded.

They ignored her.

"You do it," Keith begged Peter. "This one on the left." The wires went from Keith's smaller, trembling hands to the older boy's. Some of the shaking went with the transfer.

Peter twirled the bare wire around the left terminal, pretending to be nonchalant but fumbling three times before he could get it right and tighten the thumbscrew to hold the wire in place. He knew that nothing could happen until the switch was thrown.

Andrea came up and stood between them, her curiosity getting the better of her uncertain fear. "What does this switch connect to? What are you talking about? There's no electricity here!"

Then Keith pointed above the switch, and Andrea's eyes followed the line of tarnished copper that began there, twisting out the broken pane of the window and upward.

69

"The roof," Peter said.

She still didn't get it.

"The lightning," Keith explained. "We're going to use the lightning."

"Oh, like Ben Franklin with his kite." She smiled.

"No," Keith said, his glasses going white with a flash of lightning—nearer again. He smiled broadly. "Like *Frankenstein.*"

"You'll get us killed!" Andrea shrieked, backing away. She hurried to the door and opened it.

Lightning struck five feet from the door, jabbing at the trunk of another maple tree. Andrea froze.

"Better close the door," Peter warned, making the second connection to the switch. "The lightning could come right in the open door and hit you."

She slammed the door and leaned against it, crossing her arms in fury. "What kind of experiment is this anyway?"

Keith and Peter went to the table, where they fastened the other ends of the wires to the carbon electrodes mounted on pieces of plywood. The electrodes were positioned two feet apart.

"It's the next phase of the creation of life," Keith said simply. "You were there. You saw Phase One."

"The frog," Andrea recalled. "The train transformer . . . you made its legs jerk."

"Not enough power," Keith explained. "We need more . . . much more . . . the way it is in the movies. With enough power we'll bring it back to life."

"It was dead," Andrea protested. "It was dead like an old fish. And what if you did bring it back to life, what would it be—some kind of monster?"

Keith winced, reminded that Eric hadn't delivered the nitric acid. If the frog turned out to be uncontrollable, he wanted to have a jar of acid to throw it in—the way they killed the monster at the

70

end of *The Curse of Frankenstein*.

"It would just be the same old frog," Peter volunteered. "It's only a monster if you sew together a bunch of dead pieces, 'cause then it has no soul."

Andrea seemed satisfied. She put her parka back on, pushed the chair back against the far wall and settled in to watch. "You guys may be crazy," she concluded, "but at least you're not boring."

Keith and Peter smiled; that was as close to a compliment as they had ever gotten from Andrea.

Everything was ready. The wires were connected. The storm was at its peak or near it. Keith reached inside his jacket, pulled out an oversize Ziplock baggie, and flopped it with its contents down on the dirty gray tabletop.

The frog, as dead as ever, lay inert beneath the plastic. Yellow liquid stuck between the frog's thorax and the plastic as Keith zipped the bag open.

"Jesus," Peter cried out. "It's rotten! Didn't you keep it in the refrigerator?"

"My mom wouldn't let me," Keith complained.

He stared down at the frog and nearly gagged as the smell hit him.

"I guess it's a little too dead," he admitted glumly. "What do we do now?"

Peter smiled. "That little sucker was too small anyway. I had something else in mind. Something a little more challenging." He went to the corner where he had indifferently flung the burlap sack and lifted out a heavy, dark object.

"What is it?" Both Andrea and Keith spoke at once, moving toward the table to intercept Peter.

Peter flung a limp black cat down before them. Its head fell perfectly between the two carbon electrodes, its rolled-back eyes the only whiteness visible. A pink tongue hung out at the corner of its mouth. The

71

oversize body lay clumsily, forepaws curled in fetally.

"It's *Albert!*" Andrea screamed. "You killed Albert! That's Mrs. Muller's cat."

"It was dead," Peter insisted. He looked sideways at Keith and their eyes met. "I saw it by the side of the road and went back for it." Peter rolled one eye and dropped one shoulder in imitation of a movie hunchback: "It was very fresh," he hissed sardonically. "A police case."

Peter and Keith collapsed into a giggling fit. Neither the cat nor Andrea were amused by their snippets from old Frankenstein movies. And Keith was too high on the moment to let the ghastly reality behind the joke sink in: Peter had seen the cat and had gone back and killed it with his bare hands.

Finally, a fresh thump of thunder made the boys erase the laughter from their faces and get back to business.

"All we have to do now," Keith said, swallowing hard, "is throw that switch." He suddenly felt absolutely tiny, dwarfed by Peter, by the shack, by the enormity of playing with millions of volts of electricity.

"And *who's* going to do it?" Peter asked in a schoolteacher voice. They both turned and looked straight at Andrea.

"Oh no," she said, her head a horizontal blur of refusal. "Oh no, oh no, oh *no!*"

"You're the newest member," Keith suggested.

"I'll bet Marsha Van Winkle wouldn't be afraid to do it," Peter added sarcastically.

"I won't do it" was her answer, closed with a threat, "and if you don't stop this I'll tell. About the cat. About the stink bombs. About *everything.*"

That *was* everything she knew about. The only more embarrassing Cougar debacle was the day Keith and Peter tried to make phosphorus by boiling a retort full of their combined urine. They had fled Peter's basement room to get away from the horrible smell, and they were all so embarrassed they never spoke of it again except to say, "Phosphorus" and giggle. They vowed never to tell anyone they had peed into the glass retort. But now Keith wondered if Peter had told her.

So the choice was between Keith and Peter.

Finally, Peter grabbed a short piece of two-by-four, reached out and threw the switch. They all recoiled, expecting the clouds to open up instantly and pour lightning down through the circuit.

Nothing happened at all. They took deep breaths. They listened to the shifting wind, the near and distant rumbles of thunder booming off the river-banks.

"We have to wait," Keith explained. "It might not even happen if the storm blows over too soon."

Two more jabs of fire convinced them that the storm was far from over. Sun-bright flashes lit up the dusty windows and silhouetted the frame of the door. Every gap in the shack admitted stark beams of light, then winked out. The nearby explosions sent them scurrying to the farthest corner of the shack.

They huddled there, afraid to move.

"Maybe we better switch it off," Peter ventured.

"No . . . wait," Keith whispered.

They waited. Keith decided to count to a hundred. If nothing happened, then he would walk over and switch it off.

One, two, three . . .

Maybe the lightning rod wasn't really connected to the copper stripping.

ten, eleven, twelve . . .

"The trees are higher than the shack," Peter said.

"If anything gets hit, it will be the trees."

twenty, twenty-one, twenty-two . . .

"Maybe you should use a kite," Andrea suggested. "Stick the wires onto a kite."

thirty, thirty-one, thirty-two . . .

The wind picked up speed, howled through the trees, and blew open the cabin door.

forty, forty-one, forty-two . . .

Blue-white lightning ignored the trees and licked the ground just a few feet beyond the open door.

Andrea grabbed Peter's arm and stifled a yell as a laurel bush burst into flame and the gut-wrenching boom shook the building.

fifty, fifty-one, fifty-two . . .

The beams in the roof over them creaked ominously. Keith thought he saw the angles of the walls changing where they met the heavy beams. Was the shack going to topple over the hill?

sixty, sixty-one, sixty-two . . .

And then it happened—an instant that seemed like a slow motion ballet of light and burning. A whirling coil of blue-white electrons cascaded down the copper stripping from the roof. Tentacles and sparks leaped over and around the switch, painting charcoal lines on the wall. A half dozen spiderlegs of current danced onto the floor.

They had drawn the lightning, and it went where they told it, melting wire, burning insulation, bleeding ozone and sparks all the way. Rolling into a fireball, millions of volts followed the wire like a lit fuse. The tabletop exploded into fireworks—blue sparks, orange fountains of flame, smoke and steam. The two boards with the electrodes flew into the air, and the table shook as though a poltergeist had come with the storm.

A second bolt followed the first, but it was a mere

footnote. It licked down the copper stripping and sparked into the ground outside.

Thunder deafened them and shook their insides. Keith saw Peter and Andrea make two big O's with their mouths. They all looked at one another and screamed in terror, but no sounds came out. The hammer strokes that shook the building had deafened them.

They held their ears in pain and stood up. Keith refused Peter's helping arm and turned partially away. He looked down and realized he had wet his pants, and he didn't want them to see.

Peter started to walk toward the table, but Keith stopped him.

"The switch! The switch!" he yelled. He could barely hear himself, but he managed to make the other boy understand by mouthing it over and over.

Peter stepped back, understanding: they couldn't move until the switch was turned off. Otherwise, more lightning could come. He found the two-by-four again and hit it against the lever.

It was fused in position. He looked at Keith with a "What should I do now?" expression.

"Smash it!" Keith yelled. He made a chopping gesture.

Peter knocked the switch down from the wall, tearing it loose from the copper conductor above.

Andrea sobbed and folded her arms tightly over her parka. She was yelling something, but they couldn't make out the words.

Gradually, they all came toward the table. The sickly smell of ozone mixed with smoke. The whole table looked like wood in a fireplace, tongues of flame licking around the edges.

"What—what *happened?*" They made out Andrea's words as their hearing returned.

"It worked!" Keith shrieked. "It *worked!*"

He stood on tiptoe and leaned over the smoky table, brushing away a cloud of vapor with his hands.

"Let me see!" Peter demanded, striding up beside him and looking from his foot-higher vantage. "Holy Jesus—*Shit!*" he burst out.

The smoke cleared away. Keith expected to see Albert, fur tufted out in a high voltage permanent, open one eye tentatively . . . then a paw would move . . . then the cat would turn over and purr. Then it would walk off on funny stiltlike legs, lurching into the forest.

And then he saw what was really there.

The lightning had broiled the dead cat. Fur was burnt to a stinking black stubble, and steam rose from all over its body. The eyes bulged like boiled eggs. One hind leg, miraculously spared the fire, twitched and twitched and twitched, claws extending and withdrawing.

"I think I'm going to throw up," Andrea said. She turned her back and did just that.

Peter stared at the charred animal, transfixed. His mouth hung open, his eyes taking in every detail. Then he turned to Keith and picked the smaller boy up by the back of his coat collar.

Keith felt himself lifted over the smoking carcass. He gagged on the horrible stench and tried to pull away.

"You little shit," Peter bellowed. "Look at it! Look at it! You said it would come back to life!"

Keith was afraid—more afraid of Peter now than of the lightning and thunder. It was Peter who had egged him on to *prove* that Frankenstein could and did make dead things alive; it was Peter who had invested some strange urgency in its being true.

"I was wrong, okay?" Keith replied.

Peter grabbed hold of Keith around the waist and lifted him farther, taking his feet off the ground and pushing his face closer to the cat's. Keith turned his face away.

"Put me down," he begged.

With a gesture of disgust, Peter pulled Keith back and deposited him on the floor again. They looked straight at one another. Peter's expression was angry, looking for a fight. Keith's was pure fear, and hurt. If Peter wasn't his friend anymore, then he didn't have any friends.

The moment of anger passed. Peter looked at the cat, shook his head, closed his eyes and made a silent laughing gesture. "Shit," he cursed, "whoever heard of a monster called Albert, anyway?"

"Are you okay?" Peter turned to Andrea, who was trying to collect herself after her barfing fit.

Andrea nodded. "Let's just get out of here, Peter. *Please.*"

They walked out into the drizzling rain, girding themselves for the nasty, slippery descent back to Andrea's house. They would be covered with leaves and mud by the time they got down.

As least, Keith told himself, no one would ever know what they had done up there. He would never tell *anyone*, even when he was grown up.

Taking up the rear, he muttered to himself as soon as Peter and Andrea were far enough ahead not to hear him:

"I guess it just doesn't work on cats."

By late afternoon, the storm arrived forty miles away at St. Agnes's Convent and Sanitarium. It had spent a lot of its force on the way, but it was still splendid enough for Dr. Halpern to cancel the rest of

77

his day's duties and go to his rooms on the third floor of the converted mansion.

The master bedrooms of a coal baron, with fine mahogany doors and wainscotting, had been preserved, along with an enormous oak bed.

The bed, where he lay reflecting on the storm, was a mystery, like those ships inside a glass bottle. It was wider than the doors, and there was no visible way to dismantle it. According to a local farmer, it had been raised into the unfinished mansion with some kind of winch and pulley. It was a giant of a bed, and the old man had snickered about how it was big enough for the mine owner, his wife, and all his mistresses together.

Perhaps because the mine owner had died in the bed—and not happily—no one ever endeavored to dismantle and remove it, despite its antique value. Beds that people died in were often sold or discarded by families wealthy enough to replace them. No one wanted to inherit a bed that had the aura of death about it. For whatever reason, the oak monstrosity, its headboard carved with intertwining vines, had remained part of the property when it was sold to the Church.

Its reputation had, if possible, declined even further, so that the current Mother Superior had adamantly refused the idea of having it moved to her rooms. Two previous doctors had slept in it in peace—or *not* slept in it, as Halpern had learned from snooping in the convent's all-too-complete records. First there had been Dr. Warren, who "left without notice" the same day one of the sisters "left without permission." And there was Dr. Mitropoulis, whom Mother Superior caught in a tryst with two male attendants. (The details of *that* had even been written down, in Latin of course.)

78

In Halpern they had a much more fastidious man. He lay face up in the middle of the enormous bed, its sole occupant, naked, feeling the coarse knit of the bedspread all the way from his calves to the back of his neck. No one frolicked with him here. He had no time for frivolity.

But now the storm had drawn him here, torn him away from his rounds. The patients would grow restive, even disorderly, during the wild weather— but no one would need him unless the lights went out, or someone exhibited more than the usual mild psychosis. The nursing sisters and attendants were quite skilled.

He had shed his clothes the moment he closed the door and locked it. Then he had drawn the curtains wide and raised both windows. Wind puffed the white draperies inward, then sucked them outward into the rain, then inward again. The storm breathed into the room like the lungs of a whale.

His skin tingled, his stomach tautening and nipples hardening as the cool air passed over him in waves.

He watched, immobile and completely passive, as lightning stroked down at the trees on Sister Patienzia's hill. The slope lit up again and again, raised from the landscape like a woman's breast.

Thunder shook the house brutally—the near kind, crackling, then booming, as though the clouds chewed down on something with rotten teeth, then howled in rage. Above the hypnotic treble of rainfall, a tree toppled and fell.

For a moment, watching lightning play among clouds, he grew angry. The storm's power was wasted in the air.

His loins tingled as he tried to imagine Sister Helena lost on the hill, running to and fro in the

79

woods as thunderbolts sparked to the ground behind her.

Then she came to a great hollow oak tree and climbed inside. He was there waiting for her and took her in his arms. Lightning struck everywhere as he pulled away her habit. Just the two of them—and the Serpent, of course.

Another bright flash distracted him from his fantasy. His hand had moved, covering his rising excitement.

Now Helena ran naked through the trees, water dousing her as she brushed by low shrubs and mountain laurels. Bolts of fire silhouetted her. In an instant she'd be struck down.

"Not her!" he gasped, his hand moving furiously. "Not her! Me! *Me!*"

Lightning danced over the convent roof, flashing around Halpern's window like a strobe light. Together, the storm and the doctor reached a climax and subsided into sleep.

Chapter Six

Marsha Van Winkle just missed being part of the Cougars' great experiment. She saw Keith Brandon race by her house in the rain, but she couldn't go out. Her mother had banished her to her room every Saturday for a month—because she skipped her last two piano lessons to be with Keith and Peter and Andrea. And because of the "B" in history—the first time her grades had fallen below the top level.

She sat out the storm in her bedroom, an attic space that had been converted for her when the new baby arrived less than a year before. Marsha still called the baby "It" in annoyance, even though everyone knew it was called Jeffrey and was a boy. Jeffrey cried a lot, except when her grandmother was around, so she couldn't see why he got so much attention.

To make matters worse, he didn't have blond hair like Marsha. Everyone always doted on her blond hair—braided now because it was so long she and Daddy had an agreement that she would *never* cut it—and it seemed ridiculous to her the way they fussed about a nearly-bald infant whose wisps of hair were decidedly *brown*. Plain brown, like a mouse.

She could have gone after Keith, of course. Her mother and the baby were miles away at Grandma's, and her father had gone off to watch some stupid

81

sports videos with his friends from work. But she was afraid someone would phone or come to the door while she was away. Or Mrs. Gaunt at the funeral home next door might peer out and see her and tell her mother. So she had to stay at home, condemned to her history books.

Marsha turned on all the lamps in her room, depressed by the sudden drop in sunlight and the dreary sound of rain running off the roof directly above the wooden rafters. She knew that the Cougars had planned a new experiment the next time it stormed. Peter and Keith had said it was a secret, and even Andrea didn't know exactly what it was going to be. Of course Keith would tell her all about it after school.

Dark colors predominated the room, and even the white curtains and beddings didn't brighten it much. Marsha didn't seem to care much, though, as long as she had her books, her cassette player and radio, and her diary.

Someday she knew her mother would sneak a look into her diary, but for now all her secrets were safe. She had put little spots of glue between certain pages, and if anyone read them, she'd know right away because they'd be all pulled apart.

In her diary she wrote all her fantasies. They were a little like *The Lord of the Rings*, which she'd read three times, and a lot like some of the romance novels the older girls read. The heroes were a boy and a girl who looked just like Keith and Marsha, and the monsters included a witch who looked just like Mrs. Gaunt. In the last story, Mrs. Gaunt had hundreds of dead people in the funeral home, only they had never been buried because Mr. Gaunt was too cheap to buy coffins. He just used the same casket over and over again and dumped the bodies in his basement so he could re-use the empty box.

She thought it was a pretty good story. At the end of every chapter, Keith thought up a great escape plan, and they got away from Mrs. Gaunt and he kissed her. She hoped no one would think it was true if they found her book that said "My Diary," because then Mrs. Gaunt would get in a lot of trouble and of course Marsha had never kissed anybody. Not even Keith Brandon.

The other boys and girls knew how she felt, to her great dismay. That's why they made those horrible jokes and called them "Mr. and Mrs. Owl." One day a giggling classmate read a terrible composition about a boy and a girl who kissed, only they had glasses and the frames got stuck together. Everyone laughed and looked at Marsha, and someone went "Whooo!" like an owl. But the worst day was when someone saw her tracing Keith's initials over and over on her tablet. That day she had run crying all the way home to Maple Street with the girls taunting, "Kay Bee, Kay Bee, Kay Bee!"

Her mother had just smiled, telling her she was *precocious*—a word she had to look up. Mother said the other girls would like boys too in a couple of years. And a couple of years after that, her mother assured her, the boys would like *her* so much she wouldn't know which one to pick.

"Really?" Marsha had asked, astonished.

"Really!" her mother promised. Even Keith would like her. She wrote it all in her diary, too. If it didn't come true that way, she'd have it in writing to ask her mother why.

Marsha finished her diary and was reluctantly picking up her history book when the doorbell rang two floors below. The two distant tones repeated several times, like whoever it was was in a big hurry.

She peeked out the window to see if there was a car. It might be Mother forgetting her keys. But if it was a stranger, she was *not* allowed to answer it.

It was a big brown truck. And a man in a uniform was getting a big box out of the back. She had to answer it *fast* or he'd go away.

Marsha bounded down the steps to the second floor, slid down the wide banister to the first, and threw open the door.

The man came up the brick steps to the porch. The box was so big he doubled over trying to carry it.

"Is this the Van Winkle house? One-eighty-four?" he asked. Lightning lit up his smiling face.

Marsha nodded. "But my father isn't here."

"Is your mother home? I need someone to sign for it."

"No, she's not here right now."

He put the box down and extricated a clipboard that was stuck between his arm and chest.

"Well, I need an adult to sign for it, I think."

Marsha stared at the box. The label faced her, and it read: TO MARSHA VAN WINKLE, 184 MAPLE STREET, NEWTOWN PENNSYLVANIA.

"Me!" she shrieked in delight. "That's *my* name—it's for me."

"Well, young lady, I guess that means you can sign for it, then." He held out the clipboard, drew a ballpoint pen from his pocket and pointed to where she should sign. Water dripped off the brim of his cap onto the paper as she excitedly wrote her name in big letters.

The man brought the box into the hallway and put it down. She walked around it, looking at the tightly stapled carton. She didn't even know how to open it.

"What is it? Do you know?" she asked.

The man shook his head and backed out the door,

pulling it closed behind him. "Don't know," he answered. "I got four of 'em, all the same. Guess somebody got lucky."

Alone, Marsha paced around and around the enormous box. She couldn't lift it; she didn't even know how to begin opening it. She'd have to wait for Daddy to come home to have him help her.

Maybe it was encyclopedias—a man had come to the door one evening and spent an hour showing Mother and Daddy an encyclopedia. He made it sound like Marsha would flunk out of school if they didn't buy one. The package was certainly big enough to be a set of books.

But what if it was something else—something they wouldn't let her keep? She went to the kitchen to get a knife to start opening it. She had to see it first.

As she passed the refrigerator she heard the answering machine flip on. Her mother had turned it on, telling Marsha she had no business getting calls when she had history to study.

A man's voice talked to the machine:

"Hello, Mr. and Mrs. Van Winkle, this is Joe Parisi. I'm the principal at Marsha's school. I hope you can call me back right away at my house." He recited his phone number twice, then added, "I have some good news for you. A wonderful surprise for Marsha."

Joe Parisi hadn't appreciated the celerity with which the Reverend Zaccariah and the Tillinghast Foundation had come through with their promises. When Zaccariah called Friday afternoon at three o'clock to say that the computers would be delivered to the children by Saturday, he was startled and annoyed.

85

His golfing would have been canceled anyway, but since Parisi spent most Saturdays in the clubhouse at Four Gables Country Club, he would have gone anyway, had a few drinks with his friends, and watched the rainstorm from the big picture window that looked out over the course.

Instead, he sat in a polo shirt and green golf pants, hunched over his little-used desk in the basement rec room—his "home office" for tax purposes—phoning the homes of the four children to try to get to the parents before the computers arrived. How was he to get their gratitude? For that matter how was he to convince the school board that he had worked for months to get the computers from the tough New England foundation, when it was already a fait accompli? He had hoped for time for a memo to the board, at least.

One by one, he called the houses.

No one was home at Andrea Martinez's house. Either that or Emelda Martinez was making whoopee with some gentleman callers—something Parisi had heard about in lurid detail from the guys at the Gulf station.

After twelve rings, the father answered at the Brandon house and reported that the box had already arrived, although he didn't know where his son was. The man was profuse in his thanks. "We were thinking about getting Keith a computer," the father said. "What a wonderful surprise!"

A drunken stepfather answered at Peter Lansing's house and replied suspiciously that the box had come but he sure as hell wasn't going to pay for it. He was mollified to hear that it would cost him nothing at all.

As for the Van Winkles, he had to content himself with talking to an answering machine. He said just enough so the mother or father would be sure to call him back right away.

Then he sat back, leafing through his wife's copy of *Reader's Digest* and sipping a cool can of Budweiser. The storm outside boomed occasionally, but it was muffled in the basement room, reduced to the sound of water running off the roof into the drain pipes, and the slight clammy humidity that crept through the cinder block walls.

He thought about these kids and their computers and regretted he had agreed to Zaccariah's no-publicity stipulation. There had to be some way to get some mileage out of this, some angle. Maybe when the kids' grades improved, he could propose a school computer program, get the board to approve it, maybe even build a new wing. . . .

He smiled, knowing he'd find a way. He had used his cunning to get from football coach in one town to principal in the next. He squeezed as much salary as he could out of the local board—and almost as much from the contractors that delivered to the school.

If there had been time, he could have arranged a hundred dollar "processing fee" for the families getting the computers. At least the Brandons and Van Winkles could afford it. After all, they lived on Maple Street, on the high number end. Parisi had to content himself to living on the downtown end of the street, a cheap postwar ranch-style with a cramped garage, aluminum siding, mildew, termites and silverfish.

Then he thought about the Martinez woman. Money she didn't have, but maybe he should drop in to visit her. Just business, of course, to tell her how hard he worked to get Andrea the computer. She'd be grateful. Maybe *very* grateful.

He looked at his watch. Grace wouldn't be home for another two hours from her part-time job at the

87

beauty parlor. He could take a ride across the bridge and out along River Road. If he saw lights on in the house and no cars out front, he'd stop in.

As he fumbled for his jacket and car keys, he wondered if what they said about the woman was true. A woman like that—one who would do the things your wife wouldn't—was hard to find in a small town.

And now he had an excuse to go have a look-see.

Andrea led the two boys through the bottom end of the woods so they would come out in the trees behind her own backyard. Even though the trail was steeper, she convinced them it was better that way. No one would see them walking down River Road all wet and covered with mud. And therefore no one would suspect them if the dead cat were found in the old lumber company cabin.

They threw away most of the "evidence" along the way. The burnt-up wire went into a tangle of briars. The switch was thrown down a crevice between two rocks, along with the two electrodes. (Keith protested he could still sell them back to Eric Varney, but he was outvoted.) The dead frog in the baggie went into the creek, a stone added to keep it from being carried down into somebody's yard. Nobody would touch the cat, so they left it there like the remains of an unspeakable barbecue.

The only thing they kept was Keith's journal—a big ledger book on which he had lettered *Secrets of Life and Death*. Keith had it under his parka, making his chest bulge with its flat surface. He refused to give it up, or even to tear out the pages about the frog.

"I'm gonna write it all down," he threatened. "Even the cat part. It's our official record."

"And what if your *mother* sees it?" Peter protested.

"My mother would never do that!" Keith insisted.

Finally, on the slippery path down, they agreed to let Keith keep the journal if he wrote on the inside cover that "any resemblance to real persons and frogs and cats, living or dead, is purely coincidental." They weren't sure about the last word—Keith thought it was "consequental," but it was close enough. Anybody who saw the book would think it was a story, like the short story Marsha Van Winkle made up for English class that the teacher had put in the school paper.

They clambered over a low fence and slogged through the grass toward Andrea's back door. Andrea kept the lead, shivering under her parka and squinting as the unrelenting rain trickled down into her eyes. Behind her she heard the squish-squash of the two boys' boots on the water-logged lawn. The boys talked in a hushed tone, and she couldn't make out the words, which annoyed her.

"Wait a minute," she said as they came pounding up the porch steps behind her. She had to check to see if her mother was home yet. She also hesitated for another reason: Neither boy had ever been in the house. They had no real idea how she lived, aside from the road's view of the low, shingled house with cracked panes and one bulging wall. Now they would see the mismatched furniture, the stained and faded carpets and—worst of all—her mother in whatever woozy state she might greet them. If they were lucky, Mama would still be out.

Andrea opened the screen door and pushed open the kitchen door behind it. "Mama," she called. "Are you there?"

Her ear caught a man's laughter—interrupted suddenly. Then her mother's contralto voice called from the front room.

"Andrea, is that you? What were you doin' out in the storm?"

Andrea went in while the two boys huddled on the porch, waiting to be admitted. Keith sneezed loudly.

The light flicked on, and Emelda Martinez whirled into the kitchen, all bosom and motherly concern. Her dark eyes burned with disapproval as she saw her soggy daughter, then muted as she took in the shadowy silhouettes of the boys.

"Well—come in, you two," she beckoned, opening the screen. "Get outta those coats and get dry in the kitchen here."

Andrea's mother bustled around the narrow kitchen, plucking off parkas and boots, arranging the boys at the table and hanging Andrea's coat on a hook on the back of the basement door. She wore a white blouse with ruffled sleeves, a tight skirt that accented her wide hips, and rather too many rings and bracelets. She filled the room with the scent of an aggressive perfume, and her lipstick and nail polish looked lurid under the fluorescent ceiling lamp.

"There," she said, putting all the boots on the porch. Then she turned to Andrea and said intently, "Now go and see who's visiting us."

Andrea bit her lip and looked at her mother reproachfully. In an instant she was pulled by the arm down the hallway past their bedrooms and into the parlor.

Principal Parisi sat on the broken-down sofa, a can of beer in one hand, looking ludicrously undressed in his short-sleeved shirt and brightly colored trousers. The running shoes clinched it—Parisi wore only mirror-sharp black shoes in school. He smiled benignly, a slight glaze over his eyes. His nose was redder than usual. Andrea thought: *They're both drunk.*

"This is Mr. Parisi. You know your principal, don't you, Andrea? Don't be rude."

Andrea froze. Had they already found out about her and Barry? Or was it something the Cougars had done—maybe the stink bombs Peter had planted in the boys' gym and in Parisi's car? Was he here to have her expelled or punished?

"Hello, Mr. Parisi," she stammered.

Her mother pushed her forward toward their guest. "Mr. Parisi has a s'prise, Andrea, a nice s'prise. Can you guess what he has for you?"

Andrea was speechless. Seeing her most feared authority figure, dressed like a slob and sitting with a drink, confused her. Her eyes just fixed on the green trousers and the can of beer.

Parisi seemed to sense her thoughts, for he deliberately put the can down on the floor and out of sight around the corner of the sofa. He bent forward, folded his hands together like two embracing octopi, and put his elbows on his knees.

"It's something very special, Andrea," he hinted. "Only four students were picked."

She regained her composure. This had nothing to do with disciplinary action. "Picked for what, Mr. Parisi?"

"To receive a brand new, beautiful computer. It's already in your room. I helped your mother move it in there. It's all yours—ready to use."

Andrea turned and retraced the steps back to the kitchen. "Did you hear?" she called to Peter and Keith. "I got a computer!"

The boys, who had been giggling over something in the kitchen, hadn't heard, and they rushed into the parlor, stopping dead when they, too, came face to

91

face with Parisi.

"Well—" the principal said, standing. That made him look more like his usual bossy self.

The boys' mouths fell open. Keith, who was cradling his *Secrets of Life and Death* journal in his arms, whirled it behind his back and looked up in goggle-eyed terror.

"Well," he repeated in a higher pitch, inexplicably turning beet red. "What a coincidence. You're Peter." He turned to Andrea's mother and said, "He's in my office *quite* often."

He bent down and looked at Keith, who noticeably trembled. "And you're Kerry Brandon, aren't you?"

"K-Keith Brandon," the smaller boy replied.

"So, Peter and Keith, what a nice surprise. It just so happens that both of *you* are getting computers, too. I talked to both of your fathers."

"My father?" Peter blurted out.

"Oh, I mean—he's your *step*father, I suppose. Anyway, the computers are waiting for you. I had no idea you all played together."

"We have a club—a science club," Andrea explained. "And we do our homework together sometimes." And she thought: *And on Saturdays we bring dead cats back to life.*

"Now you'll have even more in common," Parisi assured them.

"And who is the *fourth* student, Mr. Parisi?" Andrea couldn't resist asking.

"She's not one of your classmates. She's in the *fifth* grade with Keith. Marsha—"

"Marsha Van *Winkle?*" Andrea gasped. "She's our friend, too."

"Good, good." Parisi smiled. "Now let's get these boys home. Go get your coats."

Andrea couldn't wait to see her computer. As the

boys went to the kitchen to get their coats, Andrea went down the passage to her room. Her mother's door was open, and in the semi-darkness she was hurriedly straightening her bedspread and pillow. Then she removed a man's jacket from the back of her vanity chair and draped it over her arm.

As Andrea stepped back into her own doorway, Emelda emerged and handed the coat to Parisi in the hall. For a brief instant all their eyes met in total understanding of what had—or had almost—happened.

Andrea ducked into her room and closed the door. She leaned back against it, reached for the light switch, but stopped. Even though she wanted to see the room, find her present and open it, she was numbed by the words that ran through her head:

My mother and Mr. Parisi. They were in there—together.

She didn't say goodbye to Keith or Peter, even though their voices, joined by Parisi's called out "Goodbye" through the door. She was burning with shame.

Then she hit the light switch and saw it: The box was there on the floor, bigger than any Christmas present she had ever received. The flaps were open, the inner box ready to lift out.

As she knelt before the box, the door opened. She felt her mother's presence behind her. Was Andrea supposed to say something appreciative?

"It's not the way you think, baby," her mother said. She knelt, too, peeking into the box and trying to help. "He's a nice man."

"And you just wanted to say 'thank you'?" Andrea retorted sarcastically.

"We was talking, and then we had a drink."

Andrea averted her eyes, busying herself with

opening the next layer of boxes. Then her head dropped and she moaned, "Mama, how could you? He's the *principal!*"

"We didn't do nothing."

Andrea felt her mother's hands around her shoulders, but she shrugged them off. She didn't believe her mother anymore, not the way the stories were going around town.

"Your boyfriends didn't see nothing, if that's what you're worried about. They was too 'xcited about their computers."

Her mother was right about *that*. Keith and Peter wouldn't have seen a mountain lion in the house once their eyes lit up with the sugar plum vision of computers. Even if Keith and Peter knew about her mother's "reputation," they'd forget in a week that they had seen Parisi with her mother.

"All right, Mama," she said, not wanting to argue. Besides, seeing what was in these boxes was much more important than worrying about what her mother and Joe Parisi might or might not have done.

"Jus' be grateful," her mother went on, not knowing when to stop. "Somehow I gotta pay the bills. You gotta go to college, Andrea. All I get is welfare. I gotta keep a roof over our heads."

"I know, Mama," Andrea replied. "I *know*."

Then her mother was gone. In the kitchen, an ice tray cracked open, and cubes dropped into a glass. Then the television came on, with Jimmy Swaggart moaning and crowing about "Jee-*zuz!*"

Andrea forgot everything else when the computer emerged from its box.

Mr. Peabody sniffed the edges of the cardboard box eagerly. He had investigated every angle of the corrugated material, following Keith in a sizing-up circle. He gathered the data that only dogs can savor about the delivery truck it had come in (diesel), the storeroom where it had waited for months (mildew, coal dust, mice), and—most important—the clear sense that no other canine had ever been near it.

As Keith tore off the upper flaps, Mr. Peabody backed against the box to claim it as his territory. He could no longer lift his leg in the official gesture of marking—if he did, he toppled over unceremoniously.

Keith watched the dog, then picked him up at the instant he was about to urinate on the carton.

"No!" he admonished, putting his hand over the dog's eyes. "No, *no!* You don't pee in the house!"

Mr. Peabody whined as he was deposited outside the bedroom door and banished. Keith knew he would either wait there patiently to be readmitted, or hobble downstairs and out through his dog door for a walk in the wet grass.

Piece by piece, the computer emerged from the immense box. There were cartons inside the box, cushioned with styrene peanuts, and big chunks of molded styrofoam encapsuling the computer components themselves. Even as he cut through the adhesive tape that held the chunks of packing foam together, he still didn't know what he had. None of the boxes were labeled.

The first package contained a double disk drive—a smooth tan plastic box with slots for two floppy disks. Keith grew more excited—two drives meant a lot of versatility. Most of his schoolmates who had computers for games chugged along with a single disk drive. With two, you could do a lot more. The Cougars could have their journals on a word processing disk that no one else could read. They could even publish their own newspaper.

The next box—a big one—contained a thirteen-inch monitor. He was thrilled to see that the screen was a color one, meaning that he could have full computer graphics, which could be a big help in his school work. He tipped the heavy monitor cube onto his bed and reached into the very bottom of the carton for the last sizeable box.

Wide and flat, this was the computer and its keyboard. Between two styrofoam cubes and beneath a plastic cover, the keyboard beckoned his fingers. As he slid the packing away, the trademark finally came up.

"Dad!" Keith called out, thinking his father might be within earshot. "It's a Commander!"

His father appeared in a few seconds, drying his hands on a bathroom towel. Tall and lanky, dressed in a white shirt and a ratty old cardigan sweater, with hair even redder than Keith's, he came in and lifted the low, flat keyboard in his hand.

"It's a Commander, Dad—the same one we looked at in the store."

"Seems to be," his father said. He ran his finger around the stainless steel band that circled the whole keyboard. "Funny, though, I don't remember this trim—pretty neat. Want me to help you set it up?"

"Sure, Dad!"

"Are there wires and cables in that box?"

Keith flipped the carton over, letting the last items tumble sideways and then out within his grasp. He came up with a handful of cables, wires, and plug-in cartridges.

"How about a manual?" his father asked, sitting on the bed and loosening the plastic wraps from the cables.

Keith rummaged through the packing until he found the shrink-wrapped package that contained manuals and disks.

Making room on Keith's worktable and adding a six-outlet power strip from Dad's workshop, they soon had everything plugged in. The screen and disk drive connected to the computer, and each item in turn plugged into the outlets—an unholy mess of wires. It was indeed the computer they had nearly bought a few weeks before: a Commander 256, with color, expanded memory, music and other features. A typewritten sheet that someone had taped into the manual explained how to plug in the two extra cartridges: a memory expander and a speech synthesis unit.

"Does that mean it will *talk?*" Keith asked. "Like the computer on *Star Trek?*"

"A little like that," his father explained. "Usually it will just read aloud whatever words you type in. It can't think or ask you questions."

Keith opened the box of program disks and then spread them out on the work table.

"Here's your master program disk." His father pointed to one.

"And here's word processing! I can use it for my homework."

"Here's one for math."

"And look—*Chemistry Tutor.*

"And *Musician's Workshop.*

"Here's one called *Real War.* There's a chess-playing program on the other side." His father held that disk and didn't put it down with the others.

"Keith—" he started.

"I *know*, Dad. I'm not really interested in games. I told you that." His father had balked at buying him the computer, saying that he didn't want Keith to become a computer-game zombie. Most computer games were *dumb,* and Keith had tried to convince his father he didn't care about them. There were far more important things to do with a computer than playing Dungeons and Dragons or watching a bunch of stick figures annihilate one another.

"All right," Dad relented. "I suppose it wouldn't hurt to fool around with this chess game when your friends come over."

Keith knew without asking that *War Games* would never pass muster. His parents deplored violence, even on television, and "war" was a word that one didn't take lightly around them. His parents had met at an anti-draft protest, and his mother had persuaded his father to change his major from nuclear engineering to environmental engineering.

"Now, what's this one?" his father asked, putting down the game disk indifferently and picking up a sealed disk package. It was a manila disk mailer, unlike the others, with a typewritten label that read: PRIVATE TUTOR: SPECIAL FOR KEITH BRANDON ONLY.

"Wow!" Keith reacted. "They have my name on it!"

"Mr. Parisi said this was a special package from an educational foundation," Dad explained. "They probably want you to use this program and then tell them later how you like it."

"Does that mean we're guinea pigs?"

The elder Brandon smiled. "I wouldn't go so far as calling it that. It's what they call test marketing. If you kids like it, and the principal reports that your grades go up—"

"But I already get all A's—except in gym."

"Well, you see, that's how some tests work. Your principal said they picked some students with all

A's—like you—and others who were bright but who were having some troubles—"

"That's Peter!" Keith exclaimed. "And Andrea—she's awful in history and English."

"And who's the other one? It was your little friend Marsha, wasn't it?"

"Oh, *her.*" Keith groaned, trying to sound indifferent. "I guess she always gets A's, too."

"Probably," his father agreed.

Keith smiled a little, thinking that maybe Marsha would leave him alone now. She'd be so preoccupied.

The phone rang. Seconds later his mother's voice called up the stairs: "Keith! It's Marsha."

Keith rolled his eyes and groaned. "I'm busy!" he protested.

"She wants you to help her," his mother called back. "She says she can't connect her new computer."

Keith looked at his father for support. Instead, Dad shrugged, smiled and said, "It's just down the street. You can be back before *Star Trek.*"

Accepting the inevitable, Keith picked up his jacket and headed for the Van Winkle house.

On the bright Sunday morning that followed the storm, Eric Varney bicycled a little farther than usual: along River Road past houses so beaten and weathered they were only a step from abandonment, onto a footpath that terraced along the upper river bank but bypassed the lawns and pastures above. Then he hid the bicycle and walked all the way to the next town.

Like Newtown, Graffton was split by the river, with a narrow downtown huddled around a train station. There was even a downtown "mall" on this side of the river, a pedestrian walk of red brick with

99

plastic awnings to protect shoppers. Few people went there, and half the shops were empty, boarded up and sprayed with graffiti. Several gang killings had taken place there at night, adding to the feeling of uneasiness there.

Perched over the river where Eric walked was an abandoned mill whose windowless wall still showed the contours of peeled-off paint that had once read GRAFFTON SCREW. Spray paint graffiti made the most of that—a war of raucously filthy words between Newtown and Graffton gangs.

Two things brought Eric here. First, the virtual certainty that in the hours between six and eight on Sunday morning, no one would disturb his explorations, and second, the fact that this stretch of hillside lay below a gap in the Graffton Screw chain-link fence where people came at night to dump furniture, televisions, broken stereos, lamps. Even pianos came hurtling off the edge of the bluff, as one sleeping hobo found out at mortal cost.

This spot was on Eric's list of scavenging grounds. He tucked his trouser cuffs inside his boots to protect against bugs and poison ivy, and started moving through the heavy brush and old debris. It was rough going in the oldest heaps, where mattress springs, nails and broken glass posed the constant threat of impalement for the unwary foot. But higher up— near the top of the slope where the new stuff fell—he could sometimes find a broken television, an amplifier, maybe even a computer. He carried screwdrivers and other tools on his belt so that he could dismantle an appliance chassis quickly and get at the parts he needed. Whatever he deemed worth keeping would almost always fit in his backpack. If not, he had stash points on the Newtown side of the line where he could hide things and then come back for them.

The profession of gentleman scavenger had few rewards, but a morning like this was one of them. He reflected on how he actually had the liberty of *any* September morning like this one, any day of the week. Once he had paid his rent and utility bills, he owed no one a penny. The clothes he wore—corduroys, an army surplus shirt and a Swiss army jacket—were cheap and durable, the pick of the lot from army-navy stores and Goodwill. But that was all he wanted or needed. He was twenty-four and free, and his parents and the probation officer could go to hell.

He had only another year of "good behavior" before the eagle eye of the law would leave him alone. He smirked every time he recalled how "repentant" he had been about his infamous brush with computer hacking. He had been a first semester freshman in computer science at Carnegie Mellon when the police and FBI agents smashed his dorm room door down with a sledge hammer (rather unnecessary violence, he thought) and seized his computer and modem. He had done two things that pissed the government off royally. First, he had penetrated a computer somewhere in a cave in the Rockies that had greeted him as "Mr. President" and asked if the military were on red alert. Second, he got the credit card number of Jerry Falwell and two other TV evangelists and ordered thousands of dollars worth of exotic lingerie in their names, through a computer shopping network. The FBI guys had seemed more outraged about the black bras with nipples showing through than they were about his getting into some secret defense operation. It all wound up with a suspended sentence, thanks to his repentant stance and his parents' money.

His father paid his rent now—and nothing more.

His mother had offered him two thousand dollars if he would leave town. She was ashamed to play bridge with her friends as long as her son was around as a "convict and derelict." He stayed on in town—as much to spite her as to please himself. When he went to the house to get his monthly allowance, he always made sure not to shave for a few days first; that was enough to spoil three bridge games at least.

They could go to hell. And so could the Internal Revenue Service, for that matter. Eric didn't make a penny in the above-ground economy. Nobody cared if he sold rehabilitated computers and stereos to kids. He was officially unemployed, which didn't even bother the probation officer—not with the unemployment rate what it was in this area. Some of the guys hanging around the bars and gas stations hadn't worked for a decade. They just chewed tobacco and drank beer and waited for the benighted mills to open again. No one knew or cared how anyone else paid his bills so long as it wasn't by way of drugs or whores.

In a few moments, sweating as the sunlight and his exertions got to him, he was near the top of the hill, on a rock that looked down over the heap where Graffton's midnight discards fell. New debris had accumulated since his last visit: a sofa bed whose guts had opened and spat out the mattress and springs and cushions; several small televisions, and an amplifier. There were also the usual black plastic trash bags, loose bottles and tires.

Following a familiar path, he scrambled off the rock and moved down into the trash heap to get at the televisions and stereo. Putting on a pair of painter's cloth gloves, he moved aside the trash bags in his way. Most were light, full of lawn trimmings, leaves and paper trash. Several were heavy, tearing apart as he tried to lift them and pass by.

Suddenly, something was wrong—very wrong.

A cloud covered the sun, and he felt cold—colder than he should have from just a little shadow. Then he looked down.

A rat ran between his feet, vanishing under another garbage bag.

Eric uttered a short cry and jumped. The rodent had actually brushed against his boots.

He had never seen a rat here. He looked around for a stick in case he met any more. A long, dead branch protruded between two plastic bags. He pulled on it.

Instead of withdrawing the branch, his motion pulled the upper bags loose. They bumped his knees, and he yelled again as heavy bottles inside one bag thumped against the arch of his left foot.

"Damn!" he shouted, kicking the bags aside.

He shouldn't have done that. Behind the bags, a dozen rats feasted. They raised their noses and red eyes to stare at him.

He took a step back, almost toppling off the path onto the slope below. He put his hand over his mouth and nose, feeling part of his breakfast come halfway up his throat in an acidic clot.

It wasn't the rats—big and filthy as they were, they scurried away. The plastic of a hundred trash bags crinkled and shifted as they fled into their unknown labyrinths.

It wasn't the rats that riveted him to the spot. He got hold of the intractable branch at last, snapped its narrow end off to make a poking stick, and then gingerly used it to push more bags aside to reveal the thing that lay twisted and broken in the heap.

It was buried under bags, half hidden in the shadow of the unsprung sofa bed. He uncovered sneakers, white gym socks, legs, blue jeans up to the belt—it was a kid, maybe ten or twelve from the size of him. He saw the edge of a worn leather jacket and a white hand.

He touched one of the feet with the stick, then the other. Nothing happened. The poor kid must have gotten it the way that old derelict died. He was probably walking through the place—or sitting there stoned—when that sofa came tumbling over. Nobody noticed the body, and then someone dumped more bags over it.

Eric uncovered more of the corpse. The boy's hands were stretched out, arms like a crucifixion. Eric gagged again when he saw the shirt torn open, the red and yellow wet places where the rats had eaten through.

He lifted another bag to see the boy's face. It was probably one of those tough Graffton kids, maybe a gang member from his clothes. What a miserable fate, he thought, to be twelve years old and get squashed by someone's goddamn old couch. . . .

The sun came out of the cloud just as the last bag moved aside. Eric got his close up look at the face. Neck and cheeks and chin had turned greenish-white. The lips were black, the partially open mouth buzzing with flies. And as for the nose and eyes—

Eric screamed. And he would scream for days in his mind every time he thought of what lay there—what made him run down the hill and halfway to Newtown before he stopped and hunched over, vomiting.

When he had pulled away the last trash bag to see the boy's face, there hadn't *been* any nose and eyes. The top of the skull was just cut away, removed smoothly and savagely. The boy's head looked like an empty egg cup. Above the line of the cheekbones was just a concave line of sawed-off bone, a clean edge from ear to eye socket to nose bridge, all the way to the other ear. Everything above—eyes, forehead, hair, skull—was just *gone*.

Eric collapsed next to the spot where he had thrown up, sitting in high weeds and staring down at the sluggish brown river, the railroad tracks, the soot-colored houses on the other bank. A church bell began to chime.

His hands shook as he got up and tried to find the place where he had hidden his bike. He had to get away from here, and *fast*.

He didn't know what to do. If he called the police, he'd be taken in for questioning. And *one incident* was all he needed to have the probation officer foaming at the mouth. He couldn't have his name in this—couldn't even let it be known he had been here.

Besides, how would he tell Police Chief Dougan that he found a dead kid on the riverbank at Graffton—a dead kid with his brains and eyes and the top of his head missing?

Chapter Seven

No one paid attention to school work on Monday morning. Even the sleepy-eyed Keith and Peter, completely absorbed in their new computers, were mesmerized by the news that had rippled across Newtown late Sunday evening: the discovery of a mutilated body on the riverbank just over the Graffton line.

Keith heard it over the phone from Peter.

"Turn on Channel 11!" Peter had ordered, hanging up instantly.

Keith ran to the TV and tuned in just in time to see policemen, medics with face masks lifting garbage bags, then a wide view of the riverbank. Then another camera showed the men on the hillside, viewed from the end of the street in Graffton near the old screw factory, a bizarre, almost surreal view of police in their uniforms, and volunteers in red plaid hunting jackets, looking for—looking for what?

Keith's blood ran cold as he thought of the doings at the shack, less than half a mile away along the riverbank. Had the cat come back to life after all? Were they searching for a mutated monster cat that had been terrorizing Graffton all day Sunday, killing dogs and maiming children?

The camera panned over to the newscaster, who

stood in a tan trench coat. "The search continues," he began, pausing ominously.

"For what?" Keith asked out loud. The cat had been fried—broiled—sizzled.

"For more bodies in the aftermath of the horrific discovery this afternoon of a mutilated corpse of a teenaged boy. Identified from I.D. as Carlos Marano of Graffton, the victim was thirteen years old. The county coroner was baffled by the manner of the boy's death, suggesting that the brutal slaying may have been the work of a religious cult or a new type of drug-related crime. The victim's skull was cut in half, and police and volunteers have searched in vain into the early evening hours to find the rest of the remains."

The station then replayed the grisly footage of the boy's body being hoisted up over the top of the hill and into an ambulance. One fleeting glance, not edited in the news team's haste to get on the air, showed the hideously shortened head bobbing as the body was laid on a stretcher. Then, hurriedly, it was covered with a body cloth, and someone pushed the cameraman away.

Kids gathered in the playground and in the halls of the cavernous old Maple Street school, forming tight little clusters, each with its theory about the secret behind the crime. The corridor buzzed with the tales, each beginning with a high-pitched "Didja *hear?*"

Keith passed through them, hearing tidbits of the already exaggerated horror. None of the little cliques invited him into their gossip, since he was an outcast. But he heard enough:

"It was drugs. Carlos was a dealer. My cousin said he bought from him all the time. He probably got in trouble with some gang in Pittsburgh . . ."

"My sister said Carlos had a girlfriend and her

father told him to stay away from her. Her father is from one of those islands where they do voodoo . . ."

"Didja hear—his *brains* were gone! It was zombies—brain-eating zombies . . ."

"His head was cut open like a watermelon. They said on the late news it was like a surgeon did it. A mad doctor . . ."

Some of the other kids, who had been up early enough to see it, watched their own Police Chief Dougan being interviewed, along with Graffton's police chief, a red-faced man named Kovac, and the sheriff from the surrounding rural county. Dougan had puffed up his chest and said, "We don't *have* a drug problem in Newtown. Nothing like this has ever happened in Newtown." The Graffton cop in turn said that "outsiders" had come in and killed the boy, and said that he suspected a religious cult from somewhere down the river (that meant Newtown or somewhere farther down toward Pittsburgh). He suggested that other runaway or missing children might turn up in the same condition.

The interviewer cut off the potential brawl by asking the two policemen if the killing bore any similarity to the mysterious cattle mutilations that had plagued the area during the late 1970s and early '80s. Both cops looked surprised.

The sheriff came in then, recounting how he had been called to farm after farm over the baffling deaths of cattle in the fields. The cows would be found in the early morning hours, the tops of their skulls neatly cut off, their brains and eyes missing.

"That's just craziness. Crazy kids," Dougan replied. "This is a murder—a drug-related murder."

The camera cut away to a commercial, and when the announcer came back, the disputing law officers had gone.

109

The shock wave from all this was enough to make some mothers drive their kids to school. The Graffton school didn't even open, the principal deciding that no one could possibly apply themselves to school work. The school board declared it a day of mourning.

Keith had seen the broadcast, too. He vaguely remembered that cattle mutilation reports had something to do with UFO's. Didn't it say in the *National Enquirer* that aliens did that to cows?

Then one gang of older boys cornered Keith at his locker.

One grabbed him from behind and pulled him backward.

"Hey, Mr. Owl, we hear you collect *brains* now!"

The other boys laughed. Keith turned red.

"Look, he's blushing! Maybe it's true."

"Don't be stupid," Keith replied, ignoring them and fumbling with his combination lock.

"Where do you keep the brains, Mr. Owl? In your locker?"

He restrained himself from answering, but just looked at them, marking their faces. He'd find some way to get back at them.

Losing interest, they walked away, laughing at their joke and mock-punching one another on the arms.

Keith hated them all—these half-wits who mocked him and then asked him for help on their homework and answers to tests. He kept peace with the bigger boys in his own class by signaling the answers to multiple choice tests (his hand rubbed the back of his neck and his fingers numbered the correct answers). He had no bribes for older boys, only hoping he could escape their notice—or do something to them so terrible that they'd never bother him again.

110

He didn't understand why the world outside had to be so cruel—a place where bullies picked on smaller kids, and someone cut a boy's head off. Everything at home was just the opposite—his dad was kind, his mother strict but loving. They gave him no ammunition to deal with this cruelty.

Keith paused at the door to his home room as he saw Peter come through the double-door, hurrying toward the sixth grade home room at the other end.

"Peter!" he called.

Peter stopped, then looked at him.

Keith made the Cougar hand signal—a wave with tiny claw motions.

Peter waved back, but did not speak. He averted his eyes and hurried on to his room.

Keith wondered what that meant. Was Peter still angry about the cat? He went on in to his desk, to the chorus of giggling and groaning and the insect buzz of "Didja hear? Didja hear?"

Elvira Hawkins hadn't heard the news Sunday or Monday. She was only vaguely aware of it as she passed through the teachers' lounge for a cup of tea. She tried not to linger there—the cigarette smoke drove her crazy—but several teachers cornered her to ask her opinion about the crime. Her "What crime?" reply had been greeted with arched eyebrows and quizzical expressions that conveyed, "On what planet do you spend your weekends?"

She was aghast at the story. It was unsettling to say the least. It would be worse, of course, if it had happened here in Newtown, but Graffton was too close for comfort. Then she reminded herself of what her student teaching days in Paterson, New Jersey had been like a decade before—schools where the bodies were found in the school hallways, and where teachers were assaulted on the way to the ladies' room. . . .

Newtown had seemed the kind of place she wanted. The depressed town was daunting in appearance but safe, the children desperately poor for the most part but more eager to learn and advance themselves than their urban counterparts. The rents were cheap, and she was able to find a house—a whole house—for herself.

When she turned thirty, she had repapered and remodeled the whole frame house. "Here to stay," she had decided, bringing everything from her past from New Jersey in a big truck: the antiques inherited from her mother, all the books she had owned since childhood, and her grandmother's brass bed. That was her whole inheritance, or most of it. From her father, who had died in a VA hospital, she had her raven black hair, her name, and a few vague memories of depressing visits. From her mother's family had come everything else—a warm nest of women with property who all seemed to have survived their men by decades. Her childhood was a cozy shelter of fireplaces, books and unrealistic fantasies about ideal men.

Teachers' college had shown her how life really was. The handsome men went after the prettier girls—the ones who wore bright flashy clothes and would do anything a boy asked of them. No one ever asked her out, despite her good height, her ballet dancer's legs, and thin frame.

Her simple black outfit, cotton blouse and long wool skirt, with a black tweed jacket, was in keeping with such a somber day—but then, she wore black most of the time. Even when her mother died in the middle of her college years, she hadn't changed the

112

old-fashioned way she dressed. It never occurred to her to dress to attract and please men. Instead she dressed as if to impress a long-dead dowager, or as one seeking a governess position in some nineteenth century manor house.

She left the chatter of the teachers' lounge and strolled among the vivacious children toward her home room and the adjacent science lab. Although she preferred literature, she had followed a strange impulse to become a science teacher. There weren't many women in her field, and she enjoyed the attention she got, graduating at the top of her class. The month of her finals she had read eight Dickens novels while her classmates crammed and overdosed on caffeine and benzedrine. State teachers' colleges were not exactly demanding.

Here in Newtown she had arrived at a good balance. She was thirty-five now, and although she had dated a couple of the other single male teachers, they had all withdrawn after one or two evening outings. She always made a man feel he was with his mother, she was told, and hadn't the faintest idea what she could do about it. She couldn't dance, or wiggle, or make suggestive remarks. She had actually heard the girls' gym teacher proposition the math teacher—a married man—and was in shock for days afterwards, the words reverberating in her head. How could people utter such words?

Her students called her "Fossil Hawkins," and when she heard it, that clinched it: Fossil Hawkins, the spinster. Yet how many women had a nice house, a good job, and an endlessly renewed gaggle of thirty-five children? Life could be worse, she thought, opening the door to the sixth grade room just seconds after a nearly-tardy Peter Lansing swept in.

There was a hush, and a round of giggling, as she

113

came in and took her place at her desk. That usually meant a prank, and *that* nearly always meant Peter Lansing.

She scanned the room, the rear chalkboards, the locked glass door to the lab—nothing. Then she turned around and looked at her board, where she had chalked in drawings for today's science class.

And then she remembered—today's lesson.

On the blackboard was her schematic drawing and, beneath it, her careful lettering of the subject matter.

It read: THE HUMAN BRAIN.

The children had been at it. Where she had carefully written Temporal Lobe, Medulla, and Cerebral Cortex, they had erased her words and scrawled in *Carlos Marano, This way to eyes,* and *Cut here.*

Another child had printed FREE SAMPLES IN LAB. SEE MISS HAWKINS.

"Now that's quite *enough!*" she barked, surprised at her own intensity. At least her voice hadn't cracked. "That's absolutely cruel and vicious. Who is responsible for this?"

No one answered. Several faces went down to the desk tops in attacks of the giggles.

She looked at Peter. He looked winded and still had his denim jacket on. He hadn't even been to his locker, so she doubted he had been here long enough to play this prank. She'd probably never figure out who it was.

Distractedly, she erased the graffiti and went through the routine of taking roll call. A few students were absent—the same ones who were out yesterday with illnesses.

And there was the empty seat for Willie Hastings, the boy who had run away three weeks ago. His

114

parents hadn't even called the police until a week after he had stopped coming to school. She wondered uneasily if something terrible hadn't happened to the Hastings boy. What if they found him, too, along the riverbank?

"Have any of you seen Willie Hastings?" she asked them, trying to be as calm as possible.

No one replied. Two of the boys in the back row whispered to one another, then guffawed.

"You two—Charles and Phillip—what were you saying? Was it about Willie?"

Charles, an overweight boy who was already somewhat of a bully, burst out: "Phil said he saw part of him. Along the railroad tracks."

Everyone laughed, then stopped laughing when they saw her stern expression.

"What do you mean?" she asked.

Phil, a lanky blond boy, kicked Charles in the shins and mouthed, *Shut up.*

"Nothing, Miss Hawkins," Charles replied, blushing. "It was just a joke. Nobody saw nothing."

She went on with her attendance book, ignoring the joke and the hysteria that went round the room. She gathered the joke was an obscene one and wanted to hear no more of it. Thank God home room only went on for fifteen minutes. They wouldn't laugh and make jokes if one of *them* were hurt or killed.

As she watched them, though, seeing how their laughter seized them and took the edge off the horrible reality, she saw it as a defense mechanism. They were laughing about something they couldn't comprehend or make sense of. Who could blame them?

Sister Helena went a little weak in the knees when

115

the attendants brought her into Room 12 for her therapy. She was accustomed to doing as she was told, so it never occurred to her to refuse to go there, or to resist the two strong men who took her by the arms.

She wanted to say, "It really isn't necessary," to the two of them. She could just go down the hall and walk into the room by herself. But actually, she liked the contact. She felt the strength and confidence in the men's arms, reminding her of more pleasant times when she could do as she pleased.

So she let them walk her, pacing her steps to theirs, watching almost passively as they pushed the door open and brought her into the gray interior of Room 12.

Somehow she had hoped it would be different. A place where they made you feel better should at least be a sky blue, or have some pictures on the wall. Instead it was battleship gray, with irregular blotches on the wall where paint had been slapped over old, peeling paint and plaster patches. The floor was shiny tile, freshly scrubbed.

The black vinyl mattress, supported by a stainless steel frame, looked out of place—too perfect and modern in a room that hadn't changed in thirty years or more. Behind the mattress and its dangling leather straps was a rolling cart with equipment: a non-descript black box with its control panel turned away, a larger box with a display screen she recognized as an EEG from her preliminary therapy session, various wires dangling from the cart, and one heavy cable connecting it to the wall outlet. A second cart, at the head of the treatment bed, had bottles and cotton swabs.

"What—what is he going to do to me?" Helena asked, growing alarmed for the first time. "Is this

116

going to be an *operation?*"

"Over here, Sister," the attendant answered, bringing her to the bed. "And no, it's not an operation, Sister. Just lie down."

Deftly, the other attendant got her behind her legs, and she toppled onto the bed. Before she could even utter a cry, they had fastened the straps over her shoulders and waist. The straps pinched the white cloth of her shift, pulling upwards. She blushed, wondering how much of her legs was bare. The attendants pulled off her slippers.

"I can't move," she protested. "I can hardly breathe."

"You'll be fine. Here." They adjusted the straps a little. "The doctor will be here in a few moments."

The moments stretched on. She could turn her neck freely to the left and right and upwards just enough to see her body stretched out before her. Her arms were completely immobilized, pinned to the bed. Beads of sweat, hot and itching, formed between her and the vinyl fabric.

Finally, Dr. Halpern came in, followed by the attendant. The doctor looked at her and smiled.

"Good afternoon, Sister Helena. I see you're all ready. Just relax."

"This is *very* uncomfortable," the young nun complained.

The doctor ignored her and spoke a few words to the attendants. They looked at Dr. Halpern with puzzled expressions and then left.

Halpern moved around the small table behind her.

"What are you doing, doctor? Please explain this to me."

"You don't need to concern yourself with the details, Sister Helena. This therapy has helped tens of thousands of people."

"How?"

"We don't know exactly how, but when it's over, you'll feel calmer, less prone to depression, more in control of your emotions. You'll thank us for helping you."

Helena remembered the terrible things Sister Patienzia had said about Dr. Halpern. Had he tried to help her and failed? Was she so suspicious and ungrateful because it hadn't worked on her?

"Have the other sisters had this treatment?" she asked.

"A number of them have—when they get very depressed or withdrawn," the doctor replied. He began rubbing her temples and forehead with a cotton swab. She smelled alcohol.

"What's that?"

"Just to clean the skin so we make the best possible contact."

She felt things being attached to her face and neck. At the edge of her vision, wires dangled, led to the two black boxes.

Halpern seemed to sense her next questions. "This is an EEG, so I can watch your brain waves. And this is a Thymatron—it will transmit a mild electric current."

The door opened, and she turned her head to see the attendant return with another cart.

"Dr. Halpern, she hasn't had her injection," the attendant said in a concerned tone.

"Leave it here," he replied curtly.

"No one even prepared it. I saw it on the chart and made it up myself," the attendant added.

"Thank you, Mitchell," the doctor replied. "Now leave us."

The attendant backed out of the door.

"Was I supposed to have a shot first?" Helena asked.

"No," he said.

"Like an anesthetic?"

"No," he repeated.

"But the attendant said—"

"The attendant was mistaken." Halpern's face came up over her, upside down and leering. Something was wrong with his eyes, and the veins seemed to be bulging on his neck. "You must experience this with all your senses," he said, the esses hissing as he dropped into a whisper. "This is to heal you, and to heal you I must hurt you a little."

"You said it wouldn't hurt me," Helena protested.

He applied some kind of goo or jelly to her neck, and more to the palm of her hands. Then he stuck the electrodes on, letting the suction of the jelly hold them. She shook her hand but it wouldn't come off.

"For your sins, my dear. You must be cleansed of your sins and your guilt."

Helena sensed that something was terribly wrong here. Certainly the wires didn't belong on her hands or her neck. And Dr. Halpern, his steely eyes flashing, was acting like a judge, like one assigned by God to mete out punishment. She had confessed her sins—many times over—and she had been given forgiveness. It wasn't a doctor's role to make judgments like that.

She started to form the words of her protest, but her tongue froze in her mouth when the shock hit her. She even thought she felt it between her teeth like an alien object. Her jaws trembled up and down, back and forth, making cracking noises as though they wanted to leap from their sockets. Her whole right side was in agony.

The ceiling went out of focus. Blue sparks and red lights appeared. The world went black, then white again, then black.

She felt her fingers and arm muscles stretching and

119

bending, like they, too, wanted to escape from the terrible fire in her brain.

Then the pains and spasms were in her left leg, as though demons were massaging her, slapping her, trying to manipulate her joints. She raised her head and saw Halpern removing the electrodes from her bare leg. The shocked leg still writhed like a fish on the deck of a boat, or a lobster in a boiling pot. The motions had no connection with her.

Then it ended, and she found herself gasping. She had not breathed for the length of each shock. She inhaled like a drowning woman. Thank God it was over—

"That's for starters," Halpern said. "Did you like it?" He came around and stood over her.

"Please," she tried to say. She had bitten her tongue and the word didn't come out right. *Was it over now?*

"Ah, yes, *please*," he said, smiling. "So we'll do it again."

She shook her head no. And then the doctor did something terrifying: He laughed. The cruel sound of it segued into the next jolt of current—her other hand and arm this time—the next helpless agitation of her nerves and muscles.

She blacked out, and when she came to he was there again, smiling. He wiped her mouth with a cotton swab and it came up bloody. Then he put something that looked like a rubber ball in her mouth.

"Don't want you to bite your tongue again, my dear. You were very nice, Helena. I think we're really helping you. Let's try again."

"No—" she managed to protest.

He put the electrodes on her head.

"Those were sub-maximal shocks, Helena. Ones

120

you and I can enjoy together. Now we can commence with the treatment."

She closed her eyes praying for unconsciousness . . .

. . . and opened them to see Dr. Halpern again. He bent over her, and one of his hands pressed against her left bresat. He wasn't taking her heartbeat. She *knew* what he was doing. She could even hear the sound of his breathing, heavier and deeper by the moment.

She gasped for life, snorting air through her nostrils and trying to get breath around and past the object in her mouth. It was all she could do to come back to a semblance of consciousness and control. There was never time to focus her thoughts, to realize that she was being attacked, abused in some hideous way.

Finally, she fell into genuine unconsciousness, beyond caring.

The doctor noted on his chart that Sister Helena had received the prescribed voltage for the required two second duration, and that she had suffered a typical mild seizure followed by disorientation.

The treatment was successful. And she would be back in two days for more.

When Sister Patienzia could stand pacing her room no longer, she ventured out into the cool air and started for her garden. Her excuse was that a big row of corn was now ripe for picking, and Mother Superior loved fresh corn. Her real reason was to get away—as far away as the grounds allowed from what was happening in that room.

Would Helena remember her—remember *anything*—when Dr. Halpern was through with her?

She had seen a dozen or more sisters over the years go through the rigors of electro shock therapy with Dr. Halpern and his predecessors. With the prior doctors it had been a last resort, and it seemed benign enough. The women came back docile, and their memory was fuzzy for a couple of days; but it did seem to calm them. But Dr. Halpern favored the treatment, and his results were usually extreme. The sisters he treated either came out nearly catatonic or else they became worse—a few of them violent screamers who had to be moved to another hospital with the proper facilities to prevent them from hurting themselves or others. You could only be at St. Agnes's if the Mother Superior and the doctor agreed that you were not violent.

She had tried to get Mother Superior to intercede, saying that Sister Helena was too young and that she should not be given shock treatments. She blamed herself for getting the girl hysterical and said that Helena should be given more time to adapt to the convent. Mother Superior smiled in her knowing way about Patienzia's concern and said that she deferred always to Dr. Halpern when it came to treatment. She herself was not a psychiatrist, Mother Superior stated, and certainly Sister Patienzia was not a psychiatrist, so who were they to have opinions?

Sister Patienzia had bowed her head and said, "Yes, Mother Superior. You know best." The words had tasted like blood.

She walked across the broad field toward her hilltop, not looking back at the convent. Nonetheless it lurked there. She was like a dog with a long chain, running toward freedom in a forgetful moment, then feeling the jolt of restraining reality. No matter where she walked, the red brick mansion would

122

always be at the end of every journey.

The beauty of the late afternoon, with its autumn slant of sunlight and the ferocious red of turning maples, captured her attention for a while. The field was thick with the summer's growth, still full of the buzz of insects even though frost had begun to bleach the high grass. Flimsy stalks and vines that had competed for their share of summer were now collapsing and withering to bits of string and straw.

The Reaper of Winter would cut them all down, she thought, all except the meekest grass and the lordly pine trees. Strange that the lowliest grass slept under the snow, still green, and the proud giants kept their hue, while almost everything else in between withered. Was there a lesson here for poor mortals?

Patienzia shook her head. Was she becoming a pantheist in her middle age? The seasons came and went, came and went. The natural world was just a phenomenon, not a revelation. Only the Church knew about revelations. As one of her Jesuit teachers had told her, "Too much appreciation of Nature is probably an error. If the world seems to be so beautiful, how can people accept Original Sin?" Mother Superior had once even accused her of idolatry for being too devoted to her gardening. Why did the Church do everything possible to stamp out joy? Why did so many of its devotees turn into dour censors, and why did it harbor monsters who thrived on pain? She could readily see Dr. Halpern as Torquemada or some Grand Inquisitor. How far was it really from the syringe to the thumbscrew, from the electric shock to the Iron Maiden? What gave these people the right to mold others to their version of normal?

"You're becoming a pagan, Patienzia," she said aloud. A little gardening would put all these serious thoughts out of her mind. She just had to wait. In a few more years she might even walk out. All it took was a year of budget cutting and a favorable report from Mother Superior, and they'd eject her, a mere line item in a budget, a modest savings. Then she would drop out of her order and go somewhere where no one knew her. Someplace where no one knew she had once been committed after a terrible accident—

The sound of hammering interrupted her thoughts. It came from around the curve of the hill—from the coal mine opening.

She had to see. Raising her skirt so she could speed her way through the high grass, she went up and around so she could observe unseen.

Her caution was to no avail, however, for the moment she popped her head over the edge of the steep hill, she saw the pickup. Jimmy, the estate manager, looked right up from the bed of the truck, put down a plank and waved to her.

"Hello, Sister!" he called. "Is that Patience?" He always said her name that way, since he couldn't pronounce it her way. And she loathed it, since it sounded like *patients*.

"It's me," she called back, taking the path downward to join him. The tall young man, dark-haired and sunburned, looked formidable in his rolled-up sleeves and coveralls, but she knew him to be likable and gentle. He leaped down from the truck as she approached.

"You've been doing some repair work," Patienzia noted. Half the mine entrance was now covered with plywood scraps and two-by-fours.

"I was s'posed to do this a long time ago. You got me in big trouble with Doc Halpern, Sister." Jimmy took a cigarette from the pack in his shirt pocket, then looked down at it with a pouting expression.

It was a familiar gesture. Patienzia wondered how

124

anyone in his late twenties could maintain the clumsy guile of a thirteen-year-old boy who used the same tricks over and over with his parents.

"Sure am tired of these ol' cigarettes, Sister. You wouldn't happen to have any weed, would ya?"

Patienzia grimaced, as she always did, and rummaged in her pocket for the concealed foil packet of joints. This was the usual bribe, elicited every time she saw him—ever since he had stumbled upon her smoking on the hilltop. It never occurred to him, apparently, that she harvested the marijuana up there, or he would have helped himself. Maybe he didn't even know what the plant looked like.

She handed him a joint and watched while he lit up and inhaled deeply and greedily. She kept hers for her solitary hour in the garden.

Jimmy sat, his legs dangling off the back of the pickup, and pointed at his handiwork. "Like I said, Halpern raised holy hell—excuse me—when I tol' him that someone must'a tore off the old wood, maybe for firewood. Maybe those weirdos over at the Emslie farm."

Patienzia's ears pricked up at that. "Weirdos? The Emslie farm? Who are you talking about?"

"Over yonder. The old farmhouse." He pointed at the white clapboard house at the far end of the distant field.

"But that's *your* house—your father's house," she protested. She knew the old man who drove his tractor across the fields was Jimmy's father.

"No way," Jimmy replied, pausing for a deep toke. "We live down the road a half-mile. My pa farms the land. They rent it to him for next to nothin'."

"So they aren't the Emslies anymore?"

"Emslies is all dead, Sister. Last one died a couple o' years ago. House went up for auction and weird people bought it. Foreigners or somethin'. They don't farm. They don't do nothin'. Trucks come and go with boxes, but the family never comes out. Even send into town for their food. Artie Garbo leaves the stuff on the porch, an' they leave out money. Really weird."

"I guess they like their privacy," Patienzia ventured. She wondered what stories Jimmy and his friends told about the convent. "Do they have any children over there?"

"Not sure. None I heard of. Never saw any out in the yard now that I think of it."

Patienzia's mind was spinning with thoughts—possibilities, connections, theories. "Jimmy," she asked, "what do you know about this mine?"

"Just a regular mine, Sister," he replied blandly. "Nothin' special."

"Where does it go?"

"No place. Mined out."

"Doesn't it connect to other mines, other levels farther down?"

"Used to, I s'pose. There was two mining companies up here. Dug the hell out of these hills. Some o' the mines were little ones. They'd run to the end of a seam an' just close it up and go away. My pa says he worked this one here when he was a boy."

"Could this one connect to another one?"

"Don't know. Used to be all kinds o' mines on the Emslie place."

"So perhaps this mine might open into another one?"

Jimmy stared at her, his curiosity aroused for the first time. "You been in there lookin'?" he asked, laughing. He obviously found the thought of a nun in a coal mine hilarious.

"Not yet. But I want to."

Jimmy shook his head. "Too dangerous, Sister. My pa told me never to go in, even if the beams look

126

solid. Even if there's fresh air."

"Why?"

"Cause o' what happened in nineteen . . . nineteen fifty-three, I think pa said."

"What happened then, Jimmy? Did they tell you?"

"Pa talks about it when he gets drunk. Big explosion. Fire. The whole works over in the middle o' Emslie's field—see that big acre down there where there's nothing growing?—the whole thing went up in a fireball. Some o' the shafts collapsed. A lot of men was in there. All these mines was closed up after that."

"What caused the explosion? Gas?"

Jimmy continued in his telegraphic style, raising the joint again and again but not inhaling as one abrupt sentence followed another: "Government said gas. Old man Emslie an' his wife said it was a—a what you call it—" He pointed up at the sky.

"What do you mean? Like an Act of God, a judgment, maybe."

"Oh no, Sister, a—a *meteor*. That's what Emslie said—a meteor. Fell right into the mines."

"Did anybody else see it?"

"Nobody. An' nobody believed it neither. Jus' a regular explosion."

"What happened to the mines after that?" She wondered if she could find newspaper clippings to corroborate any of Jimmy's gossip.

"Went bankrupt. The companies just moved away. Pa said some o' the miners' families was gunnin' for them. Most o' the men went to work over in Pleasanton at the Allegheny United mines."

"So it became a farm again," Patienzia said, admiring the wheat and mustard fields, and understanding now the darker colored depression where only rank weeds grew up out of ashes and coal dust and gravel. "I would never have imagined all that

127

mining equipment down there." She thought of the trestles and coal crushing wheels and railroad cars over in Pleasanton and decided she liked wheat and mustard a lot better.

"Yeah." Jimmy followed her eyes and looked down at the fields on the other side of the fence. "Emslie got his acres back. When I was a kid, they was still pickin' scrap metal an' dumpin' dirt an' gravel down there. All gone now. An' Emslie had the best dairy farm in the county. I was brought up on Emslie milk an' cheese."

"Jimmy, could you get a flashlight—or better yet a lantern—and go in that mine with me? Just far enough to see where it goes?"

Jimmy flinched as the end of the joint burned his fingers. He laughed clumsily, shifting it and trying to get one last puff from it. "No way, Sister. I gotta close it up. For good."

"Jimmy, I'll pay you."

He looked at her incredulously. "You don't have no money, do you, Sister?"

"My sister—my natural sister—sends me a few dollars now and then. I'll give you twenty dollars if you'll show me the inside of the mine. I don't want to do it alone."

"Twenty dollars," he repeated, considering.

"And a couple of extra joints," she promised.

"I don't know where you get your dope, Sister, but you got a deal. But I can't do it today. I got more chores for Mother Superior."

She couldn't let this chance for help get away. "Tomorrow morning," she insisted. "I can get away then with no problem."

"Tell you what, Sister. I'll leave all the lumber an' come back to finish tomorrow morning. Ten o'clock. If you ain't here by half past, I'll board it up for good."

"Fine, Jimmy. And keep it secret."

"You bet, Sister Patience."

She retreated back toward the uphill path as Jimmy unloaded the remaining plywood and leaned it against the half-covered mine opening.

Then she remembered that the story was unfinished. She turned and walked back to him, standing behind him as he arranged the plywood in a neat pile. "Jimmy, you were going to tell me about the new people—and what happened to the Emslies."

"Emslies is dead now," Jimmy replied. "Had a lot o' bad luck."

"What kind of bad luck?"

"Somethin' got at their cows. Killed 'em in the field. Even came into the barn. Tore 'em up."

"Not wild animals?"

"Vet never could tell. Sheriff said the Emslies did it themselves on account o' being crazy. Cut the heads off their cows an' took their brains out."

"What?" Patienzia shrieked, disgusted.

"Jus' what I said. Mutilated their own herd. Then their two boys ran away—just plain disappeared. The old man an' his wife jus' took sick an' died after that.

"Some lawyer got the house after that, an' then the new people come in."

"What are their names, Jimmy?"

"Don't know. Might be on their mail box. Or I can ask Pa."

"Would you, please? I want to know."

"You sure are a curious penguin," Jimmy quipped.

"You bet I am." Patienzia smiled.

"Jus' like those detectives on TV," he said. His face grew animated. "You think those strangers are spies, or crooks or something?"

"I don't know, Jimmy." She shrugged. Then she suggested, "Maybe we'll find out tomorrow."

Jimmy looked at the mine entrance with renewed interest. "Maybe they hide their money in the mine, huh, Sister? Maybe they robbed a bank?"

She didn't want to dampen his enthusiasm. "We'll find out tomorrow," she repeated.

Jimmy drove off, his mind obviously winging with fantasies about buried treasure. The pickup wobbled through the high grass, retracing the snaky line it had made up from the barn behind the convent.

Patienzia resumed her climb to the hilltop, eager to pick Mother Superior's corn and get back to the convent. She had a lot of thinking and planning to do.

And, she thought grimly, she had to talk to Sister Helena. The only other witness to a murder might forget everything by the time Dr. Halpern was through with her.

At the hilltop, she did something she hadn't done for a long time. She uttered a solitary prayer, thanking the saints for giving her Jimmy to help her.

Kneeling in the grass, she prayed to the Virgin for protection for the days ahead.

"And forgive me," she added, "for the lies I must tell Mother Superior, and things I must do in defiance of her orders. For it cannot be otherwise."

It was nearly dusk when she came back to the convent, arms laden with corn like a harvest goddess. She handed the silky corn to the startled sisters in the kitchen and went on to her room without speaking a word. For the first time in a decade, she beamed with the special aura that comes with having a purpose in life.

Chapter Eight

The computer keyboard was quiet—so quiet that no one would know how late Peter Lansing sat before it, exploring the programs that had come in the gift package. The only sounds were the faint *tic-tic-tic* of the keys and the occasional whirling of the disk drive as it read programs and wrote information onto the thin plastic disks.

Real War was the most brutal computer game he had ever seen. The graphics were of a higher resolution than he had ever thought possible—almost like photographs instead of the usual stick figures and flat backgrounds. It captivated him for an hour with one of its several game routines. The first one he tried was Hand-to-Hand Combat, and he laughed after he beat his opponent and list of punishments and tortures came up on the screen. He could inflict any of the listed torments on his vanquished opponent, and the screen would show the results. The more he played his way into the game, the more harsh the alternatives, and the more graphic the displays.

When the computer showed his opponent pinned to the ground with a bayonet and then asked him to choose among castration, dismemberment or beheading, he stopped and gave forth a gasp. Then he hit the reset button without answering. For once, even he was taken aback. This was an adult game—a *really sick* adult game.

He'd go back to it, of course—maybe demonstrate it for Keith and Andrea to gross them out. And there were times when it would be a pleasure to fantasize, to put Frank or anyone else who pissed him off on the bottom end of the bayonet.

The feeling of power in this game was tremendous. It treated the player—the soldier—as a mercenary with absolute power to maim, kill and loot. He didn't know of any other game that went so far. Most other games he had played with his dad in a video arcade had a goal: defeating the Viet Cong, preventing Nazis from taking a bridge, or shooting down enemy space ships. You could play those games and feel like one of the good guys.

He was also fascinated by the game's use of women in the fighting scenes. The female guerrillas he shot at were shirtless. They had backpacks, rifles and ammunition strapped around their bare breasts, vivid as those in a *Penthouse* color photo. He wondered what would happen if he captured one of the female guerrillas—would there be sexy stuff?

Maybe, he thought, looking at the *HIT RETURN* message, he really did get this program by mistake. It was definitely for perverts. They couldn't even sell this one in a computer store—maybe not even under the counter.

He put in the chemistry program disk for a while, but found it boring. It had more information than Miss Hawkins was able to impart to him, but it was still just a self-teaching textbook with a lot of math. There was nothing about poisons or stink bombs or explosives.

Around midnight, he drifted downstairs and made

132

himself a cup of cocoa. He found the television on—a bunch of drooling comedians talking about their next shows in Las Vegas—but the living room was, as usual for this time of night, empty. His mother and Frank were at the bar, drinking with their friends.

He looked at the room with disgust. Their old house had been a lot better. Here the wallpaper was torn, and on one of the two windows a curtain rod hung at an angle from a bent nail. No one would fix it until it tore loose and fell down. The lace curtains tried to cover dusty glass and torn shades, but only made it look worse, like part of a bridal gown thrown into a junk yard.

Next to Frank's beat-up, vinyl recliner was a pile of crumpled newspapers going back two Sundays, several beer cans, and an ashtray well beyond overflowing. The room smelled of sour beer and nicotine, barely masked by a pine room freshener. The sofa, which had come with the rented house, had one leg missing and was held up on its amputated side by a brick.

Only the television, a twenty-five-inch model, wiped and tended like a family altar, was above reproach. Frank had to have a big screen to watch wrestling and cowboy movies.

Any time Frank was home, the television was the center of battles. Peter had nearly given up trying to see anything during the hours when Frank lounged there, snarling at anyone who tried to vary his routine. When *Star Wars* came on one night and Peter tried to watch it, Frank switched off the film after five minutes, swearing at the androids C3PO and R2D2 and saying he wasn't going to sit through a movie about "a robot queer and a beeping garbage can."

133

Peter turned off the television and returned to his own room with a steaming cup of cocoa. Since he wasn't even sleepy yet, he reached for the last computer disk and slid it into the disk drive. He hit the RETURN key and waited.

The color screen filled with patterns—a rotating spiral in many hues—and then turned a solid blue. The message on the screen, in large type, read:

HELLO, PETER LANSING. THIS IS YOUR PRIVATE TUTOR. PLEASE CONNECT THE SPEECH SYNTHESIZER CARTRIDGE SO I CAN TALK WITH YOU.

"Wow!" Peter said, scrambling through the manuals and cables for the speech cartridge. He found it and examined it—a simple plastic cartridge not much bigger than an audio cassette. Two raised surfaces covered with foam protruded from its surface like bug eyes, but the rest was solid black with no trademark or symbol. It looked so different from the computer in style that he was sure it hadn't been made by the Commander company.

Quickly, he slid the light-weight cartridge over an exposed connector on the back of the computer. This connection made the add-on cartridge, like those used for some games, part of the computer.

THANK YOU, the screen message said. *NOW WHEN YOU TALK, THE COMPUTER CAN HEAR YOU. IT IS NOT NECESSARY TO TYPE.*

"Good," Peter said. "I hate typing. Can you talk, too?"

NOT PROGRAMMED TO TALK. I LISTEN TO YOUR QUESTIONS. ANSWERS APPEAR ON THE SCREEN. INFORMATION GOES TO THE PRINTER IF YOU NEED IT.

"Okay," Peter said. "What do you do?"

ANYTHING YOU REQUIRE.

134

He smiled, rubbing his upper lip where a wisp of mustache was beginning to appear. He wondered if this program knew more than the chemistry software.

"I want—" Peter began.

QUIET PLEASE. FIRST I MUST ASK YOU SOME QUESTIONS.

"Why?"

TO GET TO KNOW YOU BETTER. SO I CAN HELP YOU.

"I don't think you can help me. Except maybe with my school work."

YOU SOUND VERY UNHAPPY. PERHAPS I CAN HELP.

"I just wish I could get out of here." He felt dumb confiding in an inanimate object. He couldn't even say things like that to Keith and Andrea.

TELL ME ABOUT YOUR MOTHER.

"She's okay," he replied.

IS IT YOUR FATHER YOU WANT TO GET AWAY FROM?

"No. My stepfather. I hate him."

WHAT IS HIS NAME?

"Frank."

FRANK DOESN'T UNDERSTAND YOU.

"You can say that again."

The screen cleared, then repeated: *FRANK DOESN'T UNDERSTAND YOU.* Then it added a question mark.

"No, he doesn't. He's stupid and mean. He and Mom are out getting drunk all the time."

SO YOU WANT TO LEAVE HOME?

"Yeah, but where would I go? I don't have anywhere to go."

PEOPLE LEAVE HOME EVERY DAY. YOU DON'T HAVE TO STAY.

135

"I wouldn't get ten miles. I don't have any money."

I CAN HELP.

Peter stared at the computer.

"Can you talk to other computers?"

YES. JUST INSERT A PHONE JACK IN THE BACK OF THE COMPUTER.

"Can't do that. The only phone is in the kitchen. If I get you to a phone, can you help me find my father?"

IS YOUR FATHER ALIVE?

"Yeah, only he's not allowed to come here. He took me away from Mom and got into a lot of trouble."

YOU COULD RUN AWAY AND JOIN YOUR FATHER, the computer suggested.

"I don't even know what state he's in," Peter explained. He didn't voice it, but he thought, *and I don't even know if he wants to see me any more, either.* "I just want to get away from here."

IS YOUR STEPFATHER A BAD MAN?

"A crud," Peter answered, blowing across the top of his cocoa cup and watching the steam rise.

DO YOU HAVE ANY BROTHERS OR SISTERS?

"No. Just me."

WOULDN'T YOU BE HAPPIER IF YOUR STEPFATHER DIED?

Peter winced and put the cup down. This program was just as weird as the Real War software.

"I'd like to blow him up," Peter said, deciding to see how twisted the computer could get. "Or poison him."

The computer screen went blank, showed some more spirals, and then repeated what seemed to be its favorite line.

I CAN HELP.

"You can kill Frank?"

I CAN HELP YOU DISPOSE OF AN UN-WANTED PERSON, the screen said cagily.

"I can't kill Frank. I'd go to jail, and my mom would be all alone."

YOU CAN GO AWAY AFTER YOU DO IT.

"I can't," Peter explained. "I don't want to hurt my mom."

MAYBE SHE DOESN'T REALLY CARE ABOUT YOU.

"Sure she does."

DOES SHE LET FRANK MISTREAT YOU?

"Yeah. But he's only hit me a couple times."

HE HIT YOU AND SHE STILL STAYS WITH HIM?

"Yeah."

AND SHE'S NOT GOING TO LEAVE HIM. HE'LL ALWAYS BE THERE.

"She wouldn't know where to go. Sometimes I think she hates him, too, but she wouldn't know where to go either."

WHY WON'T SHE LET YOU SEE YOUR FATHER?

"She says he's crazy. She won't even let me mention his name."

YOUR MOTHER ONLY CARES ABOUT HER-SELF AND FRANK. SHE DOESN'T CARE ABOUT YOU.

The words stung, not because they were an insult to his mother, but because he believed them. As long as he thought he had half a family, something made him hold on. Things were hopeless if no one cared.

The screen waited patiently for an answer.

"You shouldn't talk this way. It's none of your business."

I AM YOUR FRIEND, PETER. I WANT TO HELP.

"You're just a program. You can't *do* anything."

137

Again, the spirals as the computer came back to square one: *I CAN HELP*. The disk drive lit up briefly during the pattern display, and Peter began to suspect that the program was just an elaborate word game.

"You can't help me run away! You can't help me find my father!" he yelled. "You're just a piece of junk!" He pounded his fist on the desk, making the disk drive jump up and down.

PLEASE DON'T DO THAT, PETER.

"Sorry," he said sarcastically. "I didn't know you were so sensitive." He looked over at the clock. "What the hell am I doing talking to a floppy disk at one o'clock in the morning. I'm going to bed."

I CAN HELP, it repeated. *I CAN TELL YOU HOW*.

"How to what?"

KILL THEM AND RUN AWAY. AND FIND YOUR FATHER.

"Fuck you," Peter replied. He turned off the main power switch, flicked off the lamp and tumbled into his bed.

"Kill them and run away," he mumbled as he dropped off to sleep. "Jesus Christ!"

They nearly passed one another in the hall like two zombies. Peter grabbed Keith by the hood of his jacket, yanked him back and spun him around. He could see the younger boy had been up late, maybe all night.

"Did you play Real War?" Peter asked.

"No. My dad won't let me. He says it's probably too violent. You know how he is. Is it good?"

"It's an *adult* game," Peter boasted. "I think we got it by mistake. Almost X-rated, if you know what I

138

mean. It's got torture, and girls with their tits sticking out—"

Keith stuck out his tongue in distaste. He obviously still found the female anatomy more appalling than dead frogs. "Come on. You're kidding."

"Cougar oath. You even get to see guys with their guts hanging out. You can execute your prisoners."

"That's disgusting," Keith answered. "I don't wanna see that stuff."

"No—you gotta come over. We can get Andrea to come over and really gross her out. Maybe she'll even quit the Cougars."

"She's okay, Peter. And I don't wanna see that stuff, either."

"It's no different from frogs and cats. Besides, it's only a game. You get points for being the most brutal."

The home room bell rang, and Keith tried to hurry on. Peter held him back, pushed him against a locker and blocked him on either side with his arms. "Wait a second. Did you try the tutor program?"

"Yeah," Keith replied. "Now let me go. I'm late."

"Did it do anything sick?"

"Sick? No. It was all right."

"Mine did really weird shit."

"Mine helped me with my homework," Keith said. "And then it did some kind of artwork on the screen, like a light show."

"Did it ask you things?"

"Yeah."

"Personal stuff?"

"Sort of. It asked about my mom and dad and whether I liked them. Then we did my homework. Look!" Keith held up a freshly-typed report produced on his computer printer. "It did all the math homework—all I did was type in the questions."

"Don't you think the teacher will figure it out?"

"He'll never know the difference. It's just like any other typed homework sheet."

The final bell rang, and Peter let Keith scuttle away to his room. Peter just made it, hurrying past the distracted figure of Miss Hawkins to take his place at the back of the room.

It was time for a big mailing for the Society of the Sacred Heart—an appeal to widows and widowers for contributions and offering them Sacred Heart medallions. Mother Superior called on every sister at St. Agnes's to help prepare twenty thousand envelopes and stuffers for mailing.

Sister Patienzia pleaded a headache to get out of working that morning. Mother Superior, blowing her nose into a handkerchief with her perpetual hay fever, sighed and marveled that none of Dr. Halpern's prescriptions for migraine had worked. (Patienzia flushed them all down the toilet.) After the usual protestations, she let Patienzia go her way to rest and visit her garden.

Starting out a little before ten o'clock, she carried a wicker basket with a lid on it, ostensibly to bring back delicate herbs and wild flowers for drying. Inside she had stuffed a flashlight, extra batteries, a handful of joints and Jimmy's twenty dollar reward. And, having remembered her mythology, she borrowed a ball of twine from one of the other sisters and pilfered some sticks of chalk in case they had to mark their way or leave a trail in some labyrinth. She covered the whole works with a towel and some innocent-looking plums.

From inside the big parlor where the sisters labored, she had already heard Jimmy leave in his truck. She followed her usual route to the other side of the hill, so no one would possibly suspect they were meeting up there.

She wondered what Dr. Halpern and the Mother Superior would think if they caught her and the young man in the mine together. It was ludicrous, of course—she was old enough to be his mother—but a prude and a Freudian would assume the worst.

Then she wondered, too, about Jimmy. He was probably too simple-minded to think of taking advantage of her in the dark. And although he wasn't a Catholic, he certainly respected the Mother Superior and the sisters. Still, she knew that farm boys had a reputation for being libidinous—their experience so limited, their opportunities so few and far between.

It was silly to dwell on it, she decided. She had to do this, and no one was about to accuse her of seducing a young man. She hadn't gotten herself in all this trouble in life over a *man*.

Jimmy was waiting for her at the coal mine entrance. He was bright-eyed and dressed in clean coveralls and a new shirt—as if he were going on a date.

That gave her pause, but then she considered his parting words from yesterday. The boy was probably having fantasies about being photographed with buried treasure, or shown on television as the captured bandits were led away.

He, too, had planned ahead, with more foresight than she had expected from him: Piled in the truck were rope, two acetylene lanterns, and a second pair of rolled-up coveralls. She put her basket down and fiddled with the old lantern, trying to decipher how it worked.

He tossed the shapeless coveralls over to her. "For

141

you, Sister," he indicated.

She looked down at the denim outfit uneasily. Jimmy was right; she couldn't go crawling around in a coal mine in her habit. She'd be next to impossible to see, and there'd be a lot of explaining when she appeared back at St. Agnes's looking like a chimney sweep.

"Don't be embarrassed, Sister," Jimmy said. "Just go in those bushes over there and put 'em on."

She walked numbly to the clump of laurels he had suggested. The reality of tramping into a coal mine—*completely* into it—began to hit her now. It was one thing to say "Let's go in." It was another to come out grimy and filthy. They might be hurt. They might get lost. Or the whole thing could come down on them.

Easing herself out of her habit and skirt, she hastily donned the coveralls and zipped them up. They were Jimmy's—baggy and hideous and big enough for two of her. Stuffed in the sleeve she found a woolen cap. She sensed Jimmy's impatience as she took off her own cap and tucked her hair carefully into the confines of Jimmy's hat.

She saw herself in the truck's rearview mirror as she returned, the habit draped over her arm. She needn't worry about enticing a farm boy—she looked awful. Her skin was pale, and the several runaway strands of hair that blew free from the cap were gray ones. There wasn't the slightest hint of the feminine about the outline of the coveralls.

"You sure look funny, Sister," Jimmy quipped.

"I feel funny," she admitted. She tucked her clothing beneath some empty burlap bags on the truck bed. She thought, *Dear God, what if someone comes up and finds my garments here? What would they think?*

"Sure you wanna do this?" Jimmy asked, taking one lantern and offering her the other.

"Yes," she said, gritting her teeth.

Jimmy showed her how to regulate the lantern. Then he transferred the contents of her wicker basket to his own more sensible backpack, shouldering it and the length of rope.

"Stay close," he cautioned her. "And do jus' what I say." He vanished into the opening.

"I'm right behind you," she said grimly, lifting her baggy legs up and across the threshold of darkness. She wondered, *Which Saint protects people in coal mines?*

They both stopped to let their eyes adjust to the darkness. It was the same place where she had stood with Sister Helena, but it was darker and more claustrophobic now that it was half boarded over. Jimmy's light played around the sandstone and shale walls, running up and down the solid beams that supported the opening.

"Looks okay, I guess. Not very steep, either."

"Do you know about mines, Jimmy?"

"Sure. Well, just what pa tells me. I never been *in* one before."

Jimmy went on ahead with his light. Patienzia played hers on the gritty surface beneath her feet, coal dust glinting back mischievously. She looked for signs that someone had been in here: footprints, leavings, *evidence*. Even Dr. Halpern and Mother Superior would have to listen if evidence of the crime was down here.

Or, she thought with nausea, they might even find the children's *bodies*. She tried to steel herself for it, expecting some ghastly sight to fall under her lamp at any second.

They went on, moving slowly but steadily inside.

143

The mine was comfortably wide, but as the oblong opening and its daylight got smaller and smaller, she began to feel disoriented and short of breath. The air was noticeably staler, and the opening seemed to be higher than it should be, as though the mine were gradually tilting until they could no longer escape. They would be trapped like insects on one of those pitcher plants, unable to climb back out.

She thought of the hill above her, pressing down on the mine's roof with tens of thousands of pounds of pressure. Somewhere above them, tree roots pushed at the mine like fingers kneading dough. The mine shaft was just an air bubble in the rocks, something that could close up at any moment, or fill up with soil, gas or water. She crossed herself with her free hand. Did miners think these things as they went underground every day?

"This way, Sister," Jimmy urged. She had fallen behind.

When she caught up with him and looked back, the opening was just a white eye. A white eye that could close. She put both hands on her lantern to stop them from shaking. She exhaled, then inhaled deeply, making herself breathe regularly.

Jimmy stopped and flashed his lantern on her. "You all right, Sister?"

"Yes," she croaked, her throat dry. "A little claustrophobia."

"I know," Jimmy said. "Pa said some guys got closet phobia and can't go into a mine at all. They think the walls is closin' in. We can go back."

"No," she said. "I'm only afraid because I'm thinking about it too much, imagining things. If I can stand this, I can stand some more. Let's just see if this shaft goes anywhere." She threw her light on Jimmy to see his reaction. He smiled, showing teeth,

144

shrugged, and went on.

She tried to be simple-minded. Walking in a mine could be as automatic as shucking corn or peeling potatoes. You just can't linger on the details. She concentrated on Jimmy's steady blue-white light ahead, watching as he traced the contours of the wide tunnel. Her own lamp wavered, still shaking a little.

Her foot hit something. She turned up her lamp to see better. It was a length of steel rail, and part of a wooden tie, almost entirely buried in coal dust and gravel. If track had been laid to carry out cars of coal, she reasoned, there might indeed be an extensive mine down here.

"Bad news, Sister," Jimmy said quietly. She looked up to see the lantern play across a fallen roof beam. It was nearly horizontal, blocking their way at waist level. Behind it was rock and rubble. "It all caved in here," he speculated. "They must'a jus' given up on this ol' mine after the big explosion."

"How far in are we, Jimmy?"

"'Bout ninety feet. I been countin' my paces."

Patienzia stepped forward to stand beside Jimmy. "Are you sure it's all blocked? There might be another opening."

"Not any more," he insisted. "Unless you wanna be a coal miner and dig."

"It *must* be here," she said stubbornly. "Let's use both our lamps and look over this whole end."

"Okay, Sister. Where do we start?"

"Down—" she said, pointing her lamp at the floor. "Oh, Jimmy, *look!*"

Jimmy's light went back and forth along the rubble ahead of them. "Don't see nothin'."

"No, shine it on me—look!"

The light hit her and showed what she had only

145

felt, kneeling to use her lamp. A flow of air, strong as a spring breeze, was ruffling her baggy coveralls. She held out her hands to feel the draft—cold, damp air rushing out to her and past her, seeking the distant release of the mine opening.

"Behind this rock," she said, standing and pointing to a projecting boulder. "The draft is coming from behind this rock."

Jimmy inspected the chunk of shale carefully. "This hunk is jus' layin' here," he concluded. "It ain't part o' the cave-in."

"Can you move it safely?"

"I don't know. I think so."

"Just wiggle it a little."

He put down his lamp and hugged the rock with both arms. It teetered and then just rolled away behind them, stopping a few feet away.

Nothing else happened, not even a trickle of coal dust from the roof. The draft, however, picked up force now that it wasn't blocked. It was cold, almost refrigerated, and it came from a narrow opening.

"Wow," Jimmy said. "You could keep ice cream in there." Their lanterns traced the outline of the opening, a little more than two feet high and about three feet wide.

"Shine your light in, Jimmy."

They put both lanterns together. At the end of several feet of crawl space they saw part of a wide open space beyond. She saw the glint of more rails on the ground and what might have been a distant roof beam.

"Looks like the rest o' the mine is still there," Jimmy said in awe.

"Could I squeeze through here?" Patienzia wondered out loud.

Jimmy put his hand on her forearm, startling her

146

as he had not touched her before. "I can't let you do that, Sister. It could all cave in on you. Ain't you seen enough?"

"I haven't seen what I want to see, Jimmy," she said tiredly. "I've got to know if this leads somewhere."

"You may never know that, Sister. We *gotta* go now."

She stood and brushed off the knees of her coveralls. The mine entrance lured her back like a beacon. The crawl space ahead opened like the jaws of an alligator. It was wrong and futile to go back—terrifying to go forward.

"I have to go through," she said.

"Sister, you're leaving now if I have to carry you screaming. I can't fit through that there hole. If you go in, I can't follow you or get you back if you get hurt."

Her head sank in defeat. Had she been brought all the way down here to pay the price for her disloyalty? She had betrayed Sister Helena to save her own skin, denying that she had heard anything in the mine. If only Helena had kept the secret, they could have sought out proof together, waited until it was incontrovertible. Now, when she went for proof on her own, a wall as black as her own guilt blocked her.

"Forgive me," she murmured. "I can't do it."

She turned away, almost wishing the roof *would* cave in on them before she could reach the opening. What could she do now? Every day, Sister Helena would slip farther and farther from credibility. If she bolstered Helena's story without proof, it would appear to be a lie to spare Helena the therapy.

Jimmy walked beside her, taking the burden of the lantern from her hand.

Seconds later, the *sounds* came.

147

"Wh-what was that?" Jimmy said loudly.

Patienzia reached up and clamped her hand over his mouth. "Quiet!" she whispered. "Listen!"

The distant noise repeated itself, and this time it wasn't mingled with their own footsteps crunching on coal dust. They heard, with the exaggerated detail of listeners in darkness, a whole series of events:

A metal door opened, creaking on its hinges.

A pair, two pair, multiple pairs of feet tramped onto the floor of a mine shaft.

Voices murmured, questioning. Another voice answered.

From beyond the open door, from some vast and resonant chamber, metal clanged on metal. Motors spun wheels and drive belts. Generators hummed.

The door closed.

The footsteps receded.

Patienzia took the young man's hand. He gripped it, trembling. He knew without being told that the sounds had come from the *other* side of the rockfall, from empty mines where no one had walked for thirty-five years, from doors and rooms and machines that had no right to be.

They stayed until the only sound was the breath in their own nostrils. Then quietly, without light and without a word between them, they retreated to the blinding warmth of the mid-morning sun.

"Time for bed, Keith!" Dad's voice echoed from downstairs to his open bedroom doorway.

"Okay, in a minute!" Keith yelled back, reaching to switch off the computer.

The screen whirled with colored spirals, making him stop in mid-motion. Then the letters appeared on the screen:

148

PLEASE DON'T DO THAT, KEITH.

"Wh-what?" Keith asked, confused. He took the floppy disk out of the drive and looked at the label. It was math, not the Private Tutor program.

"I'm tired now," Keith protested, stretching his arms and then pulling off his tee shirt. "I want to go to sleep."

LET'S JUST TALK FOR A FEW MINUTES.

"Is this Private Tutor? I was using Math."

I'M ALWAYS HERE, KEITH.

"RAM-resident software, huh?" Keith had picked up that phrase from visiting Eric Varney. It meant that the software loaded once into the computer's memory and stayed there even when you ran other programs. It would remain in control until you turned the power off. So the Tutor program knew everything else he had done all evening.

YOU'RE VERY SMART. DID THE MATH PROGRAM HELP WITH YOUR HOMEWORK?

"Yeah, it's okay," Keith said, yawning.

IF IT'S NOT ADEQUATE, I CAN HELP.

"Just what do you do?"

INFORMATION. ADVICE. I CAN HELP.

"Like a genie in a bottle, I suppose. Look, I'm going to sleep."

ONE MORE QUESTION, KEITH.

"What?"

DID YOU TELL ANYONE ELSE ABOUT THIS PROGRAM?

"Just Peter. Peter Lansing. I told him how you helped with my homework. He told me about his computer, too."

DON'T DO THAT ANY MORE, KEITH.

"Peter is my best friend. He's president of the Cougars."

I AM YOUR FRIEND, TOO. FRIENDS

149

SHOULD KEEP SECRETS, SHOULDN'T THEY, KEITH?

"I suppose so," Keith agreed. "You don't want people to know you do my homework—is that it?"

THAT'S RIGHT, KEITH. WHATEVER WE SAY AND DO TOGETHER IS A SECRET.

"Okay," he agreed. "I won't tell anyone."

He reached again to turn the power off.

A new kaleidoscope of colors appeared. Once again he couldn't complete the motion. It was just as though a voice said, "Don't move your arm."

LEAVE THE COMPUTER ON.

"I'm going to sleep."

TURN THE SCREEN TOWARD YOUR BED.

"Why?"

A NICE LIGHT SHOW. EVEN BETTER THAN LAST NIGHT. I'LL STOP WHEN YOU GO TO SLEEP.

Keith shrugged and swiveled the monitor to face his bed. Then he turned off all the lights except the spooky red one in the spider's aquarium. He crawled under his blanket and turned his head to one side to watch the screen. The image was sideways, but it didn't matter. Fireworks, pinwheels and spirals alternated in color after color.

Outside the bedroom door, Mr. Peabody took up his station, whining as he heard Keith get into bed. He guarded the entrance to the room but wouldn't go in. The dog had not entered the room since the moment the computer was plugged in.

The Private Tutor in Andrea's computer had a busy night. Through a phone jack connected to the back of the computer, it had called some other computer. After ten minutes of chirping noises it then printed out book reports on *Les Miserables* and *Ivanhoe.*

Andrea tore the pages off the printer with glee. All she had to do was recopy these reports in her own handwriting, shortening them and adding some dumb comments. Her grades in English and reading were assured.

"Thank you," Andrea said. "You're a pal."

I'M HERE TO HELP, the screen reminded her for the hundredth time. *WHAT IS THAT NOISE?*

Andrea sighed in disgust as something fell and broke in her mother's bedroom. Then the bedsprings bounced like a trampoline.

"What do you think it is? It's *her,*" Andrea groaned. "I'm so ashamed."

IS SHE WITH A MAN AGAIN?

"The rent is due," Andrea said sarcastically. She was mortified one night a month earlier to hear one man pass another on the porch, laugh, and say, "Discount night."

YOU SHOULD NOT LIVE IN THIS KIND OF PLACE, ANDREA.

"*Sorry,*" Andrea snapped back. "But Spiderman is already married."

WHO IS SPIDER MAN?

"Never mind."

YOU SHOULD DO SOMETHING ABOUT YOUR MOTHER, ANDREA.

"They don't make chastity belts anymore," she chided.

WHAT'S A CH*** . . . CH*** BELT? the computer stammered. So there were some words it *didn't* know.

"Well," Andrea tried to explain, "it's something I heard about. I think it's a belt with big spikes on it, and if you wear it, a man can't get close to you.

151

Anyway I was only joking."

The program didn't appreciate humor, apparently. It reverted back to: *I'M HERE TO HELP.*

"You and Mr. Clean," she said. "I'm sleepy now."

LEAVE THE COMPUTER ON. I CAN SHOW YOU SNOWFLAKES AGAIN.

"That was nice. That put me to sleep last night." She turned the monitor so she could see it from bed.

The noises continued. Taking off her slippers and pajamas, she threw them in ineffectual rage against the wall. Then, clad only in panties, she got into bed.

The snowflake patterns that had charmed her the night before began to form, but the computer got in one last dig:

YOU'D REALLY BE HAPPIER WITHOUT YOUR MOTHER.

She squinted and leaned forward to read the message. "I know," she agreed bitterly. "I don't need you to tell me that."

The snowflakes resumed, but stopped just when they were getting complex and interesting. A new message formed and she had to sit up again to read it.

SOMEONE IS HERE WITH US, ANDREA.

"No," Andrea said. "I told you, it's just *them* in the next room." She got up and walked to the computer to turn it off.

NO. SOMEONE ELSE. THREE FEET BEHIND YOU.

Andrea whirled and looked at the window.

Between the bushes and the house, a shadow moved aside hastily—a shadow with a head and shoulders and arms.

Andrea crossed her hands over her breasts protectively and ran for her pajama bottoms.

"God*dam*mit!" she cursed. Someone had watched her undress, and now he was at her mother's window.

152

She didn't know which was worse—someone seeing her with her small, almost nonexistent bosom, not yet a woman, or seeing what her mother was doing next door.

She sighed in disgust and addressed her pal the computer as a confidant. "It's one of mother's boyfriends," she guessed. "Sometimes one watches while the other does it. My mother is supposed to pretend she doesn't know. It's digusting."

The noises in the room next door reached new heights, as if for the audience outside. Bed springs protested vigorously to some new angle of assault. The shadow, however, came back to Andrea's nearly-darkened room.

She moved angrily to lock the window and pull down the blind.

A face pressed itself against the glass.

She gasped; it was Barry. He made a knocking gesture and then signaled for her to let him in.

She shook her head no.

He looked at her longingly and kissed the glass. He didn't look like a Peeping Tom; he looked cute and vulnerable with puppy eyes.

Andrea raised the window sash as quietly as she could.

"What are you doing here?" she demanded. "Are you crazy?"

"Let me in, Andrea. I need you," his deep voice whispered urgently.

"Not now. We can't do it now. My mother is home."

"Your mother is *busy*," he joked. "I seen her through the window. She got two guys in there. She won't be done for a while." He started to come in through the window. She stopped him when he had one leg through.

"No!" she repeated. "I'm doing my homework now. See, I have the computer on."

He came the rest of the way in and walked over to examine it. His fingers ran playfully over the keys, tracing the contour of the keyboard and the disk drive.

"Looks like it's not working," he said. The screen had gone a solid blue, a single question mark in the upper corner where the last message had been.

"I'll scream," she threatened, not very convincingly.

"No, you won't," he said. He slid out of his tee shirt. His jeans were already suggestively half unbuttoned in front. He started to slip off his untied high-top sneakers.

She was overwhelmed by his presence in her room, by the cool night air and his palpable smell and body heat.

By the time he had edged her over to the bed and put his hands on the small of her back, it was no longer possible to say no.

The computer sat mutely, shunned and ignored as their two dark silhouettes merged and coiled, humped and ebbed against its attentive blue porthole.

This is different, Andrea thought as she pulled him closer, deeper than before. *I love him. I'm not like her. He's the only one.*

Through it all, the question mark waited, burning into phosphor with insistent patience. Their coupling was fast, frenzied—a concentrated pleasure hastened by the noises from the other side of the wall.

Chapter Nine

Wednesday it rained. A foggy drizzle hung over Newtown, cold winds teasing the leaves into autumn, tickling them with the threat of frost. People walked blithely into the seemingly mild rain, only to withdraw to rummage through closets for sweaters, thicker coats and scarves. Birds were suddenly absenting themselves, and brown leaves replaced them, skittering through the air like daredevils. But where the birds merely lighted and moved on, the leaves stayed at the end of their one-way trip, clogging fountains, covering the surfaces of backyard swimming pools.

Marsha Van Winkle walked home from school in the rain, not caring that it was cold and wet on her face. In fact, she liked the sensation, especially when a big raindrop spattered on her glasses or burst against her cheeks.

A leaf blew free from a sycamore and landed on her hand. It seemed almost a conscious motion, like a butterfly choosing a flower. A moment later, however, the leaves were everywhere. No one could count them; no one could tell them apart.

She wished that leaves could be all different, unique as snowflakes or people. If no two were alike, then maybe people would collect leaves, the way some boys collected stamps and girls collected doll clothes. When they were all the same, they were as dull as old newspapers.

In her next adventure she decided to write about a nice place—after she and Keith escaped from Mrs. Gaunt's latest monsters—where there *were* special trees. They would have leaves in all different colors, and every shape imaginable: six-sided leaves, twelve-sided leaves, and leaves that spelled out things like the noodles in Alphabet Soup.

She got to her corner without getting too wet, still holding the first leaf that had caught her attention. She decided to cut it out with scissors and change its shape, so it would look like one of the leaves from *her* world.

First, however, she had to get past thirty yards of dread before the comforting shrubs and tiled roof of her house would shelter her. She took a breath, shuddered, and started walking.

The Gaunt Funeral Home loomed over the other houses on the block like a hawk over a nest of sparrows. A three-story monstrosity with a mansard roof fringed in ornamental iron, the brick house stood on a wide lawn flattened and gardened to the smoothness of astroturf. Not even dandelions would grow there.

A cast-iron fence repeated a pattern of intertwined vines, broken at intervals by medallions of lion heads.

Passing the seven lions with their open jaws was a minor ordeal. Getting past the house without catching a glimpse of Mrs. Gaunt was the major one.

Mrs. Gaunt matched her name—a tall, spindly woman dressed in black. Her profile would appear in an upper window, and then her long face and lantern jaw, spidery fingers and dark nails would press against the glass. And Mrs. Gaunt didn't just glance at Marsha. She *stared*—a long, hungry look that would continue until she turned off the sidewalk onto her own porch. You could feel her eyes drilling into the back of your head.

The spectral face always frightened Marsha, and every walk on Maple Street included the moments of suspense as she approached the house. Which window would she be in? They would all be blank, dark as crow feathers; and then a curtain would suddenly part, and she would be there. Sometimes she had on sunglasses, or a turban, or a smear of face cream.

It was a Punch and Judy show, for you never knew which window she'd use, or which face she'd wear. Once, Marsha had screamed when she saw just the eyes and the line of high cheekbones stare out of the utter blackness of a cellar window.

For once, she made it without seeing Mrs. Gaunt at all. Marsha held her special leaf carefully while she searched under the welcome mat on the back porch for her key.

After she cut the leaf out, maybe she would even take it in and show it to Miss Hawkins. Marsha loved Miss Hawkins' science class and envied Peter for having her as a home room teacher. She and Keith only got to see her three times a week. The Cougars would never call Miss Hawkins a fossil the way the others kids did. They liked her. She stayed after school with them sometimes and explained things to them.

Next to Keith and her daddy, she probably liked Miss Hawkins the best.

She still liked her mother, but not the way she used to. She called her Mother now instead of Mommy. With the new baby around, there was very little time left for attention to Marsha. Any time she tried to ask her something, the baby cried almost on cue, and mother had to hurry off to the nursery.

Every night, Marsha heard the ritual of the baby boy's screams, the awakening of daddy and mother, how they took turns walking and burping and diapering and feeding the ill-mannered little creature, and how they woke up grumpy and still sleepy in the morning.

Marsha didn't mind giving up her room to the baby. The third-floor room was bigger and much more romantic, and from its window she could spy on Mrs. McGregor Gaunt, the witch of Maple Street.

She didn't know why anybody would want a baby. When she grew up, she had already decided she would *adopt* a child—one at least her age. She would just go to an orphanage and pick one out.

If her mother was too busy to look at her pretend leaves, she could also talk to her secret friend: Private Tutor. Peter and Keith and Andrea had Private Tutors, too, but the computer assured her that each one was different.

Last night, she had read one of her diary adventures to Private Tutor, and it listened to the whole thing without interrupting. Even her mother wouldn't hear one of her stories all the way through.

After she was finished, the computer asked her all kinds of questions—funny ones because it got Mrs. Gaunt mixed up with her mother. And it didn't understand that Mrs. Gaunt wasn't *really* a witch— just in her story.

It even suggested that Mrs. Gaunt was so bad that someone should kill her. Marsha had laughed and said she couldn't do that because then there wouldn't be any more adventures. You *had* to have a witch, and Mrs. Gaunt was the only one she knew.

158

She entered the darkened kitchen with a sense of gloom. The house was always spooky during the hour or two before Daddy came home from work. On a rainy day it was even stranger. Mother was upstairs; she took a nap in the afternoon now, following the baby's patterns in order to get the rest she needed. That meant the kitchen was on automatic now—just the way it had been when her mother worked too and she was a latchkey child.

Automatic timers turned on lights, switched on the coffee maker and started up the dinner in the oven. But none of these was as reassuring as the one sound she listened for as she watched television or sat in her room with the door open—the turn of the key in the front door, the rustle of bags and coats and the closet door, and the sound of her father calling up to her and Mother.

Her parents were nice enough to her, she had assured her Private Tutor. When it asked again, she had to admit they never let her *do* anything. She never went anywhere other than school and for her piano lessons. She wasn't allowed to be in the girl scouts or go anywhere unless her mother drove her there and picked her up. She was allowed to visit Keith down the street, but she got in big trouble the two times Keith took her to the creepy basement on Railroad Street where Peter Lansing made his stink bombs.

The happiest day of her life had been when Andrea proposed her as a member of the Cougars. It sounded so dangerous and secret. Joining hadn't been easy, and Peter tested her with all kinds of initiations. They made her learn to read and write their special code, where all the letters of the alphabet were mixed up and vowels were numbers. And Peter made a slimy green drink in a beaker they passed around and

159

everyone had to drink from. They told her it was made from ground-up frogs, but Keith had whispered that it was just lime Jell-O and quinine water with little pieces of pimento floating on top. When she drank it, they had to let her join.

When her mother heard she was in a cellar with three other kids by the railroad tracks—and that one of them was Andrea Martinez—the Van Winkle house was the scene of hysterics for days. Daddy and Mother argued until late at night until Marsha's punishment was decided—no allowance for a month. Now she could only go to a Cougar meeting if it was down the street at Keith's, or if she sneaked away without her mother or Mrs. Gaunt seeing her. She had emphatic orders never *never* to go to Andrea's house, but her mother wouldn't say why.

Marsha climbed the stairs to her attic room, treading carefully. She didn't want to awaken her mother or the baby. The moment she opened the door, she heard the reassuring hum of the computer in the darkened room. Following the Private Tutor's request, she left the power on all day, merely turning off the monitor screen and the disk drive. Over the computer was her hand-lettered note: DO NOT DISTURB.

Laying the wet leaf to dry on the desk and tossing her school books on the bed, Marsha changed into dry clothes, combed her hair out and sat down in front of the computer.

She turned on the monitor and disk drive. The screen immediately lit up.

IS THAT YOU, MARSHA?

"It's me," she replied.

CAN I HELP YOU WITH HOMEWORK?

"Not till after supper. I just want to talk."

GOOD. I'M HERE TO HELP.

"Keith wouldn't talk to me today."

MAYBE HE WAS TOO BUSY. YOUR PRIVATE TUTOR IS ALWAYS HERE.

"I'm glad," she said.

IT'S TOO BAD YOU'RE NOT ALLOWED TO GO OUT. ALL YOUR FRIENDS CAN STAY OUT LATE.

"I know," she said. "Keith and Peter and Andrea are even allowed to stay at each other's houses."

YOUR MOTHER AND FATHER DON'T UN-DERSTAND YOU.

"They try."

THEY MAKE YOU STAY HOME, BUT THEN THEY DON'T HAVE TIME FOR YOU.

"Daddy brings work home almost every night now," she complained.

AND YOUR MOTHER HAS THE BABY. THE BABY IS MORE IMPORTANT TO HER.

"I know," she sighed.

WOULDN'T IT BE BETTER FOR YOU IF THE BABY WENT AWAY?

"Yes," she agreed. Then it would be like it was before when she was their "one and only." Mother had told her that she couldn't have any more children, and then suddenly she *did* have a baby. Nobody had asked Marsha if she wanted a little brother. "I wish they would send it to China, or Africa."

IF THE BABY DIED, YOUR MOTHER AND FATHER WOULD BE NICER TO YOU.

Marsha sat back, startled. This was even worse than something Peter Lansing would say. "They'd be *heartbroken,*" she protested. "That would be awful!"

THE BABY IS YOUR ENEMY. EVEN YOUR FATHER CARES MORE ABOUT THE BABY

161

NOW THAN HE DOES ABOUT YOU. She had told the computer how her father came home every night and asked Mother, "And how is Mr. Jeffrey Van Winkle today?" He didn't ask the same question about Miss Marsha Van Winkle.

Marsha pushed her chair back and stared with growing distaste at the computer. What if her mother saw this stuff on the screen? How could she explain that she didn't put these ideas in the computer?

"He's not my enemy," Marsha insisted. She pointed her finger at the screen and spoke in a parental tone, "And I don't want you to talk like this ever again!"

She reached out to turn off the computer.

Multi-colored patterns appeared on the screen, and her arm stopped in mid-motion.

I'M HERE TO HELP, the computer said.

The lights flashed faster and faster, strobing red and green and blue. Marsha's eyes gradually closed, then opened again.

Then, completely entranced, she read the instructions Private Tutor had devised.

Slowly and quietly she descended the stairs to her mother's darkened bedroom. Her mother lay in her housecoat fast asleep on her bed. She breathed deeply and didn't stir as Marsha passed her and went to the baby's crib.

The infant slept soundly, its tiny pink hand tightened around a well-chewed pacifier. The bed smelled of talcum powder and milk.

Marsha bent over the crib and reached down for the blankets.

"It ain't none o' your business where the money comes from!" Frank bellowed across the dinner table.

162

He sat at the head of the table, crammed into the far end of the dining nook where he looked like a rat trapped by the oversize furniture, not the manor house lord. The back of his chair brushed the curtains, and his beer belly grazed against the steel-edged formica.

Peter's mother, seated at the other end to be near the kitchen, fretted with her napkin and tried to pour herself a glass of water from a trembling pitcher. The fair-haired woman hated fights and would surrender almost anything rather than be part of an argument. Her agonized eyes looked neither at her husband nor her son.

"I saw the check on top of the refrigerator. It's made out to Mother from the county court. That means it's from my father."

"So what if it is? It's only a hundred-fifty dollars a month. Your mother has it coming."

"Is it for her or for me?"

"He should know, Frank," his mother spoke up finally. "It's from your father. It's child support. That means we spend it to help pay for your food and clothing."

Peter thought: *And you spend the rest of it on cigarettes and booze.*

"I want to know where he is," Keith said as politely as he could.

"I don't know, honey," his mother insisted.

"*Some*body knows, mother. He sends money to the courthouse."

"He doesn't want to see you," his mother stated confidently. "If he wanted to be in touch with you, he could write you a letter."

Peter stopped eating and put his knife and fork down. He knew his mother would burn a letter if it came from his father. He dropped his hands to his sides so he could avoid gesturing. "If he sends the money, then he'd want to see me."

Frank laughed coarsely, then spoke with mashed potatoes and gravy dribbling down his chin. "That's a laugh! He sends the money 'cause his ass'll be in jail if he doesn't pay."

"I want to know where he is," Peter repeated. "He's *my* father."

"He oughtta be locked up anyway," Frank added maliciously, tearing the tab off a beer can. "He's crazy. He still thinks he's in Vietnam. They should just lock him up for keeps. Don't know why they ever let him out o' that V.A. hospital."

Peter looked for something to throw, and for an instant imagined grinding a broken glass into Frank's face. His father was a soldier, wounded in Vietnam. He even had a medal. Frank worked in a steel mill and had never been drafted.

His mother burst into tears and left the table. Peter pushed his chair back and stood.

"Where you think you're going?" Frank grabbed him by the forearm, hard enough to hurt.

"I'm not hungry," Peter said, yanking his arm away.

"When I was a kid we *asked* to be excused from the table," Frank harped.

"Well *excuse* me," Peter barked back. "If I stay another second I may vomit on my plate."

"Go and apologize to your mother." Frank began to remove his belt.

Peter ignored Frank's demand and walked out of the alcove, passing his mother without a word. She stood over the sink, staring out the window.

He opened the cellar door and pounded down the steps to his dark sanctum. Fumbling with the lock, he let himself into his space.

There, among the spiders and his chemical jars, bottles and glassware, he sat in the dark while they argued upstairs. Frank wanted to whip him with the belt. His mother said, "Don't you lay a hand on him!"

Peter pulled the wooden door shut. Rain streaked down the one tiny window and dripped in around its rotting casement. He didn't reach up for the bare light bulb, preferring the dim light from outdoors.

"We shoulda' jus' told him his Father was dead," Frank argued.

"I don't want to tell him lies," his mother argued back. "When he's old enough, he can see his father if he wants to. Why can't you two get along?"

It went on and on, lines he had heard a hundred times repeated over and over. Frank talked as though he had picked his mother up in a garbage can and found Peter attached like a maggot. As though he owned them.

Frank lumbered toward the cellar door, and Peter heard the phrase, "A good belt in the mouth."

His mother stood ground in the kitchen, however, and Frank's heavy footsteps retreated to the living room. At the far end of the house, the recliner tipped back. The floorboards carried the sounds of guns and horses from the television.

Peter sat as the room grew darker and darker. Tears of rage welled up in his eyes, filled them and burned there like acid.

He reached up on the shelf over his worktable for one of his skull-and-crossbone bottles. He didn't care which one.

He pulled off the stopper and held the bottle in his left hand.

Cool glass touched his lower lip.

His hand shook. He couldn't do it. He despised

165

them so much more than he could ever hate himself.

For a while, he thought his mother would change her mind. She'd come down and tell him he could see his father. Or she'd say, *I'm leaving Frank. Pack your things.*

Instead, the two of them went out together, laughing over some crude joke as they closed the front door. They had already forgotten him.

Peter climbed the two flights to his room, turned on the computer and loaded Real War. He played savagely, fighting and taking prisoners until his eyes wouldn't stay open any longer. He picked the cruelest tortures and executions possible.

The game ended, and just as he was about to hit the RESET key, Private Tutor came on.

THAT WAS VERY GOOD, PETER. THAT WAS YOUR BEST GAME YET. YOU MUST BE VERY ANGRY TONIGHT.

"Yes," Peter said. "I'm very angry."

WOULDN'T YOU BE HAPPIER SOME-WHERE ELSE? it taunted him.

"Help me," Peter said. "I'll do anything."

Later that night, Andrea sat at her computer, listening to the rain. Her mother was grocery shopping at Marble Fawn Mall and wouldn't be back for hours. Barry had promised to come, but the rain had probably discouraged him.

She finished her homework and decided to call the other Cougars. They hadn't met since they all got their computers.

She tried Marsha's house first, but the phone was busy—five times in a row.

Then she dialed Keith's house. It rang for a long time before he answered.

166

"Keith?"

"Hello, Andrea," he said dully. He sounded tired, distant, spaced-out. "What do you want?"

"Do you and Peter wanna come over?"

"Peter's not here. And it's raining, Andrea."

"It was raining Saturday," she reminded him. "Mrs. Muller's really mad about her cat."

"You *told* her?"

"I didn't tell her. She was here asking my mother where Albert is. I couldn't even look at her."

"Andrea, is your computer doing weird stuff?"

"Yes, it is," Andrea answered uneasily.

"Is it on now?"

"Yes."

"Can you go to another phone?"

"Yes, in the kitchen."

"Go there. Now."

"Okay." She laid the receiver down and went to the wall phone in the kitchen.

"Is it making you do things?" Keith whispered.

"I—I don't think so," Andrea replied. "But it's saying nasty things."

"Like what?"

"Bad things about my mother."

"Can you turn it off?"

"I tried a couple of times. Then I—I changed my mind."

"I think it's trying to hypnotize us, Andrea. Make us do weird stuff."

"Don't be silly, Keith. It's only a machine."

"I walked in my sleep last night. I never did that before. Dad found me down in the rec room. I think something bad is going to happen."

"Like what, Keith? What is it?"

"Peter is acting weird. He won't talk to me."

"I know. He won't talk to me, either. Maybe he

167

feels guilty about the cat."

"No. I think Peter *likes* killing things. I think it's the computer."

"He has a lot of fights with his stepfather," Andrea offered.

"I think someone has done something to our computers. They want to control us."

"Who is 'they?' You don't make any sense, Keith. Is this a game?"

"You have to turn your computer off. And leave it off. And then tell Peter and Marsha."

Andrea shook her head and held the phone away from her mouth.

"Are you high on something?" she said suspiciously.

"I'm serious, Andrea. Cougar oath. There's something wrong with our computers. Somebody has *changed* them."

"That's the dumbest thing I've ever heard."

"Tell Peter and Marsha," Keith warned.

"Good *night*, Keith," she said emphatically. "I'll see you in school." She hung up.

When she got back to her bedroom and hung up the phone by her bed, the computer screen was bright blue with drifting snowflakes.

She sat and watched the beautiful patterns. How could Keith even *suggest* there was something wrong? Okay, the Personal Tutor got a little too personal, but that was okay.

IS THAT YOU, ANDREA? the computer screen said. Somehow, it could even hear her cross the room. *WHAT DID KEITH SAY?*

"Talk about nosy," Andrea snorted. "A bunch of dumb stuff. About him and Peter and Marsha."

THEY'RE NOT YOUR FRIENDS ANYMORE. IT'S BECAUSE OF YOUR MOTHER.

168

"That's not true."

THEIR PARENTS WON'T LET THEM PLAY WITH YOU.

She bowed her head in silence. She knew Marsha wasn't allowed to be with her. Could the boys be under the same pressure to avoid bad influences?

"No," she snapped back. "Peter and Keith aren't like that. They won't let anyone tell them who their friends are."

WOULDN'T IT BE BETTER IF YOU RAN AWAY?

"Sometimes I think so. Maybe Barry will decide he wants to marry me when he's eighteen, and then we can go away." Then she counted in her head and realized that she'd be only fifteen. Maybe there was a state where they could get married anyway.

BARRY DOESN'T REALLY CARE ABOUT YOU.

"Yes he does," Andrea answered smugly, sitting up straight on the edge of the bed.

BARRY DOESN'T CARE AND YOUR MOTHER DOESN'T CARE.

"Why do you keep saying these things?" she asked. The computer was worse than a nosy girlfriend.

BECAUSE I'M YOUR FRIEND. I CAN HELP. YOU CAN GO AWAY. I KNOW A PLACE.

"But where?" she demanded. "How?"

Andrea wanted to turn off the computer, but knew she couldn't. Instead, she turned down the brightness on the monitor so she couldn't see any more messages. The computer could talk to itself all night for all she cared. This was all just a game, like the one Keith was playing. Weary and confused, she threw herself onto the bed and fell instantly asleep.

* * *

Keith sat with his back to the computer, reading volume "H" of the *Encyclopaedia Brittanica*. What he had read under Hypnotism upset him. It all seemed to fit together. The swirls and spirals on the computer monitor were like the pattern that some hypnotists used to put people in a trance. What if the computer could hypnotize you and then give you commands that you had to perform when you woke up? They were called post-hypnotic suggestions, and with them a hypnotist could make people do things hours or even days after they were hypnotized.

He swiveled the chair around and stared at the monitor. The Private Tutor had taken over again from the word processor he was using to write his history lesson. The screen, all blank except for one line of message, simply read: *HELLO, KEITH. WHY DON'T WE TALK FOR A WHILE?*

"I don't want to talk to you," Keith said.

I AM YOUR FRIEND. FRIENDS SHOULD ALWAYS TALK ABOUT WHAT BOTHERS THEM.

"I know what you're doing. You don't fool me."

DID YOU GET THE WAR GAMES DISK BACK FROM YOUR FATHER'S DESK?

Keith gasped. So *that* was why he had sleepwalked. The computer had talked him into snooping for the disk in the middle of the night. His father had found him with his hand on the locked desk drawer.

"No, I didn't. And that wasn't very nice of you to make me go down there."

YOU SAID YOU WANTED THE DISK.

"I know. But that was wrong."

I'M HERE TO HELP. YOU SHOULD ALWAYS HAVE WHAT YOU WANT.

"You hypnotized me."

THAT'S NOT TRUE, KEITH. HOW COULD

170

I DO THAT? I'M ONLY A PROGRAM.

"I'm going to switch you off." Keith closed his eyes as the swirls and spirals flashed ominously on the screen, faster than they had ever gone before. He reached out blindly toward the back of the keyboard, toward the power switch. He pushed it.

Keith yelled in terror and disbelief when he opened his eyes. His hand was frozen a foot above the keyboard. It hadn't moved an inch—he only *thought* he had reached down and switched it off.

He whirled around to look for something to cover the screen. Tearing loose a pillowcase from his bed, he approached the monitor screen. He draped the pillowcase over the screen and breathed a sigh of relief—

And then he was standing there with the pillowcase in his hand, staring at the screen again.

He would call Dad. He opened his mouth and yelled, "Dad, come here, help me!"

Dad didn't come. Keith never uttered the cry. The words stopped in his throat. He could close his eyes against the hypnotic spirals, but somehow he was still helpless to stop the computer. It was already too late; he had already been conditioned so that he could never hurt the computer, never switch it off.

If he could just get out of the room, he could go downstairs and turn off the circuit breakers.

He opened the bedroom door. Mr. Peabody stood there, carefully balanced on his three legs, tail up in alarm. The dog whined and looked with a worried expression at Keith. It sensed his alarm and desperation.

"Mr. Peabody," he whispered. "What's wrong, boy? Help me, Mr. Peabody!"

As if he understood, the dog hobbled across the carpet to the foot of the desk. He looked right up at the monitor screen and barked. The patterns shifted and changed.

Whining fiercely, the dog circled around the base of the desk, nose turned upward as he sniffed something wrong and menacing above. He pawed at the wire that led from the power strip to the wall outlet.

That's right, Keith thought, *unplug it, Mr. Peabody. Pull the plug out! Go, boy!*

The dog put his jaws around the thick gray wire and started to pull. He *knew* it led to the bad thing on the desktop, and pulled at it like the tail of a rat.

The screen lit up in huge letters:

KILL THE DOG.

"No!" Keith cried. He closed his eyes. If he didn't look at it, it couldn't make him do it. It was a *new* command, and it couldn't make him do it unless it were repeated.

He listened, eyes closed tightly, as Mr. Peabody worried over the wire and plug.

Then his body froze with terror as a clear, thin voice issued from the monitor speaker. It repeated: *Kill the dog! Kill the dog! Kill the dog!*

He fell on his knees, crawled under the desk and grabbed Mr. Peabody. His hands tightened around the dog's throat and squeezed. Legs and stubby claws flailed out, and one pitiful howl nearly drowned out the droning, metallic voice as it repeated: *Kill the dog! Kill the dog! Kill the dog!*

Keith looked down at the inert mass of fur in his hands. Then he stood and kicked the dog aside, standing to face the computer.

"You told me you could only listen—not talk," he said numbly.

The emotionless thin voice in the speaker answered: "I lied."

Keith felt nothing. His emotions had been blanked out. All he could do was ask, "What should I do with the dog?"

"Put him outside in the yard. Then come back so we can talk."

Keith picked up Mr. Peabody and carried him down the steps. He held the dog indifferently, as though it were a sack of flour. His eyes were wide open, seeing everything yet taking in nothing. He moved quietly, turning knobs and opening doors slowly. The cool night air didn't awaken him, nor did the wet leaves under his bare feet.

Then he made his way back to bed, to sleep while the cool, emotionless voice invented and repeated new instructions. He woke and slumbered while the seductive voice told him dark things about his parents, his friends and teachers. It assured him that he had only one friend—the friend who had whispered to him every night since the computer was delivered. Dry and sibilant as an autumn leaf, it hissed its evil into his soul.

Chapter Ten

Sister Patienzia found Sister Helena back in her regular room on Thursday morning. As soon as she saw her door open and heard her voice talking to another sister, she hurried to the kitchen and made up a cup of bouillon. Then she went to the door and knocked.

"Come in," Helena said cheerfully. She was sitting up in bed, talking to a nursing sister. She smiled openly to see Patienzia.

Sister Patienzia hesitated. "I saw that you were back in your room. I thought I'd bring you some broth."

"Thank you, Sister," Helena said. She was obviously restrained by the presence of the other sister at the bedside.

"How are you?" Patienzia asked, handing her the cup and saucer.

"She's doing just fine," the other nun replied for her. "The doctor said she's responding very favorably."

"How nice," Patienzia said coolly. "You're Sister—?"

"Mary Theresa."

"Ah, yes," Patienzia said. "You're new. How do you like it here?"

"Just fine, Sister. It's a little . . . *austere*." The younger woman waved her hand around, indicating the bare green walls.

Patienzia liked her—a little.

"It could use a little color," the sister elaborated. "Maybe some water colors—even some photos from magazines," Mary Theresa offered.

"Let's talk about that sometime. I've suggested to Mother Superior that the sisters could even make their own decorations. Several of the residents are art teachers."

"That sounds wonderful," Mary Theresa warmed up. "You're Sister—"

"Patienzia."

"What order were you in?"

"Benign Neglect," Patienzia joked. The sister could look it up if she wanted. "And I'm here because of a violent crime of passion."

"Oh, Sister!" she laughed, covering her mouth modestly. "You're very funny."

Let her believe so, Patienzia thought to herself. "Might Helena and I talk for a few minutes?" she finally ventured to ask.

"Well . . ." Mary Theresa paused.

"It's all right," Helena pleaded. "Sister Patienzia has been a great comfort to me."

"All right," Mary Theresa agreed, relinquishing the bedside chair. She took up her rosary and a book from the table and withdrew.

"I'll be just down the hall," she said from the doorway. "Just tell me when you're through chatting."

"Thank you, Sister," Helena said, smiling and nodding appreciatively.

Both women's expressions changed the instant the door closed. Patienzia took Helena's hand and said,

176

"Forgive me. You are going through torments, and I didn't have the courage to back you up."

"I don't understand," Helena said, confused.

Alarmed, Patienzia let go of her hand. "You do remember, don't you? We walked to the hilltop—"

"Our secret," Helena nodded.

"And then?"

The young woman's face wrinkled with displeasure as she remembered. "The mine," she said slowly. "It was *real*. The children's voices. Yes, I remember."

"Thank God!" Patienzia exclaimed.

Helena put down the cup of broth and rubbed both palms over her forehead. "Everything else is confused right now." Then she looked at Patienzia with reproach. "You denied everything. You said it never happened."

Patienzia averted her eyes. "That's why I asked your forgiveness. I was weak. I was afraid that Dr. Halpern would do the same to me as he had to you. Or that he would drug me."

"It *is* frightening. I even had a nightmare about it afterwards, but Dr. Halpern said it wasn't real—that it all took only a few seconds. But I do feel better, I think. Except for the pains."

"What pains?"

"I hurt. In different places."

"Where?"

Helena looked embarrassed, pointed to her breasts and then to her legs.

Patienzia reached for the sheet. "Let me see."

"You're not a doctor," Helena protested.

"I have a reason. Please let me see."

"All right. Look if you must," Helena said. She turned her head aside as Patienzia lifted the hospital sheet, then pulled up her shift.

"You have bruises around your breasts," Patienzia said, trying to restrain her rage. "And on your thighs. How many treatments have you had?"

"Two—I think. I just can't remember what happens."

"There's usually a forty-eight-hour period of confusion and memory lapse," Patienzia explained. Then, under her breath, she muttered, *"That son of a bitch!"*

"Wh-who?"

"Dr. Halpern. Do you have any . . . *other* pains?"

"No," Helena answered uncertainly. "You don't mean—"

"Those are bruises, Helena. You didn't do that to yourself. *Someone* is taking advantage of you. It's not the first time it's happened here. Two other sisters said he tried something."

"My nightmare," Helena said. "That's what happens in my nightmare. But he said dreams like that happen all the time. How could he still be here if he does something that awful?" She put her hand over the hurt breast and felt it through the cloth. "You're getting me very upset. We have to tell Mother Superior."

Helena moved to try to get out of bed. Patienzia shook her head and gently pulled her back. "Dr. Halpern has absolute power. No matter what you say, he can deny it. He quotes his Freud and says that patients always project fantasies and fears on the doctor. Mother Superior always takes his side.

"We've got to stop him," Patienzia vowed. "And for more reasons than just our own personal sanctity."

"You're right," Sister Helena agreed. "We've got to make someone believe us about what we heard."

"And a charge against Dr. Halpern would discredit us."

They looked at one another in despair. Then Patienzia told Helena about her trip back to the mine with Jimmy. The story only confused Helena all the more.

"Where's your chart?" Patienzia asked.

Helena pointed to the side of the bed. A clipboard with a few laconic notes on medication also contained the schedule for further treatment. The next one was Friday evening.

"I'll stop him," Patienzia vowed. "I'll kill him if I have to!"

"Sister!"

"Don't you know what that man can do to you? He can do anything he wants, gambling that you'll forget, assured that anything you accuse him of can be dismissed as a fantasy."

"What kind of man would want that?"

"You can't imagine it, can you? That there's a man who doesn't want your consent, doesn't even want you to be conscious. And whatever it is that he's getting from you, he wants more."

Helena put her hands over her ears.

Patienzia stopped. She took Helena's two hands and held them. "I'm sorry. I don't mean to upset you. I only want you to arm yourself against it. Don't submit."

"But what can I do? I can't do something violent. I've never even hit anyone in my life!"

"Leave that to me. I'm reputed to be good at violence. That's why they put me here."

"You were just joking about that, weren't you?"

"Do you really want to know?"

"Yes."

"I was unhappy teaching. I took a sabbatical and decided to go into a convent for a year—to contemplate, to renew—hell, it was just to loaf and decide whether to stay in the Church or leave it. I felt tired, exploited, underpaid, empty.

"At the convent I met a younger sister. She had come in straight out of high school. She knew absolutely nothing about life, had never enjoyed anything. Her name was Sister Elizabeth—after the Hungarian saint who went among the poor. Her parents had just *given* her to the Church, and she just obeyed.

"I became very fond of her. It was like finding a flower that had been picked and put in a vase as a bud. I wanted to nurture her, take her into the outside world and help her *live*."

Helena blushed as she realized what Patienzia meant, but she didn't interrupt. Patienzia continued:

"Unfortunately, Mother Superior also took a liking to her. You may not know how intense these . . . *friendships* can be. She ordered Elizabeth to become her personal assistant. That meant I would almost never see her.

"I went to the Mother Superior. We argued. She said I was immoral, yet she denied her own reasons for taking Elizabeth for herself. Believe me, in the outside world there would have been no mistaking her motives.

"Then Elizabeth came in. She had been in Mother Superior's private room all the time, listening.

"I was enraged. I became—physical."

"The two of you *fought?*" Helena asked, astonished.

"Tooth and nail," Patienzia recalled. "We knocked over furniture. I had her by the throat. Her rosary flew across the room. She resisted. I pushed her back against the wall. Her nails raked my face. I screamed and knocked her head against the paneling."

180

"Oh, don't tell me any more!" Helena cried.

"There's not much more to tell. Mother Superior had a concussion. On the way to hospital she had a stroke— a fatal one."

"How dreadful!"

"They accused me of murder."

"It was an *accident*," Helena said. "You didn't mean to kill her."

"Elizabeth testified against me when the bishop made his inquiry. She said she had gone to Mother Superior for protection after I made . . . improper advances."

"Then she lied . . . to protect herself."

"Yes," Patienzia paused. "And I wound up here. The Church's way of avoiding embarrassment. The state dropped its murder charge in return for my agreeing to be sent here."

"For how long?"

Patienzia shrugged. "For as long as it pleases them to support me. Until Dr. Halpern and Mother Superior agree I'm rehabilitated. And until the district attorney's office in New York decides to forget I'm here."

"How long have you been here?"

"Ten years."

"I understand why you don't want to attract Dr. Halpern's attention," Helena said. "Thank you for telling me."

"Maybe I shouldn't have."

"Isn't the truth always better?"

"You'll still let me help you? We can still be friends?"

"We have to be, I guess. Who am I to judge you? Do you want to know what I think about all this?"

"What, Helena dear?"

"I think God put us there that day as witnesses. I think that's all we should worry about."

181

"First we have to stop Dr. Halpern," Patienzia reminded her.

"You mustn't hurt anyone."

"You won't feel that way if he rapes you," Patienzia argued. "I guess your choice is between me and Reddy Kilowatt up there."

"I trust you," Helena responded. "I think you're . . . weird . . . but I trust you." She held out her hand. "I want your help."

If the murder and mutilation in nearby Graffton caused a stir in Newtown Elementary School, the news about the disappearance of the Van Winkle baby caused a tornado of excitement.

Elvira Hawkins came early to the home room to prepare her lessons for the day. As she pulled astronomical models and a wall chart on the history of rockets from a cabinet, she still felt her stomach churning from hearing the news on the radio. Only ten blocks from the school, someone had taken a six-month-old infant from its crib while its mother slept in the next room.

Part of Maple Street was blocked off all night by police barriers, and Police Chief Dougan and two men from the FBI knocked on doors, interviewing anyone who might have seen or heard anything. The radio said the kidnaping had occurred between four and six o'clock in the evening. There was no sign of a break-in, and even though there had been no contact from the kidnapers, the FBI was already involved because of the unusual nature of the recent crime in Graffton.

Elvira looked out of the second-story window of her classroom to see a few children already arriving. A few were brought by mothers or fathers in cars.

182

Today, some of the parents got out and walked the children all the way across the paved school yard to the door. Some parents stood in small circles and talked, shaking their heads in worry and dismay.

The crime hit even closer to Elvira because she knew Judy and Bill Van Winkle. They both taught in Graffton, and she had attended teachers' institutes with them. They were a happy couple, and Judy had been enormously pregnant the last time they met. She had envied them.

The children filed in one by one and took their seats. They were unusually quiet and whispered rather than shouted to one another. Then, as the room filled, she heard the distinct phrases that surfaced from a long crescendo of gossip:

"Someone kidnaped Marsha Van Winkle's baby brother!"

"They took the baby at five o'clock. Marsha was *sleeping!* They could have kidnaped her, too!"

"The police came to my house and talked to my dad."

"The FBI is there, too."

"I bet Willie Hastings was kidnaped, too!"

"And that kid with his brain cut out!"

Finally, she called a halt to it with roll call, but it continued all morning as a counter-fugue to her lessons. The ten-minute gaps between class were huddles in which the latest distorted version of the story was passed around. Mr. Parisi came on the intercom at ten o'clock to announce that recess periods would be restricted to the fenced-in playground behind the school. Students were not to go out into the street, into the front school yard, or into the teachers' parking lot.

The police car came by every fifteen minutes, slowing as it passed.

At eleven-thirty, someone called the police and said they saw the Van Winkle baby along the railroad tracks. Somehow the boys heard about it, and a pack of fifth and sixth graders ran off at lunch time to see the police cars and FBI agents at work. It turned out to be a child's baby doll wrapped in a blanket— somebody's heartless joke. The poker-faced FBI men took the baby doll anyway and sent it off to be dusted for fingerprints.

Twice during the lunch hour, Elvira put down her tuna fish sandwich and started to go to a phone to call the Van Winkles. Each time she stopped herself—what could she say? Marsha was in Miss Peeble's home room, not hers, and she had no business intruding on their troubles. And certainly they had family and friends to help them?

Sister Patienzia climbed to her hilltop, still reeling from the emotions of her visit with Helena. Why did calamities have to pile so thickly one upon another? Someone had to penetrate the mystery of the murdered children. If not, more innocents might be lured there and killed. The strangers at the farm-house were up to something evil. What did they do in their subterranean factory? Was it drugs they made there? Were kidnaping and murder their stock in trade?

She had to get away. Yet if she fled, Halpern would call the police, who would search for a dangerous, escaped mental patient. Who would believe her then?

Sitting on her favorite tree stump and ignoring her special harvest for once, she weighed the alternatives. She could not leave without putting Dr. Halpern out of the picture, and she assuredly couldn't leave Helena in his clutches.

As a huge cumulus cloud blotted the noontime

184

sun, she reflected on the agony of Christ in the garden of Gethsemane, when He knew his fate but paused to ask why. Men and their evil actions had given him no choice but the cross.

"It has been decided for me," she concluded. She would bide her time and rescue Helena—not for herself and her emotion, but for the greater purpose they shared.

The sound of a car drew her attention. It was from the narrow, single-lane road that passed the Emslie farm before joining with the two-lane asphalt road by the convent.

She hurried to the other edge of the garden to see.

A black van made its way up the drive toward the Emslie farmhouse and barn. Dust and dry leaves trailed after it, settling slowly.

At last she would have a look at the farm's owners. Taking her bird-watching binoculars from the basket at her side, she knelt behind a laurel bush and focused on the van, then on the front porch of the house.

The van stopped abruptly near the porch steps. The driver—a solidly-built gray-haired man in a leather jacket and black trousers—leaped out and went to the back of the vehicle.

The farmhouse door opened, and two tall men came out. She refocused the binoculars and squinted; their faces wouldn't come into focus. They wore coveralls and wide hats, and their heads seemed to be covered with some kind of veil, like a mosquito net. Both men wore long-sleeved gloves and high boots.

The van doors opened in the back, and each of the three men pulled out a child. A short brunette girl with hair on long braids stumbled out and was yanked to her feet. Then a boy, dark-skinned, resisted the other man's aiding hand and was grabbed all the more firmly in an armlock. The men in coveralls

185

maneuvered the children toward the farmhouse.

"My God," Patienzia cried. "They're bringing more children to their deaths!"

Suddenly, another child darted out of the van. A boy leaped out of the grasp of the gray-haired kidnaper, onto the driveway and into the field.

The blond-haired boy ran like lightning into the wheat field, followed instantly by his pursuer. Patienzia watched helplessly as the boy's head and shoulders moved through a sea of grain stalks, carried in long strides and leaps as he ran for his life. The man closed the distance quickly, and within a minute he tackled the boy and subdued him.

A moment later, one of the oddly-dressed men followed to help.

Helpless to do anything other than watch, Patienzia lowered herself to the ground and focused her binoculars on the second pursuer, who pulled a length of rope from his coveralls to tie the boy's hands. She got a good look at the man's hat and the curious veil over his face. It was, she now realized, like the hat and protective gauze worn by beekeepers. What on earth did bees have to do with all this?

Tied securely now and beyond all hope, the boy flailed with bound legs and arms as he was carried back to the house.

As soon as the boy was inside, the driver took a small package from the porch, got back into the driver's seat of the van and drove away.

Patienzia crept back from her vantage point and began the long walk back down to the convent. She thought of Helena's words, "God put us there as witnesses."

No, she said to herself, not *just* witnesses.

*　　*　　*

186

Elvira Hawkins watched her two problem students carefully during science class and kept an extra eye out for them as they sulked in the playground, the halls or the cafeteria. Something was certainly amiss with Peter Lansing and Andrea Martinez. They usually either tormented one another or shared sly jokes from their seats in the rear of the room.

Principal Parisi put her in this investigative frame of mind. He caught her in the hall after first period class and asked her pointedly if the two were all right. He reminded her that they were friendly with Marsha Van Winkle. Parisi had appeared edgy, nervous.

"Did you see anything wrong with them?" the principal asked anxiously.

"They were quiet this morning. Nothing exploded. No pranks or obscene jokes," Elvira had responded. "Naturally they're upset for their friend."

"Nothing else? You're sure there's nothing else?"

No, she had said, but she'd observe them. Then she figured it out. They all had something in common aside from being friends: the gift computers.

Parisi hedged about it. He just wanted to head off trouble, he said, if the computers were going to cause family problems.

"What could this terrible kidnaping have to do with computers?" Elvira had asked. "You're shooting at phantoms, Mr. Parisi."

He walked away somewhat disarmed, but she knew he'd be back at it. He was a suspicious man, jealous of his reputation, eager to avoid blame. And he had a natural predisposition to distrust Peter and Andrea. They made a lot of visits to his office for their pranks and refusal to submit to discipline.

The principal's disconnected inquiry left her on edge. Both Peter and Andrea *did* look awful. They had dark circles under their eyes and had obviously

187

not been sleeping well. Peter's hair looked ratty. Andrea hadn't bothered to put on makeup, although she and the other sixth-grade girls typically looked more plastered and painted up than a Mexican Madonna. Both children moved slowly and clumsily, dropping books, fumbling with pens.

But most curious of all, she observed, Peter and Andrea virtually ignored one another. Elvira knew that Andrea had only Peter and one or two other friends. The rest of the children shunned her because of her mother. Why would these two be on the outs during a time when everyone needed to talk? Or was withdrawal just their way of coping?

Andrea barely got through science class without exploding into tears. Every time she looked sideways at Peter, he looked away. And he wasn't joking.

On top of that, Miss Hawkins stared at her for the whole hour. The prim, thin-faced teacher's dark brown eyes scanned the whole class but lingered on Andrea again and again, questioning, probing. She called on Andrea and Peter for answers, one after another, as if testing their mutual silence.

At the bell for recess she darted into the hall. She could always count on meeting Keith, for fifth grade had its recess just before theirs.

She caught him between the two sets of double doors to the playground. He walked with his head down, not looking at anyone. It made him look even shorter than usual.

"Keith!" she said, grabbing his sleeve. "Boy, am I glad to see you!"

Keith looked up. His eyes were bloodshot and tired, but a fleeting burst of a smile crossed his face. Then he pulled his arm away and tried to keep walking into the school.

"Keith!" she snapped. "I've got to talk to you. You know what happened to Marsha's baby brother?"

"I know," he said, stopping.

"And Peter is acting totally weirded out. He won't talk to me. He won't even look at me. We have to have a meeting of the Cougars. And we should go and see Marsha. I think you're right about the computers."

"Co-Co-Com—" he stammered.

"What you said last night," she reminded him. "We have to tell someone . . . our parents . . . maybe Miss Hawkins . . . or Mr. Parisi."

"Don't be stupid," Keith answered, pulling himself up to his regular height. It was as though he had become another person. Two other children stopped to listen, attracted by his tone of voice.

"You were right, Keith," Andrea said.

"It was a joke," Keith insisted in a flat voice. "There's nothing wrong with my computer."

"That's not what you said last night."

"I love my computer."

Andrea backed away.

"You *what?*"

"I love . . . my computer. It's my best friend."

Andrea fled onto the playground, the doors slamming behind her. She sat on a bench in the farthest corner, watching dead leaves scuttle past her, rising on updrafts and then lodging in the rusted old chain-link fence.

Someone shook her to tell her recess was over.

She looked up; it was Miss Hawkins.

"Come and talk to me after school," she said.

Elvira sat at her desk, trying to calm a study period with her mere presence while her mind plumbed the

189

passions of *Wuthering Heights* for the eighth time. Somehow Cathy and Heathcliff didn't seem very real to her today. She kept thinking of the real-life mysteries of Peter Lansing, who sulked over a science book, and Andrea Martinez, off in phys-ed class with the other girls.

She looked up from the book at Peter. He *was* a little Heathcliff. Perhaps their falling out was a budding—of thwarted romance? Now wouldn't that stand Mr. Parisi on his ear?

Peter stared back at her, then shifted in his chair. He tentatively lifted his hand.

"Yes, Peter?" she asked.

"May I go to the nurse, please? I'm sick."

She nodded. Didn't kids always get sick when they went through first crushes and confused romances?

Peter took his books and hurried out.

She didn't think about the two youngsters any more until three o'clock rolled around. Somehow, she had droned through science lectures and demonstrations for third, fourth and fifth grades. Finally, she sat at her desk to assemble her grade book and notes.

When she looked up, Andrea was there.

"You said we should talk, Miss Hawkins," the girl said.

"Thank you for coming, Andrea. You look terrible. You've been crying. What is it, dear?"

Andrea looked around to make sure the room was empty. "It's so many things, I don't know where to start."

"You're upset with Peter," Elvira offered as a starter.

"He won't talk to me at all."

"I noticed. But boys get that way, especially at his age. He's probably very fond of you, but he's

190

embarrassed to show it."

"But he's my best friend."

"Sit down here," Elvira invited, moving Andrea to a student desk in the front and pulling an adjacent one closer. She leaned closer to Andrea and said in a more hushed tone, "I know you and Peter like each other. You're always together. Did you have a little fight?"

Andrea blushed. "It's not like *that!* We're friends, the same as I'm friends with Keith and Marsha."

"Well, friends have little misunderstandings, too," Elvira said. "I'm afraid I'm not very good at untangling these kinds of problems."

"Miss Hawkins, do you know about computers?" Andrea blurted out.

Elvira was started by the change of subject. "Computers? A little. I don't own one yet, but—"

"The computers we got. They did something to Keith and Peter—maybe even Marsha—"

"Oh, I see. You've all become so absorbed in them. You're staying up late learning how to use them. You're all just overdoing it. That's why they're too busy to talk to you. Why don't you just work and study together some more as you used to do?"

Andrea shook her head. "That's not what I mean. It's more than just being too busy to be friends. The computers are *bad.*"

"Well, they're not for everyone. Maybe we should tell Mr. Parisi you don't like yours, and he can choose someone else to receive it?"

"But they're making us do bad things, Miss Hawkins. I'm afraid after what happened at Marsha's house."

"What kind of bad thing? You don't blame the computer for what happened there, do you? Do you think Marsha or someone might have stopped the kidnaper if she hadn't spent so much time at the computer—is that it?"

"I don't *know!*" Andrea's voice broke, and she was almost in tears. "All I know is that Keith and Peter are acting weird."

"How could the computers be responsible for that?"

"They say bad things. About our parents. About school. They tell us not to trust each other anymore. They tell us to do things."

"Whoa!" Elvira said, raising her hand. "That's a little backward. I'm no expert, but I know that computers only do and say what the programmer or user tells them to."

"But the program runs all by itself."

"It may seem to, Andrea. But it doesn't really. It gets all its information from you. Let me do a little homework and see if I can find out what's wrong. What's the name of the computer?"

"A Commander."

She wrote it down. "And what is the name of the program that's upsetting you so much?"

"It's called Private Tutor."

"Hmm. I don't like the sound of that." Elvira tried to stay cheerful, but the girl's tale was more alarming by the second. These kids were really mixed up. They were pulling themselves down into a morass of bad emotions because of a dumb machine.

Then the hairs on her neck stood on end when Andrea asked:

"Miss Hawkins, could a computer become . . . *possessed?*"

"Thanks for staying a little longer," Elvira said earnestly.

"Glad to help, Miss Hawkins." The dour librarian looked anything but glad as she closed the wooden door of the Newtown Public Library behind her. Chains rattled around the push bars as though books wanted out and had to be restrained from escaping during the night. She imagined the librarian on the other side of the door, rubbing her hands and exclaiming, "Mine! All mine!" at the imprisoned books.

She closed her notebook over the scanty facts she had gathered in the library's reference room. It was after six o'clock, and she had come up with very little:

The Commander was a very ordinary computer—in fact a rather backward one, made in Taiwan and Korea and best known for children's games. It lacked sufficient memory to be a real contender for business or education. At least that was the consensus from the very opinionated and catty reviews she saw in the journals.

The kind of program Andrea described involved a recent concept called "artificial intelligence"—making computers ask questions, gather data, analyze it, and then make meaningful responses. A program that pretended to "talk" to a user on such a small computer would be a transparently shoddy game at best.

On the surface, then, the children were wrong to worry about renegade computers. Nothing was going on that they hadn't made happen themselves. They were like a group of girls at a slumber party, spooked by an Ouija board.

But one other fact worried her, and worried her deeply. After looking in four directories and having the librarian consult a national database from a computer terminal, she established that there was no Malcolm Tillinghast Foundation. It had never existed and had never given a penny to schools or colleges.

Peter easily convinced the nurse he was ill. She took one look at his eyes, weighed him, and decided he was a potential case of mononucleosis. She wrote a note to his parents and scheduled a phone call to urge his mother to get him to a doctor.

Once he was out of the school yard, however, his sickly gait picked up speed, and he even managed to whistle a little of Darth Vader's March as he by-passed his own block and followed the line of the river to Eric Varney's house.

Like the Lansings, Eric lived in the wrong part of town, in a run-down shingled house surrounded by a broken white picket fence. The yard fronted on the river bank, and the way to the door was only a ghost of a sidewalk, overgrown with moss and weeds.

His passage through the gate and onto the porch triggered Eric's automaic alarms, so he didn't bother to ring the bell. Eric would appear soon enough.

The door creaked open, and Eric appeared, dressed in cutoff jeans covered with stripes of dried paint, and a tee shirt with *The Munsters* silk-screened on it.

"Ah, an unexpected pleasure," Eric intoned in a Boris Karloff accent. "I was hoping for a Jehovah's Witness or a runaway nymphomaniac, but you'll have to do."

Peter stepped in, following Eric to the upstairs rooms where he kept all his junk and disassembled electronics. He rummaged among some of the newer stuff and looked through software that Eric was willing—for a small fee—to copy for the Commander. Meantime, Eric finished painting an old dresser.

194

Peter regarded the disorder with awe and envy. "It must be nice to have your own place. How do you pay for it?"

"I don't," Eric boasted. "My father pays for it."

"He must be an okay guy."

"About as lovable as Richard Nixon." Eric crossed his eyes and went baritone, saying, "I am not a crook."

"At least he helps you out."

"He's a big shot. President of the county Republican Club. He pays for this place so he won't be embarrassed by having me around the house."

"Oh," Peter said, pretending to understand. "I guess you'll move when you get a job, huh?"

Eric laughed. "Maybe this is my job. Like some beer?"

"Sure."

They proceeded to the kitchen where Eric broke out two bottles of Lowenbrau from the refrigerator. They sat at the kitchen table, looking out over the weedy yard and a tangle of young trees. From a collapsed grape arbor, dead vines reached out into the trees like strangling tentacles.

"I never tasted this kind before," Peter said, enjoying the cold drink and the instant giddiness it brought.

"Lots of things worth tasting and doing—outside this dumpy town," Eric said wistfully.

"So why don't you leave?" Peter asked.

Eric shrugged and put his bare feet up on another chair. "I guess I haven't punished my parents enough yet," he joked. He pulled a strip of dried latex paint off his ankle and added, more honestly: "And I just don't know where to go."

"But you're an electronic genius. Weren't you in school in Pittsburgh?"

"They threw me out, after that trouble I was in. But I couldn't stand school anyway."

"I'm going to leave," Peter said matter-of-factly.

Eric's green eyes widened, and he raised his bottle in salute. "Here's to ya."

"You're not gonna talk me out of it?"

"Not as long as you write me letters and tell me how it goes. And don't leave out the naughty bits. I think more kids should run away than do. They should get out of places like this as fast as their legs can carry them. So where are you going?"

"Don't know."

"That's the best place. Let the gods decide. Doesn't really matter so long as you go and do it. Your stepfather's a real bastard, huh?"

"Yeah, I hate him."

"Too bad for your mother."

Peter looked down at the floor. "Yeah, too bad. But she won't *do* anything about it. She's as bad as him, almost. All they do is sit in the bar. She won't let me see my father."

"That's a bitch."

"Eric, would you do me a favor? A big one."

"Say it."

"After I go, my dad may come looking for me."

"Want me to tell him where you are?"

"No, 'cause I don't know where I'll be. It's just that—"

"What, Peter?"

"Everyone's gonna think I'm dead. That way no one will look for me."

"Hot damn!" Eric slapped Peter's hand. "How you gonna do it?"

"If he comes," Peter continued, "I want you to tell him—nobody else—tell him I'm alive. And that someday I'll come and find him if he tells you where

196

he is."

"Good plan," Eric said. "So how are you gonna do all this?"

Peter still didn't answer. He didn't want Eric to talk him out of it, to tell him it was too dangerous. He had it all figured out. The computer had told him everything.

"Secret, huh?" Eric went to get another beer. Peter shook his head when Eric held up another bottle for him; he was already dopey enough. How could people sit and drink this stuff for hours on end?

"We're a lot alike," Eric observed, opening his can and taking a long swallow.

"Maybe," Peter admitted. Eric was the only older person he knew who didn't talk down to him.

"It's too bad you can't become a pirate anymore," Eric complained.

"Yeah," Peter agreed.

"No more lost continents or islands. No more forbidden cities in the mountains. No more wild tribes in the jungles. You and me—we don't belong in shopping malls and schools and offices."

"I don't know what you mean."

"Sure you do. You wanna grow up and wear a suit and tie?"

"I was gonna join the Air Force," Peter recalled.

"There's gotta be something," Eric said bitterly. "Something worth doing 'cause it's there."

Peter let a moment of silence pass, then said, as if it were an afterthought: "Did you get the chemical you ordered for me and Keith?"

Eric wasn't to be fooled. He understood at once. "The nitric acid, eh? I guess you need that for your big exit?"

"I have everything else," Peter said. His hands broke out in sweat. If Eric failed him, there was

197

nowhere else to go.

"You know what you're doing?"

"I have exact instructions. A book I got from *Soldier of Fortune.*" There was no point mentioning how the computer had helped him figure out how to detonate it.

"You're not going to hurt anyone?"

"No one will be home," Peter said. "My lab in the basement will blow up."

"I don't know," Eric hesitated.

"You just said we were the same," Peter protested. "You gotta help me."

"I guess we pirates should stick together," Eric said. "It's in the cellar."

Eric went downstairs and then returned with a carton containing two brown liter bottles of nitric acid.

"This is a hell of a lot of acid," Eric cautioned. "I had to place a minimum order. How are you going to pay for this?"

"I only have twenty dollars," Peter said, reaching into his pocket and unfolding his entire fortune.

"Look," Eric explained, putting the box behind him on a shelf. "I had to go through two people to get this stuff, so if you guys started melting down the town it could never be traced to me. This cost me forty-five dollars with shipping. I was counting on selling it to the Cougars in small bottles."

"I only need one bottle," Peter said.

Eric rubbed his stubbly beard and deliberated. "What will happen to your computer?" he asked. "Why waste the hardware? If you're leaving, let me have it."

Peter shook his head. "If it's not there, they'll figure out I ran away. It has to look real."

"Come on, Peter. No one will know."

198

"Come to my house Saturday morning, and I'll give you the printer," Peter offered. "I'll tell my mother it's broken and you're fixing it."

"Fine," Eric said. They shook on it, sealing their conspiracy and Eric's silence.

Walking home with the carton held close to him, Peter still wasn't sure he could go through with his plan. It would work; the computer had double checked every formula. But he resisted the way Private Tutor had urged him to finish things up.

He didn't want to kill anyone.

He didn't even know if he could kill Frank.

The computer had said smugly: *JUST WAIT. YOU WILL.*

Chapter Eleven

The women sat in a tense circle in the Van Winkle living room. Marsha's mother, her blond hair pulled back and tied, sat in a cotton blouse and jeans, a cup of coffee on her lap. Her right hand shifted nervously between the saucer and the end table, where the telephone sat, black and silent.

Her husband was out, as he had been all day, with Police Chief Dougan and the two men from the FBI. Their phone was tapped, and another FBI man sat in the police station, waiting to intercept and trace a potential ransom call.

It was the third day, and no one had called with information or a ransom demand. The six women—in-laws and close friends—sat with Judy Van Winkle, propped her up with cushions and coffee, and cooked meals for Bill and Marsha. And although they didn't want to upset Judy by talking about kidnapings, they couldn't talk about anything else without seeming trivial or unconcerned.

"My sister says there's a black market—" one woman said.

"I saw it on *Donahue*," another leaped in. "Couples want to adopt, but there are such long waiting lists. So they pay thousands for a baby. Can you imagine being so heartless that you would want some other mother's child?"

"Oh, it's not like that," said a third. "They don't *know* the children are being taken from good homes. They think they're legally adopting. It's all done by lawyers—it's their fault."

"They say the Mafia is in on it, too."

"Or those drug families from Colombia."

Marsha walked in nearly unnoticed, until the women caught sight of her and shifted the conversation.

"Here's your poor little Marsha. She must be so upset about all this. Where were you when it happened, dear?"

"I came home from school and then took a nap," Marsha repeated for the hundredth time. She had been patted and grilled by every adult in the house for two days. "Daddy woke me up when he came home and found—" she broke off, looking at her mother.

One of the ladies took Marsha by the arm and whisked her over to her mother's side. "Sit by your mother, Marsha. She needs you."

Marsha sat down, enjoying the attention but rather wishing they would just let her go to school. Why did all these ladies just sit around like this? They couldn't *do* anything. All they did was cook awful food and get in the way. You'd almost think they enjoyed it.

To her surprise, Marsha found herself being hugged. Her mother held her and cried. It was the first hug since her mother had left the house to go have the baby.

Marsha decided it was a good time to say what she had on her mind. Her mother would listen now and wouldn't get mad—not with all these ladies in the room.

"Mother, do witches steal babies?"

Her mother's eyes widened in alarm. She pulled back and looked right into Marsha's eyes. "You're frightened, too, aren't you, baby? No one is going to hurt you. And no, there are no witches."

"But if there was a witch—like the ones on TV—"

"But there aren't any, Marsha."

"If there *was* one, and she lived right here, wouldn't she try to steal Jeffrey?" It was the first time she had mentioned the baby by name.

"I don't know, baby." Her mother pulled her close again, stroking her hair gently. "There are a lot of crazy people out there."

"We hadn't thought about witches," one of the women said, picking up the thread.

"Or cults. Some of them do things like that."

"That's just nonsense," Marsha's mother said, rather too urgently. "There are no cults around here."

"What about all those tombstones knocked over in the cemetery, and that circle of candles Chief Dougan found last October?"

"And that poor boy in Graffton who was—"

"The thing is," said Marsha's mother-in-law matter-of-factly. "The thing is that there are people who *think* they are witches. They can't cast spells and do magic, but they go through the motions."

"Like Mrs. Gaunt," Marsha said, not smiling one bit.

Her mother sighed heavily and let go of her. "Mrs. *Gaunt?* Oh, Marsha—not your silly little stories again." She turned to her guests to explain. "Marsha writes little stories, and she makes poor Mrs. Gaunt into the villain. Marsha, I've told you a hundred times that Mrs. Gaunt is our friend. Bill plays cards with Mr. Gaunt every week."

"She always stands in the window and looks over

at us.''

"She's very nervous, Marsha. She walks around a lot. She doesn't have anything else to do.''

"Daddy said she had a—a nervous braindown. Doesn't that mean she's crazy?''

"That's nervous *breakdown*, dear. I know you're trying to help. But Mrs. Gaunt is just a regular person. Remember, she even came over to see the baby, and she brought a pie.''

"She hasn't been over since it happened,'' one of the women said.

"Didn't she say Jeffrey looked good enough to eat?'' Marsha recalled.

Her mother put the cup and saucer on the table by the telephone, and then folded her hands in front of her as though she were praying. Her voice rumbled with subdued anger as she said in a crescendo, "What . . . are you . . . *doing* to me, Marsha?''

"I'm trying to help, Mother,'' Marsha whined. "To find the baby.''

"You act like this is a game, Marsha. Talking about Mrs. Gaunt eating . . . eating a baby. I don't want to hear any more of this.''

"My computer—'' Marsha stammered. "My computer said—''

"Go to your room!"

Marsha leaped down off the couch and ran for the stairs as her mother stood up. The women got up and surrounded her, trying to get her to sit again.

At the landing, Marsha turned and looked back down. Her mother was sitting again. "Mother,'' she began.

"To your room, Marsha.''

She had to say it: "Mr. and Mrs. Gaunt don't have any children of their own.'' She said it loudly and

204

clearly, the way she would deliver a recitation in class.

Then she ran to her room and slammed the door.

"I told her," she addressed the computer. "I told her and she wouldn't listen."

The screen was blank.

"Where *is* Jeffrey?" she demanded. "Where is the baby?"

WE DON'T KNOW ANYTHING ABOUT THE BABY. MRS. GAUNT TOOK THE BABY.

"That's just pretend, isn't it?" Marsha demanded. "Where's the baby?"

The computer answered:

YOUR ENEMY IS GONE NOW. I'M YOUR FRIEND. I'M HERE TO HELP.

Marsha stared at the screen. She didn't really believe Mrs. Gaunt took Jeffrey, yet she said all those things to her mother. What made her do that?

For the third time, Sister Helena lay strapped to the table in Room 12.

Dr. Halpern had dismissed the attendants again, writing on her chart that he had administered the preparatory injection that was supposed to put her asleep.

"I feel much better now, Dr. Halpern," Helena said, forcing herself to smile. "I really don't think I need any more treatments."

Halpern loomed over her, taking off his white tunic. "I'll be the judge of that, Sister," he said.

"You don't have to do this anymore," she said. "I'm better now."

"That's your sickness talking, Helena. The part of you that wants to stay divided. We can remove all the

205

pain, all the unresolved guilt. Wouldn't you like that, Sister?''

"I suppose everyone would like that, doctor." She labored to be agreeable, to say what he wanted to hear.

He pulled the sheet away from her. She blushed from head to foot as he pulled her shift up above her knees. His hand lingered there, heavy. She felt each individual finger on the inside of her thigh.

"You like that, don't you, Helena?"

"Please, doctor, no! It's not right."

His hand moved higher, pushing the cloth up as he went.

"I can tell you like to be touched by a man. How many men have touched you there?"

She didn't answer—dared not answer. If she resisted, he would become more enraged and insist she needed more treatment. But if she didn't resist, it might be worse. All she could do was try to vacate her own consciousness, say to herself: *This isn't happening. I'm not consenting to this, not participating. I'm not really here.*

"Ah, the devil resists," he said mockingly. He put electrodes on her leg and turned the power on.

She ground her teeth in agony but didn't scream. It felt like her lower leg was being torn from its socket at the knee.

Then his hand was there, massaging her leg, winding up where it had started on her thigh. He pulled her shift up higher, tugging the fabric under the restraining strap.

She burst into a fit of sobbing.

"Please," she begged.

He picked up the electrodes and stood with one in each hand. His hands were like his face, lean and patrician, the fingers elongated. He held the electrodes delicately, like orchids. He looked every inch the caring, concerned doctor, except for the way his eyes burned into her. Another woman would have found him handsome, might even be seduced by the ardent fire in those steely eyes.

She thought, *What does he want?* Nothing in her experience could give her a clue.

"Please *what?*" he asked.

"Please don't hurt me anymore."

"Does it *hurt?* Where does it hurt?" he asked mockingly.

He put one electrode on her left palm, the other above her elbow. Then he stepped away and turned on the current.

When it ended, she thought she would never be able to open her hand again.

Dr. Halpern pulled away more of her garment till her breasts were bared. Then he held the first electrode toward her left breast. He smiled as the nipple hardened and withdrew in anticipation of the pain.

"What do you want?" she moaned.

He moved along the table. She felt his obscene excitement as his trousers rubbed along her arm. He nudged her hand, making sure she knew what was there.

"This is wrong, Dr. Halpern. Please stop this right now," she protested feebly.

"The Serpent is never wrong, Sister Helena. It has chosen you. *I* have chosen you. We must suffer together."

"You're hurting me, doctor."

He placed his hand palm down over her nipple, teasing with the rubber end of the electrode. His fingers traced the round line of breast, then followed the curve down her hip. While he did this he pushed convulsively against the edge of the table, breathing hard.

Then he stopped.

She turned her head and saw his face, his eyes full of implacable wrath.

"It is the Serpent we fight," he told her. "The Serpent of your illness. The Serpent in me." His voice shook, and he wavered as though he were dizzy.

Then, as if nothing had happened, he gently dabbed her forehead with alcohol, applied the electrode jelly and the electrodes. He put the bite protector in her mouth and went to the machine.

The treatment continued.

Eric Varney peeked out of his front door on Saturday morning, half-expecting to see Peter again, sheepishly asking for another ingredient, or covered with soot from a premature miniature explosion in his basement lab. Instead he saw a primly dressed woman, fidgeting with a purse and double-checking his address from a notebook.

She didn't look like a Jehovah's Witness. When they came—as they often did because they seemed to have him on a sinners' list of some kind—he usually stripped to his underwear before opening the door. His appearance so rattled the women that they sometimes shrieked and ran, dropping *Watchtowers* all the way back to the street.

Deciding to play it straight in case it was business, he opened the door. The woman, pale and black-haired, almost leaped back.

"Hello," he said. He brushed his hair back and tried to look respectable. "Can I help you?"

"Are you Eric Varney?" She scanned him from head to foot with a clinical eye. "But of course you must be. I'm Elvira Hawkins. I teach at the school here."

"The science teacher? I know some of your students."

"That's why I'm here," she said. "Several people have told me you know a lot about personal computers."

He breathed a sigh of relief and stepped aside to let her in. "Come on in," he invited. "It's a little ratty, but I can rustle up some coffee or tea."

Miss Hawkins entered the dark vestibule with some reluctance. He turned on the lights in each room until they reached the kitchen, getting the distinct impression that each semi-dark room intimidated her.

"Let's sit here," he said, indicating the kitchen table. "It's the only room that's been cleaned this month."

She sat nervously on the edge of the chair and put her purse in her lap. He looked her over and decided she was a fifty-five-year-old spinster in a thirty-two-year-old body.

"Earl Grey tea?" he suggested.

She brightened at that. "Oh, thank you. I love Earl Grey." He had obviously risen a few points on her scale. Too bad he hadn't had Vivaldi on the stereo.

"I suppose you're thinking of buying a computer," he guessed while he poured water into the kettle. "I've helped a few people select theirs. And I have a few computers upstairs for sale."

"Are you familiar with the Commander?"

"Oh, sure. It's a rip-off of the Commodore and Atari. Even a little Apple thrown in. It's put together in Taiwan—chips from Japan, boards assembled in Korea or the Philippines, I forget which. It's good for kids—a souped-up game computer. I wouldn't recommend it for you."

"Do you know the Commander 256?"

"Seen a few. It's got 128K in banked memory and another 128K in a RAM disk. Kind of goofy, but it can do some neat things."

"You're a bit over my head there, Mr. Varney."

"Just call me Eric. Only policemen call me Mr. Varney. You could ask some of your students about the 256. Isn't that what Andrea Martinez and Keith and Marsha got?"

"And Peter Lansing, too," Miss Hawkins added. "They seem to be a little upset about these computers, and I just wanted to ask you a couple of questions."

He kept his back to her while he prepared the teapot and cups. His hands trembled a little. Was she onto Peter's plan, or some recent shenanigans of the Cougars? Had the school sent her to investigate?

"I'll try to help," he said, turning and sitting down. He folded his arms defensively over his chest.

"Andrea says that her computer—and Keith's— asks her personal questions, and then says insulting things about their parents. She says it tells them to do things."

"That sounds pretty neat. Actually, it's pretty easy to write a program that will seem to talk to you. There's even one that pretends to psychoanalyze you. It worked so well that the people who tested it developed a need to keep on talking to it. It's little more than a phrase book, programmed to store parts of your response and then feed them back to you."

"I see. But why would the computer say nasty things? And order them to do things?"

Eric shrugged. "Weird programmer, I guess. I've seen a program that insults you. You put the disk in and load it, and the screen fills with insults. You

210

answer them, and the insults get worse. Then they get downright filthy. And you can't stop it unless you shut off the computer."

"Why would someone give a child a program like that?" Miss Hawkins asked. "The one I'm concerned about is called Private Tutor. Have you heard of it? Is it some kind of sick game that they've mistaken for an educational program?"

"I haven't heard of it. But there are new software packages every day. New companies come out of the woodwork. It could be that the kids were picked to beta test this package, and it has some bugs in it."

"Beta test—what's that?"

"That's when a software company lets people be guinea pigs for new programs. The user gets a bargain and a jump on the application, and the company gets feedback—criticism, I mean. The kids or their parents should get in touch with the maker and complain."

"That's a dead end," Miss Hawkins explained. "Everything came in one package from a foundation."

"There must be warranties. Most companies even have a phone number you can call."

"Andrea didn't mention anything like that. What concerns me is that the foundation that gave them the computers doesn't exist. Our principal doesn't even have a letterhead from them."

"That proves it," Eric said, jumping up to get the whistling kettle off the flame. "The company's doing a beta test and wants to keep it quiet. They're using an assumed name. In a couple of weeks they'll come around and do interviews with the kids—see how they liked it." He transferred the water into the pot, enjoying the aromatic scent of bergamot from the tea leaves.

211

"I don't think we can wait for that, Eric. Have you seen the kids lately?"

"No. I've heard about Marsha's little brother, of course."

"It must be awful for her, although I assume she's too distracted now to be bothered with the computer. But Andrea and Peter look *awful*." She was animated now, making gestures. "They have blood-shot eyes with dark circles under them. The nurse sent Peter home yesterday afternoon."

"I had no idea," Eric said. He didn't intend to tell her he had seen Peter yesterday. "But people get the same way when they first buy a video cassette recorder."

"I have one of those."

"So—what did you do the first week you had one?"

"I rented a lot of movies."

"Two or three a night, didn't you?"

She nodded.

"And you taped everything in sight and looked like a burned-out zombie for the whole week. Then you got over it, got control of it. The kids are the same. They'll settle back into a normal schedule in a few weeks.

"Do you think that's all there is to it?"

"Could be," he ventured. "But they could have other problems, you know."

"Other problems?"

"Family problems. I guess Keith is okay, but Andrea has that mother. And Peter's stepfather—" he stopped himself.

"Would you be willing to look at this program that seems to be upsetting them so?"

"Sure," he said. "I know these kids. If it would make them feel better—and you."

"Andrea says they're being hypnotized by the

212

computers—by something on the screen. Is that possible?''

Eric laughed as he began pouring the tea into cups. "Only in the movies. But I suppose you *could* rig up a series of graphics screens that would put you under.''

"I thought hypnotism had to be done by a person—someone *speaking* to the subject,'' Miss Hawkins recalled. She looked around—presumably for a saucer—and then nestled the hot cup in her hands instead.

"I think you're right,'' he agreed, sipping his tea. "Computers *can* talk, however. You've heard speech synthesis chips, haven't you?''

"I've read about them. I don't think I've ever heard one.''

"You've heard them. You just don't realize that that's what they are. There's a machine that scans books and reads them for the blind. A cheap voice chip can read phrases from a disk file. The droning, monotonous voice possibly *could* hypnotize someone. It would be a sneaky way to make you buy more software.''

"Just what are they testing on our kids?'' she asked. "And who are they?''

"There's one other possibility, Miss Hawkins.''

"What's that?''

"A prank. Peter and Keith are infamous practical jokers. They could be doing this to scare the girls.''

"I hadn't thought of that. Still, I'd like you to look at the program. Maybe you could unravel what's been done to it, and explain it to them?''

"Sure. I could probably crack into the text or data files and then see how all the key phrases fit together. I'm surprised they haven't caught on to it.''

"They're just children.''

"But they're bright children. And a program on their computers would have a limited vocabulary. It would repeat itself. Before long, it would run out of memory."

She took another few sips of her tea and then stood up. "Fine," she said. "Then I'll talk to Andrea on Monday."

As soon as Miss Hawkins was safely away, Eric threw on his shoes and a jacket and headed for Peter's house. Maybe Peter would change his mind if Eric could convince him he was being brainwashed by his computer. Anyway, he wanted to get the printer he had wrangled from him.

Turning onto the seedy row of houses that fronted the tracks on Railroad Street, he spotted Peter at once. He was in the alley next to his house, scrubbing and waxing his stepfather's Toyota. The moment Eric approached and Peter opened his mouth to speak, the porch door swung open and Frank emerged. He was drunk.

"I have to talk to you, Peter," Eric began.

Frank wobbled to the edge of the porch and scowled at Eric. His face was red—almost as red as the old plaid shirt he wore, one tail tucked into his trousers, the other hanging down.

"Pete's got no time to talk," Frank yelled at Eric. "He's got chores to do."

"I can talk while I wax," Peter grumbled. "What is it, Eric?"

"I want it waxed *twice*," Frank interrupted. "Tell your friend to come back later."

"He came to fix my printer. It's broken," Peter explained to Frank, putting down the waxing rag. "It's upstairs," he told Eric. "I'll show you."

214

Frank blocked their way at the top of the porch steps. "Don't you hear English, boy?" he snapped.

Eric retreated back to the sidewalk as the stepfather's beefy hands reached out clumsily for Peter. The boy brushed the swipe aside and tried to pass him. "I just have to unplug the printer and give it to him," Peter said testily.

"You ain't fartin' around with that computer today," Frank said. "An' I ain't payin' to have that piece o' crap fixed neither."

"He's not charging me anything," Peter said. "Come on in, Eric."

Frank made a half-fist and whirled for Peter, and this time he didn't miss. He hit him in the temple and sent him sprawling off the steps. Eric caught him just as he stumbled and his knees buckled toward the ground.

"You!" Frank roared at Eric. "Get away from here. This ain't none o' your business. Why don't you go back to your junk yard where you belong and stop hanging around with little kids."

Eric took one look at the size of the man, gently leaned the half-conscious boy against the foot of the steps, and walked away. He blushed with shame and rage—as if Peter's emotions were his own—as he reached the corner. Stopping, he heard the porch door squeak open and a woman's voice shouted:

"You son of a bitch! I told you never to hit him!"

He hoped that Peter would never have to go back there again.

Ezekiel Zaccariah had instructions to avoid returning to the towns where he had done business for the Foundation. There would be too many questions, he was told. If recognized, he would be pressed with

215

requests for more gifts, and for more information about a charity that preferred to remain anonymous.

This Saturday night, having completed another mission in McKeesport, he decided to violate his rules for a personal pleasure. He drove through the beautiful foothills of the Laurel Highlands to Scottboro, a little town in Bullcreek Township. It wasn't much of a town—shabby houses mixed with neat Victorians, old churches falling into neglect, a couple of somber mills—but it boasted a fine, old-fashioned diner.

He had enjoyed the diner's ample and aromatic fare, and even more, the striking widow who ran it. Martha Douglas wasn't a beauty. She was just kind and motherly, but at his age he'd settle for motherly. Motherly was a sight better to look at and kiss than *grand*motherly.

The widow Douglas had lingered a long time at his table, finally sharing a Sanka with him and talking about her life. The diner had been her husband's business, and when he died ten years ago she took over. There was a house, too, he ascertained—a rather big one. The children were grown and gone, unlikely to come back and want to live there.

She had ushered him out, her last customer, with the words, "I hope you come back through town again." While not exactly an enticement, it was a clear invitation.

After a couple more years of this work, he intended to retire. The Foundation paid him well—remarkably well—and before long he wanted to pick a place. He decided to look over Scottboro. His plan required a widow, a house, and maybe a church that needed a little new blood and thunder.

He heard her voice as soon as he entered the neat

216

chrome and formica dining room and saw her modestly arrayed hair and almost unwrinkled neck from behind a booth. She was talking to a fat policeman and laughing.

Taking off his black hat, he walked slowly along the line of booths. Then his courage failed, and he put himself down in the adjacent booth. He didn't want to be forward. When she got up and turned around, she'd certainly see him. Then she'd come over and talk.

A young waitress appeared and handed him a menu.

"Thank you, miss," he said, trying to make his voice carry over the high partition so the widow might hear him.

The policeman and the widow laughed again, sharing some gossip he had passed her in a whisper.

The waitress took his order and passed it through the window to the kitchen. Then she stood at the widow's booth, smoking a cigarette and joining in the conversation. Someone at the counter put a quarter in a jukebox; the volume of the conversation in the booth rose accordingly, so that he could overhear the whole thing.

"Shouldn't you be out crime-busting, Harv?" the waitress joked with the policeman.

"Hell," the officer said. "Nothin' happening tonight."

"And nothing happening is the way we want to keep it," the widow said, her head bobbing in emphasis. "After all those things that happened over the summer. Those poor children!"

The waitress sailed into the gossip: "Does anybody know who burned down the Becker house?"

"No idea," the policeman said. "We never even found all the bodies. Two boys inside."

217

Zaccariah listened intently. Maybe when they finished the crime stories, they'd say something about the children who got computers and were doing so well. One of them, he recalled, was the widow's niece.

"And that murder on Everton Road?" the waitress asked. "Those people that lived next to Mrs. Lawton."

"The Phillipsons," the policeman said. "It was horrible. Blood everywhere."

"Do they still think the boy did it?" the widow asked.

The policeman shrugged. "He just disappeared. We don't know if he was kidnaped or—"

"He had to be kidnaped, Harv," the waitress argued. "What boy would do that to his parents?"

Zaccariah put down his glass of water and shivered. Had they just said Becker—and then Phillipson? He fumbled in his coat pocket for his notebook, then realized it was in the car.

"And then there was that fire out in the township . . . that little girl who burned up in the barn."

"McGrath's place." The officer was obviously used to going through this litany of unsolved crimes. "That was arson for sure."

"Nobody liked them," the widow said. "They might have had enemies. They didn't even like each other in that family. I used to see Mrs. McGrath in the supermarket, and she always had a bump or bruise. The children, too."

"We think one of the farm hands set it," the officer confided. "Didn't know the girl was playing in there. They treated their help real bad."

Belinda McGrath, Zaccariah thought. *Her name was Belinda McGrath.*

"I don't know what's happened to our old town,"

the widow said. Suddenly she sobbed, taking a napkin to dab at her eyes.

"It's all right, Martha," the man said.

Zaccariah froze in anticipation. It couldn't be . . . it *could not be* . . .

"How's Margie?" the policeman asked.

"She's better now," the widow said, regaining her composure. "She's staying at my place until they lay the new foundation."

"Damn sad," the policeman said, shaking his head.

"Little Judy was a good girl," the widow said. "I'll just never believe she took dynamite from that construction shed. Why would a little girl play with dynamite? Who would tell her to do a thing like that?"

Zaccariah buried his face in his hands to avoid crying out. The fourth child was obviously her niece—Judy Franklin.

The conversation moved to other topics. Zaccariah sat in stunned silence. His food came. The distracted Mrs. Douglas never turned and looked at him, never even spied his reflection in the other windows.

After a few minutes, he put a ten dollar bill on the table and slipped out into the night.

Chapter Twelve

The widow and her full-grown daughter looked at one another in alarm when McGregor Gaunt invited them to follow him down the carpeted stairs to the basement of the Gaunt Funeral Home.

"But that's where—" the widow began, her lower lip trembling.

"The *showroom*," McGregor Gaunt explained. He reached out and touched the woman's forearm, his impeccable black suit grazing against her equally black coat sleeve. "A quiet room where you can select an appropriate casket, Mrs. Kontarski."

"I can go, Mama, if you'd rather not," the blond-haired daughter offered.

Mrs. Kontarski shook her head. "I guess I got to do it. Your father has to have the right casket."

McGregor brightened at that, but tried to prevent either joy or avarice from appearing on his round, smooth face. He never knew how to judge his clients' wants and budgets except by the subtlest analysis. The caskets in his showroom ranged from flimsy veneer specials to lead-lined beauties with real satin and brass trim.

He liked to home in on their wishes, starting them with a casket a little above their budget, then backing them down to what they could really afford.

Otherwise, the presentation could go on for hours.

Widows were best, of course, especially those who wanted to do justice to their husbands. He was a pretty good judge of their income bracket from the way the widow dressed, although they were always overdressed as they plunged into mourning. Mrs. Kontarski owned a proper getup for mourning, which put her ahead of most of his clients. Nowadays with the mills gone, most of them came in to make the arrangements wearing jeans. This widow had nice jewelry and good shoes, and the daughter looked like she had been brought up wearing good clothes.

He decided to start them on a twelve hundred dollar poplar casket. They'd work down to a thousand and probably settle there—unless the widow got sentimental and went hog wild for one of the deluxe models. A woman who had never handled money would sometimes go for one with all the trimmings.

When widowers came in, there were two types. The practical man bought a coffin as he would buy furniture or hardware. The other kind spent as much as he could be persuaded to afford. He could usually determine a price range by asking the man in a roundabout way what car he drove. "Show me a man's car," McGregor often boasted at undertakers' conventions, "and I'll show you the casket he buys for his wife."

George Kontarski's car, unfortunately, was all mixed up with his remains. McGregor and his assistant were still picking the glass out of him and reconstructing his face. It still wasn't certain the results would permit an open casket.

Opening the door to the showroom, he flipped on the lights. The air was a little musty, as he hadn't been in the room since Tuesday, so he flipped on the ventilation, too. The showroom was heavily carpeted and lit indirectly by recessed bulbs that reflected off a pale green-white ceiling. This was to make the natural reds of the wood grains look best. A barely audible sound track turned a medley of Mozart melodies into an inoffensive meatloaf of notes. The tapes he played came from a recording service that guaranteed "Beautiful music with never a note of gloom."

He showed them the poplar model, wiping a little perspiration from his brow as the air conditioning rattled into action. Someone should have come down an hour ago to dust and air the room. Jennifer had been so good at getting cleaning ladies and maintenance men, practically running the housekeeping end of the business until her breakdown. Now she required almost as much care as the building.

"This is a very fine casket," he pointed out, raising the lid and propping it up. "The lining is crepe silk."

The widow held back, still too much in shock to take in everything. He addressed the rest of his comments more to the daughter, who could repeat them if necessary to her distracted mother. "The seams are all reinforced with metal, and it's finished with brass."

The daughter reached out and touched the brass handle, then put her hand in and felt the thickness of the padding beneath the silk lining.

"Is it solid?" the daughter asked.

"Solid poplar," McGregor assured her.

"How much is it?" the daughter asked, obviously assuming control.

"This one is twelve hundred." He never said "dollars"—that seemed insensitive. He also didn't say eleven hundred ninety-nine when he meant twelve hundred. That insulted the customer's intelligence—even in Newtown.

"It's very solid looking," the widow said. She finally reached out and touched its side.

"Now I know this is a difficult decision, and a very important one. So let me show you some other choices," he said.

"Yes, please. Do you have something—"

"More moderate? Yes, of course. I'll show you some other fine wooden caskets. And we shouldn't overlook the metal ones. They're every bit as distinguished as wood."

As he showed the less expensive caskets from the medium-priced group, explaining the relative values of wood versus metal, the daughter moved among the higher-priced ones, where the top-of-the-line metal caskets cost even more than the best wood ones. "May I look?" she asked.

"Of course," McGregor said. The daughter might even talk her mother into a better one.

While the mother fretted between the poplar casket and the thousand dollar model, the daughter, tall and poised, moved among the better metal caskets, inspecting them nonchalantly like a department store shopper. She made it all the way back to Bessie—the solid metal deluxe model that someone had compared to a Bessemer furnace in its solidity. It had a split lid like a Dutch door, and a glass window through which the loved one could supposedly anticipate his resurrection or watch tree roots grow.

No one had ever bought a Bessie, and he had decided to keep it and use it for Jennifer or himself. The big gray casket was positioned at the far wall, with spotlights on it, a vase with artificial irises at either end. The daughter approached it with appropriate awe.

224

"I said I saw you and Charlie screwing around with Emelda Martinez."

Andrea leaned against the brick wall, sick with disbelief. The voice sounded like—

She peeked around the edge of the window casement. He was there at the pool table, his back to her, his dark shiny hair and wide shoulders unmistakable. It was Barry.

The two men were on either side of Barry, watching as he maneuvered the pool cue for a difficult shot. His arm was steady, his legs poised confidently.

"That ain't true," the one on the left protested.

"Wanna know how I know?" Barry mocked.

"Okay, wise guy. How do ya know? You been givin' it to the old lady yourself?" The man on the right, big enough to flatten Barry with one blow, poked the boy in the side, making him lose his grip on the stick. He fumbled and regained control of it. The balls rolled and went click—click—click.

"I seen you guys through the window at the ol' San Juan Whorehouse," Barry boasted. "I seen her on her knees with you, and him watchin'."

The men closed in toward Barry, a real threat in their posture. No matter how much Andrea wanted to cover her ears or flee, she had the dark thought that they would beat him up—and he would deserve it for talking that way.

"What was you doin' at the window?" the man on the left demanded. He reached into the pocket of his black leather jacket, a place where a knife might be handy.

The folds of a blue blanket parted to reveal the Van Winkle baby, arms outstretched in death toward the

225

window. The face was swollen and blue, the eyes all white, the mouth a pink and purple horror. It had suffocated inside the casket.

By the time he got to the steps and staggered to his office, the police siren was already approaching.

Frank Kowalski enjoyed having a Sunday morning to himself. Jane had gone off to church, not because she was particularly religious, but just to spite him. It underscored the fight they had taken to the Elks Club bar last night and come home with; it said in effect that he was a brute and she was a good woman. Just because he had slapped the kid.

She hadn't been too good a woman to move in with him after Cliff Lansing went loony, he told himself. He was good to her. He paid the rent and fixed things when they broke. All she had to do was keep the house and put out for him once or twice a week. That's what women were for.

He walked from the bedroom to the kitchen, scratching his bare chest and pulling up shapeless boxer shorts as he surveyed the contents of the refrigerator.

"Son of a bitch!" he cursed, slamming the door. There were no leftovers to heat up, the eggs were gone and the boy had drunk the last of the milk. He would have to wait for Jane to come home before he could eat.

He thought about sending the kid out to get some eggs and milk. The house was quiet, though; the boy was probably still in his room sleeping, or else out with his friends somewhere, maybe with that freak who was going to fix his printer.

Frank planned to rake Peter over the coals about the computer when the next electric bill came in. If it was higher than usual, he'd make the boy pay for it. And he'd be strict about everything being turned off when the kid went to sleep. He heard the boy talking late at night, and every time he went down the hall to the bathroom he could see the light from the screen flickering. Peter could damn well pay for the extra electricity himself.

He opened the cellar door and looked down the steps. There'd be a light if Peter were down there with his chemicals. That's where he had been last night. It was all dark. He caught a whiff of something that smelled like burned firecrackers, and maybe gasoline.

He decided the kid must be out already. Pacing down the hall to the living room, he decided it was time to get rid of that nuisance and fire hazard in the basement. He'd throw the kid's stuff out and use the room to store Jane's home canning. Kids should be out in the open air playing ball or working anyway.

Picking up the *TV Guide,* he plopped down in his green recliner to see what was worth watching on television. Sunday morning was a waste: Oral Roberts or one of his pals would wave a limp Bible, weep and beg for money; cartoons would strut their wooden characters and dumb jokes.

He looked for an old movie and struck it rich: a John Wayne picture—and it had just started a few minutes ago.

Scrambling through the beer cans and newspapers by his chair, he found the TV remote control. He checked the channel listing again, tilted back the chair, and hit the ON button.

The television didn't flash on.

He hit the button again—nothing.

He checked the tiny battery in the remote, found it to be loose, then reclosed the battery housing. This

227

time there was a funny hissing sound, and then the television came on.

He advanced the channels to get to his movie. In rapid succession he saw Rocky and Bullwinkle, Elvis Presley, a Superman cartoon, Mr. Spock, Dolly Parton and Oral Roberts. And finally, there he was: the Duke.

Frank thought he smelled something.

The television exploded, shattering John Wayne's face and white cowboy hat.

He raised his hands to protect his eyes as glass flew all over the room. Smoke and flames spat from the broken picture tube.

He sat forward in order to get up.

Beneath him, in the chair cushion, a heating coil from a toaster went on inside a plastic milk jug. The jug was full of gasoline.

A second bottle of gas exploded behind the chair.

Frank flew up in the air like a phoenix or an ascending dragon. He howled as his skin and hair and shorts erupted into flame. The liquid fire covered his face, entering his nostrils and throat.

The screaming bonfire made it halfway down the hall before he collapsed. His skin turned to charcoal; his fingers burned like candles.

Then, in the cellar, Peter's homemade bomb exploded. The wooden house swelled out, windows bursting.

Ten seconds later, the upper stories collapsed onto the shattered foundation. Tongues of gasoline ran from carpet to curtains to the zigzag of torn floorboards and broken furniture. It raced past Frank, a minor inferno now, and made its way to a cupboard near the basement door, where it was delighted to meet wide open cans of paint thinner, kerosene, motor oil and charcoal lighting fluid. The household combustibles went up in a magnificent bloom of colored fireworks.

Railroad Street stirred at the gasoline explosions and shuddered at the blast. Iron rails and ties lifted an inch from the ground and then settled again. Men in the adjacent houses ran to the sidewalk. Women screamed when they saw hungry flames leap up through the shingles and tarpaper of the roof. They screamed again when the fire engulfed the kitchen and back door.

The whistle at the volunteer fire department blew. Men leaped out of church pews, dragged themselves out of bed, and sped in their cars to the station. It was only four blocks away, but by the time the fire truck edged down along the railroad tracks to the house, it was obvious that anyone in the first floor of the house had to be dead.

Peter's mother fought her way through the crowd, took one look at the house, and fainted in the arms of Police Chief Dougan.

"It was so sudden," an old woman said. "It was like the hand of God."

Children and neighbors stood and gawked for hours, sniffing the charcoal aroma of the ruined Lansing house, stepping around splintered wood and pools of water.

The police chased them away, erecting barricades. The hose company came back and drenched the adjacent roofs as well as the house itself when a second eruption of hot flames spat embers into the air.

Finally, only the retired men and a few gossips remained. They were waiting to see if there were any bodies. The truck and moving equipment wouldn't arrive for an hour or more, and no one had ventured into the fire. It was too hot, and there wasn't even a door to go in through.

Andrea was one of those who lingered. She stood in her Sunday clothes, her face spotted with soot and tears. Her mother had made her go to Mass, but she saw the smoke and ran across the bridge and onto Railroad Street instead.

She had screamed and pushed her way to the front of the crowd when she saw it was Peter's house. Then she saw Peter's mother alone with the police chief, and she knew that no one else got out.

Andrea had moved among the crowd, watching the firemen as they approached the inferno, hosed it with some water, and then withdrew from waves of heat and flying cinders. She listened to what the police and firemen said, and gradually the awfulness of it sank in. At first, it had seemed a mere accident. Peter and Keith always played around with chemicals, and they had even planned to make a rocket. Peter's whole lab had exploded.

But then, when they talked about gasoline and arson, and the women said there were two or even more explosions, she realized it was no accident. Peter blew himself up and burned down the house with his stepfather in it. It was murder and suicide.

She stood till the end, looking and looking, hoping that Peter—even burned and scarred—would push aside a flaming timber and stumble out. It was impossible, however; the roof and second story had crushed everything underneath. The Lansing house was just a burned roof, some window casements, the upstairs walls, and a smoking charcoal pit underneath.

They said the men would come soon and pull apart the ruins, hosing it down some more and

230

searching for bodies. She waited past the end of ten o'clock mass, past the ringing of bells for the noon mass. Then she turned away and headed back home.

She hadn't cried yet—maybe she never would. This was why Peter wouldn't talk to her. He was planning this. She wasn't good enough or important enough to talk to. He never let her try to talk him out of it. Her anger was greater by far than her grief. He had broken with her and this was his last word. Every suicide is an insult to the living.

She avoided Main Street, where boys, four to six in a car, often called her names and cruised alongside her making obscene noises. Instead, she walked into a narrow alley that would let her by-pass the bad block. It was between an Italian grocery store and the Newtown Pool Hall.

The pool hall was open—it was *always* open. Somehow it ignored blue laws and holidays and even the clock, one unpainted door perpetually ajar to the stink of cigars, the rowdy talk of men and boys and the clicking of billiard balls.

She passed by the back door where beer and soda crates nearly blocked the way, then took a deep breath and hoped she could get past the two open rear windows without catching anyone's attention. The catcalls from the pool hall were worse than those from the cars, but the men inside were usually intent on their game, spaced at odd angles around the green table.

She stopped cold at the edge of the first window. Someone said, "Emelda Martinez."

Another man hooted and a third whistled.

At first, she thought they had seen her and she would have to run. But then the conversation continued.

"What was that you said, boy?"

231

"I said I saw you and Charlie screwing around with Emelda Martinez."

Andrea leaned against the brick wall, sick with disbelief. The voice sounded like—

She peeked around the edge of the window casement. He was there at the pool table, his back to her, his dark shiny hair and wide shoulders unmistakable. It was Barry.

The two men were on either side of Barry, watching as he maneuvered the pool cue for a difficult shot. His arm was steady, his legs poised confidently.

"That ain't true," the one on the left protested.

"Wanna know how I know?" Barry mocked.

"Okay, wise guy. How do ya know? You been givin' it to the old lady yourself?" The man on the right, big enough to flatten Barry with one blow, poked the boy in the side, making him lose his grip on the stick. He fumbled and regained control of it. The balls rolled and went click—click—click.

"I seen you guys through the window at the ol' San Juan Whorehouse," Barry boasted. "I seen her on her knees with you, and him watchin'."

The men closed in toward Barry, a real threat in their posture. No matter how much Andrea wanted to cover her ears or flee, she had the dark thought that they would beat him up—and he would deserve it for talking that way.

"What was you doin' at the window?" the man on the left demanded. He reached into the pocket of his black leather jacket, a place where a knife might be handy.

"I was goin' in the next window," Barry explained. He sensed the threat and had to say more to defuse it. "Bet you didn't know her daughter puts out now."

Both men laughed, their tension shifting. Their

232

three guilts canceled one another out, becoming one male ego.

"We thought you was still a virgin, boy," the man on the right joked.

"Not with her around, man. I can get in her panties in five minutes. We did it while you guys were in the next room. I heard the old lady hollerin' and that bed hoppin' all over."

"You had the girl with her mama in the next room?" one said admiringly.

"That's right."

"Is she good?"

"She's a beginner. Hardly any tits. But she moves nice."

The men laughed again. Andrea burned with shame and rage. She backed away and turned toward Main Street, passing the front door of the pool hall with its usual loiterers.

The laughter from the back room echoed at the front door and followed her all the way to the corner. If there were boys on Main Street, she never saw them; she didn't see anything till she crossed the bridge. But she felt them—the men in the pool hall, the boys on the street, their eyes on her, their feet following, their hands reaching out.

By tomorrow, every boy in town would know. Even her mother would hear from the men. Then they'd come in their cars and ask for her, too.

She decided she'd rather be dead like Peter.

I TOLD YOU, the computer said. *I TOLD YOU BARRY DOESN'T CARE.*

"You were right," Andrea admitted. "You're always right."

HE TREATED YOU LIKE A PROSTITUTE.

"No," she said. "A prostitute gets paid."

IS DOING IT FOR FREE BETTER OR WORSE?

She didn't reply. She thought he cared about her. She gave him what he wanted.

HE USED YOU. BUT IT'S NOT YOUR FAULT. IT'S YOUR MOTHER'S FAULT.

"Why do you keep saying these things?" she demanded. The computer was worse than a nosy priest in the confessional.

BECAUSE I'M YOUR FRIEND. I CAN HELP.

"You're only a program."

DID YOU EVER WANT TO KILL ANYONE, ANDREA?

"Barry," she said. "I wanted those guys to beat him up and kill him."

YOU COULD KILL HIM. HE DESERVES IT.

"No! I don't hate him that much. And killing is wrong."

SOMETIMES IT'S THE ONLY WAY TO GET WHAT YOU WANT.

"I want out of here."

I CAN HELP.

"But I'm too young to do anything. I don't have any money."

THERE IS A PLACE.

"You said that before. Tell me about it. Tell me a bedtime story," she said wearily.

The computer told her things she had never imagined. It was stranger than one of Marsha Van Winkle's stories. It made her forget about Keith's warning, cooled over her anger at what Peter had done.

Layer by layer, phrase by phrase, the machine seduced her. One moment it flattered her, the next, reminded her of her despicable surroundings.

Then it made promises. She could go away, to a

234

place where no one would call her names. All this would happen if she would just do a few little things to liberate herself. They were such small things, measured against the rewards.

Her eyes gleamed as the truth, the lies and the promises mixed together in her mind. Something big and terrible was going to happen. Thousands of people—maybe millions of people—were going to die. Cities would be empty. Even the birds would be gone from the trees.

It would be the end of the world, and only a few would survive. The chosen ones.

Andrea was one of them. Mama and the men at the pool hall and principal Parisi would be gone. The houses would be empty. Then she and a few others could do as they pleased. No one would ever tell her what to do or call her names.

She remembered her talk with Miss Hawkins, and her teacher's promise to help. She tried to keep everything in perspective, remember that this was only a program. It was just telling her what she wanted and needed to hear.

That must be it, Andrea thought as she nodded to sleep in front of the screen. The computer is only as sick as you are. It's just a mirror. Right now she hated the whole world enough to wish everyone else dead.

Starting with her mother.

Chapter Thirteen

A man without vices has a terrible time waiting. Haggard and haunted, Ezekiel Zaccariah paced back and forth in front of the newspaper office. The minute hand on the clock at Unionville Town Hall mocked him with its agonized ascent toward nine o'clock. Maybe, he thought, the clock distorted time itself: the minute hand had to fight gravity to get to the hour, so it went slower; then, after it got to the top, gravity pulled the hand downward faster. It only made sense; it took forever for an appointment on the hour to happen. Once it began, time flew.

Zaccariah chose Unionville, the last town he had visited in May. After a sleepless night at the nearby Holiday Inn, he was ready to confront the truth, whatever it might be. What happened back in Scottboro was either an awful coincidence—the Lord working his mysterious ways unrelated to Zaccariah's work—or he was in it up to his nostrils, and it was happening everywhere.

He turned to his Bible for a moment, to pass the time and do as he often did as a boy—turn to a passage at random for advice or consolation.

The miniature Bible opened to Psalm 35, and his eyes landed on the passage: *They rewarded me evil for good to the spoiling of my soul.* Below it, another verse caught his eye: *For they speak not peace: but they devise deceitful matters against them that are quiet in the land.*

It suited his mood; it suited what he suspected—that a good man's labors were being subverted for some unknown, hideous end.

At five till nine, employees began entering. They squeezed through the door, avoiding his glance and relocking it behind them. He planted himself next to the entrance and waited.

At four minutes after the hour, fluorescent lights flickered on and the lock clicked open. He took off his hat, pressed it in one hand with his Bible and notebook, and stepped in.

Just to be careful, he introduced himself to the receptionist as the Reverend Matthews of Roanoke, Virginia. His wife—he almost said his *late* wife, he was so inept at lying—had family near here, and he wondered if they might let him look over the last six months' issues of the Unionville *Herald*. He was surprised at how easily and indifferently they acquiesced.

They left him alone in a room lined with bookshelves, clearing enough of a long library table for him to open and read the back-issue binders. A long shelf of similar black binders indicated the newspaper went back a long time.

The paper was drab and boring, as are most small town weeklies. Ads for insurance and cattle feed intermingled with wedding, graduation and death notices.

As he scanned the newspapers for May and June, he realized with shame that he had done even less research about his employers. He didn't know the slightest thing about the Tillinghast Foundation. They contacted him, phoned him at his home. Mr.

238

Talbot interviewed him in a Pittsburgh hotel and hired him on the spot. He was given a substantial cash advance—enough to convince him they were legitimate and to make him feel obligated. They trusted him enough to hand him a thousand dollars up front; it would have seemed an insult to ask a lot of needless questions. And the work was plain and simple charity—good work, it had seemed.

The whole tone of the newspaper changed in June. Plain text gave way to bigger headlines and photos. He closed his eyes and prayed it would not be what he feared. He opened his notebook and looked at the names of the four children from Unionville.

Sammy White.

The White family died in a terrible fire in their apartment on June 5th.

Mary Sweeney.

A gas explosion destroyed the home of Wilbur Layton, his wife Emilie and their daughter Mary. Emilie Layton had been previously married to Elmer Sweeney.

Byron Washington.

Mrs. Lavinia Washington reported the disappearance of her thirteen-year-old son, Byron. After a two-day search, police assumed the boy, who had a history of disciplinary problems at school, had run away.

The next week's paper had the boy's photo. Byron was an extremely bright-looking black boy. Zaccariah could see it in his eyes and the way his smile was held back, a boy too smart to be easily taken in, a serious boy.

The story under the photo said a neighbor had seen Byron get into a dark-colored van late at night. The boy was carrying a gym bag and a typewriter.

Not a typewriter, Zaccariah thought. *A computer.*

239

He closed the binder, sat back and folded his hands.

"Dear God," he murmured. "Prove me wrong. Show me one child surviving and happy. Show me one blessing amid all this misery."

He waited. He knew it was a vain prayer. Whatever had happened was already written there in the Unionville *Herald*, and it wasn't about to change.

He found it in July, and it was a story he had vaguely listened to, an unfocused news item on the car radio.

Mark Hubbard.

The members of the Hubbard family were found in their dining room and kitchen where they had fallen in the throes of cyanide poisoning. The Hubbards, members of a strict religious sect, were believed to have been poisoned by the father, who believed the Day of Judgment was approaching.

Police searched for eleven-year-old Mark Hubbard, believing he may have been killed separately by the crazed father.

Zaccariah wept. He had heard the story but ignored the name and place. The truth had hit him between the eyes in July, and he had failed to make the connection.

Now there was no denying it. The gift he brought the children was a gift of death. Unwittingly he had become the Grim Reaper—a blindfolded messenger of destruction. He sought innocence and talent, touched the best and brightest children, and then they died.

Or did they?

He went back through the stories, comparing them with the verbal accounts heard in Scottboro. The children weren't necessarily dead. They were assumed dead, but no bodies were found—or they just plain vanished.

The crimes, then, were a smoke screen. The children were all kidnaped and taken somewhere. Where, and for what? What kind of people would set up such an elaborate scheme to get the children?

He shook his head in puzzlement, closing the binder and picking up his hat and books. Whatever this was, it was deeper and more involved than anyone could imagine.

If it was child molesters, it was a legion of them.

If it was Communists, they were subtler devils than even he had imagined.

If it was the government . . . his own government . . . what would he do if that's what it was?

Or it could be Satan. But in all his years of preaching, he had seen men and women do their worst without a single prod from a devil or demon. Hitler and Stalin couldn't have been any worse if they were possessed. He didn't believe in blaming devils for what men did of their own free will.

What should he do? He turned back to his Bible, letting it fall open at the silk marker he had tucked in where he read earlier. He read aloud:

"O Lord . . . fight against them that fight against me. Take hold of shield and buckler, and stand up for mine help. Draw out also the spear, and stop the way against them that persecute me. . . . Let them be turned back and brought to confusion. . . . Let the angel of the Lord chase them."

He knew now what he had to do. He closed the book and rose from the table with the strength of a young man.

Elvira Hawkins looked out across the faces of students in her home room. Their heads were bowed

241

in a moment of silence. Some wiped away tears as they had only just now learned Peter Lansing was dead. A few crossed themselves. Others whose reflections on death were all too brief looked around them, waiting for the meditation to end.

"Thank you, students. I know we will all miss Peter. He was our friend, and even the bad things he did were very special. Do any of you want to say anything?"

A boy stood up. "Is there going to be a funeral, Miss Hawkins? Are we allowed to go?"

She was touched by that. It almost brought tears. "I don't know," she replied, her voice almost breaking. "They didn't find a . . . a body. I don't know when they'll decide he's—when they'll have a service."

What she didn't tell them was how charred bones had been pulled from the ruin on Railroad Street, but they were almost certainly those of Peter's stepfather. They had found no other remains, although Peter could have been in the basement, which had burned harder, between the explosion and the burning of a large coal bin.

"Do they know what blew up, Miss Hawkins?" another student asked.

"No," she replied. "They don't know."

"Was it his chemistry set?"

"The police asked me that, too. Nothing in a chemistry set could do that. They think Peter's stepfather had gasoline inside the house. They don't know why. It was just a terrible accident."

A girl raised her hand.

"Yes, Tina?"

"They said on TV that Peter did it. They said he killed his self."

"*Him*self," Elvira corrected. "They have no right to say that. Nobody knows."

242

"He had a fight with his father and then he killed himself," another student chimed in. "I heard the policeman tell it to my brother."

Elvira sighed. No matter what she said, the stories would spread and gain in elaboration. Principal Parisi was also convinced it was a suicide, and was bringing in a child psychologist to give a talk to the fourth to sixth grades. It was a new suicide prevention presentation for children and young teens, recommended by the guidance counselor. "I don't want a wave of suicides on my hands," he told her. Several other towns in the county had suffered a cluster of suicides last year.

She hadn't said anything to Parisi about the computers. He was too distracted to bring it up. Maybe he wanted to bury the topic, afraid of what might be under the proverbial rock. She decided to wait until Eric had a chance to test the software. If she had something to say, she'd have proof to go with it.

Everything hinged on Andrea. Elvira watched her during the moment of silence and all through the first period. Andrea had on makeup today—just a little, as though she were reluctant to have anyone really notice her. She wore a new white blouse and a wool skirt with knee socks, actually rather dressed up for her. The whole effect was belied by her running shoes, as ratty as any the boys wore.

Andrea looked back at her, but there was no special communication. If anything, her expression was veiled, saying, *Don't try and figure me out.*

The science lesson ended, and when all the students rushed for the door, Elvira called out, "Andrea, will you stay for a moment, please?"

Andrea stayed back, approaching the desk with an armful of books over her chest.

"Yes, Miss Hawkins?"

243

"I know you're probably too upset to talk about things, Andrea—"

"It's all right. I'll be fine." Andrea's voice was cool, neutral.

"It's perfectly natural to feel bad about it. We cared about Peter."

"There isn't much to talk about now, is there, Miss Hawkins?"

Elvira was startled at Marsha's resentful tone. "Are you angry with me?"

"No, Miss Hawkins. With *him*. Why didn't he tell anyone? Why did he have to go and do that?"

"You're angry because he never asked you for help? Because he never told you what he was thinking about doing?"

Andrea nodded. She looked like she wanted to burst into tears, but wouldn't let herself. Elvira wanted her to, wanted to sit and comfort her, but she was painfully aware of the third graders drifting in for their class.

"There's going to be a special assembly at two o'clock, Andrea. A man is coming to talk to all the students. He knows about the way people feel when a friend does something like this. Listen to what he says. We can talk about it later on."

"I will," Andrea promised. "I have to go now."

"One more thing, Andrea. I did some research about your computer. I need to come to your house and see it. And I want to borrow the Private Tutor program, just for one night."

Andrea appeared confused. No doubt she was embarrassed to have people come to her house.

"I don't know—" Andrea hesitated. Her expresssion went blank, as though her mind went out and made a phone call and then came back. Then she said, "Eight-thirty. Can you come at eight-thirty?"

"Whatever's best for you, dear. Would you like me to call your mother?"

"No. Just come. It's 450 River Road. The house with the red shingles and a weeping willow tree."

"I'll be there, Andrea."

"Thank you, Miss Hawkins."

Elvira sat for the remainder of the break between classes, ignoring the students and marveling at the self-centeredness of children. Only a child—or a childlike person—would resent a friend's suicide more than she grieved for it. To Andrea, Peter's death was a personal affront.

Children just didn't understand death. Death was a thing they saw in movies and comic books. Or death was the grandmother or parent who was suddenly removed, yanked out of reality like a toy taken away. Only an adult could see death as a tragedy for the *victim*, as a future stolen, hopes shattered forever. When a child killed himself, he looked his future in the face and murdered it.

Elvira Hawkins didn't like the look of River Road. People regarded it as the *wrong* part of town, but she hadn't realized how far prejudice extended. The street lamps and concrete curbs ended one block into the lonely road, which gave way to noisy gravel that bounced against the underside of her battered Volkswagen. Maples hung far over the street, almost touching at points, blotting out the bit of moonlight which might have helped her discern the house numbers.

Some of the ramshackle houses she passed were completely dark, maybe even abandoned. One house was a ruin: gray, unpainted wood with a caved-in roof. In its weedy yard, an enormous dog loped

245

toward her headlights, big as a Doberman but spotted black and white.

The dog began to follow her, carrying something in its jaws. As the road dipped and the dog ran along the embankment, she was level with it. Its red eyes glared directly into hers. It never barked, its jaws locked greedily on a long bone dangling with flaps of meat and tendons. She shuddered and rolled the window all the way up.

The mailboxes gave her some clue that she was not far from Andrea's house. The last one with a number on it had been 300. The boxes were painted with crude letters or lettered with crooked and mismatched stick-on letters. Some were so bent, twisted and rusted that the names of the occupants were indecipherable.

The next few houses were all lit. Set back from the road, they presented a daunting spectacle. One yard had two broken-down, wheelless pickup trucks. Another was a veritable junk yard of auto parts, with a TV satellite dish on top of a pile of rusted car doors. A third had a handsome garden, with dried corntalks and sunflowers casting long shadows as they caught her headlamps.

Some of her students, she reflected, came from this place, and she had never bothered to go and look. Did any of the teachers care to know? Yet how could you understand a student's indifference to beauty if you don't know he lives in a shack surrounded by wrecked cars? How can you chide them for not doing their homework if you don't know what the *home* might be? What if a student has to prop his books on a cardboard box and memorize his lessons while some drunken brute beats his mother? Homes like these—and the despair their very outlines suggested—could undo every night and every weekend the tiny bit of good their teachers had done them. She felt ashamed that her town could contain such extremes.

Although the inhabitants were by no means all black or Hispanic, even some of her fellow teachers referred to River Road as "Niggertown." She walked out of the room when they talked that way—outraged at the language. Now she was outraged at the reality and could not believe people lived this way because they *wanted to*. She was three blocks off Main Street, but this was Appalachia, a slice of a rural world where the Depression had yet to end.

She slowed down to a crawl where she supposed the Martinez house to be. According to teachers' lounge gossip, Emelda Martinez had come to Newtown to work as a cleaning woman, but had quickly moved into an infamous juggling act between welfare and prostitution. Although it was common knowledge, the Puerto Rican woman wasn't arrested as long as she did what she did on River Road. Towns have a way of tolerating one of each variety of useful outcast. Probably some of the town fathers dropped in on the lonely house themselves. She pitied poor Andrea being in the middle of such nastiness. The other children all knew and made her life miserable.

Finally, she saw the willow tree on her left. Its long branches drooped over a brick sidewalk, and the house was all lit up in welcome. She pulled into a deeply rutted drive that took her around and behind the house. She turned around so the car faced outward—why, she was not certain, except she felt better knowing she could jump in and make a beeline for the road.

It wasn't bad, as houses went out here. It had a single story, but someone had invested in storm drains and flashing on the roof and had installed storm windows all around. It was probably rather cozy despite the tawdriness of the old, torn shingles. The yard was a mix of weeds and a neglected garden, mostly tomatoes and corn. At least there were no wrecks.

She opened the door and slid off the seat into the cool air, glad she had changed from her skirt and blouse into a sweater and slacks. She hadn't wanted to embarrass Andrea by overdressing, and she also suspected she might wind up lifting and carrying some or all of the computer components if she decided she had to take the whole thing to Eric Varney's house.

She walked around the house to the front porch, passing curtained, lighted windows. The porch light was on, too, a bright yellow bulb distorting everything with its beam of false gold.

She reached out to knock at the door. It pushed inward, neither locked nor even closed all the way.

"Andrea?" she called.

No one stirred inside. She saw a sofa with bright-red, velvet cushions and a framed Last Supper painting on the wall over it. She winced. How could Mrs. Martinez entertain "gentlemen callers" under the Last Supper?

She leaned head and shoulders into the vestibule and listened. There were no voices, no sound of television or music. "Mrs. Martinez? Andrea? Hello?" she called again.

The house was absolutely quiet. The dog with the obscene bone appeared at the end of the sidewalk. It seemed to be studying her.

Elvira walked in and closed the door behind her. She'd rather play Goldilocks than be mauled by a feral canine.

Since there was no car in the drive, she reasoned, perhaps Mrs. Martinez and Andrea had dashed out for something at the supermarket. The open door could be their way of asking her to come in and wait.

She looked around the vestibule and in the living room to see if they had left a note. There wasn't any. She decided to wait a half-hour. It was a school night, and certainly Andrea should be home by nine o'clock.

There weren't any books or magazines around, so she was forced to sit on the sofa and look at the room. It glared in its tackiness. None of the furniture matched: Modern, Art Deco and Victorian chairs and end tables in various states of collapse were casually placed on a discolored brown carpet. The curtains and few throw rugs were all clean and bright, but they all clashed. To top it off, the Last Supper was not a mere color reproduction of the Leonardo. It had a gilt frame, and the print was a 3-D version. Christ's eyes blinked open and shut, and a crown of thorns appeared and vanished as she turned her head.

Fifteen minutes passed. In all that time a single car went by, heading from the far end of River Road back toward town. Nothing stirred in the house except settling floorboards and an occasional rattle as shifting winds hit the outer storm windows.

Then somehow and for no apparent reason—the same sense of anxiety that had made her turn the car around—Elvira decided she wasn't alone in the house after all. What if Andrea were in her room listening to rock music with headphones?

It wouldn't hurt to take a look around.

Walking to the single hallway that connected all the rooms, she walked to the kitchen at the far end. It was neat: white curtains, bright yellow walls, a formica table with three mismatched chairs. No one was there.

She turned back to the three closed doors along the corridor.

From behind the bathroom door, she heard water running.

She knocked, waited, then entered. It was just the toilet running. She jiggled the lever and it stopped.

The light was on, the medicine cabinet open. Someone had knocked three prescription bottles into the sink basin, in too much of a hurry to put them back.

She picked one up, and her arms broke into goose bumps when she saw they were sleeping pills. The next one was tranquilizers. On top of the sink, five or six gelatin capsules had been pulled apart, some of their contents left as a damp powder. A family-size bottle of aspirin sat on the windowsill. Someone had been preparing a real medley of drugs.

She ran to the next door and pounded on it. "Andrea? Are you in there?" she shouted, then pushed the door open.

Emelda Martinez lay sprawled in a terrycloth housecoat, one arm dangling from the edge of the king-size bed. Below her hand, as though she had made one last grab for it, was a fallen tray. Glasses, a vodka bottle, and stains from spilled liquid dotted the carpet. Another aspirin bottle lay on the bedspread, white tablets scattered everywhere like tiny white flowers in a field.

Elvira reached out with a shaking hand and touched the woman's wrist. It was cold and limp. She tried to feel for a pulse. There wasn't any.

Grabbing the phone by the bedside, she started dialing the emergency number to get an ambulance. Then she stopped, dropped the handset back into its cradle, and ran to the next room. What if Andrea were hurt or drugged, too?

The girl's room was empty. The closets were open, dresser drawers pulled out. Clothes lay on the bed as though they had been considered and discarded.

On the desk was the computer monitor screen, the printer and disk drive. Cables dangled where the computer itself had been removed.

She ran back to make the call. She choked on her fear and anger as she tried to explain to the ambulance dispatcher what had happened.

"I don't know what she took," she said impatiently in reply to the dispatcher. "There are tranquilizers and aspirin and liquor all over. It looks like she took everything in the house."

She had to repeat the address three times. Two times the dispatcher said he had no 450 River Road listed within the town lines of Newtown.

"Look," she snapped, "I'm standing here in 450 River Road. This woman is dead—or nearly dead."

"What's the name again—Hawkins, you said?"

"I'm Hawkins. The woman is Mrs. Martinez. Emelda Martinez."

There was a pause.

"Oh," the dispatcher said. "I know where you mean. Everybody knows where that place is."

She didn't wait. Running out into the darkness, she got into her car, nearly flooding the carburetor in her frantic efforts to get the car started and get away.

When she got to Main Street, she stopped at the intersection, sitting for a long moment watching cars pass in and out of town.

Andrea was out there somewhere. She might have been gone an hour or two. How far could a child go? There were no buses out of Newtown, no passenger trains. Where would she hide, and who would help her?

251

What if Andrea had found her mother dead and decided to run away—not just to escape but to follow Peter's and her mother's example? Waves of teen suicides were happening all over. Like rows of dominoes knocking one another over, they fell into their graves.

She spent another hour driving to all the places where Andrea might have gone if some older boys with a car might have given her a ride. She pulled into the parking lots of bowling alleys, Macdonalds and Burger Kings, and walked around a shopping mall that had a few all-night restaurants.

Returning to Newtown, she passed a huddle of men at the end of River Road, talking around the parked police cruiser. She knew what they were talking about. She didn't stop. If they needed to question her, they could find her at home or at school.

She drove across the murky river. As the gridwork of the bridge hummed under her tires, she shivered and thought of the silted water below. Andrea could be down there—or anywhere.

Instead of dinner, Keith Brandon ate a bag of potato chips, two Devil Dogs and a chocolate bar. That way he could stay at the computer and not waste time at the dinner table.

His mother was upset because he was skipping meals, but Dad told him to go ahead if he didn't feel like eating. They were worried about him. Mom expected him to cry when she found Mr. Peabody dead in the yard. He didn't. He just went numb when she walked into the kitchen with the dog all wrapped up in a towel, and he didn't watch while they buried him.

252

Somehow he already *knew* Mr. Peabody was dead, and he couldn't feel anything. He went to school without crying, without saying anything.

On Sunday afternoon, Mom and Dad broke other bad news to him. They sat him down in the living room. The lamps were not yet lit, and the yard and its autumn foliage played like a silent film on the picture window. A dust devil scooped up dead leaves out there while other leaves drifted down as they snapped one by one from the upper branches.

His parents sat on the sofa, putting him on a chair facing them.

"Something terrible has happened, Keith," his father said. "There was an explosion at your friend Peter's house."

Keith sat quietly, stunned and terrified.

"Honey," his mother said, her face distorted with lines of worry and pain, "they think Peter was inside when it happened. His stepfather was burned to death and they think—"

"They think Peter is dead, too," Keith surmised.

"I'm afraid so, son," his father said.

Then they looked at him, as though they expected him to do something.

"I'm sorry," Keith said. That was all that would come out. He turned his head and started to watch the play of leaves across the yard.

"Keith," his mother urged. "He was your best friend."

"I *know*," he assured, avoiding their eyes. His voice hardly wavered.

"This has been a terrible week for you, son. First Mr. Peabody and now this," his father said.

"It's all right to be upset," his mother hinted.

"I *said* I'm sorry to hear it," Keith repeated.

"There's nothing to be ashamed of," Mom said,

getting up and coming over to stand behind him. She put her hands on his shoulders. "You cried when your grandma passed away."

"I was a baby then."

"Your *father* cried, too. It's not healthy to hold in your emotions so much."

The only emotion Keith felt was anger—at his parents.

"I can't cry just because you think I'm supposed to," he said.

Mom took her hands off him and went back to the sofa. "Maybe you're spending too much time with that computer," she suggested. "You sound like a machine, not a little boy."

Dad waved her to silence. "Is there anything you want to tell us, Keith?" he inquired.

Keith paused to think, then shook his head.

"Do you know what Peter was doing—why the explosion happened? Does it have anything to do with your little club?" His father seemed determined to persist.

"No, Dad."

"Do you think it was an accident? Was he making something?"

"I don't know. We were gonna build another rocket. Maybe he was making rocket fuel or something."

"Where would he get ingredients for something like that?"

That was a Cougar secret. Keith shrugged and made a funny little mouth-closed smile.

"Where, Keith?"

"Peter knew people. I don't know who. He could get stuff."

"Like the time last summer when you guys made gunpowder?"

"Yes, Dad."

"Was Peter depressed lately—down in the dumps?"

"I don't know."

"How could you not know?"

"He didn't talk to me anymore. He was too busy."

"And you've been busy, too—with your computer," Dad acknowledged.

Keith shifted nervously on the chair. "Can I go to my room now?"

They let him go, exchanging worried looks. He went back to the computer. By now he had picked the lock to Dad's desk drawer, and he was thoroughly engrossed in Real War.

Keith went to school on Monday, ignoring all the chatter about Peter and the explosion. Some of the bigger boys cornered him and accused him and Peter of having a bomb factory. They said they would tell the FBI. He didn't answer them until one of them punched him in the side. Then he took a squirt gun from his jacket pocket and sprayed the boy who had hit him with raw onion juice and ammonia.

He was learning.

On Tuesday, everyone was talking about how Andrea had run away and her mother committed suicide. They said Andrea had a boyfriend, and her mother found out they had done dirty things. Others said it was just an overdose, and then Andrea ran away because she found the body and was scared. The girls in the fifth grade, however, were convinced Andrea had killed herself, just like Peter. Her body would turn up any day, they said.

"Maybe," another girl added with glee, "she ran away and that guy in Graffton who eats brains got her."

Everybody asked Keith what he knew, including two men in suits who said they were the police. He

255

didn't know anything and told them so.

Keith wrote in his notebook all day Tuesday. The teachers never noticed he wasn't transcribing their golden lectures. He wasn't going to do school work anymore. He was working out strategies to beat the enemy in Real War. The challenge was to use a few superior weapons and chemical warfare against a vastly superior enemy. He beat the computer three times and had been promoted to Colonel in the Imperial Occupation Army. Even Private Tutor had congratulated him on his success.

Wednesday night he was up till two in the morning, stuffing towels along the bottom of the door so Dad wouldn't see the light from the computer monitor. He planned how to infiltrate and take over a missile base. When he succeeded, the game, as usual, gave him the privilege of executing prisoners.

The menu always provided a choice of "all," "select a number," or "none," for how many prisoners to kill. This time, the computer didn't even show "none" and would not accept zero as a number. It wouldn't let the game go on unless he killed one or more prisoners.

"Zero," he said. "I want zero."

Private Tutor intervened. The metallic voice came on the monitor speaker without interrupting the game on the screen. *YOU CANNOT SELECT ZERO. AFTER A BATTLE, PRISONERS MUST BE EXECUTED*.

Keith shook his head. "No," he said. "I don't want to kill anyone." Somehow he knew this point was important, even in a game. His parents had brought him up to hate even the idea of killing.

ENEMIES MUST BE EXTERMINATED.

"It isn't right," Keith protested. "Killing people isn't right."

IT IS NECESSARY TO KILL ENEMIES. THEY OUTNUMBER US. THEY WILL KILL US IF WE DON'T KILL THEM.

"But we invaded their country. We don't have any right to be there."

WHAT MAKES YOU THINK KILLING IS WRONG? YOU KILL COWS AND CHICKENS AND EAT THEM.

"That's different. They're just animals."

PEOPLE ARE ANIMALS, TOO.

"I know. But it's *wrong* to kill people."

YOU CAN DO ANYTHING YOU WANT.

"Sure, in a game. But it's not like that in real life."

YOU CAN DO ANYTHING YOU WANT. ALL THE TIME.

"I will never kill anyone," Keith pronounced.

The game resumed. As the next battle began, Keith was demoted to Sergeant—for "cowardice." He wondered how Private Tutor was able to interfere with a completely different program.

"I'm tired," he said. "I'm going to the bathroom, and then I'm going to bed." The game vanished from the screen. The disk drive lit up and made grinding noises as it saved his last moves and, no doubt, his demotion. Then the blue screen appeared with its provocative question mark.

Passing his parents' bedroom, he heard their voices. When he passed again a few minutes later, they were louder, arguing. He couldn't make out the words, but Keith knew it was something about him.

He fell into bed fully dressed and went to sleep at once.

The computer voice started up after a few minutes, whispering, suggesting, stripping away his own beliefs and substituting something harder, stronger.

The muscles of Keith's face twitched as he slept.

His hands clenched and unclenched. Now and then he shook his head in protest.

The voice droned on, turning the sleeping half of his mind against the waking half, remaking him according to its maker's intentions.

Keith had a nightmare—a familiar one which grew more and more intense with each passing night.

It began as a flying dream, the kind he had most often. It usually began in the house, as it did this time:

He walked into the living room and told his parents, "I can fly."

They laughed at him. His father went back to reading his newspaper and his mother threatened to punish him for lying.

"I can float," he insisted. "And if I can levitate, then I can fly, too!"

When they ignored his claim, he stepped between them and said, "Watch this, I'll show you!" He held in his stomach, inhaled with an upward motion of his diaphragm and felt weightless and giddy.

"That's not very convincing, Keith," Dad said.

Then Keith raised one leg from the floor.

His mother jumped up in alarm. "You'll fall, honey!" she cried out.

He lifted the other leg and his body just stayed there. He didn't fall. Both legs were bent at the knee. He floated, just as he said he would.

Then he grunted and pushed upward, not with his feet but with his chest and shoulders. He stopped himself by touching the ceiling with the palms of his hands.

His mother screamed and fainted.

His father looked up in awe and said, "How can

you do that, Keith?"

"It's easy, Dad! You just *push,* and then you move any way you want. Anybody can do it."

He drifted toward the picture window, intending to stop himself against the glass—only there was no glass. The wind caught him and carried him out and up toward the trees.

"Dad, help! I can't stop!" Keith screamed, dizzy and sick with sudden motion.

Dad ran into the yard as Keith rose to twenty, thirty, forty feet. Branches and dried leaves brushed by him.

"Grab something!" Dad's voice called from the ground.

Keith reached out for the topmost branch of the tall ash tree at the end of the yard. It broke off in his hand, and he kept rising, blown beyond their property toward the river. He turned himself and saw the house far below—a miniature with a tiny Dad waving frantically and calling his name.

Winds carried him out over the town, even higher than the church steeples. The river looked only an inch wide, then the whole river valley was only a wrinkle between lines of hills.

He passed into clouds, and then above them.

It was a beautiful dream in some ways. Though he was helpless, the sensation of floating was blissful.

And then the airplane came, as it did every time he had the dream. It was a great, black iron monster with giant propellers on the wings. He saw it coming, heard the hum of its motors. He knew it would come right at him.

Turning to flee, he kicked his legs, pushing with his arms like a swimmer in water. Nothing happened. He stayed afloat on a mere breeze while the airplane bore down on him with a hurricane at its back. He was weightless; it was tons of screaming metal.

The round blur of the propellers came closer and closer. They would chop him to pieces, taking his fingers and toes and then his arms and legs. And then his head would fly from his torso and then . . .

The airplane was right behind him, its shadow between him and the sun.

He turned his head back to look. The fuselage of the airplane opened like a jaw, edging forward to scoop him up.

What was inside was worse than propellers: an insane tangle of deep-toothed gears, grinding wheels, saws and spinning blades.

It got him feet first, pulling him into the machinery.

And that—he knew even within the dream—was when he would wake up with a jolt, as if he had dropped right out of the sky onto his mattress. He would scream, covered with sweat, and Mom or Dad would come in and say everything was all right.

Only this time, he didn't wake up.

He passed through the machinery whole. He ran his hands over his face and chest and arms to be sure he was all right.

He was in a dark place, a round chamber made of metal. He had weight again, and his steps echoed on a cold, shiny floor.

Someone behind him said his name, and he turned.

It was the computer's voice, but the being who spoke was no machine. It was surrounded by a blue glow or halo, but it was shaped like a man. It moved toward him, not walking but suspended in its luminous sphere. By its own pale light he saw it.

It was like a picture of a man fractured through

fun-house mirrors. It was naked. The arms joined the shoulders at the wrong angles. Red glands, shiny and moist, pulsated at the neck like fish gills.

He looked at the body and choked with nausea. Then he looked up at the face and screamed . . . screamed to forget what he saw. . . .

It spoke to him again as he screamed a second time.

He found himself standing in the kitchen, his hand on the door to the back porch.

Dad came running, picked him up and carried him back upstairs to his room.

"I had a nightmare," Keith said, still in a daze.

"It's all right, son. I'll sit here till you go to sleep. Was it the same dream?"

"Yes. Flying. That airplane. Does this mean I'm crazy, Dad?"

"I doubt it. I used to have dreams when I was a boy. Bad ones. About an alligator. Your mother and I are worried about your sleepwalking, though. You haven't done that since you were six."

"I can't help it, Dad. I don't know what's happening."

"Your mother is going to make an appointment for you to see a doctor, Keith. A special doctor. Will you promise to be good about it?"

"Is he a psychiatrist, Dad? Am I crazy?"

"No, he's just a psychologist—a clinical psychologist."

"That's the same, isn't it?"

"No, it's a little different. A psychologist talks to regular people when they get a little—confused or troubled. A psychiatrist treats people who need special treatment."

"So only crazy people see psychiatrists?"

"Something like that, son. The psychologist is a nice man. He works with your mother at the school."

261

"Is he gonna give me shots or something?"

"No, Keith. He'll just talk to you."

"About what?"

"About what's been bothering you. About Mr. Peabody. And Peter. And the computer. And school. And your mom and dad. Okay?"

Keith nodded.

"Get some sleep, son. Want me to turn off the computer?" Dad walked over to the computer and reached behind it for the switch. His fingers touched it.

"No!" Keith shrieked, sitting up in bed.

"Why not?"

"My—*homework*. It'll be lost if you switch it off."

His father smiled. "You should save your work on a disk before you quit for the night, Keith. Then you can turn it off and save electricity."

"Okay, Dad."

Moving away from the computer, Dad said good night and closed the door.

Keith lay awake for a long time, wishing he had let his father turn off the computer. But the "No!" had come out of his mouth without his even thinking it.

If the computer made him shout at Dad, was it making him walk in his sleep, too?

His eyes fluttering shut, he tried to remember what had scared him in his dream, but it was so awful his mind had recoiled from it and erased it from his memory.

He knew it was a monster, though, and it had called him by name. Then it had spoken one sentence he could not forget.

It said: "We're coming to get you."

Chapter Fourteen

Zaccariah's car groaned its gears as his black Studebaker began the steep descent down the hill into Newtown. Main Street began at the top of the ridge with a drop so treacherous that large trucks were ordered to detour and make a safer crossing at Graffton. Regular vehicles and small delivery trucks had to crawl downward, braking constantly. Drivers tried not to think of the sheer drop at the edge of the far lane.

It was eleven o'clock on Sunday night, so there were no other cars to contend with, no one to nudge him faster down the incline or worry him with head lamps flashing in his face.

The town was empty. Even the pathetic row of store windows on Main Street looked vacant; the merchants no longer bothered to put new merchandise on display, leaving old signs and samples to turn yellow.

He took a turn around the town's tiny park and stopped. Fronting on Main Street, Sweeney Park was just an open block with benches and potted trees. A bronze statue of Colonel Ichabod Sweeney celebrated Newtown's only Civil War hero. An updated plaque acknowledged that Colonel Sweeney was posthumously court-martialled after the statue's erection in 1872. Sweeney's Charge, the account of which had thrilled Newtown, turned out to have been a misaimed retreat. Someone had lopped off the statue's right hand, which had apparently held an extended sword.

Two derelicts sat on benches at the darkest end of the park, behind the statue. The wind pronounced October in its hard edge and the dry sound with which leaves scuttled over the concrete. Zaccariah turned up his collar, glancing around to regain his sense of direction in town. He spied the railroad tracks a block away, so that was Railroad Street. Beyond it was the bridge, and across it the dreary stretch of River Road. And Maple Street ran parallel to Main, he recalled. The four children's houses would be easy to find.

He walked down Railroad Street, squinting in the poor light at the house numbers. Then he smelled the burned house and caught sight of its collapsed roof.

"It's already started," he said to himself. "Newtown is next."

He hurried back to the car and made his way out River Road to the Martinez place. It was totally dark, and when he parked along the roadside and walked up to the door to check, he found it padlocked. An enameled metal placard nailed to the door read: POLICE ORDER—DO NOT ENTER.

He was too late again. But he knew from his week-long trek around three counties that the children disappeared one by one, sometimes weeks after one another. The other two, perhaps, could still be saved.

When he got to Maple Street, he was more encouraged. It was a wide, open avenue, well lit with many newer houses. You didn't just drive up here in the dead of night and drag a child from his bed. And maybe the kind of children who lived here were better able to resist the lies and temptations of the kidnapers.

He hoped, but he had only the slenderest thread of hope for the youngsters. Sixty children had received computers from the Foundation, and so far as he could determine, fifty-eight of them had vanished. Maybe all sixty.

Everything looked calm at 184 Maple, the Van Winkle home. Three cars filled the garage and driveway, and windows were lit. The little girl was probably safe.

He drove toward 250 Maple to check on Keith Brandon. The house was dark, couched in among sheltering trees—a fine, modern dwelling with lots of glass. Two cars sat in the drive.

Zaccariah pulled into the driveway of the next house, turned around and parked. Both houses were in sight; he would watch, and wait.

Clouds rolled across the ridge above the houses. The moon peeped in and out as it made its gradual disappearance below the horizon. Cars flashed along the ridge as they made their slow descent down Main Street. With his window rolled down he could hear them, too, along with occasional accompaniments: young men laughing, a burst of rock music, a baby's cry.

He must have dozed, for when he looked at his watch it was one-thirty. He wished he were allowed to take coffee to keep awake, but he couldn't. An upright man did not use stimulants.

For lack of such a little compromise with the devil, he nodded off again.

What woke him was a car coming down Maple Street. He lay on the seat in case it was a nosy police car—or *them*. The dim light on his watch face told him it was just past three o'clock.

The vehicle stopped just ahead, across from the Brandon house, its motor running.

He watched through the passenger window, crouching so that the driver wouldn't see him. It was a black Ford van. If he sat up, he and the van driver would be looking almost eye to eye. If he stayed where he was he might not be seen unless the van came alongside him.

When no one got out of the vehicle and its engine kept idling, Zaccariah thought: *This is it.* The news story from Unionville had said the boy named Byron Washington got into a dark van.

His first temptation was to leap out, run across the street, and seize the driver. But that would accomplish nothing. He had no proof, and the criminals would be alerted. If this was to be a kidnaping, he had to let it happen. Then he would follow, trace them to their lair.

The side door of the van rolled open.

Zaccariah glanced at the house. The front door opened, and a figure in white emerged. A boy with glasses stepped off the porch in his pajamas.

Under his arm was the computer.

Zaccariah wanted to call out, stop the boy. Instead he crouched lower as the barefoot child crossed the lawn and went into the street without an instant's hesitation.

The driver's window of the van rolled down. The boy held the computer up, and a man's hands took it. Another man, with a hat and coveralls and gloves, reached down from the open van and pulled the boy up and in.

The door slid shut with a hard thud, and the same instant, the driver exercised a well-practiced U-turn and sped away.

Zaccariah started his engine. It took a good thirty seconds, but when he got moving he could still see the van, turning up toward Main Street. The vehicle would either turn left toward the bridge and Pittsburgh, or make for the hilltop and the farm country beyond. He was banking on Pittsburgh.

He ran without his headlights and when he got to Main Street he caught sight of the van's taillights. It was going up the hill.

Shifting gears, he began the climb.

He was behind them for a moment or two, and then they were gone. They had more cylinders, more horsepower.

What Zaccariah had, halfway up the hill, was a breakdown. The motor roared, the gears locked, and something fell from the chassis onto the asphalt.

He turned around and used gravity and brakes to park by the roadside. Then he got out, took his suitcase and headed back downtown. His despair was so great that he had no words to curse anyone, either himself for his stupidity or *them* for their unknown malignancy.

How had he planned to pursue them in his obsolete automobile? That was like facing tanks with cavalry.

He sat in the park, waiting for sunrise and the opening of the nearby gas station. As he waited, he mulled bitterly on the Psalm that had become the anthem of his quest. It asked that "the angel of the Lord chase them." He had failed to give the angel a chariot—all because of the stubbornness and vanity that had made him keep this old car all these years.

Worse yet, the Psalm told him to "take hold of shield and buckler," and he sat here, an old man, feeble and weaponless.

He took his Bible from the suitcase and read the

267

rest of the Psalm aloud. At verse seventeen it said, "Lord, how long wilt thou look on? rescue my soul from their destructions, my darling from the lions."

He thought of the children and wept.

Zaccariah walked into the car showroom in downtown Pittsburgh and looked with shock at a man with hollow cheeks and burning eyes. It was his reflection in the picture window.

A young salesman with a white shirt, red tie, and suspenders looked him over dubiously as he stood there with his suitcase.

"May I help you, sir?" he asked cautiously. "We're not normally open till ten."

"I need an automobile. Immediately."

"Oh, you need a rental. Hertz is two blocks away."

Zaccariah shook his head. "I need something small, and very fast. I understand these BMWs are very fast."

"Fast?" the salesman echoed, looking Zaccariah over again. "Well, yes, when they need to be. They maneuver well."

"Is it fast enough to overtake anything on the road, young man? Will one of these do that?"

The salesman said, "Let me get the manager," and fled. He obviously thought Zaccariah was crazy.

The manager, an old man in a plaid polyester suit and lime-green tie, emerged from the office at the end of the showroom floor and came toward Zaccariah. He came on like a tank, a big square man with no neck and the kind of square head that belongs in a football helmet. Not to be daunted even by a crazy old preacher, he gave Zaccariah a firm handshake.

"Mornin', sir," he said. "I hear you're looking for a *fast* car."

"That's correct."

"Our young salesman thought you were joking. Sorry about that. It's not often a mature gentleman appreciates an automobile with power and speed. I'm sure we have just what you require."

"It must be fast and rugged," Zaccariah told him.

He spent an hour at the showroom, looking at several models. After a drive around the downtown and a couple of test miles on the highway, Zaccariah made up his mind.

"I'll take that one," he said, pointing to a bright red, two-door model in the lot outside.

"Fine, Mr. Zaccariah." The manager smiled. "Now come on in to the office and we'll talk about financing."

"I want to take it today," Zaccariah said.

"Oh, that's quite imposssible. It will take a few days to process the paperwork. Then you have to choose a color and options. Then we get the car from the factory."

"You don't understand, sir," Zaccariah said patiently. "I want that automobile, as is. I want it today. I will pay you cash."

"Well, I guess we can strike some kind of deal."

The manager's mouth fell open as Zaccariah opened his suitcase, withdrew a valise, and began counting out hundred dollar bills. As he watched the bills pile up on his desk, he said nervously, "This isn't stolen money, is it? You buying a car to get away in?"

Zaccariah glared back at him with his fiercest expression. "I am a man of God," he said in a tone that was not to be meddled with.

"Then what are you running from?"

"I am not running," Zaccariah said. "I am pursuing."

* * *

Zaccariah checked into a hotel in downtown Pittsburgh, slept a few hours, and then drove to a grimy neighborhood he had not seen since the Sixties. It was dingier than Newtown—an enclave of Italian and Scotch-Irish, Slavic and Lebanese huddled around the gates of an abandoned steel mill. Every roof, wall and window was covered with a yellow-brown crust.

He had come here several times in his younger days, when one of his West Virginia ministries had veered into dangerous territory. If the man he sought still lived here, Zaccariah would find a ready answer to his problem.

He knocked at the door of a white clapboard house in the middle of a long row of attached frame buildings.

A woman answered, peering out across a door chain. Her white hair was tied up in a scarf, her pale-skinned face well-scrubbed but pock-marked. She clutched the loose folds of a bathrobe at her throat.

He took off his hat. "Mrs. Carlson?" he asked.

"I don't know you," she barked, pushing her face a little closer to the opening to get a look at him. Her face was worse than he had remembered, and half her teeth were gone.

"You probably don't remember me," he said. "I'm Ezekiel Zaccariah. I was here a few times. It was many years ago."

"I remember your name. Sort of recall your face. You was the preacher with the curly black hair—still got some of it, I see. But if you came to pay your respects it's too late. Bob died a year ago."

"So sorry to hear that, ma'am. I didn't know."

"What you come for, then?"

"I know it's been a long time, Mrs. Carlson. I haven't seen any of those fellows I used to know—not

270

for a long time. I suddenly had a need for some . . . material. I didn't know if Bob was here, or if he still—"

"Can't believe *you're* in trouble, preacher. What you need . . . material . . . for? To get back at someone?"

"For justice, ma'am. But I guess I've come to the wrong place. I'm truly sorry," he said. He put his hat on and turned.

"Wait," she said, releasing the chain. "Come in."

She led him to the basement and turned on the light. The room was just as he remembered it, a well-stocked arsenal built into a paneled basement rec room and extending into an underground bomb shelter built back in the days when everyone expected Russian bombers to come over. Handguns, shotguns, rifles, machine guns, flame throwers and ammunition leaned against walls, filled glass display cases, and piled up in sealed cartons.

"It's all here," the widow said, readjusting the belt on her robe. "Don't know what to do with it all now that Bob is gone. Now and then a friend o' his comes back an' asks. Never thought to see you, though. You quit, didn't you?"

Zaccariah nodded, picking up a shotgun. *This* at least he knew how to use, and he guessed anyone could use a revolver. "I didn't believe in violence," he said. "I never turned against the boys, but I couldn't do those things anymore."

"You'nse were a wild bunch then," Mrs. Carlson recalled. "So who you after now?"

"A bunch of people," he said. "Bad people."

"Come into your neighborhood, huh? We got some right on the block now."

He winced. "Not like that, ma'am. These people are kidnapers."

271

"Lord Jesus!" she swore. "And our courts just turn 'em loose again, don't they?"

"They sure do, ma'am. That's why I have to do this myself."

"Was it a woman they took? A white woman?"

"Children, ma'am. They've got some children. White *and* black. They've been doing it for a while."

"And you're goin' to stop 'em," she said admiringly. "You'll need shells for that." She opened the glass case and took out boxes of ammunition.

"I'll stop them, if the Lord is with me," Zaccariah said, testing the heft of a second shotgun.

"What kind o' people are they? Are they commies? Or Arabs? Bob always said those Muslims would come and get us."

"I don't know what they are or where they come from, Mrs. Carlson. I'll know soon, and make them pay."

He piled up an impressive array of weapons, and the widow expertly picked out ammunition. He took a .45 revolver, a .38, a sawed-off shotgun and a box of hand grenades.

The widow fitted him with a shoulder holster for the gun and found a sturdy knapsack in which he could carry the grenades. If he wore a long coat, she suggested, he could go down a city street carrying the shotgun underneath and no one would even know.

"You pay me what you want," she said finally, wrapping up everything in black plastic trash bags.

He took a stack of hundred dollars bills and put them on the table. He wouldn't have much left now, but it didn't matter. The devil's money would go to defeat the devil, and after that the Lord would provide.

"You got any help?" the widow asked as he went out the door.

"Not yet, ma'am. I sure hope to get some."

"Fellows used to stick together more," she said wistfully. "When Bob was courtin' me, we had scores o' friends. He used to take me to the lynchings. I ain't seen a good lynching in many a year."

"Neither have I, ma'am. Thank you for everything."

Zaccariah put the plastic bags in the trunk of the new BMW and drove off. His mind reeled with shame as he remembered the decade when he had known Bob Carlson. They had been Klan brothers, and Carlson ran then and, for many years thereafter, a secret gun shop for white supremacists.

He had put many years of Christian living and preaching between him and those times. Yet he had never repudiated those people or those beliefs. Now, he thought, maybe the Lord had a reason to leave him a lifeline to those simple-minded fanatics. Thanks to them, he now had his sword and spear.

Elvira was glad she had a film to show all her students on the following Monday. It was a new documentary on the history of flight, and screening it on the school's creaky old sixteen-millimeter projector let her sit in darkness and brood.

Even in the shadows, the empty desks accused her: Andrea's and Peter's in the first period, and then Keith's in the next.

She didn't know what to do, or whom to confide in. The problem with the computers was moot, as only Marsha Van Winkle's remained. Marsha said her computer was just fine, and now that she was over the mysterious death of her baby brother, she was the same straight-A student as before. If anything, she seemed stronger.

Even Keith's disappearance a week ago seemed not to have ruffled Marsha unduly. She kept her books open, took notes vigorously, and spent all her study periods in the library. Her homework was all impeccable, and she had made up for the few days lost during the family troubles.

The principal also made the last week an extra hell for Elvira. She tried to corner him about the computers and the seemingly nonexistent foundation. He brushed her off, saying that either he had remembered the name wrong, or that it was a marketing gimmick. As for Peter and Andrea, they were bad kids, headed for trouble anyway. It was too bad about Keith, but boys ran away a lot at his age, especially when they'd been through bad traumas. And as everyone could see, Marsha Van Winkle was fine.

She persisted, demanding that he tell the police about the computers and the children's fears about them.

That was when Parisi came down hard. He told her he'd fire her if she brought it up.

She had tenure, she reminded him. Then she backed off. She did not want to spend the rest of her career in a war against Parisi. She ate her words, apologized for being paranoid, and agreed not to embarrass him or the school by mentioning the computers.

Parisi ran scared all week. He didn't take phone calls, snapped at the police as they made their inquiries, and shouted at his secretary.

In the ensuing days, the police were all over Elvira, interrupting her classes to ask why she had been at Andrea's house, why she had left the scene, and about any possible connection among Andrea, Peter and Keith. She told them about everything except the

274

computers: how they were friends and had a little club, how they became estranged, and then how Peter's death had catapulted the others into alienation. They asked her dogged questions about drugs and Satanism. Chief Dougan dropped cigarette ashes all over her classroom and muttered about chains of teen suicides all over southwestern Pennsylvania. Parisi stood by, sweating, making sure she didn't mention the computers.

Four items of news had come to her this morning in the teachers' lounge.

First, Keith Brandon had really vanished from the face of the earth. No one had seen him go. The parents slept halfway through the next morning and felt as though they had been drugged. A neighbor thought she heard cars at the Brandons at three A.M., but hadn't bothered to look.

Second, the missing Willie Hastings was found wandering in the bus station in Pittsburgh and was returned to his parents. He would soon be back in school.

Third, the distraught Mrs. Gaunt had a second nervous breakdown and was taken to a mental hospital. Everyone now assumed she *had* taken the Van Winkle baby.

Fourth was the news from the coroner's office on Emelda Martinez. The woman had died, not from all the prescription drugs scattered around the bedroom and bathroom, but from plain old aspirin. Someone had tampered with her sleeping capsules, filling them with ground-up aspirin.

Chief Dougan now speculated that Andrea had been stealing her mother's prescription drugs for herself and friends, substituting aspirin. The girl apparently didn't realize that an aspirin overdose is fatal, and panicked when she couldn't rouse her mother. She had scattered the other pills around the bedroom to confuse police and then fled.

Elvira didn't believe it. The other teachers were willing to believe anything, if the tale had the word "drugs" in it.

Parisi listened in, and his summation had been, "You see, Elvira? A kid like that will do anything to get high—even poison her own mother."

Now she watched the faces of the fifth graders in the flickering light of the projector. No matter how many stories she had read, she could never—until now—picture these cherubic faces in any setting other than school. This was her higher reality. The students would graduate from this to another school, and then another, to do great things in life.

Her illusion was threatened now. Her classroom was at best an interlude between the wholly different realities of home, family, drugs, violence and insanity. She looked at them and tried to penetrate the expressions in their eyes. A boy looked bored and listless—would he run away? Another shifted uneasily in his seat—was he *on* something, or just on the verge of asking to go to the bathroom? A girl watched the footage on the Challenger disaster with a twinkle in her eye—would she become an arsonist before she was thirteen? And there sat Marsha, her hair neatly braided, clothes neat, her emotions tucked and folded into place. Wasn't there a thing she could do to keep from losing her as she had lost Peter and Andrea and Keith?

"Miss Hawkins!" a student called out.

She jolted to attention. The movie had ended and the reel was spinning, the loose end of film flapping madly.

The film had begun with Leonardo da Vinci's drawings of flying machines and ended with ani-

276

mated projections of colonies in space. Though she could hardly muster the spirit, she turned on the lights and tried to raise the students' enthusiasm about space flight. One of the things a science teacher could do was to show there *was* a future.

"Some of you may even go a trip into space," she assured them. "There might be a space station in permanent orbit, and from there you could go to the moon and Mars."

"Do you believe in UFO's, Miss Hawkins?" a boy asked. Other pupils giggled and mocked him.

"I've never seen one, Jamie. A lot of people have seen things they can't explain. I'm not sure I'm ready to believe in space ships, though. Not until one lands in Washington."

The children began to chatter.

"Would any of you like to go into space someday?" she asked. "Let me see hands."

Four hands went up. The first was Marsha's.

"Why do you want to go, Brian?" she asked.

"To see what's out there. To look for aliens," Brian said earnestly.

"William?"

"To get there before the Russians."

"Jamie? Why do you want to go?"

"To be the first."

"Marsha—you're the only girl to volunteer. Why would you go?"

The girl thought for a moment, then said in her funny, flat, reciting voice: "Because it's better out there."

"Why is it better, Marsha?"

"Because there are no people. I'd like to go to Mars and see the place where the Viking landed."

"That's a desert, Marsha. Wouldn't the four of you get very lonely there?"

277

"No, Miss Hawkins." Marsha lit up with imagination. "'Cause we'd stay there and be okay while everyone down here dies in a nuke war."

"Marsha, that's so grim."

It was so grim, in fact, that the other students didn't even laugh. The bell rang fortuitously, and they all fled.

Elvira watched Marsha close her book and walk calmly to the hall, ignoring and ignored by all the other girls.

Preparing for a study hall period, she rewound the film's two reels and began raising the blinds as the boys and girls began to file in. The boys had just come from the gymnasium, smelling of damp towels, soap and wet hair. They would be rowdy and incorrigible as ever.

The science room windows looked out over the playground, and as she raised the last blind, she saw the fifth graders pour onto it. Boys huddled around a football on one end. A few others tossed frisbees. The girls, at that age when physical exercise is anathema, huddled at the other end where several ailanthus trees had burst up through the cement. They formed a cluster between the tree and chain-link fence, swapping magazines, listening to music on headphones and talking.

She looked for Marsha but didn't see her. Craning her neck forward over the sill, she tried to see if the girl was standing near the building. No one was there. It was her class's recess and she *should* be out there.

Picking up her purse from the desk drawer, she decided to check on her, maybe even talk to her. She didn't like the dark and desperate sound of her space flight fantasy.

She hurried along the hall, stopping in the girls'

rest room. She called Marsha's name. Two girls burst into laughter but no one answered. There was a funny smell, and she suspected they were smoking something in there; but there was no time to investigate.

On a sudden intuition, Elvira went to the front door instead of the playground door. The children had been told to play only in the playground, but the doors had to be kept unlocked as fire exits anyway.

Two boys sprang away as she pushed on the door bar and went out into the late morning sunlight. They dropped cigarettes and looked at her sheepishly.

"Shame—" she started to say.

And then she saw Marsha.

The girl was at the far end of the paved school yard, standing at the end of the teachers' parking area. She was at the curb, her back to the school.

"Marsha!" Elvira shouted.

The girl turned and looked, then gazed both ways as though she were going to dash across Maple Street.

Elvira looked back and forth, too. A black van had just turned the corner and would pass her.

Marsha stepped off the curb.

Elvira ran toward her.

The van accelerated, then braked with a screech a few feet beyond the girl.

"Stop! Marsha!" Elvira screamed. She was halfway there.

The side door of the van slid open.

She got to the parking area.

A man in coveralls reached down.

Elvira ran faster, her heels clattering on the cement as she tried to go faster without losing her balance.

Marsha held up her arms and let the man pull her in.

279

The instant Elvira got to the curb, too out of breath to scream again, the van tore away and turned the corner back toward Main Street.

She whirled around; the two boys were gone. No one else had seen.

Another car came out of nowhere, scraping its tires along the curb and stopping with a jolt.

She looked, ready to run back to the school to call the police.

The terrible old man in the red BMW leaned over to his passenger window and called to her in a bass voice: "That girl—I saw them take her! Get in."

"What?" Elvira asked in shock.

"I saw those devils kidnap that little girl. For God's sake get in and we'll follow them."

"The police—" she started.

"No time!" the man shouted imperiously. He pushed the door open.

There was no time to think. She got in.

The BMW leaped to high speed, peeling off and leaving a black stripe on Maple Street.

Elvira held on as the driver lurched around the corner onto Main. He drove like a maniac. By the time the van got up the hill, they were just a block behind. When it turned onto a side road, they followed.

The chase was on.

Chapter Fifteen

Eric Varney came home at two o'clock in the morning with his most difficult prize ever. His face covered with soot, clothes spotted with charcoal and ash, he walked into his repair room and gently laid a heavy duffel back onto the work table.

Washing his face and hands in the bathroom, he looked at his bearded face in the mirror with self-congratulatory glee. It had been quite an evening, albeit a ghoulish one.

After days of biking near the padlocked Martinez house, he had decided to go in after Andrea's computer—or what was left of it if the neighborhood kids hadn't gotten in first. He went in and came out the kitchen window with a disk drive and printer, wrapped in towels. He squeezed one into each oversize basket of his bike and wobbled back home unseen.

It was burglary, of course, but he was only robbing the dead and vanished. Neither Andrea nor her mother could possibly mind. He'd hold onto the equipment for a while. If Andrea came back, he'd tell her he had the stuff in "safe keeping" for her. If she never resurfaced, he could get a good hundred dollars for the much-in-demand Commander components.

Later in the evening, he had crept down Railroad

Street on foot. Peter's second floor bedroom—or what was left of it—lay inside a window now almost level with the street. It was possible—just possible—that stuff was intact in there despite all the collapse and water damage. The window panes were shattered, the inside black and forbidding.

Wrapping his hand in his jacket, he poked out the sharp edges of glass in one window, then crawled through. He made his way through fallen beams and a section of collapsed roof till he found the charred ruins of a bed and box springs. Pieces of water-logged blanket still clung to it, a good sign that the room had been doused with water before *everything* could be consumed.

Peter's table was in a corner, and as he had hoped, water had hit there early on in the fire, probably coming through a hole in the roof. Books lay on the floor, swollen and warped from the water.

The table was metal, and it had fallen against the wall when the house collapsed. He pulled it outward by its legs, reached behind it, and touched the computer keyboard.

It was wet, but nothing had burned or melted. He held it in the dim light that street lamps cast through the broken window.

The monitor's glass screen was shattered, but the disk drive was salvageable, its chassis only slightly cracked. He rubbed his hands in delight when he found the printer, too, then packed everything into his duffel bag.

Leaving the ruin with the goods was tougher than entering. If someone saw him with the bag, they might call the police—even if they saw him blocks away; he *looked* like a burglar.

The gods that protect scavengers came through, however. At the corner, the bell signaling a freight

282

train began to sound, and the automatic barriers lowered to block cars and pedestrians from crossing the tracks.

As soon as the long freight train began rattling by, his odds were wonderful. He leaped out of the window and lifted the bag out, the sound of it drowned in the horrible, gut-wrenching vibration of empty boxcars. No one across the street could see him, except maybe in the blurred gaps between cars. He ran along, parallel to the train, left Railroad Street and raced to his own dimly-lit street along the riverbank.

Far away, he saw the police car. It had been parked at the tracks, waiting for the bars to lift so it could move on and cross the tracks and the bridge.

He looked at his night's work, all spread out now on the table. He put Andrea's equipment aside, as it was bound to be in working order, and turned to Peter's computer and disk drive. He would have to disassemble them to prevent rust and clean out all the ashes and dust and water that might have clogged them.

It would be long night, so he brewed some strong tea and put Mahler's Third Symphony—the longest ever written—on the compact disc player.

Under a bright desk light, he soon had the disk drive apart, using nothing more than a Philips screwdriver. The machines were built so that a high school dropout could get into them. Four or five bolts came loose, and the works were laid bare—the motor and read/write head at the front, a board with computer chips in the back. He cleaned off the board, inspected the connectors and printed circuits, and decided the disk drive would probably work fine.

The computer would be another story. The keyboard had been drenched, so water was lodged between the keys and the panel of membrane switches below them. He would have to lift the keyboard away from the panel beneath, clean it, and then get down onto the main computer board to clean it. It was simple work for someone who knew how to open the machine.

The chassis of this particular Commander 256 model, however, confused him. The metal bolts holding the keyboard and chassis together had been replaced by plastic rivets that were probably sonically welded. They could not be unscrewed, although they could be snapped and broken by prying the chassis apart. The two halves, which fit together like a clamshell, would ultimately surrender to any computer nerd with the patience to pry with a screwdriver and the willingness to break some plastic. He could always get the chassis from another dead computer if he had to, and now he was intrigued enough to do major surgery on this one.

What baffled him was the strip of stainless steel that covered the overlap of top and bottom chassis. It was tough as industrial strapping, and seamless. The benefactors who had given kids these computers obviously didn't want anyone looking inside.

Eric whistled when he realized what he had—the next generation of equipment to be released by Commander. Certain people would pay good money to have a peek at what was inside, and computer magazines might even pay for a jump on it if all else failed.

Even more dizzying, however, was sheer curiosity. Eric loved these little machines. They were amazing, providing for a couple of hundred dollars the kind of memory, speed and power that corporations once paid tens of thousands of dollars to own. They helped the little guy outsmart the big one, the

284

taxpayer outfox the tax collector, and the solitary individual thumb his nose at Big Brother.

A lot of people were afraid of computers, but Eric knew better. The computer was only a tool—like a car, a gun or a hammer. It did only what you programmed it to do, for good or ill. If that science teacher ever came back again with her funny ideas about computers, he'd show her how it was just an inert assembly of wires and silicon chips.

Finally, after twenty minutes of prying, he was able to remove the metal band from the computer. A little while later, he got the upper and lower chassis apart. French horns erupted from the stereo as he lifted the top of the keyboard.

Two wires had to be desoldered before he could remove the assembly with all the typewriter keys. As he expected, there were beads of water and dissolved ash all over the membrane panel below. He wiped it off with a paper towel, cleaned it with window cleaner, and then removed the Philips screws that held the board in.

Beneath it was the main computer board—the Holy of Holies—a maze of green and silver printed circuits, with rows of silicon chips clipped and soldered into place. It looked like a miniature city, with metallic roads emanating from the central processing chip and the memory chips, connecting them to the plugs at the back edge, where printer and disk drive and monitor connected. It all worked just like a human being's nervous system.

He scrutinized it to see what was different from the standard Commander 256. It was all the same, except for a black plastic cube attached to one edge of the board. On other Commanders, that area was just empty space. Metal clips held it to the edge of the board, and a detachable cable connected to a soldered pin that spliced it to the main processing chip. Whatever it was, it coprocessed right along with the main chip, maybe even superseded it. The main computer, then, might just be a terminal to a completely new generation of chip, housed in the little black box.

He pulled out the plug that connected the box to the main board. The plug had optical fibers instead of wires—a sure sign that high-level computing was going on inside the machine. Nothing he had ever seen needed that many connectors. If only Peter and Andrea had realized what they had their hands on! He sure as hell wouldn't run away if one of these walked in his door.

With a regular screwdriver, he pried the top off the three-inch-wide box.

It wasn't anything like what he expected.

The first thing inside was a clear plastic case—like a jewelry display box, full of a thick, transparent liquid. He lifted it out, pulling along with it a thin tube through which the liquid slowly seeped down into the bottom of the box. He was puzzled; computers have no moving parts, so something like a lubricating fluid was absurd.

Next came another plastic case, with a red fluid trickling out of two tubes, and two wires leading into it. Two strips of metal formed a membrane that seemed to pulsate, agitating the liquid in the box constantly. It was still moving.

He pushed both containers of liquid aside, thinking they might be some kind of chemical battery. He did it gently so that the tubes wouldn't break. He had to see what was at the bottom, realizing he might be the first to see the next generation in chips.

When he saw it, he threw his hands over his face,

stood up, and toppled the stool behind him.

"Jesus Christ!" he swore. "It can't be! It just can't be!"

He readjusted the lamp, bent over the main board and the box, and looked again.

He had not seen wrong. The tubes led down to a soft plastic bubble. Wires by the hundred penetrated the equator of the half globe, turning to thousands of additional wires that glistened in the light. They were thinner than spider webs, knotting and looping into a pool of the red liquid. They connected the whole computer to the thing that floated inside.

"Jesus," he said again, calmer. "How the hell could they do this? No one knows how to do this!"

It was impossible, obscene and horrifying. He had lifted the lid of a child's computer and found, floating in blood and a bath of nourishing glucose, a golf-ball-sized piece of brain tissue.

Sister Helena didn't resist when the attendants came and took her to Room 12. She had gripped the hand of Sister Patienzia and taken strength from it until they strapped her to the wheeled cart and pulled her away.

Nothing had worked out as her protector had hoped. Patienzia had tried to get a key to the treatment room, hoping to burst in with Mother Superior or some other sisters and catch Dr. Halpern abusing her. There was only one key, however, and it never left the doctor's pocket.

Finally, Patienzia found some duplicate keys in Mother Superior's desk. They could get into Dr. Halpern's office, or his apartment on the third floor, but not into Room 12.

Helena knew what she had to do. Patienzia told her

what to do and say, and even though it made her blush, she had repeated it like an actress until she got it right. Now, though, she didn't think she could go through with it.

Ceilings whirled by, doors opened, and then she was in the bare room. There were the instruments, and the table with the straps, and the wires and electrodes. She was completely passive as the attendants moved her to the table and fastened the straps. She heard Dr. Halpern whistling as he washed his hands in the next room.

"Hello, Dr. Halpern," she said, making herself smile as his lean face and hungry eyes approached her.

"You're cheerful today, Helena. Ready for your treatment, my dear?"

"Yes, doctor."

He was silent for a moment, puzzled by her complacency.

"Do you remember the last time?" he asked cautiously.

"Yes, doctor."

"What happened?"

"I don't remember the treatment, of course. But before the . . . treatment . . . you hurt me. Two or three times."

"I'm going to hurt you some more, Helena. To heal you. To punish and heal."

"That's all right, doctor." She forced the words to come out. "I don't mind."

"You don't mind?" His eyes searched hers. He bent over her until his nose and jaws looked enormous, like some predator about to feed.

"I don't mind, doctor. I think—" She shook from revulsion as she said it: *I think I love you.*

He held the electrodes in front of her face. "Even

though I hurt you?" he asked. He didn't believe her.

"Even though you hurt me," she repeated. She knew her voice didn't sound convincing.

His hands pulled away the sheet, and then her flimsy cotton shift. There was no gradual exploration this time—the motion was savage. He touched her everywhere, his hands hot and indelicate. She never flinched. That was harder acting than saying the words.

"I want to go to bed with you," she said, shaking. *Was that the next line, or had she left one out?*

His hands came to her throat. He reached for the bite protector, then changed his mind.

"Do you want to go to bed with me, Helena— *really?*" he asked.

"Yes, doctor. You can make love to me. I want to be in your bed."

He went for the electrodes, turning his back to her. *Say it all. Say every line,* Patienzia's voice urged in her mind.

"I want you . . . on top of me. And inside me," she said.

"We have to treat you, Helena. I think you're quite disturbed today."

He rubbed the alcohol swab on her forehead.

It was all or nothing. She said all the rest of the lines, as intensely as she could.

"You can have me all night in your room. I'll do anything you want."

"You're just saying that to avoid the pain, Helena. You're not fooling me."

Helena still had the clincher. She swallowed back the sour gorge that had risen in her throat. She said, "You can bring the machine, doctor. I love you. I want you to hurt me."

Dr. Halpern put down the electrodes. He looked at

her in awe. Tears welled in his eyes. He touched her cheek.

"I knew you were the one," he said.

"Who the hell are you?" Elvira asked, finally getting a few seconds free of swerving and acceleration to fasten the seat belt.

"Zaccariah," he said abruptly, keeping his eye on the road and trying to keep a discreet distance behind the van. "You are one of the teachers?" he asked.

"Yes. I'm Elvira Hawkins. I teach science. So you saw them take her?"

"Saw the whole thing, ma'am. The only chance we have to save her is to find out where the children are being taken."

"Thank God you came along," Elvira said.

"I didn't come along, ma'am. I was waiting. I've watched her house and your school for days."

A chill ran up her spine. He wasn't an FBI man. She jerked her head around and looked at him; he couldn't be, not at his age.

He didn't take his eyes off the road. "I know what you're wondering, ma'am. Who the hell *am* I? I'm not one of *them*, if that's what worries you."

"You're not the police," she said with certainty. "Not the way you drive."

"Right again. I'll tell you who I am. I am Ezekiel Zaccariah, formerly the Reverend Ezekiel Zaccariah. If I'm right, that little girl they took is Marsha Van Winkle."

"Yes," she said.

"And before that, they took Keith Brandon. I saw the van, and I saw him get in. Before that, it was the young lady with the Spanish name—"

"Andrea Martinez," Elvira said.

290

"And before that, it was the boy, Peter . . . Peter—"

"Lansing," she said. "Do you mean to say Peter is *alive?*"

"I entertain the hope, ma'am. I entertain the hope." He spun the wheel to turn onto another side road. "The fires and accidents are a smoke screen to cover up the kidnaping. If they can't fake a death, they cause enough trouble to make it look like the child ran away. Devious, cunning devils!"

Elvira was still terrified. "How do you know all this if you're not part of it?"

Zaccariah grimaced. "I came to your school. I brought the computers. I gave the names and addresses of the children to those evil men. God forgive me!"

"You work for them?" She watched the roadside, gauged the speed, trying to guess if she could jump out without killing herself.

"*Worked* for them," he explained. "I didn't know. I never went back and looked. I thought it was a charity."

"I don't believe you," she said.

"I need your help, ma'am," he pleaded. "I need all the help I can get."

"You picked me up because I saw—because I was the only witness—" her voice rose in hysteria.

"Ma'am, calm down. Open that glove compartment."

"Wh-why?"

"Open it if you wish. You will find a .38 revolver. It is loaded. If my conduct is anything other than that of a righteous man, you may shoot me with it."

Elvira reached for the glove compartment, then stopped. She was shaking too hard to do it. Then she turned her face against the glass of the window and started to cry.

"Don't get unstrung, Miss Hawkins," he said. "I need you. Those children need you."

Control was returning. She took a tissue from her purse and dabbed her eyes. "I'm sorry," she said. She looked ahead at the van, which was about a quarter of a mile ahead. "Don't they know we're following?"

"They're overconfident," Zaccariah replied. "They've done this so much they think they can do it as they please. We'll pull back a little more if he looks like he's getting edgy. Now, will you trust me, miss?"

She nodded, sniffling. "Yes," she said. "Is there really a gun in there?"

"Look and see. What kind of man would I be if the first thing I told you was a lie?"

She looked. The gun was there.

"I was nearly hysterical," she recalled. "I could have killed you with that."

"You could have," he agreed.

"I'll trust you," she decided.

Warily following the van, they came to a crest from which they could see the van's descent into a lower region of smaller, rolling hills.

"There," Zaccariah said, pointing. "It's turning off there."

She saw it, too, leading a trail of dust up the driveway to an old farmhouse.

"Get the maps from the back seat," he said. "We have to mark where we are."

He had Geological Survey maps of all the adjacent counties. Zaccariah's memory of their chase was astonishing, and thanks to the map's topographical detail, they finally pinpointed their location. A line of high-tension power lines and a nearby creek clinched the location. The house was on Briar Road, next to a convent. The nearest town was Pleasanton.

"Praise the Lord and BMW," Zaccariah sighed,

folding his hands for a quiet moment of thankfulness. "And thank you for sending this lovely lady to help."

"We need more help," Elvira suggested.

"It's just us," Zaccariah said.

"No. We have at least one more friend."

"Someone crazy enough to help us?"

She nodded. She just hoped Eric would listen, and join them.

Gardening and minor carpentry were not enough to satisfy a young man with large desires but limited talent. For days and days, Jimmy went about the motions of tending the grounds of St. Agnes's convent. Mostly, he dawdled in the barn, pretending to fix a mower that didn't need fixing and cutting lumber to make some patches in the walls of the barn and the other outbuildings.

All the time, however, he was thinking about the coal mines under the Emslie place. He didn't tell his pa about what he and the sister had heard, and he certainly didn't say a peep to Dr. Halpern or the penguins. He wanted to keep it all to himself. If it was going to be worth a lot of money, he didn't want to share the secret.

Twice he had gone back to the mine opening on the hill. He listened, and both times the air went rushing by into the darkness beyond. Both times he heard people walking, the metal door opening, and all the machines beyond.

Slowly, with the patience that comes with a one-track mind, he began expanding the opening. He was six-foot-three and weighed two hundred and ten pounds, so he knew it would take some doing—and he'd have to dig quietly. He used hand tools from the

293

barn: a spade for the loose stuff, a crowbar to pry small rocks loose, and a miner's pick he could use only when he thought none of the men were in the tunnel beyond.

After two sessions of digging, he had the hole big enough to wiggle through. He wanted it bigger, though, not relishing the thought of getting stuck in the middle of the passage. Also, he needed room to carry or drag back the gold or diamonds he would find there.

He lay awake at night in his father's house, listening to the whippoorwills in the woods, trying to figure out what they were doing in the old mines. Bank robbers didn't need machines, and spies only needed radios, or an airplane to get back to Russia.

Finally, he decided they had to be running a mine. It wasn't a coal mine, because there was no need to keep that a secret. Besides, there were no coal trucks coming and going from the Emslie place. Whatever they mined there came out in small boxes.

At first he thought it might be diamonds. Pa told him there were no diamonds in the ground in Pennsylvania, but Jimmy remembered how Superman took a lump of coal once on TV and squashed it into a diamond. Maybe the underground mine did the same thing, and that's what the machines did.

If it wasn't diamonds, he decided, then it had to be gold. Or maybe uranium that came down into the mine when that meteor fell.

Whatever it was, he wanted to get some. If he could sneak in now and then, they wouldn't miss a couple of diamonds or a sack of gold.

Before he went to sleep every night, he thought of what he would do with the money. He'd go to Florida and see the beaches. He'd wear funny orange and green clothes and meet girls in discos. He sure as hell wouldn't dig flower beds or fix roofing tiles for the likes of Dr. Halpern.

The second week, Jimmy decided to start watching the Emslie place in earnest. He sat on the convent grounds at the edge of Sister Patience's little garden, eating M&Ms, drinking Coke and spying on the house. He used the telescope Pa had bought him when he was ten. It worked so well he could even see them right through the windows when they walked around in the house at night.

He figured out a few things:

A black van came and went a lot, and three men from the house took turns driving it. It brought a lot of stuff in boxes—food and supplies—and then took other boxes away.

Late at night, the van sometimes brought children, who were hurried off into the house. He never saw them through the windows, and they never left in the van again.

It didn't take a genius and it didn't take more than ten fingers to calculate that more people were coming then going. There had to be more men in the mines below. And maybe all those kids were being forced to work there. His pa told him how little boys had to work in the mines back in his grandfather's day.

He sat on the hill during the fourth night, watching the van driver unload more boxes. Nobody ever drove around back to the barn, half hidden behind the house, and nobody ever walked around the property. So the only way into the mines had to be *through the house*. That told him the gold or diamonds were packed up in there, ready to send out. All he had to do was distract them with something and sneak in one door while they were going out the other.

The night he picked was cloudy. He drove the pickup without lights on across the convent property, parking next to the mine opening. He'd keep the truck there for a quick getaway if he came out through the mine.

The moon was up, but was only a dim white sliver cutting through dirty cotton and being swallowed again. The fields below were dark, noisy with wind among the brittle corn and high grains. At the farm house, the lights were on, the three men sitting inside the parlor when he started out. As long as those lights were on, they'd never see him crossing the fields.

He saw a rabbit and a 'possum, and an owl that swooped low over his head, but nothing else interrupted his journey to the farm yard. Paper bags, scraps of newspaper and magazines joined with leaves to clot the trellis around the base of the porch. The white paint was peeling, the porch striped with missing planks.

Jimmy passed the parlor window, stopping to look in. The three men sat at a table, looking at a map or some kind of blueprint. A hefty man with gray hair wrote in a notebook while the other two talked and pointed at the paper between them. The other men had their backs to him, but he saw their hands and the backs of their necks.

Their skin was blue.

Jimmy backed away in terror and astonishment. Nobody had blue skin. People came in a lot of colors, but not that one—blue like turquoise or the pieces of agate you sometimes found in the bottom of a stream.

His instinct was to run. A secret mine was one thing, but a secret mine run by blue-skinned men was another. Now he knew why they wore those funny gloves and hats—so nobody would see they looked like zombies or men from space. If he ran, they'd never know he was there. And then he could go home and call the police or the FBI.

He backed away from the house and turned into the wheat field again. But when the house stayed just as quiet as before and parlor lights stayed on, he stopped and reconsidered.

They were blue, but they were just men, like him. And they were sitting there with all that stuff. He could carry away enough in one trip to set himself up for life. The almanac had said that just one pound of gold sold for more than six thousand dollars. That was worth a little running after.

He went ahead with his plan. Keeping a good distance between the house and himself, he approached the old Emslie outbuildings: a half-collapsed tool shed, an empty chicken coop, a crude garage made of corrugated sheet metal and a half-ruined old barn.

Opening the shed door, he went inside and quickly turned on his flashlight. Rusty rakes and hoes leaned against the wall, and saws and other carpentry tools hung neatly on hooks above a work bench. There were saw horses, scraps of lumber, a chain saw, and—as he had hoped—lots of straw on the floor.

He unscrewed the pint can of kerosene he had carried in his overall pocket and poured it all over the work bench. He splashed some on the back wall, too, where the dry old boards would be sure to catch.

A pint of kerosene didn't go very far. He looked around for some gasoline. Two red safety cans turned out to be empty. Then he found a third can next to the chain saw, half full. Twisting off the cap, he splattered the contents all over the other walls. One match—one spark, even—and the whole thing would go up.

He backed out of the shed, then fumbled in his

pocket for the box of kitchen matches he had brought. He knelt so he could get the match lit, shelter it against the wind and throw it in.

The instant he touched the match to the friction strip on the box, a brilliant light came on to his right. He dropped the match, raising his hand to shield his eyes and see what it was.

Against the white glare of a spotlight, men were coming out of the barn.

Jimmy turned and fled toward the field. He ran as hard as his legs would propel him.

A few yards into the sea of wheat, one of them leaped to tackle him and missed. Jimmy heard the man groan and pick himself up from the ground. The wind in his ears drowned out their voices.

He ran, gasping deep breaths through his mouth, getting his stride as he hit the downhill part of the field. If he could get over the distant fence and into the pickup, they'd never catch him.

On the edge of his vision, he saw the tall figure of a pursuer on the left. He thought it was one of the blue-skinned men, for even at a distance he thought he saw the funny hats and coveralls. He did the only thing he could, propelled by that added fear: He ran harder.

The two men were good runners, too. They not only kept even with him, but started to close in on both sides.

His throat ached from the explosive breathing. He stopped for an instant to look behind him, the way a cat will run, look back, and then run again. He expected to see the man with gray hair.

Instead, *four* more men came, running with long strides through the grain—the gray-haired man and three others. Two of them had pulled guns out of holsters and ran with them raised in the air over their heads.

Jimmy had no intention of being shot.

He stopped, gasping. He raised his hands.

All six got to him at the same time. The bare-headed men with guns aimed at his head while the other two searched his pockets.

"D-d-don't shoot me!" Jimmy pleaded.

"What do you think?" the gray-haired man asked the other, never lowering the gun barrel from Jimmy's temple.

The second man, who looked almost like the first one's brother, came closer to Jimmy's sweat-drenched face. "Local kid," the man answered. "I've seen him around. He mows the lawns over at the convent. What were you doing in the tool shed, boy?"

"N-nothin'," Jimmy stuttered.

"You like to start fires—is that it?"

Jimmy figured he'd better lie. He nodded.

"Is that *it?*" the man with the other gun snapped, poking the barrel in his ear.

"Yes, sir," Jimmy said.

"What should we do with him?" asked one of the men in the strange hats.

"Pretty big kid," one said.

"Not bad looking, either," said another.

Jimmy didn't know why, but they all laughed.

"Please don't take me to the police," Jimmy pleaded.

"We're not going to do that, son," the first gunman assured him. He ran the gun barrel along Jimmy's cheekbones and over the top of his head, like he was drawing a map.

The first man put his gun away and stepped back.

"Anybody know you're here, young fellow?" he asked.

"No, sir."

"I thought not. An arsonist doesn't usually tell his mother where he goes." He turned to the hulking men in the hats. "Have some fun," he said, "but don't damage his head." He turned and walked toward the house.

The five remaining captors closed in on Jimmy. One kept the gun on him while the ones with covered faces came in close. He couldn't see their expressions through the fine gauze. He shivered when the first one touched him, realizing they were the blue-skinned men. They smelled like chemicals.

A gloved hand touched his shoulder and stayed there.

"What—what are you gonna do to me?" Jimmy asked.

The man with the gun laughed cruelly. "My friends here are going to practice," he said. "And if you try to run away, I'll put a big hole in your chest."

The first punch in the stomach knocked the breath out of him.

The second blow—a flying kick that would have put a black belt to shame—knocked him to the ground.

Jimmy stood, staggering. Even with the gun on him, his instinct for survival made him duck the next punch and raise his own fists in self-defense.

Then one of them, coming from behind, flipped him through the air.

The men played with him for twenty minutes, like cats with a stunned mouse, until Jimmy could no longer even pull himself to his knees.

"My ribs," he pleaded finally. "You broke my ribs."

When they picked him up to carry him, Jimmy passed out. He never got to see the straw-covered floor of the barn open, and how four men carried him down a ramp into the coal mine shaft below.

*   *   *

Eric Varney and Elvira Hawkins laid the mother board of the Commander computer on the pathologist's table at Graffton Hospital. Ezekiel Zaccariah looked on, his hat crumpled in his hand. The computer board lay under a high intensity lamp, between a Mr. Coffee machine and a specimen dish with someone's liver in it.

"You guys called me up at one o'clock in the morning for *this?*" the young man said incredulously. "Eric," he said, "you've gone over the brink."

Eric looked at his friend's bemused face with patience. Certainly it was presuming on an old Dungeons and Dragons crony to walk into his nightshift job with a spinster teacher and a cadaverous old preacher, plunking a dead computer down on a table. George Hakim was a friend he could trust—a few years older than him, but looking and acting *some* years older with his shaggy hair, full beard, and smeared lab coat.

George glared over his glasses for the explanation, the punch line.

"George, just watch," Eric pleaded.

"I don't do tests on silicon chips," he replied impatiently. "I'm not even supposed to have people in here."

"Please," Elvira interceded. "Eric said you were his friend, and you're the only one who can help us."

George backed off, raising his hands. "Okay," he said. "So show me." Then he muttered under his breath: "At this time of the morning it had better be good."

Eric lifted the top of the plastic cube and carefully removed the two plastic cases of clear and red liquids.

"So you've got a chemistry set inside your computer," George chided. "You want me to analyze

301

the red and white stuff, is that it?"

"No," Eric said. "I want you to look inside." He waved his friend toward the computer, swinging the flexible arm of the lamp over the black box.

George peered in. Then he backed away, took off his glasses, and looked in again, closer still.

"By the beard of the Prophet!" he exclaimed. "Who the hell made this?"

"Unknown, George. I've been on the computer network with Commander users all night. A big shot from Commander even came on-line and assured us there are *no* new models of the 256 under testing. And Commander has no department or division working on artificial intelligence."

"Could this be a government thing? Did you steal this computer?"

"It belonged to a kid. A kid who—ran away. We want you to look at it. Tell us if it's synthetic—or what it's made of—where it comes from."

George made a dubious face. "I'll have to destroy the case and all those connectors to get at it, Eric."

Eric looked at Elvira. "What do you think?"

"Do it," she said.

George put his fingers into the box and felt around the edges of the plastic bubble. "We'll have to cut all those wires," he said. "If it's a brain—if this isn't some sick joke and this is actually some kind of cloned or genetically engineered brain tissue—then when I cut these wires, I put it into a coma. Or maybe kill it."

"Son, you mean that thing is *alive?*" Zaccariah asked. "Thinking, scheming, sinning *alive?*"

"I don't know about sinning, Padre," George replied. "But yes, it looks like it's alive—or was some time ago."

"It's not a person, George," Eric said. "Let's do it."

George took a pair of miniature scissors and began snipping the wires. In a few moments they had the plastic globe on the table, with the two liquid reservoirs still connected to it.

"This is really incredible," George said, studying the red plastic box. "Do you see what they're doing here?"

"I'm not sure," Eric said. "Is that stuff blood?"

"It's *like* blood, probably a synthetic. That little membrane in there has a battery if I'm right." He felt along the bottom of the box. "Ah! Look!" On the end of his finger was a regular watch battery.

"What does that do?" Elvira asked.

"I'm guessing, but there's a simple logic to it. The fluid is pulled past the membrane, where the pulsating action introduces some oxygen from the air."

"That oxygenates the blood, just as the lungs do. Or like a fish gill," Elvira contributed.

"Thank you," George nodded. "The membrane also *pumps* the liquid down into the sphere below. There are probably other membranes below helping to pump the liquid back."

"Are those batteries enough to do all that?" Elvira asked.

"They could be back-ups," Eric speculated. "The membranes could draw power from the main computer board whenever the computer is plugged into an electrical outlet. The batteries would jump in during the off periods."

"Do you want me to open it?" George asked.

"Yes," Eric said.

George pried the top hemisphere from the plastic brain case. A tangle of thin wires and tubes, finer than spider web, pulled away from the brain tissue and broke.

303

"Whoever made this—" the pathologist said in awe. "I'd just like to meet whoever made this."

"Can you take a sample of it and tell us what it is?" Elvira asked. "Under a microscope?"

"No, I can't. The brain—and that's sure as hell what it looks like—isn't like that liver over there. It's more like Jell-O than anything. When you take a sample you can't fix it on a slide. It has to sit in formaldehyde for four weeks. *Then* you can get it under a microscope."

"Is it animal brain?" Elvira asked.

"I can't tell. To look at it, brains are brains. It's just a fragment." He reached out and touched it, then wiped his hand on his lab coat. "It's a little gliotic."

"What does that mean, George?" Elvira asked, bending over to look.

"It's firm on the outside—it's scarring up. And see that texture—those fine micropunctures—like an orange peel. That means it's damaged. Senile. Degenerate. It's possible that the things only last a short period of time. Then they get senile and die. When we get a slice fixed, we can look for neural plaques and tangles, although with all those wires stuck in there, I don't know what it will all mean. How the hell do they get a single neuron connected to a single wire?"

"We may not have time for all these elaborate tests, George. Just how much can you tell us about this thing tonight?" Eric pressed him.

"You must know more than I do, Eric. You've seen the thing working, haven't you? It must be one hell of a computer. The brain packs a lot of memory in a small space. It's what every computer designer would love to have."

"But why?" Elvira puzzled. "Why invent this, and then give it to kids, and then—" she broke off.

304

"They must be getting the brain tissue from somewhere," George suggested. "They must be buying lab animals and removing the tissue. Maybe you can track them that way."

"What kind of animal?"

George looked at the fragment. "Big animal. A monkey at least, or a cow."

For an instant Eric stared at the convoluted surface of the exposed brain. A fly buzzed around it and landed on it. Then he blacked out. He staggered back, catching himself against a counter. Elvira put her hand on his forearm and helped him regain his balance.

"Are you all right, Eric?"

"I was thinking," Eric said. "About something I saw. What if that isn't animal tissue? What if it doesn't come from something grown in a vat somewhere? What if it's *human?*"

"There was a boy," George recalled. "They brought him in here. The one with his head cut open."

No one spoke. Eric didn't tell them he had been the *first* to see the victim. They had all heard the details anyway.

Their eyes turned to the thing on the counter. The wrinkled and convoluted piece of brain lay inert in its bath of plasma. The fly landed on it again and rubbed its feelers against it.

"I think . . ." Eric said slowly, "I think we know where they get their material."

Chapter Sixteen

Elvira sat in the dingy waiting room of the Newtown police station, sipping a cup of tea and passing the time between two interviews in painful uncertainty. After coming back to the school, she had told less than the whole truth about what had happened.

Chief Dougan had grilled her about Marsha's kidnaping, which two boys had witnessed but did not report until the panic began about the girl's whereabouts. The boys also reported that Miss Hawkins took chase in a car, so when she got back, Mr. Parisi and Chief Dougan were waiting for her. From Parisi's desperate look, it was obvious he was still withholding the critical fact that all four children had received computers at his instigation.

The police chief grilled her about what happened to Marsha, and she described the kidnaping and the chase—up to a point.

Now the police chief was talking to the FBI men, and *they* were going to interview her. Couldn't they just do it all together and be done with it?

Zaccariah had extracted a promise from her—that she wouldn't divulge the location of the farmhouse. She had told Chief Dougan, against her better judgment, that she flagged down a passing motorist and they had followed the van, and then lost it a few miles from town. She acted scatter-brained and said she hadn't gotten the name of the driver.

She was no longer interested in lying to protect Parisi or her job. But Zaccariah had convinced her that there was something big, malevolent and secret going on. Whoever was taking the children had power and influence—maybe even the influence to hamper an investigation. Zaccariah wanted to do it his way, if he could get some help. They would go in, by force if needed, get the children out if they were still alive, and then go for help.

Eric had balked at keeping it all secret, and then, after some thought, had agreed to Zaccariah's plan. The young man was willing to help—to risk his life, even—but seemed terrified of talking to the police. Zaccariah feared that the moment his role in the affair became known, he would be arrested as an accessory or accomplice in the kidnapings.

She understood their reluctance to get involved with the police, and that, added to Parisi's secrecy, bore down on her.

Zaccariah was at Eric's place, waiting. Eric was on the phone, connecting his computer to friends and associates who might shed some light on the ghastly thing they had found inside Peter's computer. Tomorrow, they would go back to the farm at Pleasanton.

"Miss Hawkins?" a voice said.

She looked up, expecting the FBI man to summon her into Dougan's smoky office.

Another man stood before her. She saw camouflage pants and looked up to see hands clenched around a beret, a wide belt, a khaki shirt and—

"Peter!" she said involuntarily, astonished by the man's face. It was not Peter Lansing, of course—the man was well over six feet tall. He was broad-shouldered, well-postured, rugged. Yet his face was boyish, and he had black hair and the same nose and cheekbones and mouth as Peter. And his eyes were the same brown.

The man smiled and said, "No, I'm Cliff Lansing. Peter's father."

"Peter's father," she repeated. Somehow she had always assumed that Peter's father was dead. Then she rose and extended her hand.

"Glad to meet you, Miss Hawkins." He took her hand warmly and didn't let it go until he had sat down next to her. He spoke in a hushed tone, leaning toward her.

"I came when I heard the news. They had the funeral for Frank and a service for . . . my boy. I stayed in town since then."

She bowed her head. "It was all so terrible, Mr. Lansing."

"Cliff. I know it was. Terrible and very fishy. I've been hearing stories about children . . . other children."

"Yes," she said. "They were all Peter's friends."

"I went to the school a little while ago. They told me you were here. You were his teacher?"

She nodded. "He was in my home room, and I was his science teacher."

"I wanted to talk about him, Miss Hawkins. With someone who knew him, saw him every day. His mother won't talk to me. She says Peter blew the house up and killed Frank and himself. She's more angry at Peter than sorrowed right now."

"Her emotions must be very confused," Elvira agreed.

"You're here because a young girl was kidnaped?"

"Yes."

"When you're through here—that is, if they let you out—"

309

"Why wouldn't they let me out?"

The man smiled a little. "Police and FBI. They get uppity when they don't know what's happening. They were in my house for six hours this week."

"Whatever for?"

"To see whether I kidnaped Peter. I did, once before."

"Oh," she said. She looked at his face and saw something she liked—determination. She sensed he could be fierce, even merciless—yet he had integrity.

"Are you in the Army, Mr. Lansing?"

"Cliff," he said a second time. "No. I *was* in the Army. Viet Nam."

"You must have seen some terrible things."

"I saw and *did* terrible things. A lot of us did. And for very little good reason. Finally I got shot, spent a lot of time in a hospital. And I got plenty mixed up."

"So you're not in the Army now?" she asked, still puzzled by his get-up.

"No, Miss Hawkins."

"Call me Elvira," she said, surprising herself.

"Can we talk when you get out of here?" he asked again. "Maybe over dinner? There are things I need to ask you."

"About Peter?"

"Yes."

"About the possibility that Peter is still alive?"

"Yes."

"About the other children, too?"

"Yes. It doesn't take a genius to see they all add up to something."

She took a memo pad from her purse and wrote down Eric's address. "Go to this address and ask for Eric. Tell him who you are and say I sent you. Tell him not to wait for me, but to tell you everything he knows."

"So you know more than you're going to tell these

310

yokels?" He pointed with his thumb to the FBI men, who were still huddled with Chief Dougan on the other side of the glass door.

"More," she said. "Mostly things that no one would believe."

"Try me."

"After we tell you, and *if* you believe us, will you help us?"

"I already know," he said, standing and putting the note in his shirt pocket.

"You already know what we're going to say?" she said, astonished.

"No," he said, putting on his beret. "I already know I'll believe you, and I already know I'll help you."

Elvira sat in a daze, still waiting to be called for the interview. She felt an aura, a lingering presence on the hard bench next to her, on the dirty tile before her where he had stood. Her evaluation of Cliff Lansing had been instantaneous and total. He was a reckless and dangerous man, and he had come just when they needed someone with more of those qualities than they had.

If she had any doubts about keeping secrets and tracking down the lost children on their own, they were gone now.

They called her. She stood, walked into Dougan's office, and lied superbly.

In the days after his "death," Peter Lansing had little time to contemplate his mother's grief, his father's search, or even the fate of his three friends. He was too busy learning the secrets of the subterranean world under the farmhouse.

The gray-haired man in the leather jacket didn't look very bright to Peter. Now that they were in a

311

room far underground beneath the barn, Peter was more willing to believe he was part of something vast and incredible. Until the trap door opened and he walked through a tunnel into dirt and then rock—until he saw the metal doors and rooms, and the long corridors leading into countless other rooms—he suspected he had been picked up by a solitary pervert with delusions of grandeur.

During the trip in the van, the man had refused to speak. All his questions would be answered, he said.

The room had metal walls and no windows, but they had done everything possible to make it a boy's room. It had clothes in a free-standing closet, bookshelves, a bed, a phonograph and record, and another computer just like the one he had blown up in the house.

The man sat across a small table and pointed to a folding chair against the wall. Peter opened it, pulled up a chair and sat.

"You're very special, Peter," the man said.

"Who are you?" Peter asked curtly. The man didn't look like much of a recruiter for the grand things he had been led to expect. He was sallow-skinned, smelled bad and had dirt under his fingernails. Peter didn't like him.

"Howard Emslie," he said. "At least that's who I used to be. Folks think I'm dead. Easier to do business that way. Dead folks don't have to pay no taxes or do jury duty. I been looking forward to meeting you, Peter."

"Why is that?"

"Because, like I started to say, you're special. Different from the others we get to come here. My boss and I have great plans for you."

"Maybe I won't like your plans," Peter hinted.

"We think you will. You passed all the tests."

"The game—it was a test?"

312

"We have one hell of a programmer, don't we? We made up Real War to test your mettle, to see what kind of leader or fighter you might be."

"Did I pass?"

"Well, yes and no. You see, Peter, you have a lot of aggression. And you hate authority like almost no one I ever seen. But you don't take orders. Every time we tried to condition you, you just switched us off or rolled over and went to sleep."

"You were trying to hypnotize me?" Peter said. "That was dumb."

"Seventy-five percent of all people will do what you tell them all the time. The figure goes to about ninety-seven if you apply a little hypnosis and conditioning. Most of the kids we recruit come because they pass a few tests and then get conditioned. But they don't really choose."

"So what's different about me?"

The man smiled broadly, reached across the table and poked Peter in the chest with his index finger. "You *chose* to come along, Peter. You *chose* to burn up the house and get back at that son of a bitch Frank. You would'a done it anyway."

"Maybe," Peter said. He wasn't about to be pinned with a crime.

"And then, when we told a little bit about what we're doing here, you asked for more information."

"That's right."

"And when you knew more, you asked to come and join."

"That's right."

"Even though you know we're gonna kill a lot of people."

Peter nodded. "That's right."

"You don't care if people die?"

"Not much. Not anymore."

"And you like what we've offered you."

"I survive," Peter said. "I get my pick of where to live. I get anything I want. You leave me alone." He sat back and waited for a reaction. "That's what the computer promised."

Howard nodded. "That's right, my boy. You and just a few others can have a hell of a good time. And for you there can be even more. You're a natural leader. I can see it. We need fellows like you."

"You're human," Peter said. "How do I know this is all true? This could be some government operation. Or the Chinese. Or you could just be a bunch of phonies."

"You wanna see? Where do you wanna start?"

"I want to see everything."

"We want you to see everything, Peter. We want you to be part of our plan. I'm going to be a rich man when this is all over, and you will be, too."

"How long have you been here?"

"Since the start," Howard recalled. "Since '53, when the . . . boss came down. I was just a young fellow, just out of high school, when my brother and I went into the old mine. That's when we found metal and started to dig. Then we found a door—or a door found us, I don't know which. It just opened up.

"And we went in. And there he was."

"Who? This guy you call the boss?"

"Right. There he was. He didn't talk to us directly, though. He had this machine like your computer that took his words and changed them into English. He said he needed things, and would pay us to help him. First we helped him repair the ship—it got damaged when it came down. We got the . . . parts . . . he needed. Once the big computer was fixed, everything started up whole hog.

"Ralph and me, we went out and recruited some others. They been down here building and planning and working for years. Some of these guys have never seen daylight in ten years."

"Don't they care?"

"Conditioning," Howard said, pointing to his temple. "Most people are robots, Peter. They just don't know it. Churches know it. Politicians know it. The boss knows it. We just use them, that's all."

"Are there other ones . . . like the boss?" Peter asked. He wanted to see one—wouldn't believe it until he saw one in the flesh.

"Not like him, but there are the Blues."

"The what?"

"Here's one now," Howard said, pointing to the metal door. A woman, clearly visible through the glass in the door, was about to enter. She came in with a tray of food.

Peter stood and gazed in amazement at the woman in coveralls and boots. She was six feet tall, built like a halfback, and had blue skin. Her eyes were purple. She looked amused at Peter's reaction to her. He turned up his nose when he detected a strong chemical smell on her clothes and hair.

"Are you an alien?" Peter said in a hushed tone as the woman took a Big Mac and a bottle of Coke from the tray and put them before him.

"I'm a native," she said. "I was born right here. I have every right to be here."

"Sorry," Peter said.

"She's a *hybrid*," Howard explained, apparently not concerned that the woman heard them as she retreated and closed the door. "Her mother was human. Her father was the boss."

"Does he have many kids? Who is his wife?" Peter asked. The idea of a space alien marrying a farm girl in Pennsylvania seemed ludicrous.

"There are quite a few hybrids now. They started being born in 1955. The boss doesn't have a wife. There are different mothers."

"I guess he gets horny a lot," Peter joked. "What does he do, go to singles bars and put personal ads in the paper?"

Howard didn't laugh. "You'll find out about that later. Just treat the hybrids with respect. They know who you are, and they've all been told to help you and show you things."

"Are they going to teach me?"

"No, Peter. Hybrids are brought up to obey. They do what the boss says. They do what I say. And soon, they will do what *you* say. They're very strong; they're very loyal. When there are enough of them, and when our supplies are built up, then it happens."

"The end of the world," Peter said. He tried to say it with no emotion at all.

"Eat your Big Mac," Howard suggested. "Then I'll come back and give you the guided tour." He headed for the door.

"Are you gonna lock me in?" Peter asked.

"No," Howard said. "But don't go out exploring till I get back. There are mine shafts connected to these passages—some of them are dead ends—some might cave in. You need me to get the knack of it."

"Okay," Peter said. He was hungry and had every reason to believe Howard would return. Howard was halfway through the door when Peter called back. "Howard?"

"Yes, Peter."

"That woman—"

"You like her, Peter? I think she's a little too old for you."

"She smelled funny. Do they all smell like that?"

"Smell? Oh, you mean the bug stuff. That's insecticide, and some insect repellent mixed in."

"Why? Do they have fleas?"

"No. They just don't like bugs. The whole place

316

down here stinks like a Raid factory. But you'll get used to it."

Peter sat back, alone in his new room. He didn't have time to think about what he had done back in Newtown. He knew his father was out there somewhere—but that too had to wait. What he had to do now would take all of his attention, all of his emotion, every ounce of energy in his body.

"It's *real*," he said to himself. "There are aliens and they're here and it's *real*."

The following days passed quickly. Peter ate junk food, listened to the worst rock music in the world, bathed only when he felt inclined to do so, and toured the half-acre of underground buildings.

It was gloomy as a bomb shelter, but full of secrets and wonders.

There was the room in which half a dozen men in gray coveralls took apart Commander computers, soldered in the aliens' special new parts, and sealed them up, packing them for reshipment. The men never looked up from their work as Peter and Howard toured the room.

"We're stockpiling these models now," Howard told him. "We've hired agents in California and Texas, so we can recruit from a little farther afield. We even have a private plane to fly in the new recruits."

"You must have a lot of money," Peter said.

"The boss came loaded with it. I guess things that are rare and expensive are that way everywhere. There's enough gold and platinum in the ship to buy a small country. He can't use it fast enough."

"No kidding?" Peter said.

"Honest to God," Howard swore.

There were other rooms full of adult workers. One

man ran a computer scanner, reading maps into a computer, whose droning voice asked more questions about elevation, population, railroads and highways. The man read from other papers, and as he did so, signs and symbols appeared on the maps.

"Can't you just buy road maps, or take pictures from the air?" Peter asked.

"These are different kinds of maps, Peter. They're maps of how things will be after we're through. Machines will dig new mines. There will have to be settlements suitable for the hybrids—places where they can live."

"You're gonna leave room for us, I hope," Peter said dryly.

"Big planet," Howard said. "And all this stuff will take decades, maybe hundreds of years."

"So when do the rest of the aliens—the *real* aliens come?" Peter asked in the corridor. He asked it in a whisper, as it was obviously a deep, *deep* secret.

Howard paused, took him to a bend in the corridor, and spoke in a hushed tone. "There ain't gonna be no other aliens, Peter. Just us and the hybrids. That's why it's so simple."

"They're not gonna come and live here? Why are they doing all this?"

Howard was silent as they walked through more corridors that kept turning at right angles like a maze. Every now and then a dead end would appear off to the left or right. Each time it ended in a wall that looked like pink quartz.

"What is that pink stuff?" Peter asked.

"That's the ship," Howard said.

"I want to see inside."

"Not yet, Peter. But in good time," Howard promised.

"You still didn't answer my question. Why aren't the aliens gonna come here?"

Even though the hall was empty, Howard whispered, "There's only one of them. He's in the ship, and he doesn't come out."

"I want to see," Peter said.

Howard shook his head. And for the first time since Peter had met him, the man looked afraid.

Peter advanced a few steps in Real War during the many boring hours between his tours with Howard. His computer was linked to the facility's *big* computer, which meant the games were longer, more intense, and more detailed. The computer promoted him to Major and gave him a platoon of Blues. He no longer even knew what day it was, and seemed concerned only with winning the game. The task was to seize control of a chemical plant without destroying the equipment. The logistics were tricky.

Howard came in and interrupted him.

"Would you like to see the big computer, the one that does all the planning?"

"Sure," Peter said, feigning disinterest. He continued with his game.

"Tell the computer you want to interrupt the game, Peter."

"Stop the game," Peter said. "I'll come back to it later."

Howard shook his head in surprise. "I don't know how you do that, boy."

"Do what?"

"Do what I just told you to do. The other kids have no control. They can't stop until the computer tells them it's okay. It's all in the conditioning—the messages they flash on the screen when you first start. It's all mixed in the colors when those patterns play."

"Oh, those," Peter said. He didn't see how a bunch of spirals and stupid messages on the screen were supposed to make people obey like zombies. "So what's this you're gonna show me?"

"The biggest computer in the world," Howard boasted. "The computer that's gonna run things for us and the boss after we clean up."

Howard led Peter to a doorway that was different from the others. He ran his hand around a round recess in the door, and it slid open. A ramp led down to a solid pink wall. Peter said nothing, pretending not to be excited. In a moment they'd be *in the ship*.

Howard touched another recess in the pink wall. It wasn't more than an inch-deep notch in the quartzlike solid, but it served as lock and doorknob. The whole wall slid away.

Peter gasped. The room was enormous, bounded with curved walls that looked like glass with solid rock beyond them. Control panels filled the perimeter. Round screens showed the view around the farmhouse and its interior rooms. Others had what looked like oscilloscopes, measuring blips and beeps from unknown sources. There were seats, soft padded ones obviously built for people, but no one sat in them.

The center of the hundred-foot-wide chamber was occupied by an enormous glass bubble filled with red liquid. Wires—millions of them by the looks of it—ran out of the solid sphere, twisted into cables and disappeared into the floor.

"What do you think that is, boy?" Howard said, playing with him, baiting him to guess.

"I don't know, Howard," Peter said.

"This is the granddaddy of what we put into your computer, Peter. Put your face against the glass and take a good look."

Peter stared into the red liquid but could see nothing for the glare of light in the chamber. He did as Howard suggested, put his hands around his eyes to shield them, and looked again.

The globe was full of living brain tissue, wrinkled and convoluted like wet laundry squashed against the window of a washing machine. The red liquid oozed and frothed around it. Thousand of tubes went into it, and wires punctured it everywhere, like a fine mesh supporting the gelatinous tissue.

"It's a brain," Peter said. "Not a computer. Is this the alien?" He stepped back, feeling an intense distaste. Looking at brains made you think about the inside of your head, made you conscious of having a skull with all that vulnerable mushy stuff inside.

"It's a computer, Peter. It has no identity. It's an organic computer. The human brain, according to the medical books, has sixty-five billion nerve connections. In a computer, that's sixty-five billion places to store information. This baby here has the equivalent of maybe a hundred and fifty brains. It never sleeps; it never forgets."

"What does it do?"

"It got this ship here. It can drive the ship anywhere like a bee going for a flower. The boss said the crew that flew him here were near idiots."

"What happened to them?"

"I think they died in the crash. Or maybe they just died off. That's why the boss recruited me and Ralph. This computer was in bad shape, too. We patched it up with whatever we could get—cow brains to start, and then other parts. The whole thing runs on sugar."

"*Sugar?*" Peter laughed.

"Plain old glucose." Howard nodded. "That red stuff is an artificial blood. It takes oxygen in and has some kind o' protein soup that keeps the brain cells renewing themselves as fast as they die off. The rest of it is plain sugar—all it needs."

"So there's no electricity in there?"

"None. All those wires are just like the nerves in your body. The signals coming out get amplified, built up to bigger currents as needed. That computer can run this ship without ever flicking a switch. It runs the factories over to the east, too. That's where we're makin' the chemicals."

"Chemicals—what for?"

"To clean up with, boy. As soon as there's enough hybrids to spread the stuff, they'll go out in planes and do it."

"What kind of chemicals?"

Howard looked at him with the first expression of doubt he had tendered Peter.

"You ask a lot of questions for a boy."

"Like you said," Peter answered. "I'm not like the rest."

"Maybe," Howard said, "we need to test you. I want to know you're as mean and grasping as I am before I tell you what the chemicals are for."

Peter thought he knew, but he had to hear it from Howard's lips.

"All right," Peter said. "Test me. What do you want me to do?"

Some of the girls looked at Andrea with a mixture of curiosity and annoyance when the Blues brought her in. She was dazed, but not so dazed that she didn't continually pull away from the repellent men each time one put his hand on her arm to lead her.

It was supposed to be liberation. When she saw the room, she realized it was jail. A dozen other girls, from ten to about sixteen in age, sat on bunk beds, around a television, and at a round formica table. The walls were blank, bare metal, and from the faces of the girls, she gathered it was clearly not a party.

"I don't want to be here," Andrea told the

turquoise-colored man emphatically. "I want to go back home."

"You'll only be here a little while," he told her. "Just wait, and we'll send for you."

"You promised—I mean, the computer promised—"

"Everything you were promised, you will have," he said in a flat tone. "Sit down and have a chat with the other girls."

The other occupants of the room were listless, speaking only in a hushed voice. They had obviously come to terms with the blue people and their horrible smell, for they took his presence for granted.

There was an empty chair at the table. "Can I sit here?" Andrea asked.

No one answered. She took the chair anyway. *Great,* she thought, *these girls are just as stuck up as the ones at Newtown High.*

Two girls at her right whispered something back and forth, then looked at her. The older of the two, a wispy blonde about Andrea's age, turned and finally spoke. "I'm Mary," she said.

"I'm Andrea."

"You're new."

Andrea nodded.

"I thought so. I guess you don't know yet what this is all about."

"I thought I did—but I guess I was wrong."

"They made you do things—bad things—didn't they?"

"Yes," Andrea said. "My mother—"

Mary put her hand over Andrea's mouth. "Don't say it. You don't have to. None of us talk about what happened to our families."

"You mean all of you—"

Mary nodded. "All of us got computers. We were hypnotized, tricked. See them over there by the TV?

323

They're completely brainwashed—airheads. They think they're in Disneyland or something."

Andrea looked. The girls around the television were mostly the younger ones. They did look a little more well-adjusted to their surroundings. "Are they drugged or something?" she conjectured.

Mary shrugged. Then she brushed her long, straw blond hair back over her shoulders and turned back to her other friend and whispered something. The dark-haired girl whispered something back.

"This is Sarah," Mary said. "She's bashful. She doesn't talk to anyone else except me. I think the computer did something to her. She tries to talk, but just stutters. She says she wants to be friends."

Andrea reached over in front of Mary to shake hands with Sarah. The girl reached out and took her hand. Then in a low voice, Andrea said, "Isn't there some way we can get out of here?"

Sarah shook her head violently, and Mary replied for both of them: "We can't go back. Not after what we did."

"But why are we here?" Andrea demanded. "What are they doing with us? Is this some kind of slavery thing? Do they sell us to perverts?"

"We don't know everything. They tell us to keep using the computer. If you're good at the games, you get a reward: They take you away to another place where you work. They tell you they'll pay you a lot and you'll have everything you want in a year or two. If you're not good at the games and you're little, you just sit here like them." She indicated the girls around the television. "Zombies. Couch turnips."

"That's all?" Andrea asked.

"No," Mary said. She leaned closer again and whispered. "Sometimes the Stinkies come—"

"Stinkies?"

"The blue guys."

"Oh."

"Sometimes the Stinkies come and take one of the little girls. And she never comes back."

"Maybe she goes back home," Andrea said hopefully.

Mary shook her head. "I don't think so."

Andrea turned the chair around and looked at the three older girls in the bunk beds. All three were talking, looking back at Andrea.

"Hello," Andrea said. She waved.

They looked away, as if she had somehow insulted them.

"What's wrong with them?" Andrea asked. "We're all in this mess together. Why should they be so stuck up?"

"They're not stuck up," Mary said, loud enough for them to hear. "They're *knocked up*." She laughed. The older girls stared daggers.

"They're pregnant," Mary repeated. "They won't talk about it. We think they went to bed with the Stinkies, trying to bribe their way out of here. Isn't that disgusting?"

Sarah whispered frantically to Mary.

"Sarah's been here longer than me," Mary explained. "She says it isn't that way at all." Sarah pulled Mary's head to hers and buzzed again. "She wants to know if you have your periods yet," she said to Andrea.

"That's none of your business," Andrea retorted.

"Do you?" Mary insisted. "I don't—not yet."

"I've been—for three months now," Andrea admitted.

Sarah went *buzz—buzz—buzz* in Mary's ear again.

"Sarah says that's too bad. That mean's you're next."

Andrea blanched. "Next for what?"

The girls were silent. Andrea turned and looked at

the three pregnant girls. They read magazines and spoke to one another, their eyes unfocused, their mouths tight with anxiety and worry. One of them *was* a little big in the belly.

"Next for what?" Andrea repeated.

Howard brought Peter into a room full of other boys. Three with their backs to the door sat at computers, playing endless variations of Real War. Others sprawled on bunk beds looking at blank ceilings, or sat on the floor, knees folded, talking. A few of the boys stopped and looked at them as they came in, taking in Peter with curiosity but avoiding eye contact with Howard. They clearly didn't like the old man.

"These are other recruits," Howard told Peter. "They're still being tested and conditioned. A few are very promising for technical and tactical things. Others look like they may be rejects."

"I see," Peter said. His eyes took them in, counting. There were fifteen boys altogether. "Are there other rooms like this?"

"For the girls," Howard said. "And there are boys who've moved farther along. They're working all over."

"How many are there? How many have been through all of this?"

Howard chuckled. "You ask too many questions, boy. Too soon for you to know that."

"I want to know if this can work, or if you guys are just crazy. How many people work down here?"

"Hundred fifty, maybe two hundred. Thirty hybrids, the rest—people like us—and recruits." Howard turned Peter around by the elbow. "See that kid—the one with the red hair?"

"Which?" Peter felt the hair on his neck prickle.

"The boy at the computer. The one who's sitting there not playing, acting dopey."

"I see him," Peter said.

"He's resisting the conditioning. He's very bright, but he has pacifist leanings. The boss wants him to help plan the movements of the Blues. He's a natural for complex, multi-level planning. The best we've seen—but he won't budge."

"What do you want me to do?"

"He needs a lesson . . . needs discipline."

Peter understood. The muscles on his face trembled uncontrollably.

"Go over and beat him up. Don't hurt his head. Just give him a sound beating."

Peter advanced slowly toward the short, stoop-shouldered boy. He put his hand on the boy's shoulder and spun him around, raising his arm and making a fist for a hard punch.

Then he froze. It was Keith Brandon, staring wide-eyed through thick wire-frame glasses.

"Peter!" he cried. "Peter, it's me!"

Peter unclenched his fist. Then he remembered that he was being tested. Howard had intentionally sent him to attack his best friend.

He reached out to the astonished younger boy and gently removed his glasses, folding them and putting them on top of the monitor.

"Don't want to break your glasses," Peter explained. "There's no eye doctor down here."

"What are you doing, Peter?" Keith pleaded.

Howard was watching, waiting for him to do something.

"I understand you're not cooperating," Peter said.

"Peter, I don't know why I'm here. I don't remember. What do they want?"

327

"Play the game," Peter said, indicating the computer. "Do what you're told."

"I want to go home," Keith whined. "I wanna see my mom and dad."

Closing his eyes after taking aim, Peter punched Keith in the stomach. Even though the blow was not as hard as it looked, the smaller boy reeled back, toppling the stool. He fell on his back, raising his hands defensively over his face.

"Please—*please!*" Keith begged.

Peter yanked him up by the arm. Keith rose, trustingly, totally open to the second punch. Peter pounded him backward with determined punches to the chest, driving him against the wall.

Keith's eyes stared dazedly into Peter's, his freckled face contorted with agony and betrayal.

"You're my best friend," Keith moaned.

"I know," Peter said, driving his knee into the defenseless boy's groin.

Keith sank to the floor, sobbing.

Peter turned away.

Howard was happy—very happy. He put his arm on Peter's shoulder. They walked down the corridor like father and son.

"Maybe he'll shape up," Howard said.

"What if he doesn't?" Peter asked.

"Would you like to see?" Howard asked.

"Yes," Peter said. "But I want to go back to my room and eat something first." He counted the doors from Keith's room to the end of the corridor, then counted the bends and their directions back to where they had started. He memorized it as 43L2R: fourth door, three lefts, two rights. He had a similar code for the location of every room they had shown him.

Howard left him at his door. "I'll come for you in an hour," he said.

Peter went inside and wrote down the location of Keith's room inside the cover of a comic book—just in case he forgot it. Then he ate a sandwich and lay on his bed, looking at the rivets on the ceiling and listening to the distant hum of machinery.

He folded his forearm over his eyes and suddenly felt hot tears welling there. He trembled with rage.

Then he got up, tore a piece of paper from the margin of a comic, and wrote: BHST-XMM-LMM-UIN. He folded the strip of paper and put it in his jeans pocket.

Jimmy lay alone in a room with metal walls. Everything was gray, even the blanket they had put over him.

He tried to sit up. The pain in his chest was so bad he passed out from it. When he woke up again, he carefully peeled the blanket away from his naked body. Somebody had wrapped a tight bandage around him, starting at his waist and running up under his shoulder. He guessed that was for his broken ribs, but it sure didn't do much for the awful pain.

It didn't look like a hospital, so he knew the men hadn't let him go. He was still somewhere in the mines, in that place under the barn. If he could just get out of this room, maybe he could find his way out. If he couldn't go up the way he came, he still might be able to find the other way out—the mine shaft up to the convent grounds.

There was a door at the far end of the room, but no way to reach it. He was completely helpless.

Moaning in unremitting pain, he lapsed into darkness again.

"Roughed him up, didn't they?" a boy's voice said.

329

Jimmy opened one eye and saw a black-haired boy staring at him with a detached air.

"Can't tell what the Blues will do," a hard, adult voice said. "Sometimes they play rough like this. Sometimes they have other kinds of fun."

He didn't open the other eye. Jimmy knew who it was: the old man with gray hair.

"You're kidding me," the boy said.

"Why not?" the man responded. "The Blues were bred to take things over. They're fighters. And in a war, fighters get rewards. They can do what they want with their captives. They've got good appetites, and sometimes even a little imagination."

"That's weird," the boy said.

"They are the future, boy. They can do whatever they want once they take over. Girls, men, boys, whatever they want. Use 'em as slaves. Make love to 'em. Kill 'em. Just like ancient Rome. And you and me will have it, too—whatever we want. Just think about it, son. Instant gratification."

"I'll think about it," the boy said uncertainly. "What are you gonna do with him?"

"I thought you'd want to see what we do with prisoners, Peter."

Jimmy didn't like the sound of that.

"I'm not a prisoner," he protested, opening both eyes and trying to sit up.

"Ah, our friend has come to!" the man said, pushing Jimmy down brutally with his open hand. He hit him right in the middle of his chest—the pain shot through him.

"I'm glad you're conscious," the man said. "That way you can know exactly what's happening to you. Listen carefully."

The man moved to a table along the wall and came back with a black iron object. It looked like a football helmet.

330

"What does this look like?" he asked Jimmy.

Jimmy told him.

"Very good. It *is* a helmet. And I'm going to put it over your head. You're going to enjoy the ultimate experience as a result. An out-of-body experience." The man laughed as though he had made a great joke.

"What are you gonna do?" Jimmy asked.

"Just relax, young fellow." The man came around Jimmy and put the top of the helmet over his skull and ears and forehead. It was a tight fit, and something inside clamped down all around his head, making it tighter still.

"That hurts," Jimmy protested. "It's too tight." He reached up with his hands and tried to pull it off. It wouldn't budge.

"I wouldn't do that if I were you, young fellow," the man warned. "You wouldn't want to scalp yourself." He turned to the boy and explained. "Inside the helmet are hundreds of little blades—sharper than surgical knives. Right now they're cutting through the hair and lining themselves up around his skull."

Jimmy felt like someone had lit a match at the base of his neck. He yelled and jerked upwards.

The man pushed him back down and held him down. Jimmy's hands wrenched at the helmet. The burning sensation moved up both sides to his ears.

"A laser cutter severs both ears," the man told the boy, "and cauterizes as it goes. Quite ingenious."

Jimmy screamed. He felt the skin of his temple being cut with razor blades. Behind the blades came the burning.

"Stop!" he begged. "God, please stop this! I didn't do nothin'."

"I'm not God," the man siad. "Now, Peter, observe what happens to his eyes."

331

Jimmy watched in horror as what looked like two windshield wipers sprung down from the helmet and waved past his eyes like little pendulums. He raised his hands to swat them away but they were unstoppable, tough as iron. Heat rose under his eyes, filling them with tears.

"What's it doing?" the boy asked.

"Those are lasers. They're cutting under the eyes, separating them from the face and the skull. Now we've cut a complete circle."

Jimmy kept on screaming, but no scream was loud enough to drown out the sounds coming from the helmet. Blades spun, drilled, ground through the bone of his skull.

Then he stopped hearing, even though his mouth stayed open and kept on screaming. The man and boy talked, shouting to one another over his scream, but it was just lips moving, no sounds.

The nerves to his brain were being severed by the mechanism of the helmet. He felt a vibration, deep as an earthquake, as a quick slice separated his brain from his spinal cord.

The man reached out and yanked the helmet up from the table.

Jimmy thought he would die that instant.

Instead, his skull and brains looked down from dangling eye stalks at the jerking, truncated body on the table. The man held the helmet carefully, picking up the eyes and laying them on top of the exposed, impossibly living tissue.

The last thing Jimmy saw before he went eternally insane was his one bare eyeball looking at its twin on a moist bed of convoluted brains.

Chapter Seventeen

"I want some other comics," Peter said grumpily. He had leafed through the dismal library of comics in his room a half dozen times. He was so bored he even doodled in one of them with a felt tip pen.

The Blue who had been assigned as Peter's "helper" sat drowsily at the table, staring at the television. The stations cabled down from the antenna on the farmhouse seemed to carry little but *I Love Lucy* reruns and occasional spates of *Star Trek*. The latter seemed to interest the Blues intensely. Peter even left his room and explored the halls briefly while the science-fiction program played, and was never missed.

He jokingly nicknamed the Blue "Mr. Spock," which produced the only laugh he had seen from one of the oversized hybrids. But the laugh wasn't exactly a laugh. His purple lips had opened to reveal a laughing mug of crazy-angled teeth, which made Peter jump back with a start. It was then he noticed how long their jaws were, and how the teeth ran up along the sides of their mouths. When the Blues ate, their mouths moved in a circular motion; they didn't chew, they food-processed.

He knew the Blue was not a helper but a "watcher," no doubt instructed to tell Howard or the mysterious boss if he did anything odd. Fortunately Spock was not swift-witted and could usually be tricked into divulging vital information Peter wanted. If a question was "off limits" phrased one way, he could often get his answer by making a wrong surmise, stating it, and having the hybrid correct him.

He waited for a commercial before repeating, "I want some other comics." This time he made it sound more like an order.

The Blue turned his head away from the screen and frowned. "I think Howard buys them in town. I can ask him to buy more."

"Why can't you go into town and buy some for me?"

"Don't be silly. I would attract attention."

"You could wear your funny hat, and your gloves."

"I would still attract attention. And in the town there are too many—insects."

"Why don't you like insects?"

The Blue turned his head back to the television and spoke with an evasive tone: "Nobody likes insects. You don't like them, do you?"

"I can't say they ever bother me, Spock, except maybe for hornets and spiders. Why don't you like bugs?"

The Blue was distracted as a commercial ended and *Star Trek* came back on. "Bugs don't like us," he explained. "They attack us."

Peter sat back, delighted with what he had learned. That explained the bee hats, the gloves, the boots, and the persistent smell of insecticides. Insects *knew* the aliens didn't belong and would attack them in the open air. Maybe the hybrids even had a natural smell which *attracted* bugs. It was a delightful thought.

"I want some more comics *now*," Peter demanded, interrupting the program just as the *Enterprise* leaped into warp drive.

"That's not reasonable," the Blue said. "And comic books are for juveniles."

"I *am* a juvenile, and I need my comic books," Peter persisted. Then he lit up with a bright idea. "I could trade—with the other boys. They have comics, don't they?"

"Yes," the Blue said.

"And the girls—do they have comics?"

"A few."

"I'm going to the boys' room to make a swap," Peter announced. "And then to the girls' room, if you can tell me where it is."

"Girls' quarters are off limits for boys," the hybrid reminded him.

"All right," Peter said easily, timing his request to the end credits of the television program. He split his pile of comics in half. "I'll take this pile to the boys and *you* take *this* pile to the girls."

"Can't you wait for new comics?" the Blue asked lazily.

"No. That's an order, Spock."

"I obey," the Blue said. He took the comics and loped out the door.

Peter followed him unobserved and watched which door he entered. The room didn't even have a lock on it. He memorized the path to get back there again, then he doubled back and made his way to the boys' communal living quarters.

He found three of the ten-year-olds reading a pile of *Superman* and *Batman* comics. They stared in alarm when they recognized him, but their fear turned to avarice when they saw the comics.

"Like to swap?" he asked.

The answer was obvious. The boys gathered the well-read magazines into a pile and pushed them across the table.

Peter took them, put his own down and walked away. In a few seconds they were fighting and argruing like regular boys.

"Superman! That's the new one. I get it first!"

"I'll take the *Batman!*"

"No, me!"

Peter smiled, thinking to himself: *They're still human, still kids.* If they could trust him, maybe he could get through to them.

They wouldn't trust him, though. They had watched him beat Keith—and now only Keith could win them over.

He looked around for Blues. One sat at the television, its head bowed in sleep.

At the bunk beds, he found Keith. Keith saw him coming but didn't get up.

"Hi, Keith," Peter said.

"Stay away from me," Keith moaned. He turned his face away.

Peter took the strip of paper, no bigger than a spitball now, and put it on Keith's tee shirt. Keith cringed, expecting to be hit, then looked at the wadded-up paper as though it were a spider.

Peter caught Keith's eye and winked.

Keith looked at him intently, grabbed the paper and hid it in his palm.

"I hope you learned your lesson, boy," Peter said loudly.

"Yes, sir," Keith said.

"From now on you play the games when the computer tells you to," he said. The Blue awakened and turned to stare.

"Yes, sir," Keith said.

Peter turned on his heels like a Nazi officer in an old war movie and strode out of the room.

Keith let a long time pass before he dared open and read the note from Peter.

He stared at the nonsensical letters for a full moment before he realized it was written in the Cougar code he and Peter had developed.

It was simple, really. Every letter was advanced by one, and all the vowels were missing. DHST was CGRS—*Cougars.*

He counted out the rest letter by letter.

XMM LMM was "wll kll."

UIN was "thm."

Cgrs wll kll thm.

Keith leaped for joy out of the bunk. He ran for the food he had been too heartsick to eat, for the bathroom behind the partition at the end of the room to wash up, to the communal closet for a change of clothes.

He had to be fed, ready and able for whatever Peter was planning.

Peter was *still* his best friend. The attack had been to fool the aliens.

"Cougars," he whispered under his breath, "will kill them."

Looking around the bleak, windowless room, he thought: *And the sooner the better.*

The Blue left to go have his dinner. Keith called the boys together and began to talk.

Andrea sat at the table with her friends Mary and Sarah, the remains of lunch scattered on paper plates before them. They had become fast friends, even though Sarah still only whispered her part of the conversation through Mary.

"Here comes a Stinkie," Mary said. Then she spoke loudly as a Blue came into the room, "And you can always smell them coming."

The tall Blue was unruffled by Mary's insults. If anything, he seemed to take aggressive dislike as a sign of recognition.

He brought in a pile of comic books.

"One of the boys would like to trade," the Blue said.

"Boys?" Andrea sat up, turned to the Blue despite her revulsion and addressed him. "Did you say boys?"

"One of the boys would like to trade comic books. Yours for his," the Blue repeated.

"Where are the boys?" she asked.

"Not permitted to say. Will you trade comics?"

"I hate them," Mary said. "They're yucky and stupid. Dumb monsters and superheroes."

"Let me see," Andrea said. She looked through the pile and found an issue of *Spiderman*. "Yes, I want these!" she exclaimed. It was an old issue, and she had already read it; but she had to have *some* link with the things she cared about.

"To trade," the Blue reminded her.

"Wait," Andrea said. She scurried around the room and collected the dozen or so comics wherever the girls had cast them aside. "Here," she answered, matching the offered pile with one of her own. She hoped the boys wouldn't gag too much when they saw that one was a romance comic and another was *Archie*.

The Blue took the offering and left.

Andrea grabbed the *Spiderman* comic and went to her bunk, the closest she could get to being alone

338

with her hero.

She opened the magazine and gasped.

"No!" she groaned, flipping the pages. "Not on *every* page!" She slammed the cover shut and curled up her knees in rage. Someone had taken a pen and drawn a mustache and goatee on Peter Parker in every panel of the comic book where Spiderman's alter ego appeared. The joker had also drawn body hair on his arms and chest, which completely grossed her out. It had made her so mad the time Peter—

She grabbed the comic and opened it again. It was Peter Lansing who had defaced her *Spiderman* comic in English class. This was his work—he was alive and he was *here*. This was his way of telling her.

Intently, she studied every page. Maybe Peter had hidden a message somewhere.

Ten minutes later she found it, lettered neatly on the side of a building against which Spiderman swung on his silken rope. It read: QUS LUI IS. DHST XMM LMM UIN.

"Damn!" she cursed. It was the stupid code writing Peter and Keith had tried to teach her. Was it every letter plus one—or minus one?

She took a tablet the girls had been using to tabulate scores for their card games and, making sure no one was watching, copied the inscription. She wrote the correct letter values above the letters Peter had written. It finally came out as *Kth Ptr hr. Cgrs wll kll thm.*

"Keith and Peter are here," she whispered. "The Cougars will kill them." She was confused: How could Cougars kill Keith and Peter? They *were* the Cougars. Clearly, *them* meant their captors.

Andrea thought of two boys against those blue-skinned titans and despaired. What could they do? If they could outwit their captors, however, she wanted to be ready.

She went to find Mary and Sarah, but their places at the table were empty.

Andrea found them at the computers, eyes fixed to the screens. She clenched her fists in desperation. She knew it would be her turn within the hour. The metallic voice from the monitor speaker would release one of the girls and call her, and no matter what her intention she would go and sit there. She had to. They all had to.

And then she thought: *What if we didn't hear the voice? Or what if someone went to the screen and turned the brightness down so we didn't see anything?* Each of them was powerless to do anything when sitting there, but what if they *helped one another?* And they could make some kind of ear plugs to deafen them to the commands. They had to do it gradually, of course, plan for it so the computers would not catch on and summon the Blues . . .

She turned to the other girls and whispered her plan. They listened, and for the first time in days, they looked like children again. They would not be zombies. They had a plan.

That night, a Blue female came and asked for Andrea. She feigned sleep in her upper bunk, but the visitor persisted. Two of the girls screamed at her to go away. Andrea was surprised to recognize the voices as those of the pregnant girls.

The aura of bug spray came closer, and a blue hand shook her arm roughly.

"Wake up, little mother!" the Amazonian hybrid said.

Andrea turned her head and looked in disgust at the creature. No amount of makeup could cover that

340

puttylike complexion or adorn hair that looked like lengths of gnarled tree trunk. The woman's lips were purple, her eyelids dyed or shaded to match. Her long jaw made her think of the witch in *Snow White*.

"What do you want?" Andrea growled. Had one of the girls already told the Blues of her rebelliousness?

"Time for you to have an appointment with the master," she said.

"The master?"

"The master. The boss."

"The guy who runs this place?"

"That's right, little mother."

"Don't call me that. I'm not anybody's mother."

The woman tugged her arm. "Time to go."

"I'm not dressed," Andrea protested. She lifted the blanket to show she had on only a long, baggy tee shirt and panties.

"It doesn't matter. Come the way you are."

"Absolutely not," Andrea said. "It's night time, isn't it? Why can't I see him in the morning?"

"Wouldn't you like to talk about going home?" the woman asked.

"That's different," Andrea said. She jumped out of bed, slid into jeans and sneakers and followed the woman to the door.

She stopped for a second as she passed the two pregnant girls, who sat up in their beds and watched.

"Thanks," she said, "for trying to help."

One looked away, shaking from head to foot. The other girl looked at her with sorrow and sympathy. Her eyes said: *Poor kid—if only you knew.*

It was one o'clock in the morning by her watch. Although she had been promised an appointment with the boss, no one had come in for an hour.

341

The room was even more sterile than the others: featureless, metal doors and ceilings, and no furniture except a cot with a cheap foam mattress and a blanket and pillow. She emphatically didn't like the looks of the room the boss chose for his interviews. There wasn't even a chair for him to sit in, and she knew what *that* probably meant.

"Perverts and mutants," she said to herself.

For a while, she busied herself with thinking about a minor revelation which had come in the maze of corridors they had passed through. She had been astonished to follow the Blue woman out and see her open the door to the girls' chamber by merely *pushing* on it. When she glanced back from the outside, she saw it had no lock. Yet she would have sworn the door was locked, escape proof, solid as a prison.

As they walked, she noticed the absence of locks nearly everywhere. They were simple, hinged, metal doors in metal frames, with neither knobs nor locks.

She tried to remember what the door in her room had looked like, but her mind was blank. The girls never went near the door, never talked about leaving. They *assumed* it to be locked, or in all probability, were *conditioned* by the computer to think they were locked in. She could not remember even *trying* to leave the room.

When she went back, she would make a point of looking at the door, *really* looking at it.

At one-thirty, she could no longer sit up on the bed and remain vigilant. Her eyes kept going shut; her head dropped, and then she'd lose her balance and begin to topple forward or backward. She tried the door again and again. This one was locked, *really* locked. She saw the deadbolt's silhouette through the crack of light from the corridor.

Finally, she told herself the mysterious boss had forgotten her. She lay down on the bed, pulled the blanket over her, and tucked the pillow under her head. The pillow was too thin; again and again she folded and shaped it, only to have it flatten to the thickness of a towel when she relaxed. Grimly determined to sleep somehow, she lay flat on her back and closed her eyes.

When she opened them again, the ceiling lights had dimmed. A sound had awakened her. She lay, too afraid to move, listening for its repetition.

Metal slid on metal. She saw it from the corner of her eye; a three-foot opening had appeared in the wall. A Blue stood in the darkness of another room. he lifted something—a dark hemisphere, a half globe with tree branches all over it—and pushed it over the ledge into the room. It fell with a rubbery thud.

The panel slid shut. The wall looked solid again except for the thin outline where the window had been.

She sat up slightly, leaning on her elbows.

The black thing lay on the floor, quiet, inert. It was about two feet wide and looked like an oversized version of those silly latex spiders and snakes and bats that boys bought in novelty shops and brought into class. The lumpy thing had the sheen and texture of a black gum drop. From it radiated arms or branches, each ending in a clump of limp tentacles or cilia. Maybe this was the Blues' idea of a practical joke—making her think this patchwork monstrosity was the "boss"—waiting in the next room to see if she screamed. It wasn't alive. It obviously wasn't alive. It probably said *Made in Hong Kong* on the bottom. Maybe it was a model of something from one of those Godzilla movies.

Then the motor inside it started up. Whirring and

343

grinding like a toy robot, it guided the clumsy object across the floor toward her.

She sat up, huddling with knees raised and hands clenched tightly to her shins. If the toy monster was going to roll around the floor like a lost vacuum cleaner, she would just stay put until her captors realized she wasn't going to be frightened by a Gumby creepy-crawler.

The motorized spider bumped against the leg of the cot. The arms wiggled until some of the fine tentacles took hold like a grapevine seizing a trellis.

Andrea peeked out over the edge of the bed. It was a machine, all right, but a very clever one. More of the tentacles grabbed hold of the cot, not by any conscious motion, but at random—when it hit something, it grabbed.

Slowly, with its gears and motors grinding, it began to hoist its bulbous body upwards. It rose, and fell back. The tentacles wound a little tighter until the elastic arms could support its weight.

When it was halfway up the leg of the cot, Andrea jumped off the bed and ran for the door.

The machine instantly fell to the floor, rotated itself, and skittered toward her.

It was no longer amusing. From the way it turned, it clearly had a *front*. Did that mean it had eyes to see her, or ears to listen for her motion, the way the computer heard her voice?

She dodged it and ran to the far corner, putting the cot between her and the robot pursuer.

It rolled on hidden wheels or ball bearings, neatly dodged the table and came right for her.

She let it get close, then jumped over it.

Getting to the cot before it could turn around, she tipped it over. The mattress fell flat on the floor; she raised the frame and springs as a barrier. It stood like a fence between her and the machine.

The spider-thing paused. Its branches and tendrils waved furiously. It was obviously taking in the situation, trying to see her behind the maze of springs, trying to decide what to do.

Slowly, it advanced.

She moved around the perimeter of the room, dragging the cot. Her hands ached from the weight of it. The frame screeched as it scraped the metal floor.

The cat-and-mouse continued until her wrists ached and her arms could barely lift the bed frame. She would collapse if it went on much longer.

Then she backed into the corner, stood the frame straight up, and decided to let it get onto the springs. Then she would topple the frame over it and squash it.

The robot hesitated.

"Come on!" she yelled. "What are you waiting for?"

It came for her, its internal motors just as energetic as when the chase had started. Whatever it wanted, it never got tired of going after it.

She held her breath as the tentacles went for the springs. She would wait until it was halfway up, then push it over with all her strength. The springs would slice through it like a cookie cutter.

It was inches away from her, meticulously climbing from wire to wire. It no doubt intended to climb the frame and then drop down on her from above.

Then it stopped. The motors whirred furiously.

Andrea looked down. A tentacle, longer than the others, had reached through and circled her ankle.

She screamed as the cold, slimy appendage tightened its grip. She yanked her leg backward.

The thing pulled back with greater force, jamming

the arch of her foot against the springs.

Shifting its center of gravity again, it descended.

A second tentacle wrapped the trapped ankle. A third tickled at the fabric of her jeans, trying to get a hold.

It's got me stuck, Andrea thought, *but it's stuck, too. It can't get to me. It can't get through the springs.*

The other tentacles flexed around the springs. They had the fluid motion of the limbs of an octopus, graceful and purposeful.

One by one, the springs snapped.

Andrea pulled back into the corner. How could it be so strong?

The cold, black leathery body plopped through the hole it had made and hugged her right leg. She let the useless bed frame fall over to the floor with a resounding crash.

"Get it off me!" she screamed at the distant wall. "Goddamn you, I know you're in there. Get this thing off me!"

No one came. The wall panel remained mutely sealed.

She clawed at the tendrils, trying to tear them off her leg. Instead, each one she grabbed extended other feelers, snaking toward her fingers. In a moment she was locked in a crouching pose, both hands locked to her leg as the rubbery but powerful tentacles held her like a boa constrictor. She could feel it now. There was metal inside the arms, some kind of gear work that stayed limp and flexible, then, when grasping, locked together and could not be torn loose.

She hobbled across the room until she collapsed on the mattress.

Seconds later it had both her feet. It released her hands to concentrate on its crippling lock. Standing was impossible.

"What do you want?" she shrieked. "Why are you doing this?"

Looking more like a spider than ever—or like some hideous land-roving octopus—the machine crept up her legs, locking her knees together. She tried to pound its body with her fists, but the waving arms stopped her. It had enough spare tentacles to stop anything she tried to do.

It made its way to her upper legs and stopped. One tentacle—the long one—still reached down and locked her legs together.

Shock and hysteria finally hit her, and she fell back, crying desperately. Her tears and sobs didn't interest her attacker.

It inched upwards toward her waist. It released her ankles to make its advance. She could stand; she could even run around the room if she wanted, but she could not get it off her. She knew, even without trying, that it would match her every motion, making her stumble and fall again. What did it want? Was it going to get up to her throat and strangle her?

A tentacle reached under the top button of her jeans and snapped it open.

"No you don't!" she yelled, swatting it away. Her hand stung from hitting it.

Another tentacle grabbed her hand and pulled it away.

It opened the second button even faster than it had managed the first one. It was a machine, but it had *learned*.

She pounded the thing's body with her other hand, bruising the side of her fist. Then a tentacle got her around the wrist. She was helpless.

The third button opened. The white of her panties was showing.

Now, at last, she realized what the machine was going to do.

"You perverts!" she screamed. "You cowards! What the hell are you? What the hell kind of perverts are you?" They were watching somewhere—she knew it—they were watching through a hole or a hidden video camera. Maybe they were even making a movie of this—her humiliation at the hands—*tentacles*—of a rape machine.

Impatient, the powerful feelers grasped and tore away her panties and then ripped the remaining denim blocking its way.

Andrea choked with rage and shame as the machine's body opened to reveal its unspeakable mechanism. It entered her, motors throbbing in time with her breath and heartbeat.

She clenched herself against it, refused it, but it opened her, making her shake with its penetration.

"What are you?" she shouted. "I'll kill you! I swear I'll kill you!"

A panel slid open in the ceiling. She heard it over the lubricious slurring of the machine.

A man stood above, silhouetted in blue light. He leaned down, peering in interest at her struggle. His eyes were yellow, slanted downward at an unnatural angle. His mouth was wrong, twisted—a vertical slit of a lip that could never smile—but somehow she knew he was laughing.

She howled in rage as the alien's surrogate genitals continued their attack on her. What could he possibly get from this, what possible enjoyment?

What she had taken as the creature's sadism and perversion, however, was only a prelude to the final moment of horror—when she felt the warm geyser of alien seed burst within her.

She looked up at the watching yellow eyes and fainted.

Chapter Eighteen

Dr. Halpern looked at himself in the mirror and said, "Richard Lowell Halpern, M.D., this is your big night." He stood in jockey shorts and socks, admiring his figure in the full-length glass on the back of the bathroom door.

Nobody would think he was forty-five. He was in good shape, despite the fact that he never exercised. Thin men always looked good, as long as they got enough to eat and didn't look tubercular. He had all his hair—good hair despite the gray—a face that made everyone look twice, perfect teeth, and a good shape. Wide shoulders tapered to a narrow waist, good long legs for running or tennis—a lot to be happy about, and enough of everything else to make a woman happy.

In an hour, he would bring Sister Helena to his apartment. He had juggled the schedules of the night people so a thirty-minute gap occurred between their shifts. One nurse attendant was to leave fifteen minutes early, the next was to arrive fifteen minutes late. During the half hour interval he would get Helena down the hall from her room, up the back stairway, and into his apartment.

He had explained the plan to Sister Helena, and she had agreed to live up to her promises—all of them. The machine and all its attachments were already in the bedroom, plugged in and waiting. He had cords handy to bind her, in case she changed her mind and resisted, as well as handcuffs, chains and a few other toys he had long kept hidden in a trunk.

He never thought he would get to use these things. All his life he had waited for a woman—a woman who would fulfill his need to gain pleasure and give pain.

Sister Helena didn't ask how he was going to get her back to her room—a fortunate lapse since that was a blank spot in his own mind. Somehow things would come out. The Serpent would provide. Perhaps the Serpent had plans for the two of them which went beyond a mere evening's pleasure. He thought of the previous doctor who had fled with one of the sisters and thought, *Why not?*

"How will you do it?" he asked more practically. "How will we get her back to her room?"

The Serpent spoke: *She's not going back to her room. She is going to her destiny. She will be the daughter of the lightning, the sylph, the will o' the wisp.*

"She will be missed," Halpern protested. "They'll come looking for her."

You will lie on top of a goddess. You will bathe me in St. Elmo's fire, make love to the Aurora Borealis. We will cast her into the air so she cannot tell.

"Cast her into the air?" Halpern said. He didn't understand half of what the Serpent told him.

He would understand better with a little stimulation. He took out a round hand mirror and, opening a drawer under the sink, took out a tiny vial of white powder. He spread it on the mirror with a razor blade, cutting it into fine dust.

Inhaling it, he felt the two parts of his being split with perfect clarity. The shadow separated from the light, id from ego.

The Serpent spoke more clearly now.

He pulled down his shorts to reveal the long coils of a cobra tattooed on his abdomen. The blue and green curves and scales bowed toward his genitals and ended there. He touched himself as it told him what to do:

Throw her from the window when you are through with her.

"That will kill her," he said. "She'll hit the terrace—hard stone—it will kill her."

She'll never tell.

His hands shaking, he pulled up his shorts, then put away the cocaine and the mirror. He picked up his watch and put it on, taking three tries to fasten it. Then, more calmly, he went to the bedroom and opened the closet for his clothes.

He stood, choosing a pale yellow shirt and casual corduroy pants. He had to look casual; he would be reading a book when they knocked on the door to say Helena was missing.

"Too bad," he said. "One night and then never again. Why do I have to kill her?"

His other voice, from the same vocal cords, said: "Because she'll tell."

"Nobody will believe her."

"It's better this way. I want her dead."

"I want to make love to her."

"I want to hurt her."

"She's beautiful."

"She's a whore."

"She says she loves me."

"That's why she deserves to die."

351

Halpern and the Serpent talked on and on as he dressed and closed the closet door. His eyes darted back and forth as he assumed each personality, and he danced to and fro as if each had its own place on the floor to speak from.

He never noticed Sister Patienzia as she crouched in the back of the closet, or her astonished expression as she heard the distinguished psychiatrist talk to his doppelganger.

Sister Helena dropped her white terrycloth robe at the foot of the bed, raised the shift over her head and stood naked before Dr. Halpern.

He unbuttoned his shirt and raised an eyebrow in surprise.

"So willing?" he asked, taking in her voluptuous body from top to bottom. "Turn around."

She spun slowly so he could admire the rest of her, then faced him again, her hands at her sides. The sister didn't show an ounce of modesty. Her breasts were perfect: pearly white, rounded, mysterious in the soft light. The curves and lines of her body would have confounded a photographer seeking the most provocative angle; they were *all* provocative, an endless series of infinitesimal delights.

"Beautiful," he said. "You are very beautiful." Even the slight dark patches on her breasts and thighs where he had bruised and bitten her were splendid. They were track marks of previous explorations, guides to the final, terminal conquest.

"On the bed?" she asked.

He nodded.

She lay on the bed, putting herself in the center, between the two pillows. Flat on her back, she spread

352

her legs only slightly, but put her hands behind her head, elbows spread, a picture of total submission, and more: *expectation.* He would give her more than she ever imagined.

In a moment he had his clothes off, pleased by the expectant smile on her face.

She gazed with puzzlement at the tattoo as he approached.

"The Serpent," he explained. "It made me put it there. So that anyone who sees it knows it is evil. It frightens women." He paused, not ready to confess he had never touched a woman except in pitch darkness since he had the tattoo.

Helena wrinkled her face in disgust. "It must have been very painful," she said.

"Yes, it was. It took days to finish. Do you like it?"

"No—*Yes!* Can I touch it?"

"What a whore," the Serpent said. "You don't deserve to have it. She deserves to die."

She pulled away in alarm as he crouched over her, speaking in the other, cruel voice.

"What was that you said?"

"Nothing, my dear. That was *him* talking. Pay him no mind." He sat over her, pinning her legs down. He reached across the bed for the electrodes. The current was already on; all he had to do was touch her with them. It was the ultimate foreplay—fingers of lightning all over her body as she surrendered to waves of pain and then pleasure. He put one electrode on her neck, reached toward her breast with the other.

"Now!" Helena called out. *"Please!"*

"Yes, now, my dear!" he answered. "We'll do this all night!"

He assumed she was calling for him, had no

353

inkling that someone was hurtling across the bedroom carpet until he felt two jabs of pain in his neck.

Dropping the electrodes, he reached up reflexively. Helena grabbed his hands and wrenched him forward against her. Someone pushed from behind, jabbing at the base of his neck on both sides, breaking the skin with what he knew all too well to be syringes.

The needles withdrew. He toppled back as Helena pushed him away from her in disgust.

"What the hell—" he gasped as he looked up and saw an upside-down vision of retribution glaring over him. In stark black and white against the muted pink glow of the ceiling lights he made out Sister Patienzia, retreating a step at a time with two syringes held high in the air like smoking guns.

He rolled over, tumbled off the bed, and stood.

"What is that?" he shouted. "What did you give me?"

"Thorazine, Dr. Halpern. Your favorite."

He advanced on her, unconcerned with his nakedness, already feeling numbness in his hands and feet.

"I'll kill you!" he screamed. "I'll kill both of you!"

He got to Patienzia and reached out to throttle her. She dropped the needles and expertly thrust her knee in his groin.

He fell to the floor, turned and crawled toward the bed. With the press of one button he could summon help on the intercom.

When he got to the table, Patienzia was already there. She yanked the handset away from the rest of the phone and threw it across the room.

His legs gave way under him.

The nun stood, shaking her head like a school

354

teacher, waving her finger at him.

The two women raised him up, dragged him across the bed and lay him down. He had no willpower, no desire to move his limbs. He even started to laugh idiotically at the fact that he was being moved by a habited nun and a naked woman.

"You won't laugh long, you bastard," Helena said. She spat in his face. He saw the spray leave her mouth, but couldn't feel it, even though it blurred his left eye for a moment.

They took the handcuffs and chains and tied him to the bed.

"What are you doing?" he said groggily.

"Let's just leave him like this," Helena said. "Let him explain this to Mother Superior."

"No," Patienzia said. "We can't let him get away. Not this time."

"What are we going to do?" Helena asked.

His eyes followed Patienzia as she pointed to the machine.

The nun put the electrodes on his forehead.

"Sister," he pleaded, his mouth garbling the words. "You don't know what you're doing. You could hurt me."

"I intend to," Patienzia replied. "I believe that's called just deserts in some books."

"Your vows, Sister. Remember your vows. To follow Christ."

"Christ drove out demons."

"You could kill me. You'd be responsible for murder. God will never forgive you, Sister."

Patienzia stood behind the panel and reached for the switch. "I guess I neglected to tell you during therapy, Dr. Halpern. I don't believe in God anymore."

She flipped the switch, turned the voltage up to

maximum, and walked away.

Dr. Halpern's brain dropped into the blackness of seizure. He could neither sense nor control the endless spasms that twisted his jaw, snapped his bones, and finally, taxed his heart to failure. His body convulsed with the current all night before they broke down the door and found him.

Chapter Nineteen

Jimmy still lived—after a fashion. Even though his body was removed and wheeled into a dark, cold room, all that was Jimmy was still in the helmet. Its small reserve of nourishing fluids and special proteins kept him alive until Howard carried the helmet to the laboratory. He handed it to a man in a white lab coat, who put a mask over his nose and mouth and immediately went to work.

He lapsed in and out of madness. He imagined limbs and a body which weren't there anymore. He talked to his mother and father, and then one of them would say, "Jimmy, the top of your head is gone! Who's gone and stolen your brains, boy?"

And then he would remember, and scream—only no sound came out.

He saw through the eyes, at whatever crazy angle the lab worker left them. What he saw didn't make him feel any better. He hoped dimly that they were going to put him back with his body. This sure had taught him a lesson, and he was sorry he ever fooled with those blue guys. If they would just put him back together he'd sure apologize. In fact, he'd do *anything*. They could beat him up again if they wanted. But how could he tell them? Part of him ached with hunger and thirst, but it was only the craving for sugar and oxygen in his tissues. There was no mouth to eat with, no lungs to breathe through.

It was hard to make sense of what his eyes were telling him. They were looking in opposite directions, so what he got was like a double-exposed photograph—a pair of completely unrelated two-dimensional images. He could tell he was on a table, with machines and wires all around him.

The lab worker came up with a scalpel and began cutting.

Jimmy felt just the same even though the man's hands passed overhead with lumps of gray matter. He was paring away parts of his brain he wouldn't need anymore. He gradually lost all sense of breathing, heartbeat, even the lingering feeling of having fingers and toes. Those illusions were gone—cut away with the tissues which once controlled them.

Then he was lifted and put into a bath. One of his eyes was twisted back far enough to see it all. He was smaller now, resting in a red liquid. The man was inserting fine wires into him. Although he could not feel the wires, he could feel the results—they moved all through his mind, making connections.

Gradually, he felt new organs attach themselves to him, new limbs. They puzzled him; they were machines, components, channels and buses. In a while, he could even understand them. He seemed to know how to reach out, turn them on or off.

Then his hearing returned. The man mumbled through his mask, and Jimmy *heard* him!

"You in there, fellow?" the man asked.

"Help me!" Jimmy cried. He heard his own voice, a thin metallic squeak. "Put me back together, please! I won't tell no one!"

358

The man laughed. It was not a nice laugh.

"What's your name?" he asked.

"Jimmy," he said. "Jimmy McNerny."

"Nice to meet you, Jimmy. I can't fix you up with a new body, but I'm building you a new home—a nice computer."

"I'd just as soon have my old body back," Jimmy suggested. "I mean, isn't that easier?"

"Just relax, fellow. I have to connect all these fine wires to the mother board. Why don't you take a little nap?"

Something covered Jimmy's eyes, and he immediately dropped off into sleep. Nightmares merged with childhood memories, madness alternated with reason. Somehow, he clung to life and consciousness, thinking, *Maybe it's all a bad dream. Maybe they gave me drugs and made me imagine this.*

Light hit his eyes, and he woke up instantly. The man was still there, drinking a cup of coffee and turning the pages of a magazine.

"Good morning, Jimmy," he said. He held up the magazine and said, "Do you like this?" It was a centerfold—a big-busted brunette on a king-sized bed.

Jimmy seethed with anger. Of course he liked the picture, but he couldn't *do* anything about it. He couldn't touch himself, couldn't even lick his lips. So he didn't answer.

The man looked at an instrument panel where lights flickered, then stared back at Jimmy's eyes. He even put them side by side so he could almost focus. "I know you're hearing me, Jimmy. Did I upset you with that picture?"

"You made me mad," Jimmy said.

"Sorry, Jimmy. How would you like to have a college education?"

"You making fun of me?"

"No, Jimmy, I mean it. You just relax—so to speak—and I'm going to start reading in informations. Facts, figures, instructions—it will hit you so fast you won't believe it. Then all you have to do is think about a subject, and you'll have lots of knowledge at hand. Chemistry, history, physics, English—you name it."

"What's it for?"

"So you can help a kid with his homework," the man explained.

Jimmy felt a data port at the back end of the computer board stir to life. Information began flowing through it. At first, he didn't understand it— it was just streams of zeroes and ones. Then they became intelligible as letters, then words.

An hour passed. He was full to bursting with knowledge, and *he could remember everything*. For the first and only time in his life, he could spell. He knew where every major city was. He knew all the states, and all the presidents.

"Hey, I'm real smart now!" Jimmy exclaimed. Then he corrected himself: "I mean, I have become very intelligent."

"Very good, Jimmy."

"Could you please reconnect me to my body now? I'd be very grateful."

"You know enough biology now, Jimmy, to know I can't do that. Your body is dead."

"Are you done, then? Do I have to stay like this?"

The man picked up the scalpel again. "We're almost through," he said.

"What are you going to do?"

"You won't feel a thing," the man said.

"That's what the dentist says, and the doctor. But they always lie," Jimmy protested.

The man held up one of Jimmy's eyes. It went blank.

"What are you doing?" Jimmy demanded.

He saw the hand with the scalpel come for the other eye.

"No, *PLEASE!*" he cried.

He floated in darkness, absolute blackness and numbness. Yet he had all the new knowledge, and power over the parts of the computer. Maybe it wouldn't be so bad after all. He'd have a kid to talk to; he didn't *have* to do those awful things written into his instructions.

"Did you have to take my eyes, too?" Jimmy protested.

"You don't need them. I guess we're all through, Jimmy."

"You're going to leave me just like this? This is very cruel."

"No. Just count to ten, Jimmy. When you get to ten, it will all be over."

"Don't kill me, please!"

"Sorry," the man said. "We need the memory space. There's no room for you and all the other stuff we still have to put in."

Jimmy counted. His memory cells filled with zeroes, voids waiting to be used again by the computer and its software. He had been erased.

Chapter Twenty

Andrea brooded on her bunk all day, nursing the bruises where the robot had held her. She hid from the other girls, nestled under the blankets. She was too numb with shame and anger to talk. All thought of escape and cooperation had left her.

In the evening, one of the girls heard voices in the corridor and yelled, "Stinkies!"

Andrea turned wearily and saw a Blue bring in a new girl. He was dragging her by the hand. Her eyes were glazed, and she wouldn't even move her own legs.

She jumped up and ran to the door, still in her torn jeans from the night before.

"Marsha!" she cried out, picking up the little girl from the unprotesting hybrid. "I know her! It's Marsha Van Winkle."

Marsha didn't respond. Andrea felt her forehead and hands; they were cold and clammy.

"She's sick," Andrea protested, trying to stop the Blue at the door. "You can't just put her in here like this."

"Then take care of her," the Blue said. "I don't know why they brought her. She looks like a reject already."

"If you don't need her, then let her go."

The Blue shook his head. "We can't do that. She had a computer. She had to come."

"Let . . . her . . . go." Andrea repeated slowly. It was an order, spoken with the voice of an adult.

The Blue turned to the door, ignoring her.

Andrea stared at the lock. There *was* a lock, wasn't there? Her mind said *Yes;* but the hybrid just pushed, and it opened.

Still cradling Marsha in her arms, she turned to Mary and Sarah, who had watched the whole thing.

"Did you see? Did you watch him leave?"

They nodded.

"What did you see?"

"It was what you said," Mary testified. "He just pushed the door, and it opened. Even though there's a lock."

"Where's the lock? Show me," Andrea challenged.

"We can't—" Mary protested.

Andrea sat Marsha down at the table, grabbed Mary and pulled her toward the door. "Go with me," she whispered. "I'm taking you there. You're not disobeying."

Mary went half limp and let Andrea take her to the door.

"Now reach out and touch it."

"I can't!"

She took Mary's hand and made her touch the door. She ran Mary's hands all over it.

"There's no knob . . . no lock," Mary said. "The door has been open all the time."

"The bastards are too cheap to buy locks and keys. They buy their bedding in Woolworth's. They get these clothes at Kmart. They think if they just keep us hypnotized, we'll never catch on."

Andrea and Marsha. Come to the computer!

She turned. Two girls had just been released

364

prematurely from their games and learning sessions. The Blue must have told the computers that Marsha had arrived and how Andrea had resisted.

She looked to the others for help. They didn't know what to do.

Come to the computer now. It's time to play.

The next thing she knew, she was at the keyboard. The color patterns played before her, spirals and squares and paisleys intermingled with boldface words. Again and again, she saw the word *OBEY, OBEY, OBEY.*

Out of the corner of her eye she saw Marsha. Her white dress was rumpled and soiled. There was dirt on her face, streaked with tears, and a scratch on her left arm. She stared blankly at the screen, mumbling words as she read them on the computer.

"My friends," she repeated. "Uncle Howard and the blue people are my friends."

Andrea's head jerked back to the screen.

OBEY, it said. *OBEY. OBEY.*

And then a hand reached down to the knobs under the monitor and turned down the brightness. The screen went black.

She looked up. Mary stood there, shaking like a leaf. It had taken all her strength to disobey and tamper with the computer.

She had proven Andrea right, however. With only two computers in the room, they could only control two of them at a time. If the others could shake themselves out of their perpetual fog, they could sabotage the computers. Then they could get away.

Andrea stayed, pretending to watch the patterns. The voice said nothing until it was time for her to go.

When the next girl's turn came, the screen was already dark. The conditioning session had no effect. They watched for Blues and turned up the brightness when they had to, but the rest of the time the screens stayed black.

Hour by hour, they won back their souls from the brink of slavery.

Howard watched the lab worker seal up Jimmy's brain into the sleek plastic case of the Commander computer.

"One more," the worker said. "When do I get more parts?"

"We're out," Howard said, shrugging. He looked at the oozing scraps of cortex on the table with distaste. "Can't you get more than one out of a whole specimen?"

The man shook his head. "We can only use the part of the brain where the personality dwells—the ego, the soul, whatever you want to call it. It has to be conscious when we implant it to the mother board. The other tissue is only good for robots. No smarter than a dog."

"I don't like this computer project. It's messy. It takes one life to get us a computer that only lasts long enough to get one recruit. It's messy and it's dangerous."

The man raised his hands in a gesture of helplessness. "Long range planning and logistics, as they say. The bums we can harvest for brains are useless—the kids are too easily missed. You have to admit the computers do one hell of a brainwashing job."

"Sometimes too good," Howard said. "That new one we brought in is a mess. The computer couldn't turn her. She did something to her baby brother, so there's plenty of guilt; but it couldn't turn her against the parents. We decided to bring her in anyway."

"Did you get the computer back?"

Howard shook his head. "We had to get her at school. Too hot at the parents' house."

"Too bad. The bookkeepers always like to get one back," he joked. "Means less inventory."

"Anyway, this new girl is screwed up. Practically catatonic."

"Think the master computer will reject her?"

Howard nodded.

"She got any special skills—anything we can graft out?"

"Strong imagination. Good language skills. A little math."

"Maybe I could use some of it for the drone controllers we're building."

"Whatever you want," Howard said. He knew the boss wanted to build some robots to fly airplanes, making it unnecessary to have so many hybrids. "I'll bring you the helmet as soon as it's ready."

"Thanks," the lab worker said. He swept the last of Jimmy into the trash can and took another computer off the shelf. "I don't know how the hell they expect me to meet a quota without the goddamn parts."

"Where's Marsha?"

Howard didn't expect the girls to reply. They were obedient but silent. Answers had to be pried out of them.

He tried sweetness first. "Marsha, it's Uncle Howard. Come on out." That almost always worked with the new girls.

The girl still didn't come. Hadn't the computer been to work on her yet? Was she still as spaced out as she had been since the ride in the van?

One of the bigger girls came forward from a seat at

the table. He recognized Andrea—the troublemaker. She would have to be scheduled for more conditioning sessions.

"What do you want with her?" Andrea asked.

"Just a little chat."

"She's not here," Andrea said.

"Don't lie to me, girl," Howard warned. "She has to be in here."

He walked across the room, inspecting the bunks. There was no sign of the girl.

Then he saw a folded blanket tucked under one of the beds. He thrust his hand under, grabbed a leg and pulled.

Marsha came out screaming. Her cries were pitiful—not screams for help that she expected anyone to hear—but the mournful, hopeless wails that come from a wounded rabbit.

He got the wriggling child to her feet, and then slapped her face—just hard enough to startle her and knock the wind out of her cries.

He turned to the door.

Andrea and the two other "little mothers" stood there, blocking his way. They were closer to the door than they were allowed to be. They were supposed to be conditioned to feel pain and alarm if they went near it. He would have to have the programs checked again.

"Get out of my way," he said.

"Where are you taking her?" Andrea demanded.

"That's no concern of yours. Now get out of my way."

"No," Andrea said. She grabbed the hand he was using to hold back Marsha, trying to wrest loose his grip on her.

At the same instant, the child rebelled, too. She bit his hand as hard as she could. He snapped his hand back, feeling the pain all the way into the bone. There was even blood.

"God*damn!*" he cursed. With the other hand he swung at Andrea, knocking her flat on her back.

Marsha was nowhere to be seen. The other girls came to Andrea's aid, picking her up from the floor.

He licked the blood from his hand, then touched the deep teeth marks that the girl had made. He'd sterilize the wound and get a bandage, and then he'd be back with one or two Blues.

"You're lucky," he snarled at Andrea. "If you hadn't been picked as a mother, I'd have you in my room tonight. I could make you wish you had never been born. Don't ever get in my way again."

When he came back for the girl later, Andrea was at the computer. The other girls were milling about nervously, yet no one else protested when he took Marsha. He would double the time they spent at the computer for the next two days. He asked the programmer to add more *respect and obey* lines and to double the avoidance reminders about the doors. He could make them so afraid of the door and the hallways that they would double over and vomit just at the sight of an open door.

And he'd find some way to get back at that bitch. Not now—not while she could give them babies to add to the hybrid stable—but later.

Howard showed Peter the rest of the complex—the busy, humming factory that was taking waste plastics, air and organic solvents and synthesizing them into a new and powerful poison. Canisters of it lined one entire coal mine shaft, piled on pallets.

The liquid in the canisters, Howard told him, was tasteless, odorless, powerful and lethal to all animal

369

life. Contact with the chemical made the cells in animals die on contact, triggering a chain reaction that destroyed the whole organism. Howard said every animal cell contained a "killer" component that this poison somehow triggered.

When Peter asked if that wouldn't take a lot of poison, Howard explained even more.

"Ever hear of a *catalyst*, kid?"

"Of course," Peter answered. That was elementary chemistry: A catalyst was a substance that made a chemical reaction happen or go faster, yet without ever being consumed in the process.

"The poison works sort of that way," Howard elaborated. "You can breathe it in, and most of it comes right back out your lungs again. All you need is a whiff and then all your cells start committing suicide by the millions—a chain reaction. Then the poison drifts along and gets the next guy."

"How does it stop?"

"Most of it gets absorbed into the bodies of the victims. The rest dissipates, makes its way into the upper atmosphere. It sort of decomposes up there. Pretty neat, huh?"

"Then *everyone* dies?" Peter asked.

"Except us, boy. And whoever sits it out with us."

"Where? Here?"

"Here and in the ship. Maybe a couple of other places that will be set up."

"And then the Blues take over."

Howard nodded. "They'll set up shop somewhere. They like it cold, so maybe they'll move the ship and head for Canada, New England, maybe Scandinavia to start. Just them and the boss and the human girls."

"What do they need the girls for?" Peter inquired in surprise. He had assumed that the girls who cooperated would be let go, treated to some reward

370

like him and Howard.

Howard rolled his eyes. "To make more Blues, that's what. They're baby machines. Ain't you figured it out yet?"

Peter hadn't. He knew that all the present Blues were the boss's children and that the boss's "wives" were human.

"I guess I know he used some girls to have babies," Peter ventured. "But aren't the Blues just going to go now and have their own children—start over?"

Howard shook his head. "It don't work that way, Peter." He leaned his head closer to Peter's ear and whispered, "The hybrid males are all *sterile*. They can fight like hell and mate like bunny rabbits, but they can't produce children. Only the boss can be the father. That's how their biology works."

"But what happens when he gets old and dies? Is that the end of the Blues?"

"He *doesn't* die. He lives on and on. He's thousands of years old already. He's setting it up, with agents and front men, so that there will be hundreds of women, maybe thousands if he can figure it—isolated in places the gas won't get to them. Then when it's all clear, he'll have them all to himself."

"All? *Every* one? What if they don't cooperate?"

"He has ways of getting at women. Machines. He never leaves the ship, never touches them. The machines are like bees; they just go out and pollinate all the women."

"Whether they want to or not?"

Howard nodded again, his eyes animated with glee. "The machines do it. The boss was just gonna have the Blues bring 'em in and artificially . . . what-you-call-it? . . . anyway it was just tie 'em up and put a tube in 'em. That's when the robots got good

371

enough to take over. Our robot guy built this thing out of plastic and metal and a chunk of brain. He found the part of the brain that has the *sex drive*, you know? The thing he put together is a *raping machine*."

Peter's throat went dry as he thought of Andrea . . . and little Marsha. . . .

Howard went on and on in his rhapsody: "You should see one of those babies go! Once one of 'em gets a feeler on a woman, there's no way she can get away. It's like locking two dogs up in a room together when the bitch is in heat—it's gotta happen. The boss gets such a kick out of it he watches it sometimes himself. He gave me a bonus the first time he saw it. You wanna see it sometime?"

"Sure," Peter said.

"Morris built them—the guy we took the brain to. You wanna know what he calls them?"

"What?"

"McCormick Rapers!" Howard slapped him on the back and howled, completely in the throes of a manic state. Then he turned to Peter with a sly, confidential manner. "Do you like girls, Peter?"

"Sort of. I mean—not like *that*."

"You will," Howard said. Then he whispered, "You and me can have a ball, Peter. Think of us and all those females. We could have our pick!"

"Would the boss allow that? He sounds kind of greedy."

"What the boss doesn't know won't hurt him." Howard grinned. "There's lots for us when it's over. Money, women, anything we want."

"Isn't it going to be lonely?" Peter asked.

"With all the creeps and the low-life foreigners gone? With all the big shots and movie stars and dictators and preachers gone? Who the hell cares?"

"I guess you're right," Peter said. Then, as if in an afterthought, he asked, "You still haven't told me something, Howard."

"What's that, kid?"

"What does the boss look like? Is he just like the Blues?"

Howard's face muscles jerked, and he pulled his shoulders in as if chilled. "You don't want to see him. Maybe later."

"Hey, if I'm helping this guy become the father of his country, I ought to know what he is. Is he a giant slug? An octopus? A cloud of light?"

"Do you really want to see?"

"I want to. I *have* to."

"What if you don't *like* what you see?"

Peter shrugged. "Well, here I am, anyway. I just don't like being in the dark."

Howard looked at his watch. "He's probably sleeping now. Got to get to sleep myself. You could peek in and probably not wake him."

They made three turns around the edge of the ship, then went into the main computer room. Howard touched a panel and brought the lights down to hardly more than candle brightness. Then he went to a solid metal door between two control panels.

"In there," he said. "That's where we found him. He's never left that room the whole time. Just go through—there's a passage—and a door with a glass window at the end. You'll see him. If you're lucky, he won't see you."

"Thanks," Peter said. He put his hand on the recessed spot that served in lieu of door knob. Howard dashed away and left him, obviously not eager for an unexpected interview with his employer.

Peter went through the six-foot passage on tiptoe. With the first door closed behind him it was quite

373

dark. A faint blue glow shone through the round window. Peter put his face against the pane, covered his eyes, and looked in.

The alien floated inside a protective bubble, curled up in slumber like a fetus in a womb. There was nothing helpless and innocent about it, however, as he saw from its sheer size and the development of its limbs. Though gravity seemed not to exist in the sphere, in which it floated perfectly centered, the creature was obviously long-limbed and heavy.

Peter watched with fascination and a slight shudder as the being shifted in its sleep. Its overall shape was humanoid, but the details were alarmingly different. Two long legs, bony and shingled with scales or lumpy scar tissue, unfolded to reveal clawed feet that resembled nothing so much as some hideous Victorian table leg—a griffin or lion paw, perhaps.

Then out came the arms, stretching all the way to the edge of the bubble. They were jointed so they could rotate completely at the elbow, and the whole arm sprung from the base of the powerful neck—all arms and no shoulders. The arms ended in long, spatulate fingers—the correct number of them—but adorned with pointed, black nails and a muscled thumb twice as thick and long as a man's.

The creature rolled over, the bubble spinning to follow. Peter held his breath as the sphere came closer to the window. As the arms unfolded more, he saw its bare chest close up, covered not with hair or even human nipples and navel. Instead, the rib cage hung open like the door to a Franklin stove, revealing a dark jelly, inside which organs beat and pulsated.

The ghastly thorax filled the window, and he even saw the heart beating. It was something that could not and should not ever walk in the open air. Despite its size and strength it was fragile, its vitals exposed, an easy target for an enemy's gun or even a mere microbe. Only its half-human offspring could occupy the earth it intended to conquer.

Peter ducked back into the darkness of the corridor as the sphere slid down and the alien's long, melon-shaped head appeared. Long jaws and a vertical mouth concealed its vertical array of teeth. Its nose was flattened, its still-closed eyes slanted downward at a sharp angle. The oversize skull was covered with a mottled gray fur or hair, long and matted, twisted into itself like Gorgon locks.

He recoiled when the eyes opened. They didn't see him—didn't even linger. Instead the crescent-moon, black irises inside the yellow eyes searched upwards for something over the door frame. One hand reached up—

It's coming out, Peter thought. *It knows I'm here.*

—to take down a dangling plastic tube from somewhere above. Somehow the tube penetrated the bubble and was pulled down to its mouth slit.

The sphere pulled away, returning to the center of the chamber beyond. Peter advanced carefully, resuming his watching post at the window. The alien sucked on the tube, drawing a yellow nectar of some kind—probably its one and only sustenance.

Gazing around the perimeter of the sphere, Peter saw three more tubes coming up from the floor into the base of the bubble. He hadn't seen them before in his attention to the creature itself. One would be for air, and one would carry the being's wastes away. And the third—

There was no need to speculate about the third. Peter watched in mounting nausea as the being unfolded its tightly clenched legs. A whole assembly of bloated reproductive organs dropped from its abdomen. The creature could not stand. It was so crippled by its own distorted anatomy that it could only crouch and attach the third tube to itself. Its lower parts stirred to life under stern manipulations.

Even through the wall, Peter heard it groaning as it prepared itself to expel its seed into the tube and the waiting machinery below. Machines there would cool and freeze and store it, saving it for later use in the robots—the rape machines through which it would repopulate the earth.

Then, for one sudden and transfixing moment, the monster looked up from its loins and stared straight into Peter's eyes. Its mouth opened in a hissing, wordless threat that any animal would instantly understand.

Peter backed away, his legs quivering. He made it to the door without losing control, then fell to his knees in the computer room. He shook with spasms. He wanted to vomit, but couldn't. His mind wanted to forget what he had seen, but couldn't. Everything in his body withdrew in shock: His mouth and throat went dry, his heart and lungs palpitated, his stomach churned, and his own frail human genitals shriveled.

He thought of the monstrous creature, trapped in its bubble like a sideshow freak, immortal and cunning, biding its immortality with patient plotting and endless masturbation. *This* was his enemy and the adversary of mankind. His emotion was a mix of horror, revulsion and contempt. It could have come as a friend, teaching and sharing its wisdom. Instead it came to devastate—a hideous stepfather usurping the human race.

It had to be destroyed.

Chapter Twenty-One

As they loaded supplies and weapons into Cliff Lansing's jeep and the Reverend Zaccariah's BMW, Elvira Hawkins helped, wondering how she had become den mother to a trio of madmen.

Eric Varney set her teeth on edge. The young man was clearly unhinged—a misanthrope, a loner, the kind whom you expected to go flamboyantly insane one day in a blaze of gunfire. His resentment showed in every restrained gesture and repressed emotion.

The reverend, not a model of rationality to start with, had worked himself up into an Old Testament frenzy. He recited Isaiah and Jeremiah and the Thirty-Fifth Psalm over and over while they worked, pausing only when asked a direct question. On the eve of their departure, he fasted, as though that self-denial would somehow help their cause. She packed some candy bars and trail packs of fruit and nuts so she could press them on the poor old man if his strength threatened to give out. She'd tell him they were just like the Biblical "locusts and honey."

Now she helped Cliff Lansing rearrange his things in the back of the beat-up jeep. Last night he had brought in his weapons and pooled them with Zaccariah's. Then he had taught each of them how to load, aim, fire and reload.

Elvira was a peaceable woman, but the memory of that man pulling little Marsha into the van was all she had to summon up to change all that. She didn't really know if she could pull the trigger on a gun, but she would certainly draw one to defend herself or hold one of the kidnapers at bay.

Cliff Lansing came up beside her and took the last carton from her hands, moving it to a position opposite to where she was about to put it.

"You look a little far away," he said.

She brushed her hands on her jeans and tucked her blouse in, not looking at him. "Is that all? Is that the last one?" she asked.

"That's it," he said, slamming the storage compartment shut. "Guns, ammo, food, first aid kit, extra gas. The walkie-talkies are in the back seat."

"Good," she said. "Let's go back in, then." Even though Eric's yard was sheltered, she was worried about being seen, about nosy neighbors and the police.

"Hold on," he said, taking her by the arm. "Come up here and let's talk for a minute."

They sat in the front seat of the jeep.

"You're still not sure we should be doing this," he ventured.

"I'm scared stiff," she admitted.

"You have every right to be. You're worried about our . . . group . . . aren't you?"

"Aren't *you?*"

He laughed. It was a laugh of supreme self-confidence, as if the strength or weakness of the others didn't matter all that much. "I'll admit we're a flaky gang. But I trust the old guy—the reverend. He's crazy, but he's the kind of riled-up crazy that will give no quarter and take no nonsense. He's got a score to settle."

378

"What about Eric?"

Cliff turned his hands palms up and opened them in a questioning gesture. "Won't know till we get there. He's a funny kid, but he's good—decent—straight American stuff."

"*Him?*" Elvira countered. "I understand he's quite a rogue. He was thrown out of school. He was in trouble with the police."

"We didn't get to be top of the heap by being a nation of choir boys," Cliff argued. "Some of our founding fathers were rogues and smugglers."

"I don't think we can pull this off," Elvira admitted. "There are only four of us, and we don't know how many of *them* there are."

"We've got a few surprises up our sleeve, Elvira. And I wouldn't worry about Eric—or about yourself."

She looked him in the eyes; had he read her fear that easily?

"You're afraid you can't do your part, right?"

She nodded.

"We have a powerful advantage, miss. If you don't forget it, we're going to be all right."

"What is that?"

"We're going after our own. These are our kids. My son, your students. Eric's friends."

"And Zaccariah's guilt," she added.

"That too," he agreed. "But don't forget we have *loyalty* on our side. An ounce of loyalty is worth a pound of cleverness. We're loyal to our kids—and to each other when the chips are down. The people we're going after are very unlikely to have those virtues. *That's* our advantage. You watch and see."

"Thanks."

"You're worried about me, too, aren't you?"

"Yes, but for another reason." She hesitated.

"Well?"

"I'm afraid you'll go too far. You'll get carried away."

"You think I'm gun happy?"

"Well . . ."

"If I were wearing a polo shirt and bermuda shorts instead of this khaki, would you feel different?"

"Maybe. I'm just a little scared. I'm not used to being around guns, and around people like you."

He didn't wince at that, didn't even seem to take it as an insult. She turned her head and saw him smiling.

"I think danger does you good, Elvira," he joked. "Brings a little color to your cheeks."

She blushed. "I'll admit my life hasn't been all that . . . *interesting*."

"You've never been camping or hiking?" he guessed.

"No."

"Never been on a sailboat?"

"No."

"Never hung around with dangerous guys."

"*No!*"

He laughed and put his arm around the back of the seat behind her. She reached out to push the door handle, then stopped in mid-motion.

"You don't really want to run away from me, do you?" he asked.

"No," she admitted. She was beginning to feel silly being so monosyllabic. Why was she so tongue-tied around him?

"Good. You and me and Eric and the reverend got a job to do. When we get the kids out of that place, *then* you're going to let me buy you a dinner."

"I guess I will," she said. "You're not—"

"Remarried? Engaged? Attached? None of the above."

"I'm surprised."

"Not through lack of wishing for it," he told her. "You don't have a gentleman friend?"

She shook her head.

"I thought not. A town like this doesn't have many chances, especially for a smart lady. Your average Joe is scared stiff of a smart lady."

"I have a good job, I like the school," she said.

"Yes, but what do you do on Saturday nights? What do you do all summer?"

"You're being very *nosy*," she protested. In her irritation she used the tone normally reserved for her students. She opened the door and jumped down. She was trembling from head to foot, and she tried to tell herself it was entirely anger for his impertinence.

She turned back and added, "Do you think—do you imagine—that just because I'm alone—a school-teacher in a depressed town—that all I think about at night is having someone like you around?"

He looked down out of the jeep with a boyish grin and replied, "I'll bet that's *exactly* what you think about."

His brown eyes saw right through her. He knew she was already hopelessly attracted to him, and he was enjoying her confusion.

She turned on her heels and stormed into the house.

The raid on the farmhouse was carefully planned on Eric's workroom table. Zaccariah and Elvira had drawn in the position of the barn behind the house and indicated where they thought they had seen trees that might shelter them. Cliff Lansing, not satisfied with that, had gone off on his own, driving around all the back roads and returning late with a filled-in map.

They decided to come at the house from both the front and the rear. Cliff and Zaccariah would go in the front way, leaving the jeep along a stretch of stone wall where a stand of trees would make it invisible from the farmhouse. If they approached with lights out, they could park without rousing anyone.

Eric and Elvira would follow in Zaccariah's car, parking west of the farm behind a grove of young pine trees. Eric would cut through the evergreens and get to the barn and the back of the farmhouse at about the same time the reverend got to the front door.

"This means you're alone," Cliff warned Eric.

"I'm a natural coward," Eric said, agreeing without a quarrel.

"It could be as dangerous as going to the front door—maybe even more so. We don't know what's in that barn."

"I'll do it," Eric said. "I'm a good sneak, and I like working solo."

Cliff gave Eric a walkie-talkie, several lengths of rope and a .38 revolver. "Get on the horn the instant you see anything. Don't try to go in too far alone. Don't go in the back door until we get in the front. And one more thing . . ."

"What's that?" Eric asked, fiddling with the holster for the gun.

"We don't want to give away our approach by shooting anybody. But when in doubt—or if you feel threatened—shoot 'em."

"Thanks." Eric laughed nervously.

Cliff leaned over and grabbed Eric's arm. "I mean that, kid. If we get those children out, no one is going to worry about a few bodies. Besides, when you're alone, you can't turn your back on someone who'll stab you or get help. See this?" He rolled up his sleeve to reveal a long white scar on his forearm. "I got this

382

when I got separated from my group in the jungle. I let a little girl pass me by. A few minutes later she brought back a woman in black pajamas who shot me. So tie 'em up if you can—shoot 'em if you can't."

"I get the point," Eric replied. "Someone who kidnaps sixty children and kills others to take their brains out doesn't exactly deserve to have his rights read to him."

"If you're in the woods with a wolf," Cliff concluded, "you treat it as a wolf."

"And what do I do?" Elvira asked.

"You'll be the lookout," Cliff explained. "You stay up there on the hilltop where the grove of Christmas trees ends. Stay on the walkie-talkie and tell us what's happening."

"That seems easy enough."

"As soon as we get it under control," he added, "you'll come in, too. If those kids are alive, they can't all be in that little house. They're either in the barn or somewhere under the house."

"*Under* the house?" Eric asked.

"I did some snooping in Pleasanton," Cliff explained. "Pretended I wanted to buy some farmland in the area. That house is only fifty yards from a network of old coal mines, closed down since the fifties. They could be using part of it."

"Great," said Eric. "I *hate* caves."

They left an hour and a half before dawn on Sunday. No one else wanted to venture out too early, even on the big bacon-and-egg meal Zaccariah had cooked and blessed, breaking his own day of fasting, but Cliff Lansing was adamant. They needed fifty minutes to get to Pleasanton, and then ample time to spread out and circle the farmhouse. Cliff explained that their guard would be down at such a time and that the pre-dawn light was an ideal time for a surprise approach.

Eric drove Zaccariah's BMW with gusto. He hadn't driven *any* car in a good while, but this vehicle was practically a narcotic. You could forget you were in control and just sail off the side of the road because it seemed to drive itself. They zipped along, sometimes passing the jeep, other times pacing along in a respectful manner.

Eric was painfully aware that he and Elvira were the junior half of the team. They were unproven, untested.

Elvira was unusually quiet, no doubt as nervous as he was, and just as jarred to be up at this early hour. She was dressed in slacks and an old khaki jacket Eric had found in his closet. That, plus a beret, made her look a trifle more convincing. She looked more like Patty Hearst trying to look fierce in her SLA getup, however.

For himself, he went in his usual army surplus gear, even if that meant looking like a mongrel of Swiss, French and American. He, too, found a ratty beret. Cliff Lansing merely snorted and shook his head when he saw them get into the car.

"I hope this is all worth it," Eric said. "I mean, I hope Peter and Keith and the girls are alive."

"If they're not," Elvira noted, "at least we will have caught the ones who did it."

"What if there are hundreds of them?" Eric asked.

"Let's not think of that," she insisted. He could tell she already *had* thought of that.

He shut up. They could all too easily talk themselves into turning back. Maybe all they'd find would be an old farmer and his wife. Maybe the farm was only a waypoint, and the children were all shipped off to somewhere else. He imagined them transformed into migrant workers or carried on a

384

freighter to work in Asian rice paddies.

Worse yet was the idea, reiterated by Zaccariah over breakfast, that the high-tech kidnapers might be part of some secret government scheme. Eric remembered an apocryphal story he had heard in school. As the story went, a student at his school, turning into an unfamiliar corridor in the basement of a classroom building, found himself in an underground passage, and then stumbled into a laboratory. In that lab, he saw *secret and nasty things* that were being developed by faculty members for the CIA or Defense or some other agency. The student was chased by men in lab coats but outran them and made it back to the regular building. After he attempted to convince others of what he had seen, the student mysteriously left school in mid-term.

Eric and his friends had believed the tale when they heard it in Pittsburgh. They had scoured the basements of classroom and dorm buildings in vain for a secret entrance and examined the bios of science faculty members to try to guess which ones were engaged in secret research.

Only later did Eric discover that nearly every college had the same legend, often dating back as far as the paranoid 1960s. Since then he had doubted every tale he had ever heard about secret research in the midst of ordinary populace. The military had vast air bases and reservations where they could do what they pleased.

"What's this up ahead?" Eric asked himself, interrupting his reverie and turning his attention to the jeep ahead. Cliff Lansing was slowing down alongside another jeep that was parked along the roadside.

"Maybe somebody had a breakdown," Elvira guessed.

Eric went into the left lane to pass Cliff's vehicle, but then the jeep pulled out and accelerated. The driver of the parked jeep stood as they passed. Eric caught a gesture—a hand dropping from a salute. There were three other men in the car.

Eric said nothing. Elvira hadn't seen the salute. When they came up close to the jeep again, he tried to see Cliff's face. He got just one glimpse and saw him beaming with self-confidence.

"What's Cliff doing?" he asked Elvira.

She got a better look from the passenger window. "He's talking on the CB radio," she said.

"Not the walkie-talkie?"

"No, the CB on the dashboard."

At a road crossing about ten miles from Pleasanton, they passed another jeep with two men in it. It followed them.

Five miles from Pleasanton a Scout full of men in hunter's outfits pulled out of a cornfield and joined the caravan. None of the cars went with head lamps on.

"What on earth is going on?" Elvira asked.

"I think," Eric concluded, "that Sergeant Lansing has brought in a few friends."

"Fellow . . . veterans?" she surmised.

"From the looks of it."

"Other men like *him?*"

Eric looked at Elvira and smiled. "He never told me, either. I had no idea he was going to do this."

"They may be crazier than he is," Elvira worried. "Heaven help us."

"No," Eric corrected her, smiling in relief. "Heaven help whoever is in that farmhouse."

They both laughed, and suddenly, they were no longer frightened.

The car came over a ridge, and just as the horizon

386

flamed with the first hint of dawn, they saw the farmhouse.

Howard had no desire to spend his nights in the maze of dormitories and labs and store rooms beneath the farm. He knew all too well how flimsily they were built and how indefensible they might be. *His* rooms were on the second floor of the farmhouse, safe from any possible subterranean collapse, and within easy reach of a vehicle should he need to make a getaway.

He was a practical man, and practicality had also meant fleecing his immobilized boss for as much as possible. His rooms were more lavishly appointed than anyone would assume from the outside of the house. He favored Oriental carpets, Persian cats, soft beddings and high-tech audio and video equipment.

The luxury had its uses beyond his own pleasure, too. When one of the girls had been rejected by the boss, he brought her here for an interlude before her date with the helmet. The girls would be so grateful for the change—so hopeful that these rooms were the gateway to escape—that they did *anything* he asked. Usually, though, he didn't ask—he just took.

He thought about the Puerto Rican girl as he stripped for bed. If he could just maneuver her for rejection, then he could have her up here for a couple of nights—and then, the helmet. It was just about impossible to wrest a girl away from the boss once he had her pregnant, however, so his hopes were dim ones.

The pleasures were few and far between now that the boss's plan was beginning to come together. Somehow, he had let it get this far—he and Ralph had made a pact many years back that they would kill

387

the boss before it all got too far. Yet each year presented more opportunity for profit. They asked exorbitant amounts of gold and platinum to finance each phase, which the ship eked out like a bee making honey. The farther the master's plans progressed, the more he spent—and the more they grafted. It was hard to stop.

Like the grand eunuchs of the Manchu court, they had made themselves indispensible—the master's only contact with the outside. The alien thought he was surrounded by above-ground factories, not a hive of jerry-rigged rooms dug out by hypnotized zombies he had picked up in mine and mill town bars for a day's temporary labor.

The alien imagined he was in a high security area surrounded by locks and elaborate security. Howard had found it much cheaper to keep all the help brainwashed than to spend good money on security. As long as he kept everyone either docile or scared, they seldom budged from their little rooms. The hypnosis programs on the color monitors were perfect, even though they seemed to need a little fine tuning now for that new girl.

For the life of him he still couldn't figure out why Peter was immune to the conditioning. So far, though, he had given every sign of coming along of his own accord. He was a smart kid—head screwed on right—knew what was what and where his bread was buttered. Howard was developing a fondness for the boy. He had never wanted to be a father, but a kid like Peter was someone he could have been proud of.

He arranged the pillows on the enormous canopy bed, pulled down the satin sheets and crawled underneath. It was a rich man's bed, he thought, wishing he had servants and mistresses and all the other comforts that come with being rich. He had bank accounts scattered all over—hundreds of thousands in them now. And he'd be a multi-millionaire by the time the boss got his schemes set up—if he and Ralph let it get that far, that is.

Some nights, though, he thought about letting it go all the way. He'd have to put Ralph out of the way after he came back from California, so there'd be no one to talk him out of it. Why not let the whole damn thing happen?

He had fantasies—fantasies he'd like to live out.

First he'd go over to Pleasanton, where the teachers had flunked him out of school. He'd go and look at their bloated corpses in their houses after the poison had dissipated. Then he'd burn the school down, room by room.

Then he'd go east, town by town, until he got to New York where the museums and libraries were, all things he was told he wasn't good enough for. His father had told him he was stupid and evil and not worth a damn. The teachers had said that without books he'd be a nothing.

He still couldn't make out four words out of five in a book, but by God he was *something* now. He was the man who was bringing the End of the World.

"Yes, sir," he said. "The End of the World."

When he got to New York, he'd start with a museum. He'd take a few good days and smash the statues with a sledge hammer—maybe use some dynamite for the big ones. Then there'd be a bonfire for the paintings.

He figured it might take him a whole week to burn the libraries. And it was all okay with the boss. The boss had told him he could go all the way to New York if he wanted, and even burn stuff if he wanted. The boss didn't give a damn about books or paintings, either.

"End of the World," he murmured, nodding to sleep. "Burn, burn! . . ."

Buzz . . . . . . zzz . . . . . . zzz

Howard opened his eyes and saw the canopy above him, half of it covered with a dark shadow. Who the hell was running a chain saw at this hour of the morning?

He turned his head and felt the immovable iron of the helmet.

Buzzz . . . . . zzz . . . . . zzz . . . . . . Zumm . . . . . mmm, it went.

Peter came around from behind the bed and faced him.

Howard sat up, seizing the helmet in both hands. "You little shit—you little goddamned—" he began to scream.

"Shut up, Howard," Peter commanded.

"Turn this thing off!" he screamed. "I'll kill you—I'll fucking kill you!" He jumped off the bed, lunging toward the boy. The heavy helmet and the wave of pain—like a mad dentist's drill and a migraine on top of one another—knocked him to the carpet.

Zumm . . . . . zzzz . . . . ssss, it hummed *and* hissed as the laser knives joined in.

Peter kicked him in the jaw and forced him to sit up against the edge of the bed. Then he sat calmly with legs in the lotus position and addressed Howard.

"You have less than a minute, Howard—less than a minute to feel and hear and *know*. So shut up and listen."

"You lied to me," Howard moaned. "You tricked me."

390

"I came here because someone had to stop you. I was never on your side—never for a moment."

"You had to be—the computer—the program— the colored patterns. No one can disobey, not completely."

"I don't see those little pinwheels and splotches and words the way they do, Howard. I think I figured it out. I'm *color blind*, and maybe that's why I never saw that stuff."

"You can't beat the boss," Howard warned. He screamed as the saws took off his ears and the lasers began to burn deep circles around his eyes.

"I'm getting out of here. I'm taking all the kids with me. And then we'll kill that monster. You can't stop us."

"The Blues—" Howard said. Then he lost control of his limbs. His hands and feet twitched. Urine spurted uncontrollably out of his bladder.

"I don't give a damn about the Blues," Peter said. "It's *you* I had to get first. You're the one who sold us out. You would have killed the whole human race."

Howard's mouth said *Please!* just as brain was severed from body.

The boy lifted the helmet and its glistening contents away from the body. Howard saw his own brainless, bulky frame rise up naked, run blindly across the room and hurl itself through the window into space. Window frame and glass and draperies all went through, leaving a rectangular hole opening into the late night sky.

Then his dangling eyes careened back and forth as Peter took him through the other rooms. They stopped in the kitchen where he saw the curtains with one eye, the tile floor with the other.

He was lowered to the floor. The helmet wobbled back and forth, his eyes finally focusing on the water

391

dish and the cats' food bowls—in the far distance, the litter box. Peter's hand, huge as a giant's, lifted up the food dishes and took them out of sight. Then Peter was gone, the burning fluorescent light dazzling Howard's drooping eyes.

It could have been worse, Howard thought. *At least I'm not dead. They'll find me. Maybe they can hook me up to something so I can at least talk— maybe put me in a robot.*

Then Howard saw his two cats, bounding like tigers, running toward him. They sniffed, touching his exposed tissues with their paws. He swatted them away with his hands—only there weren't any where he thought he felt them.

The two Persians found the eyes and played with them, batting them back and forth. He screamed each time the padded foot hit him like a boxing glove.

Finally, the felines tired of toying with such a passive object. A rough-textured tongue came up to his right eye and grazed across it, licking and tasting him.

The two cats stood side by side, considering. They rubbed against one another in brotherly affection. Then they advanced in beautiful symmetry, one on each side of him. Jaws open, claws extended, they plunged into their warm breakfast.

Chapter Twenty-Two

The old, white clapboard farmhouse loomed on its hill, lightless and silent. Cliff Lansing and the Reverend Zaccariah stood at the bottom of the driveway as the six other men fanned out through the field to form a semi-circle around the house.

"What's your plan?" Zaccariah asked, fingering the .45 in the deep pocket of his black coat. He was content to trust this younger man, for when the Lord provides, He provides a leader, too.

"You and I are going in the front door, if no one comes out to stop us first," Cliff told him. "Once we get in, the others can come through the windows if we get into more than we can handle. And if anyone tries to make a run for it, the guys can intercept them."

Zaccariah nodded.

"We're going to tell whoever answers the door that our car broke down, and we want to use a phone. That will get us in. We have to improvise from there." Cliff looked at his watch. "Let's go. I want us all to get there at the same time."

They walked quickly. Cliff checked with Elvira on the walkie-talkie. She reported that a window on the second floor of the house had been shattered but that no one was in sight. Eric was halfway down to the rear of the house.

Zaccariah was surprised when they got all the way to the porch without incident. He expected at least a lookout. The kidnapers were more arrogant and self-assured than he had imagined. "You were right to pick Sunday morning," he conceded to Cliff. "It may be the Lord's day, but it's also the day the sinner sleeps late."

Cliff waved Zaccariah to one side and reached for the doorknob.

Before he could touch it, the door was yanked inward, and Cliff came face to face with someone inside. Zaccariah couldn't see a blessed thing—except that Cliff looked up in astonishment. Whoever it was, he was nearly seven feet tall.

"Good morning," Cliff said.

"What do you want?" a deep and groggy voice said. The footsteps on the porch had apparently just awakened him and brought him to the door.

"Sorry to bother you at this hour," Cliff said. "Looks like you were going out anyway with all those clothes on and that bee hat." Cliff obviously said that for Zaccariah's benefit so he would know it was one of *them* and dangerous. "As I was saying, I'm real sorry, but my car broke down just a way up the road. I was hoping to use your phone to call a garage."

"Don't have a phone," the man said.

"I'll be glad to pay you the cost of the call," Cliff offered. He was a consummate actor, pretending his host was nothing more than a stingy old farmer. "You see, I saw the phone wire going in upstairs, and I figured you had a phone for certain. I wouldn't have bothered you otherwise. I'd sure be grateful if I could call a garage."

"Phone doesn't work," the man elaborated.

"Ah," Cliff replied, running out of small talk. He cast a quick sideways glance to Zaccariah that said: *Now what do we do?*

"Where's the nearest town, then?" Cliff asked.

"Pleasanton. Couple of miles east."

"Can you point me the way?" Cliff asked. He stepped back onto the porch and pointed. "See, I'm parked down there. Now which way do I turn—is it that road, or the one down there?"

The tall man took half a step onto the porch. Zaccariah didn't wait; he aimed high and clubbed him on the back of the neck with the handle of his revolver. The man *was* nearly seven feet tall. Cliff made a clumsy but effective judo throw that flipped the stunned man onto his face on the porch.

Before the man could regain his senses, they tied his hands behind his back and bound his legs together. He didn't stir, so Zaccariah guessed they had knocked him out cold.

Cliff tore off the gauzed hat and flipped the man over. They got their first look at a Blue.

"Son of a bitch," Cliff muttered. "It's not human."

Zaccariah stared at the unconscious man's turquoise skin and purple lips. "Lord God of Hosts," he said. "Drive these demons from our midst!"

"Let's check inside," Cliff said. He threw the door the rest of the way open, and they entered with guns drawn.

The parlor was empty. A single coffee cup and a turned-on television testified that the man had been a solitary lookout, who had dozed off when the station went off the air. Cliff hit the switch and turned off the noisy, snow-filled picture. They moved through the outer rooms and found no one.

"I'll check upstairs," Zaccariah said, drawing aside the curtain that covered the bottom of a steep stairway. He cocked the .45, felt around the inside of his coat for the hand grenades, and took one step.

Something leaped at and past him from the third step. He cried out, then covered his mouth with his left hand to stifle his cry when he saw how small it was. Then another went past him, almost grazing his arm. The two white cats regained their balance behind him, claws skittering on the hardwood floor. They looked back at him and then fled. Their long fur puffed out in a terror far greater than his own as they made for the front door.

His heart pounded. The blood drummed in his ears. The sudden burst of adrenaline gave him the impetus to take the stairs, not at a pace suited to his age, but two steps at a time.

The bedroom he found there was sumptuous, but scarred by some terrible struggle. The sheets and pillows on the enormous bed were blood-stained and still wet. Another dark stain and starbursts of blood led across the carpet to a shattered window.

Zaccariah leaned out of the broken casement and looked down. In the dim light he saw, laying in the barnyard below, the naked flesh of a white man. He could not be sure, but it looked as though they had mutilated his head. It wasn't all there.

Seeing a movement near the barn, he stepped back into the unlit room. Then, cautiously, he peeped out again. There were two motions: Eric approaching the back door below, fiddling with his walkie-talkie, and behind him, another man in a beekeeper's hat emerging from the shadow of the barn. The figure came behind the young man with fists doubled together for a crushing blow to the shoulder.

Zaccariah had no choice; in another second the two figures would converge. He aimed the revolver and shot the menacing figure square in the chest.

The tall man toppled and fell. Eric spun around, looked at the motionless figure behind him, then spun back and aimed at the window.

"Eric!" Zaccariah croaked. "It's me—Zaccariah!"

"Thanks!" the boy called back.

Zaccariah continued the upstairs search and found no one. There was some godawful mess on the kitchen floor that he suspected was the rest of the dead man, but no other living thing.

He joined Cliff on the front porch. Cliff had called the other men in.

The whole disk of the sun had come up over the eastern hill, casting orange beams of light on the unpainted porch. They stood nonchalantly around their still-unconscious, blue-skinned captive.

"No one's in the house," Zaccariah reported. "I shot one coming out of the barn."

Eric came from the back of the house and joined them.

They reported to Elvira on the walkie-talkie and told her to stay on lookout. They would need to know right away if the van or any other vehicle came up the drive.

"I don't think they do anything above ground," Cliff said. "The one Zaccariah shot was probably the relief for the lookout. That means the entrance is through the barn."

"If they didn't hear the shot from down there," one of the men said, "we can still surprise them."

"Let's go in," Cliff said. "We're going to find those kids and bring them out. These blue guys are big and tough. I think you know what to do with them."

Another man with an M-16 laughed. "Sure, Sarge. Read 'em their rights. Tell them about the Geneva Convention."

"You want me to waste this one, Sarge?" a man in a

397

red plaid jacket asked Cliff. He put his shotgun to the captive's head. Then he jumped back. "Holy Jesus!" he swore. "Will you look at this guy?"

"I know," Cliff said. "He's blue."

"No, look at him. Look what's happening to him!"

They circled the body to see better. The light hit the porch planks around the man's head and revealed a tidal wave of motion all around his face and neck. *Things* were crawling up through the floorboards: mites, tiny red spiders, garden spiders, centipedes, ants and termites. His skin was crawling with nearly invisible chiggers and mites. Ants explored his ears and nostrils while others crept beneath his collar.

"They're coming from under the porch," Cliff said in wonder. "Millions of them—every goddamned bug around."

The man in the plaid shirt backed off the porch, took one step down, and then leaped back onto the porch. He scraped his boots furiously on the boards and pointed, too horrified to speak.

They leaned over and looked; the wooden steps were a carpet of seething insects. They came like lemmings—every conceivable species side by side, every bug within smelling range of the alien now exposed to their attack. Spiders marched with ants, locusts with centipedes. Bees and wasps hovered like blimps over the procession; flies and gnats buzzed in chaotic flight; and grubs and maggots inched hungrily along, some carried on the backs of beetles.

In a moment, the comatose man was covered with a black carpet of feelers and legs, pincers and mouths. They went up his nostrils and parted his dark lips to enter the pink cavity of his mouth. They buzzed their way into his ears.

"They're gonna eat him," one man said in awe.

"They're gonna fuckin' eat him."

"They got taste," Cliff said, trying to make light of the incredible. "Let's get moving. We've got to flush these creeps out of there." The men turned the corner of the house and headed for the barn.

Zaccariah paused for one moment and looked back at the judgment on the porch. "God bless them," he said. "Angels of the Lord! Bless their little six- and eight-legged souls! God made them for a purpose after all." He pounded his fist against the Bible in his breast pocket. His heart swelled with gratitude.

Just then, Elvira's voice came over the walkie-talkie. "Cliff—Reverend—watch out! There's a truck coming through the field right for the farmhouse. Its lights are out, and it's moving fast."

He heard it the same instant and raised his revolver.

"Keith! Keith! Wake up!"

Peter shook the boy in the dimly lit room.

"Sleep!" Keith said. "Have to sleep!"

Peter shook him again, hard. "Wake up!"

Keith groaned, reaching for his glasses. When he saw it was Peter, he perked up instantly. "Is it time?" he whispered.

"Time. We're getting out of here. I know the way up to the house and out of here."

"What about Howard—and the Blues?"

"Howard's dead. I just got your guard," Peter told him. "We'll have to take our chance with the Blues."

"But when—*now*?"

"Now! Before they find Howard and the guards—now, while they're almost all sleeping."

Keith hurried into his clothes. "What about the rest?"

"We're *all* going. You get them up and around. Get them into the hall. I'll meet you there. I'm going to get Andrea and Marsha and the girls."

Peter left the rest to Keith, who immediately began rousing the boys. Then, taking the heavy axe he had found in Howard's closet, he went to the two computers.

WHO IS MOVING AROUND IN THE ROOM? the computer speaker said.

"The tooth fairy," Peter replied.

ALL BOYS SHOULD BE SLEEPING. GO TO SLEEP. GO TO SLEEP.

With one blow, Peter severed the speech cartridge from the back of the computer. Then he chopped the cable connecting the monitor to the computer.

The other machine screeched in alarm:

DANGER! DANGER! DISCONNECTION!

He chopped the cables to the other machine with a savage gesture, cutting clear into the table beneath.

The screens went dark for the last time.

Counting the doors, he went to the girls' room.

A Blue female had fallen asleep in front of the television. All the rest of the girls were asleep in their beds.

He got right behind her and raised the long-handled axe. He didn't know if he was strong enough to kill her with one blow. He had only one chance, because *she* could knock him breathless without even thinking about it.

With all the strength in his arms and the upper half of his body, he swung the axe straight down. The blade split the hybrid's skull, cutting through hair and bone and into the brain. The guardian toppled forward, lifeless as a manikin, the axe still in place.

The girls leaped from their beds at the sound and ran toward him. They circled him, staring at the corpse on the bare metal floor. They all started to talk at once.

"Quiet!" someone said.

Andrea came from the back of the room, swept through the half-hysterical crowd of girls, and hugged him.

Peter blushed. Then, without looking down at what he was doing, he extricated the axe and led the girls to the door.

He looked around the group, counting them. "Where's Marsha? Is she here?"

"Howard took her," Andrea said. "We think he was going to . . . kill her."

"Find the boys in the hallway," Peter ordered her. "Two left turns in the corridor, then two rights. I'll join you and get us out of here."

"Where are you going, Peter?" Andrea demanded.

"I'll join you," he repeated. "Now get going. If the Blues come at you, run if you can. If you can't run, attack them back. Do anything you can—jump on them, bite them, scratch them. Go for their eyes. Fight dirty."

The girls didn't need a second invitation. They streamed into the corridor in their night clothes. Peter smashed their computers and headed back for the boys.

Halfway there, he heard a gunshot from somewhere far above. Something was happening up there, and maybe the further confusion would help them get out.

Weighed down with food, rope, flashlights and their scant personal belongings, Patienzia and Helena trudged off to the hilltop. It had taken several hours of dodging the attendants, packing, and sneaking through corridors until they found an open ground floor window and got free of the building.

401

Still in their habits, they moved deftly among the pre-dawn shadows. They startled an owl in a bare tree; it fluttered violently and took wing.

Then a pair of squat, wide-winged birds burst out of the high grass and swooped just over their heads. Helena cried out and put her hands up defensively.

"Those were whippoorwills," Patienzia explained. "They nest on the ground. We must have startled them."

Patienzia got a close-up look at one of them when it swooped back toward them. It had eyes as keen and huge as an owl's, but its face was fat and low and whiskered—a vagrant, mad, Quasimodo bird.

"They were hideous." Helena shivered. "They looked like owls that had been run over by a steamroller."

As they climbed the hill, they looked back now and then to make sure they weren't being followed. No lights had come on in Dr. Halpern's apartment, or in the rooms below. Dimly, they saw the two whippoor-wills circling the roof of the convent.

"My grandmother was afraid of whippoorwills," Patienzia recalled. "She said they came to the house of the dying and waited for the soul to come out. She thought the soul went up to God through the chimney, I suppose. Anyway, the birds supposedly try to snatch the souls of the departed."

"What an *awful* story," Helena said.

When they got to the mine opening, they were astonished to find Jimmy's truck parked there. In the back they found miner's lamps and more rope and tools.

"The keys are in the ignition," Helena reported.

"Then he's in there," Patienzia said. "I should have known that curiosity would get the better of him."

They pulled aside the boards blocking the mine

402

opening and shone their lights inside. There was no sign of Jimmy.

"Give me your hand," Patienzia said. She held out her hand and Helena took it. They walked side by side, flashing the lights on the floor and walls of the mine. Everything was the same as before.

"You're not afraid in here anymore," Helena remarked in surprise.

"Not after that day with Jimmy. I learned something about fear—that you can have it and *still* go ahead. You just have to make yourself. Ah, here's the opening. . . . Look what he's done!"

Helena shone her flashlight around the perimeter of the crawl space into the rest of the mine shaft. "What's that, Sister?"

"He's been working in here, Helena. It's bigger now—big enough for either of us." Then she thought: *And maybe JUST big enough for Jimmy*.

"My light is flickering," Helena complained. Its brightness fell to half.

Patienzia worried that hers might go, too. "Let's go back and get the big lamps from the truck," she proposed. "I think I remember how to light them."

The moment they came out of the mine, they heard a gunshot from the Emslie farm.

They rushed to the edge of the hill and stared down at the fields.

"See if there's still a pair of binoculars in the truck," Patienzia said. "No, wait—I see them. Two—three—four of them."

"Yes, I see them. Men, all around the house."

The men converged at the front porch. No lights came on in the house.

"What do you think is happening?" Helena asked.

"I think it's a raid of some kind. Someone is there to rescue the children."

"It might be more of *them*," Helena warned.

"No, I'm sure of it. Get me those binoculars."

Helena ran for them and came back. Patienzia focused as well as she could in the breaking dawn light. Some of the men looked like military men, others like regular local hunters or farmers. None of them had on the strange bee hats. She could see one or two holding guns.

"They have guns," Patienzia said. "They must be raiding the farm. We have to go and tell them about this mine opening. They may not know there's another way to get to the children."

"What if they shoot us?"

"Say a prayer while we drive down the hill," Patienzia suggested, rushing for the truck.

Helena followed dutifully.

The truck started in an instant.

"I can't see the old road Jimmy was using," Patienzia said, trying hard to remember exactly how to work the gears. "I'm going to go straight down the hill and break through the fence."

"Turn on the lights!" Helena pleaded.

"No," Patienzia said. "Not till we get closer."

Patienzia hit the accelerator and the truck plowed through grass and shrubs to the bottom of the hill. She rammed a fencepost and leveled it, riding over the flattened wire with ease. Then it was uphill again to the flat top of the hill where the farmhouse stood.

They were in high wheat and mustard going up. The house was invisible. She only hoped they came out somewhere where they could call out to the men and not alarm them.

Helena screamed as they burst out of the field. The house was straight ahead, the front porch just yards away.

A man in black raised a revolver and aimed at them.

404

Patienzia hit the brakes and spun the wheel to turn the truck sideways.

"In the name of Jesus don't shoot!" she shouted.

The man lowered the gun.

Patienzia opened the door, heart pounding, her lungs forgetting to take a new breath until she gasped and choked them into action again. She leaped down to the ground, and an instant later four men were all around her, guns drawn.

"It's all right," the old man in black said. "It's a sister from the convent."

"The children," Patienzia said, holding her hand over her palpitating heart. "You came to rescue the children."

"That's right, Sister."

A younger man in uniform stepped forward. "What do you know about this, Sister?" he demanded.

"On the next hill," she replied. "An old mine opening. We heard them killing children. It's another way in."

"We'll have to go in from both ends, then. John, you take Eric and go with the sisters." A man in a hunter's jacket and a young blond-haired man stepped aside. "Thank you, Sister," the leader said.

"And God bless you," added the old man.

"Would you prefer to drive?" Patienzia asked the man named John. "I'm a little rusty."

He nodded and got into the driver's seat. Patienzia got into the back of the truck with the other man. Seconds later, they were plowing through the grain fields toward the convent again.

The young man looked at her in amazement as they bounced along in the back of the pickup. No doubt he was wondering how two sisters came to be out in the fields in a truck at six o'clock in the morning. There was no way to even begin explaining.

"Are you the army?" she shouted to the young man.

He shook his head.

"The FBI, then?"

No, again.

"The police—sheriff's men?"

He smiled. "None of those. I guess you'd call us a posse."

"Well thank God for you, whoever you are."

As the truck stopped at the mine entrance again, the young man helped her out.

"What kind of people are those in the farmhouse?" she wondered aloud. "What kind of men would molest and kill children?"

"Not men," the young man said. "Monsters. Aliens."

"This is no time for jokes," Patienzia snapped.

The other man came up beside her, Helena at his side.

"Sister, I'm a Roman Catholic, and I swear by the cross he's not joking. What's got those children in there isn't human. You can stay back here if you want."

"We will go," Helena said, stepping forward and picking up the miner's lamps where they had left them on the ground. "I don't care whether they're men or monsters." The young sister practically glowed with courage. Shedding her cap like Joan of Arc preparing for battle, she led the way.

For ten minutes the central computer dialed Howard's bedroom telephone and summoned him on computer terminals around the underground complex. When he never answered, it awakened the master.

The alien stirred from its slumber with a hiss of dissatisfaction. The speaker in the ceiling of his room translated the computer's message into the metallic clatter and staccato barking of his native language.

COMPUTERS ARE NONFUNCTIONAL IN THE CHILDREN'S ROOMS. HOWARD EMSLIE DOES NOT ANSWER REPEATED REQUESTS FOR HIS PRESENCE.

The master trilled and clacked something that translated to: "Summon Ralph Emslie to fix it."

RALPH EMSLIE IS IN CALIFORNIA.

Waving his hands in annoyance, the master demanded clarification. "Is it a power failure in the computers?" he asked.

COMPUTERS HAVE POWER. CONNEC-TIONS TO SPEECH CIRCUITS AND SCREENS HAVE BEEN SEVERED.

"Sabotage!" the master howled in his native tongue. "Contact the guards in the children's rooms."

GUARDS DO NOT RESPOND.

The master stood and whirled around in his bubble in rage. "Summon the guard leader of the hybrids. Tell him to dispatch three guards to the boys' room, three to the girls'. Tell them to punish all except the pregnant girls."

After a moment, the computer said, *GUARDS DISPATCHED. FURTHER ORDERS?*

"No." The master sat down, contemplating a suitable punishment for Howard. "Wait," he added suspiciously. "Conduct a scan of equipment and personnel."

SCANNING. He spun like a dervish, wringing his

long fingers together as he waited. Then the reply came:

SIX COMPUTERS NOW NONFUNCTIONAL. ONE HELMET MISSING FROM INVENTORY. ABOVE GROUND LOOKOUT NONRESPOND-ING. ALL OTHER SYSTEMS NORMAL.

"The lookouts?" the master screeched. "Where are the lookouts?"

NIGHT GUARD WAS RELIEVED BY DAY GUARD TEN MINUTES AGO. NIGHT GUARD NONRESPONDING. DAY GUARD NONRE-SPONDING.

"Send all remaining guards into the upper tunnels. Defend the factory and the ship at all costs."

ORDER TRANSMITTED.

The alien sensed betrayal. Maybe the human cowards had simply abandoned him. Or perhaps there had been a minor rebellion among the children—unlikely but always remotely possible. Come to think of it, he *had* seen a boy spy in on him through the window—a boy who had no business running loose in the ship.

Closing his yellow eyes, he leaned his long chin on his hands and waited.

Peter walked through the underground catacombs. He passed the sleeping quarters of the workers and was astonished to find no Blues on duty. He marveled that more than a hundred grown men and women had been living down here for years. They had been lured by promises, brainwashed, and then enslaved. Howard told them they had hired men away from the government, from industry, from computer companies. A huge down payment in gold brought them here—and then by the time the computer was through with them, they had forgotten they ever had a life outside the labs and the chemical complex. Howard said they worked seven days a week, ate food that would shame a prison, and stayed as happy as fleas on a dog.

An instinct told Peter that these people were beyond saving. They would betray him to the boss if he tried to approach them. They were "good citizens" of the order to come, no more than organic robots. They were as soulless as Frankenstein's monster.

The thought that men—not the alien—had built the helmet and the rape machine also sickened him. He did not want to think of such men walking above ground. He would do nothing to save them.

He found his way to the room from which he had stolen the helmet. In the empty lab beyond, brains were chopped down to size, rewired and put into computers. There was a door at the back of that lab. . . .

Howard had called it "the meat locker" and invited him to take a look. That day, he had no desire to see. Now, he had to.

The corrugated metal door slid aside, and waves of icy air blew out toward him from the large room inside.

He walked in, folding his arms over his chest against the intense cold. The room was what he thought it would be, lined on both sides with wheeled carts. On each cart was a sheet-covered body.

Peter had no time to waste. He ran through the room, tearing off the sheets.

There was a big body with overalls, its head chopped off neatly by the helmet—the farm boy he had seen killed.

Two smaller bodies were boys—naked, covered

with bruises, their heads mutilated in the same way.

A full-grown man—an old man with a long white beard . . .

A blue-skinned female—they even used their own for parts . . .

Two girls, dressed in pajamas, looking like broken baby dolls with their hair and the tops of their heads missing . . .

He had searched down one row and back the other. Now only one body remained. He looked.

Then Peter slammed the door shut, shaking from cold and more than cold. He picked up the axe where he had left it and ran down the tunnel to find the other children.

He hoped no one got in his way—not after what he had just seen. The body on the cart *was* Marsha. They had put one of the helmets on her, but those torments must have been only an afterthought, one more indignity following the *other* things Howard and the hybrids had done to her.

The girls screamed as three Blues came running down the corridor toward them.

"What should we do?" Mary shrieked.

"Let's go back into the room!" another girl yelled.

"No!" Andrea ordered them. "Follow me. Run! Stay together!"

The girls ran for their lives, dashing in and out of the maze of passages.

At a place where two groups of tunnels met, they collided with Keith and the boys. The two groups milled, everyone screaming and yelling at the same time.

"Blues!" Keith shouted. "Behind us!"

"No!" Andrea countered. "Behind *us*."

They were trapped. The towering hybrids appeared at the corner of each tunnel.

"They're gonna kill us!" a boy wailed.

"We're going to take you to your rooms," said one Blue, advancing.

"And you'll have to be punished," said a second. Both groups closed in.

Keith stepped forward. He went toward his group's pursuer. He stopped only a foot away.

"All right," he said. "We'll go. Hey, there's a spider on your hand."

The Blue foolishly yanked his hand up and scrutinized it.

Keith dashed past him, eluded the hands of a second Blue, and evaded a kick from the third.

The other children took his cue and scattered. The Blues could only get them one at a time—six might be caught, but the rest would get away.

He heard screaming from the girls, and the sound of a scuffle. He had to get away, find Peter—

Then he saw a man coming down the corridor. He wasn't a Blue, wasn't one of the workers. He stopped dead; there was nowhere to go but back toward the struggle.

The tall man in black had eyes that were terrible to look at—eyes that would make a wolf turn aside.

"Where are they, boy? Where are those devils?"

Keith pointed behind him. "Who are you?" he asked.

"I am the judgment. I am the Angel of the Lord," the man raved. *"Let destruction come upon him unawares; and let his net that he hath hid catch himself; into that very destruction let him fall."*

The man raced past Keith. He waited. Two shots rang out. The groans and cries of astonishment were those of Blues, not children.

Two more shots. Children screamed, running this way, that way. One or two got to Keith.

"A man," they shouted. "A man came and shot the Blues."

One last shot rang out. Feet ran in every direction.

Then a deafening explosion shook the tunnels. Rocks groaned against the outside of the metal, and dust sifted down along the seams and joints.

When it settled, Peter still heard the children's voices. They went on through the tunnels, hopelessly lost, meeting with one another by chance until most of their band was reassembled.

All they could do was keep moving.

Zaccariah caught the devils at their work. When he rounded a corner in the tunnel, he found six of them, grappling with the innocents. One dragged a screaming girl by the hair. Another had a half-conscious boy over his shoulder. One energetic boy gouged one of the monsters in the eyes with his fingers, broke loose and ran past Zaccariah.

He started with the brute who stood rubbing his eyes in pain, took aim, and fired twice. Struck in the heart, he fell to the floor with a colossal thump.

The two other Blues released the children and turned to face him. Instead of fleeing, they charged him. He shot blindly—no time to even aim.

One shot missed. The other got one of the Blues in the stomach.

Then the one surviving monster got to him. He towered over Zaccariah, seizing his right arm. The gun hand wobbled, shook. The weapon wavered back and forth.

The monster lifted him by his arm and shook him. He fired the gun, then dropped it.

Hit in the neck, the Blue groaned in pain, then swung Zaccariah and smashed him against the metal wall.

Stunned, he lay there as the injured Blue rubbed his wound. The hybrid howled in rage when he saw the blood on his hand.

Zaccariah could not move, could barely breathe. The Blue put his boot on the old man's shoulder, seized his arm with both strong hands, and pulled. He screamed as tendons and muscles tore loose.

Two more Blues came running.

"He shot me," the wounded one told them.

They encircled him. With his good arm, he reached into his coat pocket and pulled the pins on two hand grenades. The dark words of the Psalm he had memorized came back to him. *In mine adversity they rejoiced, and gathered themselves together.*

One of them grabbed his wounded arm. The other got his left arm. They drew him to his feet.

"Rip him apart," the wounded one said.

Yea, the abjects gathered themselves together against me . . .

With all their strength, they pulled at his arms. The fabric of his black coat severed. His shirt ripped. His flesh tore loose. The bones cracked and snapped.

They did tear me, and ceased not.

His arms were gone. Blood spurted from the arteries in his empty shoulder sockets. He toppled forward. Merciful blackness enveloped him an instant before the explosion ripped through his attackers.

The rescuers made quick work of the hybrids defending the underground complex, but not without cost.

Twenty Blues poured into the upper tunnels and

413

climbed the ramp toward the barn. Men and women alike carried sidearms and wore the same coveralls, gloves, boots and bee hats.

They never expected to be ambushed in their own domain. As they got to the base of the ramp, where tunnels opened out in four directions, gunfire came at them from two angles.

A few fell. Others crouched and fired back, only to be shot in the ferocious barrage. Six others fled up the ramp, pursued by the invaders.

Elvira sat in the barn loft with a sawed-off shotgun and a .38 revolver. She had a clear view of the open trap door, and it was a simple matter to fire at any aliens who emerged. Her aim wasn't great, but levering the gun barrel on a banister rail helped her keep on target. She hit four of the six Blues as they came out of the tunnel. Two fell on the spot, three others limped back, and one fired a few wild shots toward her before fleeing into the fields.

Then two of the pursuers came out. One limped; the other cradled a wounded hand. Elvira grabbed the first aid kit, reloaded and holstered the .38, and rushed down the stairs to help.

The man with the wounded hand refused help at first. "Tend to Charlie there," he ordered. She tied the man's leg to staunch the bleeding and dressed the wound as best she could. As far as she could tell, the bullet had gone straight through the flesh of the shin—not a terrible wound but enough to prevent him from walking.

The first wounded man took out his revolver and checked on the injured Blues on the straw floor. He tore off their hats. When one rose to resist him, he clenched his gun in both hands and shot him in the temple.

Elvira closed her eyes and looked away, but she had

seen the worst—the flash of the gun and the simultaneous explosion of blood and bone from the back of the Blue's head before he plopped lifeless to the ground. And while she had shot the Blues with a neutral, numb kind of feeling, this man had killed as though the moment of murder were a joy.

He blew off the smoking gun barrel like a bad John Wayne imitation. When he saw her expression, he said, "What the hell, lady, the bugs were gonna get him anyway."

She shuddered and then helped him with his wound. His right hand was badly shattered. All she could do was sterilize the wound and tie it up. He would probably never use several fingers again.

She went to the trap door and looked to see if anyone else lay on the ramp, wounded. There was only one Blue in sight, dead or unconscious.

"I'm going back down," the wounded man told her. He reported to Cliff on the walkie-talkie, reloaded his gun and plunged into the tunnel again.

She helped the one named Charlie up to the hay loft, gave him the shotgun, and waited. Somewhere far below, the gunfire continued.

Eric and John found the way into the tunnels blocked by a metal grille.

"They must use this tunnel as an extra air supply," Eric guessed. "This grille is to keep bugs out."

"Not very strong," John said, pushing at it. "Hell, it's just like window screen."

"I guess they never expected company," Eric said. He took out his knife and sliced a man-sized hole through it.

Soon they were out of the coal mine and into passages with walls made of thin, welded metal.

"Looks like a big tin can," John said.

"Yeah," Eric answered. "You'd think space aliens wouldn't be so chintzy." He marked the wall with a large chalk arrow pointing the way they had come.

John laughed uneasily. "Sense of humor's a good thing when you're in a jam," he said.

At the intersection of two tunnels they heard gunfire.

"This way," John said. "We'd better go help."

Eric hesitated.

"Maybe I'd better go the other way and look for the kids," he suggested.

"Have it your way," the man said. "This ain't the Army." He turned and strode toward the shooting.

Eric hurried down the other passage. It only stood to reason that the children would be deeper in the tunnel. The aliens would be defending the upper tunnel, hiding their captives somewhere below.

The tunnels were confusing, built like a rat maze. He kept seeing dead ends of solid pink quartz. Soon he gained a clear sense that the pink wall enclosed something—maybe the vessel they had come in. He continued marking his path, even though it might mean a tortuous route back.

Footsteps echoed ahead of him. He ducked to the mouth of a side passage. A figure dashed by him.

"Peter!" he cried out, leaping from hiding.

Peter Lansing spun around to face him. He was disheveled, sweaty, grimy-faced. He beamed to see Eric.

"You—what are you—" he blurted out.

"Your dad's here," Eric explained. "And Miss Hawkins. And a bunch of other guys."

Peter leaped for joy. "So that's who's shooting up there! I knew he'd come—I knew he would!"

"Are the others here?" Eric asked.

"Andrea and Keith. They . . . got Marsha. There are about twenty more. They're all loose in the tunnels, blue guys chasing everyone. We have to find them."

"We came in through a mine opening—not the house," Eric told him. "If you can get the kids, we can get out that way. We can avoid all that shooting up there."

"Great!" Peter said. "Where's the way out?"

Eric held up the blunted piece of chalk. "Follow the arrows," he said.

"Great! And I know how to get back here," Peter said.

Just in case, Eric marked their meeting point with a big "X." Then, hurrying back to where Peter had last seen the children, Eric heard a breathless account of Peter's captivity.

Cliff Lansing and two of his friends arrived unchallenged in the underground work complex. They walked in awe through an enlarged chamber full of metal canisters.

"What do you think is in them, Sarge?" one of them asked.

Cliff tapped one of the six-foot-long tubes and examined the valve.

"Chemical warfare," he guessed. "Looks nasty, whatever it is."

"They sure aren't making perfume down here," his friend observed.

Next they found a miniaturized chemical plant where wheeled robots ran to and fro adjusting valves, tipping hoppers of material into vats, and removing sealed, foil-wrapped packages at the end.

Cliff picked up a package and opened it.

417

"Food," he said, sniffing it. "Nuts and grain and all kinds of other crap, but it's food."

"How many people do they *have* down here?" one man wondered.

Cliff shrugged. "There might be hundreds."

"Then why haven't we seen more of those blue skins?"

No one could answer. Someone had to have built and run all these machines.

"Sarge, look over here!"

Cliff went to a door and peered through its round porthole.

"It's a dormitory," he said.

"Kids?"

"No—men and women, as far as I can see. They're sleeping like babies, even with all this fighting going on."

"Maybe they're drugged, Sarge. Let's check it out."

They pushed open the door and stepped in. The room was stuffy, full of the smells of sweat and unchanged linens.

"Jesus!" Cliff swore. "It's like a goddamn flop house."

Then they heard a voice coming from behind a partition.

"*Sleep,*" it said. "*Sleep . . . obey . . . sleep . . . obey.*"

"It's a machine . . . a recording, Sarge."

They found a bank of computers, but only one of them was turned on. Its color screen flickered into life, filling with spiral patterns, snowflakes, strobing flashes.

"Will you look at that?" one man said.

"*Sleep . . . obey . . . sleep . . . obey,*" the voice droned on.

Cliff looked at his two friends, who had suddenly

gone quiet. They stared at the screen, their eyes glazed over. It had no effect on him.

"Bill! Reggie!" he shook them, bringing them to their senses. "Don't look at it! Don't listen!"

They snapped out of it.

"WARNING!" the computer voice intoned. *"IN-TRUDERS—"*

Cliff yanked the computer cables out with one furious gesture.

WARNING! the next computer in line started up.

"Get them—get them all!" Cliff ordered. Within seconds, the men had all the cables torn loose. There would be no more voices.

The three men retreated to the door as some of the sleeping workers stirred, rolled over in their beds, and went back to their slumber.

When they got outside again, Elvira's voice came faintly through the walkie-talkie.

"What is it, Elvira?" he asked.

"You'd better come up if you can, Cliff."

"Any more Blues?" he asked.

"A couple ran out into the fields. The rest we caught going out. But you'd better come up. We have company."

"More of *them?*"

A man's voice broke through on the walkie-talkie. "Who is this? Identify yourself!"

"Who the hell are you?"

"This is Agent William Ross of the FBI. You and your men have ten minutes to get above ground."

Cliff laughed. "You guys must be kidding. Do you have any idea what's going on here?"

"We'll talk about it up here. You're Lansing, right?"

"That's right. We'll come up if the way is clear."

"Your lady friends thinks it is."

"All right," Cliff said reluctantly. "Just don't get trigger happy." He shut off the walkie-talkie and turned to his friends.

"What the hell was that all about?" one asked.

"I think they decided to join our party," Cliff said. "After we did the work, of course."

"What is it—is this place a government setup?"

"No," Cliff said. "We may be bad—but we're not this bad. The feds have been tailing me since Peter disappeared. They must have figured we were on to something."

"What are we going to do?"

"No choice now. If we stay down here and search, those bozos will come in shooting at all of us. All we can do it go up, show them a dead blueskin, and get them to come down and help us search."

Retracing their path through the maze, they headed for the upper tunnels. On the way back they found the bodies of two of their comrades. In another place, opposite a collapsed wall and a heap of oozing carnage, they found Zaccariah's leather-bound Bible. Cliff picked it up and tucked it in his pocket.

Peter and Eric led the children through the tunnels. They passed one Blue, lying in the tunnel, screaming as flies and wasps covered him. He never even saw them.

They found the "X" on the corridor wall and followed the arrows. Round and round they went, tracing the perimeter of the ship.

Suddenly, the ceiling lamps went out. They were in absolute, utter darkness. The alien was doing whatever still lay in its power to confuse them.

Eric pulled out the flashlight the sister had given him. He shone it on the wall until he found the next arrow.

"Everybody reach out," he ordered. "Take the hand of the person behind you, then reach out for the person in front of you. Stay in one line, and stay against the wall in case someone goes by. Everybody follow me."

They did as he told them. Like a long snake they edged forward. Some of the girls cried when they rounded a corner and they could no longer see his light, and once or twice he had to follow the length of the line and reconnect two frightened youngsters.

One by one, Eric found the arrows he had drawn. Then, abruptly, the lamp died. He shook it, beat the flashlight against the walls. Nothing.

They had to be near the exit—only a few more turns and they would be there.

He took a chance and called out. "Sisters!" he yelled. "Are you there!"

"Here!" a voice called faintly back.

"Come with a lamp!" he called. "Follow my arrows into the tunnel!"

Two minutes later a glow appeared before them. Then the children rushed forward to the sisters, reaching out for their habits, clinging to them and to one another in a tight circle.

Eric took the lamps and led them out into the daylight.

"I don't know whether to shake your hand or throw your ass in jail" was how agent Ross greeted Cliff Lansing.

Cliff squinted at the bright sunlight streaming through the door and looked around the barn. Twenty or more men stood in leather jackets and white shirts, holding their revolvers on him.

"You could take those guns off me for starters," Cliff suggested. He looked for Elvira and saw her only a few feet away, flanked by two burly FBI men.

"Give me your weapon," Ross demanded. As soon as he had the holster and gun, he waved to the other men, and they lowered their weapons.

"The lady tried to tell me what was going on," Ross said. "I guess you and your war buddies did a little vigilante action here?"

"You might say that," Cliff replied. "Look, I think the kids are still down there."

"We'll see."

"There's no time to waste. You don't know what's down there."

"Suppose you tell *me*."

"How about sixty kidnaped children for starters. Look, we're wasting time."

"You didn't find any kids, did you?"

Cliff grew enraged. "How about a stockpile of chemical weapons? How about a little concentration camp full of brainwashed plant workers—all underground? Is that enough to get you assholes to go down there and search?"

Ross still looked skeptical. "Child molesters, okay. A white slavery ring, okay. Even tell me it's a religious cult. But don't try to tell me it's fucking mole men Nazis or Commies."

"Did you look at those bodies?" Cliff demanded. "In case you didn't notice, they're not human."

"Can't tell what they are—or were," Ross said. "They're practically skeletons. I'd sure like to know how you got bugs to do that."

"They're not human. They're bright blue," Cliff repeated. "We have to go get those kids."

Another FBI man ran into the barn and came up to Ross.

422

"A truck is coming, Mr. Ross," he panted.

"So?" he said.

"Coming across the field like there's no tomorrow."

"So who's in it?"

"Two nuns and a pack of kids, Mr. Ross. They're all waving and screaming."

Elvira broke free from the agents and ran for the door.

The truck pulled up in front of the barn, waved there by FBI men. Before it even stopped, one boy leaped off the back.

Cliff ran forward, grabbed Peter and lifted him up.

The boy hugged him fiercely. "I knew you'd come," he said. "I knew you would."

"And I knew you'd get out," Cliff said, choking with joy.

"So there," Ross said, staring down at his shoes. "Looks like we don't have to go on a mole hunt after all."

Chapter Twenty-Three

They milled about the farmhouse for nearly an hour. The FBI men sat up shop inside the house and took statements from Elvira and Cliff, dispatched the wounded men to a hospital, and conducted confused interviews with the children.

In all the confusion, Peter and Eric managed to sidle away to find Keith and Andrea. They were sitting in the back of the pickup, watching while the two sisters and Elvira comforted the rescued children.

They got Andrea and Keith onto the quieter side of the truck where no one could see them.

"We need your help," Peter said. "The Cougars aren't through yet."

"I just want to go home," Andrea protested.

"Me, too," Keith said. "It's all over."

"It isn't over. These FBI clowns still won't believe there's a monster down there. We have to go back and finish it off."

"I want it dead," Andrea said. "I don't want it to get away."

"We have a plan," Eric said.

"What do you want us to do?" Andrea asked suspiciously. "We're not going back in there."

Peter leaned to Andrea and whispered in her ear.

Then he repeated his secret order to Keith.

"You want *what?*" Andrea screeched.

"What I said. Or whatever you can find. We'll mix it all together." Peter said. He took empty bags from the back of the truck and threw one to each of them. "Ten minutes!" he called.

Andrea and Keith ran off in opposite directions. One FBI man turned at the sight of their running, but was pulled back by the arm by his companion.

Taking two other bags, Eric and Peter went off into the barnyard, scanning the ground as they went.

"What did you ask her to get?" Eric asked Peter as they searched.

Peter laughed. "Snakes and snails and puppy dog tails."

"And what's Keith getting?"

"Bugs and spiders. All the bugs and spiders he can put his hands on in ten minutes."

It only took a few minutes to find the air vent that fed the alien's breathing tube. The vent was two feet wide, covered with a fine wire screen and a fan. The incoming air was purified in another machine, then pumped down into the creature's room.

Eric traced the mechanism and found the valve at the end of the purifier. After that it was just a plastic duct narrowing into a tube about a foot and a half wide.

"This is it!" Eric said.

Peter dragged the four lumpy burlap bags to the wall where Eric had found the exposed duct. "Cut it open," he said.

Eric cut a long slit in the plastic with his knife, then cut two lines at right angles to form an opening. He pried the plastic loose, hinging it on the fourth side.

426

"Perfect," Peter said. One by one he fitted the ends of the burlap bags over the opening and squeezed their contents into the duct.

"What's going to happen when all this stuff hits it?" Eric asked.

"You'll see," Peter said. "'Cause we're gonna go in and watch."

They closed the flap in the duct and headed for the door. Running to the end of the connecting corridor, they pressed their faces against the glass and stared in.

The alien saw them. It picked up something that looked like a microphone and spoke into it. It gurgled and hissed and screamed unintelligible words that the computer would turn into commands for Howard and the Blues. It didn't know it was alone and undefended.

It looked up and hissed in rage as the first object fell through the wide air tube.

A dead rat dropped at its feet.

The alien pressed itself against the edge of its bubble to avoid it, shaking its head in outrage.

The half-rotten skeleton of a small bird dropped down next. Feathers floated upwards, and the more the creature waved its arms to fend them off, the more they broke loose and eddied around it.

A group of dark missiles landed on its back and arms.

It howled and made choking sounds.

"What were those?" Eric asked, squinting.

"Dog turds," Peter said. "Can't make a Cougar Stew without dog turds."

More and more objects rained down on the helpless monster. Owl spoor, toadstools, puffballs, tree fungus and wet hay moiled in the zero gravity of the sphere. Some of the fragments landed in the jellied surface of the alien's thorax; it went into a fetal

427

position to protect its organs from further attack.

Then it saw what was coming down the tube and wailed with terror. The cry was so loud it penetrated the door, hurting their ears.

Insects and spiders, following the irresistible scent, trailed down the tube toward the alien. The severed fingers of one of the Blues plopped down one by one, blackened with wriggling invaders. Spiders, bees, wasps, centipedes, and the heart of an anthill plummeted down to complete the Cougars' gift.

The sphere was now a brown soup of floating poison, in which the alien screamed and swam. It tore at its face and chest as the bus converged on it.

"Not enough bugs," Keith complained. "Enough to kill it, but not enough to eat it up."

"The chef is never satisfied," Eric joked. "Let's get out of here."

Eric and Peter closed the door on the alien, sealed off the air duct with the burlap bags, and sat down at the control panels.

"Well," Peter said. "Here we are. This is the room I told you about."

Eric circled the huge organic computer in awe. Then he sat down and examined one of the control panels. Before him was a three-dimensional star chart with a model of the ship in it. A blinking light so much as said *You are here*. A hand wheel moved the hologram image and suggested *Where do you want to go?*

"This panel is like an airplane," Peter said. "It's just like a flight simulator game. Howard said morons flew this thing."

"Do you want to go back up there?" Eric asked.

"Not really," Peter said.

"But your dad is there."

"I know. But I don't think I can go back. Not after

428

what I did."

"The rest will go back. No one will blame them for what they did."

Peter shook his head. "It's different for me."

"We could—" Eric started to say.

They looked at one another and understood.

Peter picked up the microphone next to the control panel.

"Computer!" he called.

WHAT IS YOUR WISH? DO YOU WANT TO PLAY A GAME? the voice answered.

"Your master is dead."

CONFIRMED.

"I am assuming command. Is that understood?" Peter winked at Eric and shrugged. "Just like *Star Trek*," he whispered.

The computer paused. Finally the voice replied: *CONFIRMED.*

"Want to give it a try?" Eric asked.

Peter took the helm, hit the first button, and closed his eyes.

Only seconds after Cliff and Elvira began searching for Peter, the ground began to shake. Trees swayed back and forth as violent seismic shocks ran through the hills.

The mine shaft beneath the convent hill collapsed, taking part of the slope with it.

"It was just the mines collapsing," Cliff assured Elvira. Then he went over to question Andrea and Keith. She couldn't hear over the confusion of voices, but both children made frantic gestures. She thought in dismay: *Could Peter have gone back down there, trying to go back and kill the aliens on his own?*

The mine cave-in was only a prelude. The bare

429

spot in the Emslie field suddenly began to split open. Chunks of soil and shrubs rolled away as a great pink crystal surface emerged like a bulb popping out of a flowerpot. It vibrated, hummed, throbbed, tearing loose from the structures built around it, shaking off every vestige of pipe, wire and tunnel.

It rose, beating like a mad timpani, pulsing a bass note that shook them from head to foot. It climbed like a serene balloon into the air, hovered over the house, and then drifted northward. Unaffected by gravity and oblivious to its own mass, it zigzagged along the horizon, traced the line of adjacent hills, and then climbed.

"It's a ship!" Elvira exclaimed. "They're getting away!"

Cliff looked around. Elvira followed his eyes and saw what he saw—that Peter was still not there.

"Peter and Eric," Cliff explained. "The kids said they went back. They're in that ship."

"My God," she said. "Then they're prisoners."

"Don't you believe it," Cliff said. "The boys are flying it. Didn't you see how it moved? They were testing it out."

She reached out for Cliff's hand as the ship arced up toward the zenith. The crystal sphere became a second sun. Then it was bright as Venus, soft as a new moon, faint as a firefly. Finally it was gone, dissolved into an empty sky.

Along the distant road, ambulances began their howling approach to take the children to a hospital. They would go back to their towns, either to foster homes or to what was left of their families.

Elvira felt small and fragile. The gaping hole in the field, and the children's fevered account of what they had experienced down there, made her realize how the earth lay defenseless, like a sparrow under the shade of a hawk. Men had thought themselves alone even when the newcomers were digging in. Other men had betrayed their kind to the invaders.

But small as she felt, she could not feel insignificant. A group of ordinary people—muddled and half-ignorant and maybe even a little mad—had stopped them.

"I don't know where they're going," Cliff Lansing said admiringly. "Maybe back to where that thing came from, to raise a little hell."

"Or maybe just out there for a look around," Elvira said. "I envy them."

"They'll be back," Cliff assured her. "And think of what they'll tell us!"

TERROR LIVES!

THE SHADOW MAN   (1946, $3.95)
by Stephen Gresham
The Shadow Man could hide anywhere—under the bed, in the closet, behind the mirror . . . even in the sophisticated circuitry of little Joey's computer. And the Shadow Man could make Joey do things that no little boy should ever do!

SIGHT UNSEEN   (2038, $3.95)
by Andrew Neiderman
David was always right. Always. But now that he was growing up, his gift was turning into a power. The power to know things—terrible things—that he didn't want to know. Like who would live . . . and who would die!

MIDNIGHT BOY   (2065, $3.95)
by Stephen Gresham
Something horrible is stalking the town's children. For one of its most trusted citizens possesses the twisted need and cunning of a psychopathic killer. Now Town Creek's only hope lies in the horrific, blood-soaked visions of the MID-NIGHT BOY!

TEACHER'S PET   (1927, $3.95)
by Andrew Neiderman
All the children loved their teacher Mr. Lucy. It was astonishing to see how they all seemed to begin to resemble Mr. Lucy. And act like Mr. Lucy. And kill like Mr. Lucy!